LONG BLACK VEIL

ALSO BY JENNIFER FINNEY BOYLAN

Remind Me to Murder You Later

The Planets

The Constellations

Getting In

I'll Give You Something to Cry About

Falcon Quinn and the Black Mirror

Falcon Quinn and the Crimson Vapor

Falcon Quinn and the Bullies of Greenblud

She's Not There: A Life in Two Genders

I'm Looking Through You: Growing Up Haunted

Stuck in the Middle with You: Parenthood in Three Genders

LONG
BLACK
VEIL

A Novel

JENNIFER
FINNEY
BOYLAN

CROWN
NEW YORK

8-8-2017

Copyright © 2017 by Jennifer Finney Boylan

All rights reserved.
Published in the United States by Crown, an imprint of the Crown Publishing Group, a division of Penguin Random House LLC, New York.
crownpublishing.com

CROWN is a registered trademark and the Crown colophon is a trademark of Penguin Random House LLC.

An excerpt from *Pale Fire* by Vladimir Nabokov, published by Penguin Random House, is used by permission.

Library of Congress Cataloging-in-Publication Data is available upon request.

ISBN 978-0-451-49632-4
Ebook ISBN 978-0-451-49634-8

Printed in the United States of America

Jacket design by Jake Nicolella
Jacket photograph by Scala/Art Resource, NY

10 9 8 7 6 5 4 3 2 1

First Edition

For

MJ Boylan, who found me

and for

Deirdre Finney Boylan, who knew I was not lost

If you are not too long, I will wait here for you all my life.

—OSCAR WILDE

1

Philadelphia, Pennsylvania

AUGUST 1980

This was a long time ago, before my first death, and none of us now are the people we were then. Instead we are ghosts: two of us dead, a third unrecognizable, a fourth suspected of murder. It would be easy enough at this hour to have contempt for those young selves, to focus instead on how much cleverer we have become here in the green pastures of the twenty-first century. But over the years I have come to believe that people are usually more deserving of forgiveness than judgment. This is not only because it's an act of grace; it's also because most men and women aren't afforded the luxury of dying more than once.

Unlike some people I could mention.

It was Rachel who got us out of our beds that hot August morning, even though our heads were still throbbing from the wedding the night before. But Rachel was a woman on a mission, and she'd decided she was going to take Quentin to see *The Large Bathers* by Cézanne, or perish in the attempt. She was all about the Impressionists then. Before we graduated, when she was in her Renaissance phase, she'd taken a crack at painting Quentin's portrait in the manner of Leonardo da Vinci's *John the Baptist,* but instead of being flattered, he got all sore about it. *That's what you think I look like?* he said, hurt that she did not see him the way he saw himself. But *hello.* Of course he looked exactly like that.

Later, it had been Tripper's idea to walk from the Philadelphia Museum of Art to Eastern State Penitentiary. It wasn't far. He'd been a history major at Wesleyan, and he'd always wanted to check out the medieval-looking ruins. The prison had opened in 1829, and closed only eight years before, in 1972. Since then it just sat there in the heart of Philly, all boarded up, while the city tried to figure out what to do with it.

Maisie looked at the sketchy neighborhood into which they had strayed. "Do we *have* to do this?" she said. She had long blond hair and a mole in the middle of her left cheek.

"When the prison was built this was all green fields," Tripper said. His nickname contained no small degree of irony, given that he was the most conservative of the group and the only trips he had any intention of taking were ones to the Grand Caymans. At birth he'd been christened Tobin Owen Pennypacker III, though, and his father (Tobin Owen Pennypacker Jr.) had taken to calling him Triple for short. Over time, "Triple" had inevitably morphed to "Tripper."

"It's *not* a very good neighborhood," noted Maisie.

"Will ye not fuck yourself," inquired Wailer. It was a rhetorical question.

A bottle smashed in an alley behind one of the row houses to their right. "Sorry," said Maisie. "I just don't like the idea of getting mugged."

"Hey man, nobody's mugged you *so* far," said Casey. He was a generously obese young man wearing a striped engineer's hat upon his head. The groom.

"But it's early yet," suggested Wailer. She was wearing black fingernail polish. The bride.

"No, we should keep going," said Rachel. She had a big head of bushy black hair, but even at twenty-two there were streaks of gray. "Quentin has got his heart set on the prison now." In her painting, Quentin had pointed with one hand toward the heavens. The other hovered over his heart. It was some likeness.

It was August of 1980. Carter was still president, Reagan an unlikely joke. There were hostages in Iran, fifty-two blindfolded souls. The Bicentennial, with its tall ships and fireworks, was a recent memory. John Lennon was alive. Now and again there'd be a story in the news about how the Beatles were going to come together once more, perhaps in order to raise cash for some charity. Everyone figured it would happen, sooner or later. Why shouldn't they?

They were six in all, plus Krystal and the boy. Quentin and Casey and Tripper had known each other since high school, out at Devon Boys' Latin on the Main Line. Later, the three of them went to Wesleyan, which is where they'd met Rachel and Wailer. They'd only graduated two months before, June first. Plans for the future were sketchy.

The day was hot and sticky. Their clothes stuck to their bodies.

On the street ahead, Rachel saw Quentin talking to Herr Krystal, his former teacher, and now his friend. The two of them had been yammering away in German all morning. It had kind of wrecked their visit to the Cézannes, in fact. All Rachel had wanted was to look upon *The Large Bathers* with Quentin, to have him see what she saw. But Quentin had hardly paid *The Large Bathers* any mind at all. Instead he just yakked away with Krystal in a language that sucked the beauty directly from the air. It was worse than the Black Speech in Tolkien. *Ash nazg gimbatul,* suggested Hitler.

Benny, Maisie's little brother, tightened his grip on her hand. The ten-year-old had a buzz cut and enormous glasses that were always on the verge of falling off of his face.

"I'm afraid of the garble," he said.

"Well, get used to it, Benny," said Tripper. There was a gold anchor embroidered on the breast pocket of his blue sport coat. "That's what the world is! Garble and gibberish."

The boy looked at him fearfully. He and Maisie had grown up in a ruined Main Line mansion, a place called the Bagatelle, out in Villanova. After the exploits of their father, "Lucky" Lenfest, it was the only asset the family had left, a haunted house with a listing Victorian tower, leaking ceilings, an attic full of crap. The heart of the mansion was an elaborate spiral staircase, carved from cherry, with a pipe organ in its center. Maisie was the only one of them who hadn't been at Wesleyan. She'd gone to Conestoga High, out in Berwyn, and dated Tripper—a scandal, given Tripper's natural predilection for debutantes.

She'd wound up at the Berklee College of Music in Boston, studying organ and harpsichord.

At the wedding the night before, Wailer had come down the cherry staircase of the Bagatelle in her bridal gown as Maisie played "A Whiter Shade of Pale" on the organ. Casey stood at the bottom of the steps, best man Quentin at his side, watching the bride descend. As she drew near him, tears of joy had spilled over Casey's eyelashes and rolled down his cheeks. Wailer's parents had not come to the wedding, being dead.

A half a block ahead of them, Quentin and Herr Krystal started singing. It was the Marlene Dietrich song from *The Blue Angel*. Quentin had gotten Rachel to watch *The Blue Angel* with him one night, in the same way that she had perhaps tried to get him to look at *The Large Bathers*. The film had seemed to demonstrate some verity of the world, in Quentin's eyes. But all that Rachel could see was a bunch of proto-Nazis, intent on breaking one another's hearts.

"Man," said Casey. "It's just like old times, the two of them, makin' sauerkraut. It's like we're in the Time Tunnel!"

"Jonny hand me yer pocketknife, will you?"

"What?" said Casey. He reached into his pocket, but his knife was gone. "Wait, no! It's gone!"

Benny held up the jackknife. It bore the initials *J. C.* "I played a trick on you," he said.

"Benny," said Maisie. "What did we say about the stealing?"

Benny wasn't moved. Casey took the knife and handed it to his bride.

"You're a criminal, little dude."

Benny pushed his glasses up his nose and smiled, satisfied.

Krystal and Quentin laughed at something in the Black Speech. Herr Krystal's hand was placed gently on Quentin's back. "*Wunderbar! Wunderbar!*" Krystal shouted.

"Bloody hell," muttered Wailer.

Since graduation two months earlier, Quentin had been living in his high school bedroom. He'd majored in modern foreign languages at Wesleyan, and was supposedly immersed in a project translating Walt Whitman into German. It didn't sound like he'd gotten very far though. He was going to call it *Der Whitman Sammelband,* which, as Tripper liked to point out, translated, sadly, as *The Whitman Sampler.* Rachel worried about Quentin, who'd seemed to have the greatest promise of their group, but since graduation the young man's boat had appeared to become hopelessly lodged upon the rocks.

"I want a kitty, can I have one?" said Benny.

"What?" said Maisie. She wasn't certain whether he was serious. Sometimes her little brother had sudden whims. "Do you think you're old enough?"

"It's a lot of responsibility, taking care of a cat," added Tripper.

With his forefingers the boy picked at the cuticles of this thumbs. There was a small wound on each thumb where he'd made himself bleed.

Quentin and Krystal stopped singing and stood still. Slowly, the others came up behind them. There they were: the eight of them, gathered together like the members of an a cappella group. Before them rose the high walls of old, abandoned Eastern State Penitentiary. There were arrow-slit windows, turrets at the corners. A central guard tower, covered with rust, looked down upon the ruins.

Tripper raised an eyebrow. He hadn't expected it to be quite so gruesome. Quentin pointed excitedly. "The entrance is around the side."

"Entrance?" said Casey.

"We don't have to go in," said Quentin. "Just look."

Herr Krystal nodded. "Hermann Hesse said that the eyes of others are our prisons, their thoughts our cages." He was tall and thin and infirm, like a human who had somehow come down with Dutch elm disease. Even though he wasn't the boys' teacher anymore, Krystal acted a lot of the time like he was still taking attendance.

"I need me fuckin' snorkel," said Wailer. "It's got so bloody deep."

They walked up the block toward the prison's old stone gates. As they walked, Maisie imagined the Rosalyn Tureck version of the Goldberg Variations in her head, which she preferred to the Glenn Gould, on account of the groaning. Over the years, the Bach had been the music she turned to in an emergency, producing in her a calm in the face of chaos. But staring up at the towers of the old penitentiary, the Bach wasn't much help. There were some things that music was no match for, and a horrible abandoned prison was one of them.

They reached the gates. Clouds gathered in the sky above them. Benny looked fearfully toward his sister.

"*Maisie,*" he said, his voice trembling.

There was a creak as Quentin pressed forward on the iron door. Gently, it swung open.

For a moment they all stood there in silence, looking at the long stone room just beyond. There was light at its far end, where a small set of stairs led out into the old prison yard. Twenty pairs of eyes peered back at them.

"*Miao,*" said the creatures.

2

Cold River, Maine

SEPTEMBER 2015

The house was dark. "Gollum," I said.

He waddled over and looked up at me with his sad, bulbous eyes. His tail thumped once against the tile floor.

"Good boy," I said, and kneeled down to hug him. He groaned piteously.

"Come on," I said, "let's go up." I left my suitcase at the bottom of the stairs. The old black lab—eleven years old now—followed me up the steps, then doddered over to our bed. Jake wasn't in it, off at a fire, I figured. Gollum jumped in, as if it were the last action he would commit upon this Earth. The dog glanced at me with his rheumy, grateful eyes, then lay his head down on my husband's pillow and moaned. *Gollum, Gollum.*

A pair of loons called to each other out on the lake, the bird-world equivalent of a married couple's late-night argument—the male laughing, the female responding with a melancholy *hoo*. It wasn't hard to translate: *I'm here, I'm here, are you listening, I'm here!* And the reply, *Yeah, I know where you are.*

I crossed the hallway to the room where our son, Falcon, lay in his bed fully dressed, arms spread like a man on the cross. His mouth was open. I stood in his doorway. It wouldn't be long now before he graduated, another nine months, and then Jake and I would be alone in the big house. On his desk Falcon's schoolbooks were piled high. His French horn lay by the foot of the bed, the case open, a music stand over by the window.

Once, he'd been a two-year-old, lying in a crib in a room not unlike this one. Back then I feared that the slightest breeze might carry him off. There had been days when I'd stood by the crib, my heart filled with equal measures wonder and fear. The sunlight had slanted through the window and reflected off of the pumpkin pine floorboards, filling his room with golden light.

Back in my bedroom, I put on a green cotton nightie with a silk-screen of a baleen whale on it, and got into bed next to Gollum. Now deep into his dotage, the black lab's face was mostly gray. I turned off the light and lay there for a moment, wondering if my mind was going to be able to slow down. I'd woken that morning in a hotel room in Manhattan, after two days of researching a story on Hart Island, the Potters Field of New York. I don't know why I thought the Hart Island story was going to go anywhere: it wasn't exactly the kind of story magazines use to fill what they call the blue pages—photos of Caribbean oceans, models luxuriating in infinity pools. Some of the things I'd seen on Hart Island were going to be hard to forget: prisoners in orange jumpsuits, coffins in a long trench, white guards with machine guns trained on black men. Even the landscape was gruesome: the summer sun shining down on the deteriorating buildings of the abandoned hospital for the insane. I'd stood for a while in front of a collapsed structure filled with rusted gears and steam engines. There was a rusted sign: THE DYNAMO ROOM.

I'd begun the day in the Algonquin, had breakfast down in the lobby, and looked over my notes, trying to figure out the hook for the story. A cat crawled around my ankles and then hopped up on the couch. Steam rose from my coffee cup.

Later, I made my way to LaGuardia. It was there, as I waited to be X-rayed by security, that I saw the headline on the front of the *Post*, and the photograph of the unearthed corpse. A sophomore from Penn named Shannon Savage had found it, an intern on an archaeology project at Eastern State Penitentiary, and she'd been digging around in one of the rooms in Cellblock 5. The skull had rolled out of the wall and stopped at her feet. She'd picked up the skull for a moment and held it Yorick-style, not believing it was real.

The photo in the *Post* was grisly, a close-up of the skull. It didn't look like the person I had known.

Of course, we'd always assumed that the day had ended in murder. So no, it wasn't exactly a surprise. But it had taken all these years for the corpse to turn up, and it was still shocking. Waiting there in the line at LaGuardia, I felt all the hairs on my arm stand up. This was it. It was all going to get churned up again.

A TSA agent yanked me out of line and said, *You've been selected for extra screening, ma'am*. I know these things are random, but it was hard not to take it personally, the suggestion that *there's something about you that's not quite right*.

People had been telling me this for years. I remember when I first got my passport, my mother had looked at my photograph and said, "It looks in this photo like you have a secret."

I'd laughed it off, but Mom wouldn't let it go. "Is there something you want to tell me? You know I will always love you, no matter what." She said this in the way people always say this, pledging their unconditional love before knowing what the actual conditions are.

I thought about my mother, wondered whether she was dead or alive.

The TSA agent encircled my body with an electronic hoop, a device that squelched and squealed at my joints and organs. The man was wearing a name tag that said NABOKOV, like the novelist. I couldn't remember what his theories were. I thought of the line from *Pale Fire*: *Was he in Sherlock Holmes, the fellow whose / Tracks pointed back when he reversed his shoes?*

Then the guard said, "Okay. You can go, ma'am."

I'd stood there for a moment in relief. Seriously? I thought. I can just be on my way? It seemed so unlikely that the thing I had been hoping for was the thing I had been given.

Now, safely home, I lay in bed for another hour listening to the loons calling to each other. I thought about the friends of my youth: Tripper and Casey, Wailer and Rachel, Maisie and Quentin. I wondered what the world would have been like, if that door in the old prison had never creaked open, and those creatures had never gazed upon us. Even now I could see those cold eyes glowing in the dark, asking the questions to which, all these years later, I still had no answer. *What is this world? What is this life?*

A loon cried in the dark night. *I know where you are.*

3

Philadelphia, Pennsylvania

AUGUST 1980

The six young men and women, and the old man, and the child, stood in the dark stone entrance. The long hallway was dark, but an open door at the far end let in a rectangle of sunlight. For a little while—five seconds? ten?—the humans stared at the cats. The felines' long tails undulated behind them.

Then Benny took a step toward them, and in an instant the cats skittered toward the far door and ran out into the prison yard. Benny ran after them. *"Kitties!"* he shouted, his arms raised high in ecstasy.

Then the cats were gone, and Benny with them. The others were left staring into the dark.

"Shit," said Tripper, and ran after the boy. He hurried through the entry chamber and ascended the steps on the far side in a single bound. "Benny?" he shouted. "Come back." The others followed in his wake, all except Nathan Krystal, who stood alone for a moment, looking every one of his seventy-three years. "We should stay together," he said, to no one.

Wailer, emerging into the prison yard, looked around and said, "Bloody hell."

The penitentiary was a block-long square of high stone walls. Behind those walls, in the center of the square, was a series of long cellblocks, arrayed like an asterisk. The cellblocks all converged at a central point, in the center of the square, and radiated out from there. In the open spaces of the square, around the perimeter, long grass grew. A few paths through the grass connected the entryway to the cellblocks and some scattered outbuildings.

"Benny?" Maisie shouted.

"Listen," said Rachel. She was standing at the end of the closest cellblock. Its door was off the hinges. The boy's footsteps could be heard from inside, as well as his high, hopeful voice. They could not quite make out his words.

"What's wrong with him?" said Rachel. "Is he—" Tripper shot an angry look at her, daring her to say it.

"He has his demons," said Tripper.

"We," said Rachel, "have to get *out* of here."

Krystal came up behind them. There was not the slightest suggestion of a breeze on that August afternoon.

"Oh, but it's brilliant," said Wailer. "In its horrible way. Do you not think it has its own beauty?"

Casey looked at his new bride thoughtfully, as if half afraid that one of the reasons she had married him was her inability to distinguish between the beautiful and the horrible. He loved everything about her, including her exaggerated accent, which consisted of varying combinations of brogue and Geordie, depending on her mood. Wailer (née Winifred) had been born in Tyneside, then raised in Cork, but had spent most of her life in the States, which explained, in part, the bizarre accent. Or, as she once described it: *I'm a naturalized citizen of the County Fuckyouvania.*

From behind the cellblock, a pair of cats appeared.

"I'm going in after him," said Tripper, swinging open the door to the cellblock, which they now noticed was marked with the number 1.

"We need to stay together," said Herr Krystal. "Togetherness. That's the thing. Why don't we count off, by twos? I'll begin. One?"

The others just stared at him. No one counted off, by anything. But Casey took Wailer's hand, and Maisie took Tripper's. After a long moment, Quentin reached out and locked fingers with Rachel.

"All right then," said Krystal tremulously. He was the only one without a hand to hold. "Forward into the breach, dear friends."

They stepped into Cellblock 1, and the temperature dropped twenty degrees. The group took five or six steps, then paused.

"Holy shit," said Casey. "Holy fucking shit."

The cellblock stretched before them. Doors to the cells opened on either side of the corridor. In the cells were the remains of iron beds, small toilets, crumbling stone walls. At the far end of the ruined little rooms were barred doors leading to exercise areas, one for each prisoner. Paint in the hallway peeled in large, lurid sheets. The place smelled like rotten mushrooms, damp earth.

"Benny?" called Maisie. Her voice echoed in the empty space. *Enny, enny* . . . There was no sign of the boy. "Benny?" *Enny, enny* . . .

"This is intolerable," said Krystal with desperation. The tall, thin man was shaking like a tree in a breeze. "We have to find that child. If we can?"

"And then get *out* of here," said Tripper.

"Ah, but look at it!" exulted Wailer. "It's brilliant! Have ye ever *seen* a thing so fuckin' 'orrible?"

They walked down the long cellblock, not speaking. Their footsteps scraped against the cracked cement floor.

"Guess this isn't how you expected to spend your honeymoon, huh," said Casey, breaking the tense silence. Wailer shrugged. Her face still showed a wicked delight. "We'll have a real honeymoon," he said. "When you get back from Togo, okay? We'll go to, like, Niagara Falls!"

"Niagara Falls," muttered Tripper. "The second great disappointment of American married life."

Casey looked confused. "I don't get it."

"Shh," said Maisie, flapping a hand at Casey to quiet him. She called again. "Benny! Come here! Now!"

In the distance they heard a voice. Was he shouting?

"What's happened to him?" said Maisie. "What's going on?"

"He's just having fun?" said Casey. "Maybe?"

"This is out of control," said Tripper. "We're not wandering around here lost. We're just not."

"Perhaps," said Krystal uncertainly, "he's just ahead, where these halls converge?"

He pointed to the area before them, where the cellblock ended in an octagonal room, the center of the prison where the spokes of the long halls connected. They walked through a crumbling portal into this central chamber, suggestive of a roundhouse. There was a door in each wall, and beyond each doorway another long cellblock.

There was a long, drawn-out moan. It didn't sound like Benny.

"Okay, that's it," said Rachel. "I'm going back. We have to get help."

"I'm not leaving him here," said Maisie. She took a step toward one of the long hallways before them.

"No one's leaving him," said Tripper. "But Rachel's right. We should get help. We don't want to stumble around here lost. That's crazy."

"Um," said Quentin. "That wasn't the sound of someone who's gotten lost exactly."

"We don't fuckin' know what that's the sound of," said Wailer. The look of exaltation had faded off her face. "That might not have even been him."

There was a pause as they all thought this over.

"If it wasn't him," said Rachel, "then . . ."

"I'm not sure," said Krystal. "But perhaps we should divide our numbers? Some of us might get the authorities. The rest continue the search?"

"I'll get help," said Quentin. "There was a pay phone on Twenty-First Street. I saw it."

Rachel looked at him. "I'm going with you." She looked at Quentin, then Herr Krystal. "Okay? Okay?"

Krystal nodded. "Yes, that will be, yes all right." His voice was shaking. The fact that he was so ineptly trying to hide his fear made things worse. "We'll meet back at this central room, this room here, the one we are in. *Nicht wahr? Doch.*"

The room in which they stood had once been known as the Surveillance Hub. The penitentiary had originally been designed so that the warden and his guards could see every cell in the entire prison from this one spot. Later, as additional wings had been built onto the original eight spokes, mirrors had been placed so that the guards could see those from this single spot as well.

"Okay," said Tripper. "We'll meet back here."

Rachel and Quentin nodded at the others. "Don't worry," said Quentin. "He'll turn up."

Krystal stared down into the dark corridor of Cellblock 7. "Where would he *go*," the man asked.

Quentin and Rachel headed back down Cellblock 1, through which they had entered. The others, standing in the Surveillance Hub, watched them recede.

"He always runs off," said Maisie. She ran a finger through her long blond hair. "He's got no sense at all." Before them, running from one side of the cellblock to the other, was a set of mangled gates bearing a faded red cross.

"What's this?" said Tripper, walking toward the gates.

"Benny?" called Maisie.

There was no response. Casey looked over his shoulder suddenly.

"What?" said Wailer.

"Nothin'," he said. "I'm hearing things."

"What do you think you heard?" said Tripper.

"I don't know," said Casey, more insistently. "Like a voice maybe."

"*Oh for*—" said Krystal. He was staring into a chamber off the right-hand side of the corridor. The others gathered around him.

Before them was a ruined operating room. A warped, rusted table stood at the center, flanked on two sides by what had once been green tiled walls. Glass bottles were strewn haphazardly on a table. There was a large dome-shaped light on a movable arm hanging down from the ceiling. Light shone through a small hole in the ceiling near one of the stone walls. Pieces of plywood leaned against the wall beneath the hole, along with pieces of rusted metal, crushed stone, and shattered plaster.

"This is where they did the operations, man," said Casey, and his voice caught.

The others looked at him. He covered his face.

"What are you crying for?" said Tripper, in a voice that sounded more critical than the situation might have demanded.

"It's okay, love," said Wailer, putting her arms around the big man.

"It's *not* okay," said Casey. "It's all *happening*."

"All right, stop that blubbering," said Tripper. "You're making things worse."

"Hey, fuck you, Tripper," said Casey. "Look at this place." He pointed at a dark patch on the broken floor. "This is probably blood, from some *guy*. Okay? Blood?" His voice caught again.

"Steady," said Krystal. "Let's find the boy. All right then? I'm looking for the *boy*."

"I bet you are," said Maisie. Tripper gave her a sharp look.

Then the air was torn by a scream. "Jaysus fucking Christ in heaven!" Wailer shouted. "Mother of—" Then she paused. "Oh, for fuck's—"

"Wailer," said Casey. "Are you all right?"

"Of course I'm all right," she said. The scream had been hers.

"You didn't *sound* all right," observed Casey.

"Look," said Wailer, and she pointed at the wall. A figure was moving there. It pointed its finger at them.

"It's a *mirror*, Winifred," said Krystal. He refused to call her Wailer, like this was a matter of principle. "It's a convex mirror. To help one see around the corner."

"Sure I know that now," said Wailer. "But when I came upon it, I thought I'd seen the devil."

"I gotta lose some weight, man," said Casey, looking at himself. The convex mirror made him look even more enormous. Casey squinted. There were words painted in faded red paint upon the mirror. "*Incoming cases have right of way*," he read.

"I guess they—wheeled people into the operating room from this hallway?" said Maisie.

"Gross," said Casey.

They turned the corner and followed the hallway deeper into the medical wing. In rooms to their left and right were what looked like the remains of rooms for the sick. There were rotted beds. Next to the beds were small tables with beakers and clipboards. Syringes were scattered on the floor.

In the next room they found an abundance of rusted medical apparatus. Against one wall was what appeared to be an X-ray machine from the 1940s.

Casey walked toward the device and inspected it. He seemed to be imagining a prisoner standing behind the machine's rectangular screen, suffering from some unknown malady.

"Benny?" Maisie called.

"He's not here," said Tripper as they reached the end of the wing. "We should go back." Before them was the door that led outside. There was the distant rumble of thunder.

"Benny?" called Casey. "Benny-boy?" He turned to the others. "Should we look for him outside?"

"*Es tut mir Leid,*" said Krystal, by which he meant *I'm sorry,* although the actual words meant *It does me pain.*

"He's *always* like this," said Maisie. "He doesn't care what he puts people through."

"Well," said Casey, staring down the long hallway, "let's keep looking. We should look some more around this, like, scary dungeon place."

"It's as scary as we make it, mate," said Wailer. "You just have to not let it fuck with you is all."

"I get what you're saying," said Casey. "Except it's kind of fucking with me."

"It's like something out of Poe," said Krystal. "Or Lovecraft."

"What's love craft?" said Casey.

"I'll show you later, Jonny," said Wailer.

They stepped back into the Surveillance Hub. For a long while they stood there, looking down each cellblock, each one more awful than the one before.

"I found a cat; its name is Creeper," announced Benny, and just like that he stepped into the hub from a cellblock behind them. He was holding a cat in his arms.

"Benjamin, my lad!" shouted Krystal.

"Where have you been?" said Maisie, her sudden relief making her cross. "We've been sick with worry."

"Well, look at you, little dude," said Casey. "You got yourself a friend!"

Maisie threw her arms around him. The cat hissed and swiped at her face with its paw.

"Ow!" she shouted.

"Bloody hell," said Wailer.

"Benny," said Tripper, "you shouldn't have run off like that. We were all very worried."

Maisie was trying not to cry, but a sob convulsed her.

"We're all fine," said Krystal. "One and all. Let's take our leave, then?"

"Miao," said Creeper.

"There are *lots* of cats in here," said Benny. "I found a room that had a hundred and seven in it." He pointed down the hallway toward Cellblocks 8 and 9, which divided at a fork about twenty feet down the corridor, one to the left, the other to the right. "Their leader is a caveman."

"Maisie," said Tripper, wiping a little blood from the cat scratch from her cheek. "Are you all right?"

"I'm fine," said Maisie, her voice still trembling. "Now can we please, please, *please* get out of here?"

"Stellar," said Krystal. "Shall we?"

They were just about to turn, to go back down Cellblock 1 to the entrance. But at that moment, from the hallway that led to Cellblocks

8 and 9, came the deep, distant moan they had heard before. It hung on the air, and then died out in echo.

"Jaysus Christ," said Wailer. "What was *that?*"

"Guys," said Casey. "There's something *in* here."

"Their leader is a caveman," Benny said.

Rachel and Quentin walked through Cellblock 1, holding hands as they passed empty cells filled with fallen plaster, broken beds, chairs fallen on their sides.

"Whoa," said Quentin. He stopped walking and stood frozen, looking into a cell to his left.

"Quentin," said Rachel, "we have to——"

"But look. Just look." He sounded so sad.

A wall of the cell before them was covered with drawings done in charcoal or thick pencil. There was a grid with numbers inside, and next to this the names of the months. The prisoner had not recorded the year.

Next to this was a charcoal drawing of a man's face. The eyes burned out at Quentin and Rachel accusingly, like whatever it was the prisoner was angry about was something that Quentin and Rachel had done. Next to this was a heart. Inside the heart was a name: GEORGENE. Beneath the heart were the words I AM INOSANT.

"Georgene?" said Quentin. "Maybe his wife's name?"

"Or his girlfriend," said Rachel. "Someone he loved."

"Yeah, maybe," said Quentin. "Or maybe it's somebody he didn't even know. Somebody he made up in his head."

Rachel made an annoyed face and took Quentin's hand again. "Come on, we have to get out of here. We have to get help."

"Right," said Quentin. "Right, right, right. Okay."

They went back out to the hall and headed toward the exit to the main yard. A black cat came out of an opposite cell and looked at them. It stared at the couple for a long second, then darted into another cell.

When they arrived in the yard, they found that the skies had become dark with thick rain clouds. To their right was the blockhouse that led to the outside. Rachel noticed, for the first time, that there was a tall tower sitting atop it. It appeared to have been built more recently than the rest of the prison.

"*I hear that train a comin'*," said Quentin, imitating with uncanny precision the exact intonation of Johnny Cash singing "Folsom Prison Blues."

"Good one," said Rachel.

"What," said Quentin. "You're not a Johnny Cash fan?"

"Not really," said Rachel.

"I like it when he says, 'I shot a man in Reno, just to watch him die,' and then all the convicts in that audience shout, 'Yeahhh!' "

Rachel looked for a moment at beautiful, raggedy Quentin. His clothes seemed to have been purchased for a man fifty pounds heavier.

"I didn't know you had a Johnny Cash."

"Oh, I got voices you don't even know about up here," he said, pointing to his brain. "I got John F. Kennedy and June Lockhart and Tricky Dick Nixon."

Rachel, still holding the man's hand, looked down at it for a moment as if it were some sort of odd seashell she'd picked up on a beach. "Who's June Lockhart?" she said.

"Mom on *Lassie*," said Quentin. "*Timmy, come back! Good girl, Lassie!*" he said. "She was on *Lost in Space* too."

"And Nixon?"

"*I am not a crook.*"

"Kennedy?"

"*We choose to go to the moon! And do the otha thing! Not because it is easy, but because it is hahd!*"

Rachel shook her head, either in wonder or sadness.

"Is that what you're going to be when you grow up? One of those guys who does impressions on TV?"

He looked hurt. "I am grown-up," he said.

"You think?" she said.

"Hey," said Quentin. He was wearing Wallabees and worn brown corduroy pants. "This is what grown-up looks like."

"You're so full of shit," she said.

Quentin took his hand away from her. "Don't be mad at me, Rachel," he said. "Just because you want me to be someone else."

"I don't want you to be someone else, I want you to be you." Her forehead crinkled into a scowl.

"Which is who exactly?" said Quentin.

"That's what I don't fucking know," she said. "You can imitate all those people, but you can't imitate yourself."

"That doesn't even mean anything," said Quentin.

"It's true," she said.

"Can we just get out of this place, please?" said Quentin, looking at the high walls and the dark clouds. "Maybe we could have a psychodrama later?"

"You mean never," said Rachel.

"I would do anything to end this conversation," said Quentin. "Anything."

"Answer me one question and I'll shut up, okay? One question."

"Fine."

"Why won't you sleep with me?"

"Why won't I—?"

"We make out, you tell me you love me, you get my shirt off, and then just before we fuck you have to go. You're always leaving. Did you think I didn't notice that?"

Quentin's face colored. He looked down at the ground.

"Is it because I'm ugly?" said Rachel. "If I'm ugly, why don't you just say so?"

Quentin's lips twitched around as if he was trying to find some syllables that kept eluding him. Then he said in a voice that was almost a whisper, "You're not ugly."

Now Rachel started to cry. "I don't understand you."

Quentin put his hands on her shoulders. "You're not ugly, Rachel. I think you're beautiful."

She turned her back on him. "Fuck you," she said.

He put his arms around her. "I do think you're beautiful," he said. "And I do love you."

She turned around again. "Then why are you so *mean* to me?"

"Because," said Quentin.

"Because why?"

"Because," said Quentin again. He was whispering now, his voice like something echoing out of a cave. "I'm afraid."

"Afraid?" said Rachel. "Afraid of what?"

The moaning voice that they had heard before now rose once more, hung in the air, and faded.

Rachel and Quentin stared at each other for a second, then turned toward the blockhouse and ran toward it, not looking back.

Rachel pushed on the old iron door, but it would not open. Quentin pushed on it too, but he could see that since they had last passed through someone had wrapped a heavy chain around the door and sealed it with a padlock.

They were now locked in the old prison.

"I'm trapped," Quentin said.

4

Atlantic Coast

JULY 1987

Quentin sat in a chair behind a set of iron bars reading a book. Mrs. Levine approached his cage.

"Hello, Quentin," said Mrs. Levine, putting the bag of money in the window slot. His name was right there on a plate: *Quentin Pheaney.* She'd made out the deposit slip.

"Hello, Mrs. Levine," said Quentin, placing the Nietzsche face-down. "And how are you today?"

"Oh, I'd complain, but who would listen?" she said cheerfully. She was a seventy-two-year-old woman with an updo and Benjamin Franklin glasses. Her clothes were gray, except for a pink silk scarf. "What are you reading today—?" She squinted at the cover of the upside-down book. "Freedrick Neetchy?"

"Neet-cha," said Quentin, opening the bag and starting to count out the money.

"Neet-cha!" said Mrs. Levine, with a smile. "If I met that Friedrich Neet-cha, I would tell him, 'Glad to meetcha!' "

Quentin nodded, counting softly under his breath. "Three, twenty-three, forty-three, sixty-one, two. Three hundred sixty-two dollars. Is that what you have?"

"To the penny!" said Mrs. Levine.

From the next cage over, his boss, Mrs. Haddad, took a glance at him. She was humming a song entitled "What the World Needs Now Is Love."

"What happened to your friend Mr. Goethe?"

He handed her the deposit slip. "I'm branching out," he said. At twenty-nine, Quentin was no longer quite the handsome young man he had once been. While his build had once been "slender," now he just seemed underfed and bony. The long hair that had seemed rakish in college now made him look a little wild. Even a stranger could discern an air of disappointment about him, some of which had to do with the fact that his mother could not afford to send him to graduate school, and some of which had to do with the events that had taken place in Eastern State Penitentiary seven years before. On this day he was wearing the same formal white shirt he'd worn that day in the prison, although at this late date, the shirt was frayed and worn. The tie covered with treble clefs that Quentin was wearing only made the shirt seem sadder.

"Oh, I hope this one is more cheerful," said Mrs. Levine. "That Goethe just seems so sad."

"He's not sad," said Quentin. "He's just realistic."

"Oh, pooh," said Mrs. Levine. "You need more sunshine and flowers!"

Quentin nodded. "You're right as always, Mrs. Levine."

"Of course I am, Quentin," she said. She looked thoughtful, as if she were going to say something, but then she turned away. "You be of good cheer," she said.

"And yourself as well, Mrs. Levine." He watched her go. She was the last customer of the day, and after she left, the guard locked the bank's revolving door.

Very quietly, Quentin spoke in the voice of Jimmy Durante: "*And good night, Mrs. Calabash, where-*ever *you are.*"

Quentin cashed out and counted his drawer. Friday was always a big day. To his right Mrs. Haddad was banding up twenties. She was still singing. *What the world, needs now, is love, sweet love.* I wonder if she knows she's doing that, Quentin thought. She'd been singing it for hours.

"Any big plans for this weekend, Quentin?" said Mrs. Haddad. She pulled the handle on her adding machine.

For a second he thought about telling her, but if he said it out loud he would have to admit he was doing it, and if he admitted he was doing it, that there was a possibility this plan might fail.

"Nothing special," he said. He finished balancing his drawer, then counted out the float. It was fortunate that he was neither over nor under today. If he'd had a serious shortage in his drawer all the other tellers would have to open up again, and everyone would have to stand around until they found the mistake. This had happened before, further bolstering the image of Quentin as a man who had his head in the clouds. One time he'd left ten thousand dollars by the coffee machine in the break room. Mrs. Haddad was the one who found it. "You'd forget your head if it wasn't screwed on!" she said. It wasn't a compliment.

Already Theodore and Kati and Mrs. Gellert were standing around the cage of Mrs. Thornton-Wilson, the head teller, with their coats on. Quentin was the last person to hand in his tally, and it was with a shared sigh of relief that she saw he'd balanced his drawer. "All right then," said Mrs. Thornton-Wilson. "We are in tip-top shape."

Everyone smiled, and Mrs. Thornton-Wilson nodded across the bank platform at Mr. Cogliano, the branch manager. Each day, Mrs. Thornton-Wilson pronounced them to be either *in tip-top shape* or *in a pothole.*

"Good night, everybody," said Quentin, heading to the door. The Nietzsche was tucked under his arm.

"Good night, Quentin," said Mrs. Thornton-Wilson.

"You take care, honey," said Mrs. Haddad. "Please?"

He smiled tightly and walked through the side door, the one that led into the concourse. Dave the guard nodded to him as he headed out. For a moment he locked eyes with Dave, and the guard looked at him uneasily, as if he could read his mind. Jesus, Quentin thought. I hope not.

He walked through the concourse toward Suburban Station. The hot, thick air smelled of deep-fat fryers and soft pretzels. His train was waiting on the track as he came down the stairs. It pulled out before he was even in his seat. They traveled in a tunnel to Thirtieth Street, paused there to take on a few more commuters, then emerged into the bright light. The art museum sat on a hill beyond the Schuylkill. Eastern State was just behind it, but you couldn't see the towers from the train. There were rowers from the University of Pennsylvania crew team on the river. They pulled as one.

To the left was the old *Evening Bulletin* Building. It had stopped publication five years ago, in 1982. There was an electronic sign on the outside of the building on which news headlines used to crawl by, but the sign was dark. Next to the dead *Bulletin* was the corporate headquarters of Food Fair, also closed. Someone had spray painted across the building's front: US OUT OF NORTH AMERICA.

Quentin opened the Nietzsche and continued reading. He was in the section called "At the Waterfall." It was a meditation on the nature of free will. When he looked up, they were in Merion.

If I met that Friedrich Neetchy, I would tell him, "Feelin' peachy!"

Once, a long time ago, he had been on this same train when it had run over someone—a girl about his age, which back then was about sixteen. The next day there had been an article in the *Bulletin* about her. She'd waited at the Bryn Mawr station for the train to come around the curve, then jumped in front of it, Anna Karenina–style. He still remembered her name: Louisa van Roden. The *Bulletin* said she'd been despondent. He remembered coming home after school and reading the paper and then going up to his room and crying his eyes out over her, a girl he'd never met. Then he came down the stairs and ate dinner with his mother. Shake 'N Bake. She asked him if anything was wrong. He'd said no.

Quentin looked out the window and for a brief second saw, down a long street, the face of Haverford's upper school building. He and Tripper and Casey used to play JV soccer against the Haverford boys. He hadn't seen either of them since the murder. If it was a murder. The difference between a murder and a disappearance being the presence of an actual body. One of them anyhow.

A month and a half after Eastern State, he'd watched the Philadelphia Phillies beat the Kansas City Royals in the World Series. He'd never gone in much for sports, of course, but that fall there was something about drinking Guinness with his mother, and watching the Phils: Steve Carlton, Mike Schmidt, Pete Rose, Tug McGraw. His sweet, buoyant mother—Grainne—had interpreted the Phillies' victory in personal terms. "You see, Quentin," she said, in her gentle, loving voice. "Impossible things happen all the time."

Quentin wasn't sure that the victory of the Phils in the World Series was evidence of the world's generosity, especially given what had happened to them six weeks earlier. He yearned to share his mother's optimistic view of the world, but he felt unequal to the task. He felt shipwrecked up there on the third floor of the old house, spending his day writing and typing, consumed with his loss.

He felt bad that his mother loved him so much, sometimes.

He got off the train at Villanova and walked to his car, a VW Golf. He'd tricked his mother into buying it for him. He'd threatened to buy a Yugo instead, and in order to keep him from buying what his mom considered a deathtrap, she'd bought him the VW. On the back windshield was a small decal featuring the face of Bullwinkle the Moose, and the words WATSAMOTTA U. He put the Nietzsche on the passenger seat and fired up the engine, then he reached into the glove box and took out the pillbox and shook some speed into his palm and swallowed the pills with a little 7Up. Then he began his journey.

He knew these roads so well by now, having spent almost every one of his twenty-nine years upon them—the exception being the four years at Wesleyan. He knew every detail of the roads that led to the turnpike—the fords in Gladwyne, the Hanging Rock in Gulph Mills. He entered the Pennsylvania Turnpike, headed west toward Jersey. The road rose upon the arches of the steel truss bridge over the Delaware, then sank to the swamps of the Garden State. He joined the New Jersey Turnpike and headed north. He passed rest areas: Richard Stockton, Molly Pitcher. He wasn't sure who these people were exactly. Quentin glanced down at the cover of *Menschliches, Allzumenschliches*.

He began to recite the beginning of the book out loud, using his Nietzsche voice, which was a kind of combination between Hitler and Jimmy Stewart.

Then he got on the Garden State Parkway, took it as far as the New York Thruway, then crossed the Hudson via the Tappan Zee. From the crest of the bridge you could just make out the city to the south, the Empire State Building, the Twin Towers orange and fiery in the sunset. He had gone to a job interview in Manhattan, once, in his early twenties, for a position teaching German at the Dalton School. The skies had opened up on him, though, and without an umbrella he'd arrived at the school like a man who'd just jumped into a swimming pool. He didn't get the job.

He followed 684 and 84 into Connecticut. The sun went down and the stars came out. On the radio he had a classical station playing softly. It was Barber's *Adagio for Strings*. It was almost unbearable to listen to. You could feel the weight of the oncoming Holocaust burdening every note. Quentin turned it up.

"Quentin, what are you doing here?" he said in Rachel's voice. He pictured her standing there in her Dorchester apartment, the oil paint still wet on her brushes.

"What do you think?" he said, in his best imitation of his own voice.

It was nine o'clock as he crossed the Massachusetts state line. He pulled into the rest stop at Charlton for gas and a cheeseburger, then got right back in the car, and headed east toward Boston. The closer he got, the faster he drove. He was doing eighty-five as he passed the 495 turnoff, ninety as he crossed the Boston city line. Quentin took the Mass Pike all the way into town and went south on 93. Years and years later this would all become the Big Dig, but in 1987 it was just a series of tunnels and bridges, lanes that disappeared or merged without warning, others blocked off with traffic cones and barriers, some that just dropped off into thin air. Boston was not like Philly, that much was certain. Philly made sense, in an obvious, demeaning kind of way. Boston, on the other hand, was an unsolvable mystery.

He got off 93 and came down Dorchester Avenue, lots of duplex houses, cars on blocks out on the street. It was just shy of midnight when he rang her bell. The house was dark. He rang the bell again. It took a while, but at last there were footsteps from inside and the door swung open. A man about his age stood there in his boxers. "Who the fuck are you?" he said.

"I'm Quentin Pheaney," he said. "I'm looking for Rachel?"

"Not here," he said.

"Oh," said Quentin. "Will she be back?"

The man was well muscled. In one hand he held a can of Pabst. "Back?" the guy said.

"I'm her friend," Quentin said.

The guy took a swig of Pabst. "Fuck off," he said. He swung the door closed.

Quentin stood there in the Dorchester night staring at the closed door. He listened as the dude went back up the stairs. Turning around, he faced the street, then slowly, aimlessly wandered down the front steps of the porch back to his car. Quentin leaned against his car, looking up at the beat-up duplex. One light was on in a second-floor window. The guy stood silhouetted in the window frame for a moment. Then he was gone.

Quentin thought about getting back in his car, but after the seven-hour drive he was in no hurry. Instead he just leaned against the hood, and crossed his arms. "Not here," he said, in the voice of the guy who'd answered the door. "Not here. Fuck off! Fuck *off*!"

The door of the house swung open again. The guy stood there. "Oh, come on already," he said. Quentin looked up at him. He'd put some pants on now.

"Okay," said Quentin, and walked up the stairs.

"I'm Backflip Bob," said the guy.

"Yeah?" said Quentin.

They walked into a living room. There was a couch with stuffing falling onto the floor, and a stereo on top of some milk crates. A cardboard box was filled with records. On every wall were Rachel's paintings. Her style had changed since Wesleyan, though. She'd turned to landscapes: docks and water and fields of Queen Anne's lace. It all looked like the work of a wounded soul. Yeah, Quentin thought. But that's where I come in.

Backflip Bob walked out of the room into a small disgusting kitchen, came back a moment later with a can of Pabst Blue Ribbon, and handed it to Quentin, who took the can and held it against his neck. The cold aluminum felt good in the summer night.

"I know who you are now," said Backflip Bob. "You were one of the, those people in the prison."

Quentin nodded. He opened the can of beer, which made a satisfying *whssst*. A small crown of foam gathered around the opening.

"You live here," said Quentin.

"Yeah," said the guy.

"Why do they call you Backflip Bob?"

The guy finished the beer. "Why do you think?" he said. He walked over to the stereo, pushed a button on a small black box. A tray slid forward.

"You seen these things yet?" he said. "Compact disc player."

"I heard about them," said Quentin.

"I only got the one CD," he said, putting a copy of *Graceland* into the tray. He pushed another button and it slid into the black box. A second later, there was the sound of an accordion and a monster drum.

"I have this record," said Quentin. "I like that one, what is it, 'I Know What I Know'?" For a few years there, *Graceland* was everywhere you went. Later, he'd think of it as the last time he knew a piece of popular music. *Graceland* was the final stop on the journey he'd begun when he was thirteen, going down to Wayne Book and Record to buy *Abbey Road*. But from now on, popular culture would have to trudge on without him.

Backflip Bob stood up, got another beer out of the kitchen, then he sat down on the busted-up couch next to Quentin. "So what's your deal?" he said. "You got a thing?"

"I don't have a deal," said Quentin.

"Liar," said Backflip Bob.

"Yeah?" said Quentin. "What's *your* deal?"

"Well, I got the backflips, for one," he said.

"I guess," said Quentin. "I haven't actually seen you do one, though."

"Fuck you," said Backflip Bob. "You want me to do one right now? Let's go." He stood up.

"Where are we going?"

"Outside."

"You can't do a backflip inside?"

"I don't *think* so," said Backflip Bob.

"How about if I just take your word for it?" said Quentin.

"Fuck you, you insulted my honor."

"I didn't."

"Yeah, you kinda did. Up."

Quentin sighed and followed the man back outside, muttering a phrase in German under his breath.

"What the hell was that?" said Backflip Bob.

"Nietzsche," said Quentin. "To honor, you must sacrifice."

"Whoa," said Backflip Bob. "I can feel my brain expanding."

"You don't like Nietzsche?"

"Yeah, I don't know," said Backflip Bob. "Did you ever notice how everybody who's really into Nietzsche is either fucking insane or, like, nineteen years old?"

"Those are the only two choices?"

"Pretty much," said Backflip Bob. "Which one are you?"

They arrived on the porch. Rachel was walking up the stairs toward the house. She stopped halfway up.

"Quentin?" she said. "What are you doing here?"

"Rachel," said Quentin. He went to her and put his arms around her. She endured this, then looked at him awkwardly. "Did you drive?"

"I did," said. "All the way from Philly."

"Why?"

Quentin looked her in the eyes, and the enormity of his miscalcula-tion was already clear to him. He already saw the entire fiasco unfold-ing before him, a fiasco that was going to end with him driving off in mortification as Rachel's new boyfriend did a backflip out in the street. And yet there was no way to stop the train. All of this felt like it had already happened a long time ago.

"To ask you a question," he said. He was still wearing the tie with the treble clefs on it, and the frayed white Oxford shirt.

"What do you want to ask me, Quentin?" she said. She sounded weary, like she knew what the question was, and the answer was no.

"Rachel Steinberg," he said, getting down on one knee. "Will you marry me?"

The question fell like a tin can tossed into the street.

"Oh, Quentin," she said. "Why would you ask me that now? Why?"

"Because we love each other," said Quentin. "Because we've al-ways loved each other."

"You're serious," she said. "You're actually proposing?"

"Man said he didn't have a deal," said Backflip Bob. He sipped some of the beer.

"Bobby, quiet," said Rachel.

Yeah, Bobby, Quentin thought. *Quiet.* It was humiliating enough to be in this conversation, but to have this other guy watching the whole thing like a foreign movie was just unbearable. There was no way out.

"Quentin. Why would I marry you?"

"Because we're soul mates?" said Quentin, and his voice broke. How was it possible, when he'd hatched this plan, that it had never occurred to him that she'd say no? Whereas, in truth, there was no possible version of the world in which she'd say yes, excepting the one that existed in his head.

"Oh no," said Rachel, tears coming to her eyes.

"Take a chance, Rachel," he said, hopefully. "Don't you remember how it was with us? I was so uncertain, for all that time. But now I know."

"Know what?"

"That we're meant to be together!" he said, but it just sounded like he was a crazy person.

"Oh, Quentin," she said. "What happened to you?"

What happened to me, he thought, and suddenly he was angry with her. It was a heartless thing to say. "You know what happened to me!" shouted Quentin. "It happened to you too!"

"All right, that's enough," said Backflip Bob. "Thanks for stoppin' in."

"Jesus, Quentin, we were twenty-two years old," she said. "Did your life really come to an end back then?"

"No," said Quentin. "Mine came to an end just now."

He walked toward his car, opened the door. "Quentin," said Rachel, "please wait."

"No, let him go," said Backflip Bob. "It's time he was on his way."

Quentin reached in, picked the Nietzsche off the seat, and threw it at Backflip Bob, who caught the book with one hand.

"Quentin," said Rachel, "you have to find a life."

He just looked at her. "*How?*" he said. Then slammed the door, and drove off down Melville. He looked in the rearview mirror. The last thing he saw was a man standing in the middle of a Dorchester street, doing a backflip. Rachel's new boyfriend landed perfectly on his feet. She fell into the man's waiting arms and started to cry.

Quentin, he said, in Rachel's voice. It was eerie how well he could do her. *You have to find a life.*

For a while he drove around Boston, uncertain what he should do next, or where he should go. Plan B had never been his specialty. He just went straight as long as the lights were green, and turned right on red when they were not. The clock on the dashboard read 2:30 a.m. He knew he should probably find a motel somewhere to sleep for the night, but the idea of waking up in the city, in this world, with this life, was inconceivable. The streets were full of revelers coming home from closed-down bars. Couples stumbled down the streets arm in arm. A man walked a Dalmatian dog with three legs. Lights clicked off in windows. The wind blew a pile of trash around in a small tornado.

He pulled over at a convenience store. Inside the world was brightly lit. Magenta and scarlet slushies churned around in plastic tubs. A young man—a boy, really—with extraordinary droopy dog jowls stood behind the cash register. Quentin went to the back of the store and poured himself a cup of coffee. Cream, no sugar. He went back to the cash register and the droopy-dog guy said, Anything else? and Quentin thought, What else could there be?

Back in the car, Quentin drove on for a while, sipping the coffee until he saw a sign for 93 North, and headed for the interstate. The road went through a tunnel and then rose up onto a bridge. The bridge seemed shockingly, frighteningly high to Quentin. On either side of him was the sleeping, beat-up city. It was nothing to him.

After a while the highway merged with I-95, and he rolled down his car window and threw the empty coffee cup out on the highway. I-95 passed through Old Byfield, where there was a towering sign for something called Bonker's. It looked like the kind of place you could take your children for their birthday, if you had some. An hour later he was in New Hampshire, and a half an hour after that he was crossing the Piscataqua River Bridge into Maine. There were exits on the highway for Kittery and Saco and Kennebunk. He did not stop.

Well, what were you expecting? That she would drop everything after all these years and leap into your arms?

Yeah, something like that.

And you expected this reception because?

Because she loves me.

Quentin, my friend. She doesn't have the slightest idea who you are. Anything she was ever in love with was only what you let her see.

And that makes me different from other humans how, exactly?

In every way. The souls that other women come to love bear some resemblance to the men those souls actually belong to. Unlike some people we could mention.

So this is the price of being in love? Having to share your darkest self with someone before they wrap their arms around you? I don't think most men approach the question that way exactly. Or women, for that matter.

Okay. So what now then?

We're not going back to Continental Bank, I can tell you that.

So where then? Twenty-nine seems kind of old to be starting your life over again from scratch.

Starting it over? I don't think we ever had one in the first place.

And whose fault is that exactly?

I know what you want me to do. But I'm not doing that.

Because your plan is clearly working so well. When's the wedding again?

Just because I know what we have to do doesn't mean that I can actually do it. I'll die if I have to do it.

Hey, whatever doesn't kill you makes you stronger.

Yeah, I know that people always say that. But what they never add is, whatever actually does kill you, kills you totally fucking dead.

He passed through the city of Portland, then Freeport and Brunswick. After that there was a long hour without a sign of human life. On either side of the interstate were thick stands of pine trees. There were no other cars on the road. He passed Augusta, Sidney, Waterville, and then once more the world gave way to nothing. A line of thick electric wires crossed the highway. Osprey nests had been built onto the towers. A huge brown bird sat in a nest, watching him draw near.

The sun came up somewhere after Bangor. It didn't look like much from the highway. A beat-up shopping mall. An Arby's.

He stopped an hour or so after Bangor, used the restroom, got more coffee. He stared at himself in the men's-room mirror. "Don't you remember how it was with us?" he said. "I was so uncertain, for all that time. But now I know."

"*Know what?*" he said, in Rachel's voice.

Yeah, he thought, know what?

You got me.

Quentin untied the tie around his neck. He held it in his hands for a moment, thinking of his mother, who'd given it to him for his birthday when he was fourteen. *It looks in this photo like you have a secret.* Then he threw it in the trash.

The sun rose up as he drove to the east and north. By midmorning Quentin had crossed the Penobscot River; by lunchtime he was in Acadia National Park. Bar Harbor was crowded, though, and when he saw a sign for the Nova Scotia ferry, he turned left and joined the line for the SS *Bluenose*. Just shy of one o'clock he parked the Golf adjacent to a flatbed bearing a monster truck with ten-foot-tall tires. On the side of the truck in garish flaming letters were the words: DONDI'S INFERNO.

He stood in the stern of the boat and watched America fade away. There was someone walking around in a moose costume on the deck, and a photographer drafted behind the moose, taking passengers' photographs. On a deck chair by herself sat a young woman about Quentin's age. She had a beauty mark on her right cheek, just like Maisie. Their eyes met for a moment and for a terrifying second he saw a sorrow in her face that shocked him. He imagined striking up a conversation with her, engaging in some desperate suicidal affair. All of that took place in a heartbeat, and then he looked away.

Shortly after the coastline of America was out of sight, the gambling began. Apparently the *Bluenose* passed through international waters, where it was all legal. The interior of the upper deck was a colorful wasteland of slot machines and cocktail lounges. There was a slot machine directly before him with a lit-up sign that read INSERT COIN. He dropped in a quarter and pulled the handle. There was a clicking, whirring sound, and first one, then two, then three cherries slid into place. A red light on top of the machine began flashing and buzzing, and coins poured out of the contraption's maw. At first Quentin took three or four steps away from the machine, embarrassed by the sudden scene. But then one of the cocktail hostesses rushed over to him with her congratulations. The woman bent down to help pick up the spewing money, and as she did he saw her soft, pillowy bosom, all that flesh just barely withheld by the crappy satin top she was wearing. The sight of her filled him with longing and sorrow. The girl stood up and handed him the giant bucket of money. It looked for all the world like a rundown version of the pot of gold you find at the end of a rainbow, the kind that might be guarded by an especially disgusting leprechaun.

"Congratulations!" said the girl. "Was that your first time?"

"Yup," said Quentin.

"Wow! What's your secret?"

He looked at her with the same expression you might see on a recently stabbed man. "Just lucky I guess," he said.

They arrived in Yarmouth, Nova Scotia, in late afternoon. Quentin followed the monster truck off of the ferry and onto dry land. The last thing he saw was that woman with the mole on her cheek, walking a bicycle down the metal ramp. As he passed her, she unexpectedly raised her hand, as if waving good-bye.

He followed the coast northward, passing through miles and miles of pine trees. Now and again, to his right, the road hugged the shoreline, and there he saw the vast gray ocean, churning up onto a beach covered with round gray stones. The sight of the ocean stabbed him to the heart, made him realize how incredibly tired he was, and not just of driving. *Oh once I sang a song about a man who got turned inside out*, he thought. *He had to jump into the ocean because it made him so very sleepy.*

He wound up in the city of Halifax after nightfall. There was a small sign for something called the Black Dog Inn, and he pulled into the parking lot and turned off the Volkswagen's engine and looked at himself in the rearview mirror. *What the world needs now*, he said, in the voice of Mrs. Haddad, *is love sweet love.*

The couple who ran the Black Dog Inn was named the Whitakers. He got the sense that he was the first guest they'd had in a while. The first floor of the place was an elaborate, overdecorated parlor, with a concert grand piano and lots of ancient photographs that showed what the place had looked like in the previous century. A small fire lay dying upon its embers. The mantelpiece held small porcelain statuettes of extinct species, including the dodo. Mrs. Whitaker asked him what time he wanted to be awakened in the morning, and Quentin said that he imagined he'd be awake before dawn, and head on his way. Mr. Whitaker looked at him gravely and asked, "Where you going, son?"

He suspected that the old man meant this question kindly, but to be called son by strangers at this late hour felt heartbreaking and strange. "North," he said.

Mr. Whitaker said nothing for what seemed like a long time. Then he said, as if pronouncing the judgment of an appeals court, "North is good."

Mrs. Whitaker, taking his plate, said, "We'll leave you some jam."

"Oh no, that's all right. I don't want to trouble you. I don't need any jam."

"Of course you do," said Mrs. Whitaker. "Everyone likes jam."

"How old are you, son?" asked Mr. Whitaker.

"I'm twenty-nine."

"Are your parents living?"

"My mother is."

"You can use our phone if you want to call her," Mrs. Whitaker said helpfully. "We don't mind."

"I'm good," said Quentin.

Mr. Whitaker nodded gravely. "Suit yourself."

"There's marmalade, strawberry, and rhubarb," said Mrs. Whitaker.

"That's good to know. Okay, well I'm going to just——" His throat closed up unexpectedly and for a strange long moment the three of them stood there in the garish parlor. Then Quentin turned and walked up the stairs to his room.

He woke in the middle of the night to find his room filled with yellow moonlight, and Quentin sat up in bed and looked around. He had been dreaming of the prison again, of the deserted hallways, the ruined cells. He'd seen the wall upon which someone had written GEORGENE. I AM INOSANT. It took Quentin a moment to remember where he was. Then it came back to him—the moose on the boat, the monster truck, Backflip Bob. From outside came the voice of someone singing drunkenly, and he looked at the small glowing clock on the bedside table. It was just after two in the morning, and the bars must've closed. The stranger was singing "Norwegian Wood," off-key.

Quentin got out of bed and walked to the window. Before him was the cruel sea, and the yellow moon shining down upon it. Okay, he thought. I get it. I get it. I get it.

He put his clothes on and went out to the creepy parlor of the Black Dog Inn. He left a twenty-dollar bill on the table and then headed out to the Volkswagen. As he pulled out of the driveway, a light went on in a second-story window, and for a moment he saw the silhouette of one of the Whitakers, watching him depart.

A long bridge joined the northern shore of Nova Scotia to Cape Breton Island. He followed a road dug into the mountainous eastern shore of Cape Breton. To his left, pine trees marched up toward a high ridge; to his right was a long drop down to the Atlantic. There wasn't much here—an occasional store selling videotapes and beer. There was a shack with a sign that read WORMS and FUDGE. He turned on the radio, but there weren't any stations.

Was it even possible, he wondered? Surely he'd get caught. Reality was unyielding that way.

But if he could? It would take cunning and care, but it was not impossible to imagine. He was not a person who had ever spent much time thinking about the future, but he thought about it now.

In midmorning he pulled over at one of the shacks and bought a six-pack of Beck's and a clam roll. Then he walked back out to the Golf and sat on the hood and ate his lunch. Before him the ocean crashed against round rocks. His clam roll was unexpectedly delicious—salty and chewy and earthy. He washed it down with one of the lagers and then closed his eyes and felt the sun on his face. From the ocean came the endless roar of the waves crashing up, and then withdrawing.

"All right," he said, and then hurled the green bottle against the rocks. It smashed into a hundred sharp shards. "I'll do it."

He found the right spot a few miles north of that. There was a small turnoff carved into the side of the cliff, and he followed this gravel drive down to a boarded-up cabin. There was a sign on the side of the cabin: NORTHERN LIGHTS.

The drive turned right toward the cabin, but he parked without making that turn. Leaving the motor running, he walked to the edge of the cliff and looked down at the churning ocean below. Waves slammed angrily against the granite rock face. Quentin looked down at the sea for a while, then went back to his car and rolled down the driver's-side window. *Ready?* He got behind the wheel and put the car in neutral. Then, climbing back out and holding on to the left side of the car, he pushed the Volkswagen down the drive. It didn't take much. Soon enough it was moving all by itself. He watched it roll away, off the gravel, across an open space blanketed with pine needles and moss, and then right off the edge of the cliff. Things were silent, and for longer than he thought, as if the Volkswagen were falling in slow motion. The sound of the crash, when it came, seemed to come from miles away.

I stood there in front of the boarded-up cabin, listening to the ocean roar. I felt as if I had become something like a light or a gas, a sentient thing now invisible. But who had I become? I knew that I was not who I had been, but I did not yet know what it would mean to exist in the world, at least not outside the private, silent realm of my own ragged heart.

I'd always liked the sound of the name Judith; it was the name I'd used in private since childhood, since my first recollection of being alive. I said it out loud, in my own voice. *Judith.* It was a voice I'd never used before, but for the first time it sounded like my own.

I wasn't quite sure what was going to happen next.

Well, I said. *I guess I'll have to find my way.*

5

Philadelphia, Pennsylvania

AUGUST 1980

Lightning flickered through the holes in the decaying ceiling of Cell-block 1. They were running. Creeper struggled in Benny's arms. Its claws came out. "Ow, ow, ow," said Benny.

"Come on," said Maisie. "Just keep moving."

"Ow, ow, ow," Benny cried again, and then the cat leapt out of his arms and ran down the cellblock. It paused about twenty feet away from them. The prison was dark now. The cat's eyes glowed, two pin-points of light in the shadows.

"Creeper," said Benny, turning toward the cat.

The wailing voice came again. The cat turned toward the sound.

"Creeper," said Benny.

"Come on," said Maisie, pulling on the boy's arm.

"*Creeper,*" said Benny.

"We'll get you another goddamned cat," said Tripper.

Creeper took off toward a door marked LIBRARY. Benny pointed at the door. Lightning flickered again.

"Come *on,*" said Maisie, pulling on the child's arm. Benny began to cry.

Rain began to fall upon the roof. Water ran through the holes in the ceiling and streamed onto the floor of the prison.

The doors at the far end of the cellblock opened and Quentin and Rachel ran inside.

"The front gates are locked!" said Quentin. "Someone came and chained them."

"What?" said Wailer. "Go on away with that."

"Well, good night nurse!" said Krystal.

"It's true," said Rachel. "There's a big heavy chain wrapped around the door, and a padlock."

"This is insane," said Maisie. "We can't just be locked in."

"Rachel and I tried all the gates. It's sealed up tight."

"That's—intolerable," said Tripper.

"Creeper," sobbed Benny.

"Shut up about the goddamned cat, okay?" snapped Maisie.

More water was dripping through the ceiling now.

"Who would bloody lock the doors?" asked Wailer.

"I should think," said Krystal, breathing heavily, "there would be . . . a caretaker of some sort."

"Are you all right, Mr. K?" said Casey. "You seem kind of—not."

"I'm a little short of breath," he said.

Thunder rumbled from the skies above them.

"So there's a guy . . ." said Casey. "Who feeds the cats?"

"Creeper," said Benny, despondent.

"This is insane," said Rachel. "We can't just wait until he comes back. This caretaker?"

"No," said Tripper. "We're not waiting. There has to be a way out."

They walked to the end of the hallway and opened the door. Rain poured from the black sky onto the broken ground. The walls of the prison seemed impossibly high.

Benny looked remorsefully down the hall in the direction from which they had come.

"Come on," said Tripper. "Let's go." He charged out into the downpour, and the others followed. They ran back toward the block-house, and saw the thick chains around the gates. Tripper shook the iron bars, then turned around and leaned with his back against the gate and stared at the innards of the prison—the high walls, the broken, junk-strewn yard, the star-shaped cellblocks.

"It's not supposed to be like this," he said.

"Help!" shouted Rachel. "Help!"

"No one will hear you in this weather," said Wailer.

"Yeah, Wailer?" said Rachel. "What's your plan?"

"I think we find somewhere dry to get tucked up and we wait for the morning. Someone will be along."

"Wait, you mean stay here all night?" said Casey.

She took the big man by the hand. "We're locked in, mate. Where else are we going to stay?"

"We aren't prisoners," said Tripper.

Quentin looked at him mournfully.

"*What?*" said Tripper.

The boys and Herr Krystal headed out to do a 360 of the prison yard, and Maisie, Rachel, Wailer, and Benny returned to the Surveillance Hub to evade the downpour. As they walked toward it, the women's eyes fell upon the open cell doors on either side, and the dark, destroyed rooms beyond each one. There were thirty-two cells on the right-hand side of the hall, twenty-five on the left. In some of the cells they could see iron posts and mattresses. But most of the cells were too dark to see anything at all.

They arrived at the Surveillance Hub and paused for a moment at the center. The arms of the prison stretched before them, most of them dark now. It was dry here.

"Why don't we make camp until the gents get back?" said Wailer. "We don't want to wander too far in case they need to find us."

"Great," said Maisie, sitting down upon the floor. Benny sat down next to her and fished around in his pocket for something. He was holding a small blue silk handkerchief in one hand. He waved the other around his fist and in an instant the handkerchief disappeared. Rachel watched, uncertain. It seemed like an odd moment for magic tricks.

"How'd you do that?" she said.

Benny looked at Rachel with his intense black eyes, as if considering whether it would be proper to reveal his secret. Then he held up his hand. "Fake thumb," he said emotionlessly.

"Fake . . ." said Rachel, "thumb?"

Benny pulled the end off his thumb. It was plastic. The handkerchief was stuffed inside. "See?" he said.

Then he put the end of his thumb back into the fake one, and wrapped his other fingers around it in a fist. He popped his thumb out of his fist—his actual thumb, and then reached into his fist and pulled out the handkerchief.

"The hand is quicker than the eye," said Benny, but he didn't seem happy about it.

A pair of cats wandered out of a cell, then stood frozen for a moment, staring back at them.

"Here kitty," said Rachel, and got up to look at them. The cats slunk away.

A set of iron stairs leading upward was visible on the right side about halfway down the hall. "I wonder where that goes," said Rachel.

"I can't believe this is how I'm spending me honeymoon," said Wailer. "Lying on the floor of this manky ruin."

The women fell silent. They heard the sound of rain trickling through the roof of the old prison. From down the hall they heard: *miao.*

"What was that sound we heard before?" said Maisie quietly. "That moaning."

They stared at one another, but no one said anything.

Rachel looked at Wailer's hand.

"Let me see your wedding ring," she said.

Wailer spread her fingers. The ring, which had belonged to Casey's grandmother, was not really meant to be a wedding ring, but Casey loved its weird beauty. There were two rubies on either side of an emerald. It was a stark contrast with her black fingernails.

Wailer smiled. "Don't be blue, Rachel Steinberg. Your day will come."

Rachel's eyes glistened with tears. "You think?"

Wailer nodded, and reached out for Rachel's hand.

"It's not you Quentin doesn't love," said Wailer. "It's himself."

Maisie ran her fingers through her brother's hair. "That's where you're wrong, Wailer," she said. "I think his own self is the only thing that boy does love."

"Yeah, well," said Wailer. "Fuck the bastard. If he can't see you for who you are."

"Which is who?" said Rachel. There was a streak of blue paint on her right hand.

Wailer smiled. "A git."

Rachel laughed. "Aren't you thoughtful."

"No joke, love," said Wailer. "You won't always be crying your eyes out over Q-ball. In years to come you'll have your heart broken by loads of boys. You won't be able to count them all. If you're lucky anyhow."

"So I have that to look forward to," said Rachel.

"A'carse," said Wailer.

The sound of rain on the roof grew slightly less intense. Maisie leaned back against the wall and closed her eyes, her arm still around the boy. Wailer glanced at Rachel, then got to her feet.

"I gotta go for a whiz," she said. "You good?"

"Yeah, I'm okay," said Rachel.

"Me too," said Maisie.

Benny, lying on the floor next to his sister, stuffed his blue silk handkerchief into his fist, and then his thumb down into the fist after it. He opened his hand. The handkerchief was gone.

Wailer walked down the hallway toward Cellblock 4. The creatures scattered.

Rachel watched until Wailer disappeared in the darkness, as Maisie shut her eyes and held her brother. Rachel got up and stood at the center of the prison and slowly turned, gazing at each long hallway in turn. It was possible, she thought, to imagine that she was not the one moving, but that the penitentiary was spinning around her.

There was a shout. Footsteps crackled against the fallen plaster.

"Wailer?" Rachel called. Her voice echoed in the empty space.

"You think she's all right?" said Maisie.

Rachel squinted into the darkness. "I'll just"—she swallowed—"I'll be back."

She walked down Cellblock 4, one hand trailing on the wall. There was a shuffling sound from one of the cells, and Rachel poked her head in. The cell was empty except for the broken springs of the bed. It had a damp, decaying smell.

Rachel looked back down the hall. There was no sign of Wailer. She called out for her again, but she didn't hear anything except the dripping of the rainwater onto the concrete.

A few steps down the hallway was a circular iron staircase.

"Hello?"

Placing one hand on the railing, she slowly climbed the stairs. The steps ascended through the ceiling of Cellblock 4, then emerged in an enclosed stone tower. Rachel circled upward. It was dark.

She emerged in a small room open to the elements. It was full of rusted-out equipment. It's that guard tower, she thought. The one they had seen from the street. It looked like it had been built a lot more recently than the rest of the prison. There was the shell of a giant searchlight on one side of the tower, covered with rust.

From there she could see the whole prison, or could have done so in the daytime. In the dark, rainy night, Rachel could only make out the high walls on all sides of the yard, and the arms of the cellblocks reaching out from the midpoint of the Surveillance Hub.

From the corner of the yard off to her left, she heard voices. There was a large maple growing near the wall there, a tree that had clearly not been its current size and shape during the years that the prison was operational. She could see two forms on the ground, looking up at the tree—probably Quentin and Casey, to judge from the silhouettes. A limb moved. Okay, she thought. So Tripper's climbing a tree?

A cold wind blew through the guard tower. Rachel watched it shake the branches of the tree Tripper was climbing. Then, with a gymnastic swing, Tripper dropped off of the tree limb and over the far side of the wall.

Quentin raised both of his arms in jubilation, and he and Casey hugged each other. Oh thank God, she thought. A reprieve.

She turned from the tower and walked back down the spiral staircase. "Wailer?" she called as she arrived at the bottom and looked around Cellblock 4. She heard the sound of the broken plaster crackling beneath her shoes again as she walked past the dark cells back to the Surveillance Hub.

There she found Maisie and Benny, just as she had left them, the young woman's arm curled around her brother.

"Tripper's gone over the wall for help," she said. "He climbed out on a limb of a tree."

"I bet he did," said Maisie. "He's so clever."

"Where's Wailer?" said Rachel.

A cat entered the Surveillance Hub, a black creature with green eyes. Its tail undulated in the air. The cat came to the place where Maisie lay with Benny and sat down. It looked at the child. He was playing with his fake thumb.

"She's not with you?" said Maisie.

"Right then," said Krystal. Somehow he had lost everyone. The young men had run on before him but he could not keep up. His heart was pounding. Krystal held on to the wall of the prison to steady himself.

Now he stood at the entrance to one of the cellblocks. This one wasn't marked. The old man looked down the long hall and saw the abandoned cells on either side, stretching toward infinity.

Krystal stepped into the cellblock and walked gingerly down its length. He reached out with his left hand and felt the wall as he moved swiftly toward the Surveillance Hub. Those girls would be at the center.

He stopped, mid-cellblock, and looked back at the place where he had been. There was a rectangle of dim light at the end where the door stood open. He thought about Quentin, his prize student. He'd been so full of promise, but now the lad was living in his parents' house, translating Whitman, eating baked potatoes.

There were times when Krystal feared he'd given false hope to Quentin Pheaney, that he'd made the young man think that it was possible to exist in the world dedicated only to one's art. He wanted to take Quentin by the shoulders and tell him of his own disappointments, the compromises he'd had to make, starting with spending his life grading papers at Devon Boys' Latin. And there were other burdens Krystal had to carry.

The first time he'd set eyes upon Benny Lenfest was at a cast party at the Lenfests' house. He'd spent a long time talking to little Benny, sitting on the couch telling the child stories. He felt he had a special relationship to the boy. I do not suffer what you suffer, Krystal thought. But I know what it is like to be the only person in the world who speaks one's own particular language—like the last known speaker of a tongue that would become extinct upon one's death. He'd put his hand on the child's shoulder, but out of what he'd thought was kindness—like the way a rescuer would reach out to another man, drowning in the ocean. The girl Maisie had seen but not understood. *Benny, you go to bed, now,* she'd ordered. Then she looked at Krystal with hatred. *You, leave now.*

Miss, I don't know what you think you saw—

I didn't have to see. I know all about you.

He had thought that this meant that he was permanently banished from their company, but then there he was, invited to the wedding of Jon Casey and the Irish girl, or the Geordie, or whatever she was, the girl with the ironically exaggerated accent. Winifred Curtin. He presumed the invitation meant he'd been forgiven, or that Maisie at last understood that she'd misconstrued his actions. But the night had passed without her talking to him. Instead he'd spent the night speaking German with Quentin. He still admired the young man, but it was true that Quentin did not make his spirits lift the way he had when he was still young, a creature still half-formed. He hated the way youth faded off the cheeks of his students, and all their glorious, vague poten-tial boiled down to dreary, fallen specificity. That was what he loved about teaching—all the hope of youth, with the disappointments of the world still to come.

Krystal arrived in the Surveillance Hub and found that the space was empty. There was nothing but the eight arches leading into the darkness of the other cellblocks. "Hello?" he called out, and he heard his own voice as if it belonged to an elderly, trembling stranger.

"I'm alone in the world," he said, and once more his voice echoed in the dark.

"No, you're not," someone said.

⁂

Rachel and Maisie and Benny wandered in the dark, calling for Wailer. She did not reply. They'd been all through Cellblock 4, then returned to the Surveillance Hub, and now were exploring another of the pris-on's radial arms, number 7.

"Wailer?" Rachel called. Her voice echoed down the long hall filled with empty cells, their doors half-open. This one was two stories. A second layer of cells, accessible by a steel mesh staircase, hung over their heads.

"I want to go home," said Benny. "But I can't go home."

"I know," Maisie said. She stopped and squatted down so that she was eye level with her brother. "This is really scary. But we're going to be all right. We just have to find Wailer, and wait for the boys to get help."

"I want to go to the magic store," said Benny.

"I'll take you there, promise," said Maisie. She gathered him into her arms and hugged him. "If we get out of here, I'll buy you some new tricks. I'll buy you a whole bag of tricks."

He looked thoughtful. " 'If'?" he said.

"What's this?" said Rachel. She was standing in the doorway of a cell at the end of the block. A little light from outside shone through an open door. Maisie stood and took Benny's hand and the two of them walked to the place where Rachel was standing.

The cell looked like all the others: a ruined rectangle of broken plaster, peeling walls. A rusted bed stood in the corner. But in one wall there was a hole, and there was dirt and sand in a pile next to the hole.

Rachel bent down and felt the edges of the hole with her palm. "It's a tunnel," she said.

"Seriously?" said Maisie. "Is it a way out? Or—in?"

Rachel touched the walls of the tunnel, and loose plaster crumbled into her palm.

"I don't think it's safe," she said.

A cat padded into the room and stood for a moment watching them. Its tail moved back and forth in a sinuous wave. Then it hopped into the tunnel and disappeared. They looked at the opening in the wall where the cat had gone. From the distance came an echoing *Miao*.

Benny reached out with his hand, but his fingers grasped at nothing.

"I tell you what," said Rachel. "Why don't we find the others?"

The moaning voice rose in the air again, and fell.

They didn't say anything. Maisie took Benny's hand and then they walked out of the cell and then outside. The rain had stopped. The moon was half-hidden behind drifting clouds.

They turned to their left and began walking counterclockwise around the outer perimeter, between the radial arms of the prison and the wall. They passed the main entrance through which they had come hours before, a stone battlement built into the wall. The doorway was still chained shut. For a moment they paused by the door. Rachel shook the gates. The chains rattled.

"Wailer?" shouted Maisie.

They walked past the entrance building and back to Cellblock 1. They looked down the hallway, but saw no one. Then they kept walking around the perimeter.

The frame of a greenhouse with all of its glass panes broken stood between the two long arms of Cellblocks 2 and 13. Old clay pots stood in rows upon metal tables. Nothing grew.

A door just ahead of them shut with a sudden clang. They stopped and stood.

"Wailer?" said Rachel. "Hello?"

The door that had closed was marked Cellblock 5. This structure was different from the others; it appeared to have been built between the radial arms of Cellblocks 2 and 13. It looked newer than the others. Rachel swung the door forward and leaned in. "Hello?" she said.

There was a vibrating sound, like a soft motor running. On one wall was a large electrical fuse box, with rusted buttons and levers. Thick cables threaded into the bottom of the box.

"Who's there?" said Rachel. Maisie and Benny followed her into the chamber.

There were six cells on the right-hand side of the cellblock. They seemed like they were in good condition. The beds still had mouldering sheets and blankets on them. One of the doors stood half-open.

She took another step in. There was a small room at the back, beyond the hallway with the electrical box. Two green eyes stared at her from its heart.

"I wonder where that caveman got to," said Benny.

Through the darkness she could now see what lay before her. A chair was bolted to the floor. Rotted leather straps hung from the arms. A metal helmet with wires dangling from the bottom was suspended at the top. A cat was sitting on the chair, staring at Rachel with a placid expression, as if to say, *Come on, have a seat, why don't you.*

Casey and Quentin were in a ruined chapel. There were two dozen pews, a crumbling altar, and what looked like a baptismal font. A large crucifix hung upon the wall. Water poured steadily through the ceiling and gathered in a pool before the chancel. Quentin sang softly in the hollow space. *"I once had a girl, or should I say, she once had me."* His voice echoed in the dark.

"We've lost our way," said Casey.

"You can say that again," said Quentin.

"Look, man," said Casey. "Nasty Bibles." There were decaying black books on the pews. Quentin reached down and picked one up.

"We hanged our harps on the willows in the midst thereof," he said. Casey didn't recognize the voice. Quentin shook his head.

"Dude," said Casey.

"For there they that carried us away captive required of us a song and they that wasted us required of us mirth, saying, Sing us one of the songs of Zion." His voice caught as he read the Psalm.

Casey looked at his friend in the dim light, a little worried. "Hey, so like, I appreciate the readin' from scripture and junk. But maybe we should, like—"

"How shall we sing the Lord's song in a strange land?" continued Quentin, as if this were the question they had been called upon to answer, and would remain imprisoned until the proper response was found.

"Q-ball," said Casey, putting his hand on the man's shoulder.

"Oh, I just can't stand it," said Quentin, and put the Bible down upon the pew. He sat down and covered his face with his hands.

"What can't you stand?" said Casey.

"Everything," said Quentin. "Nothing." He heaved a mournful sigh. "I don't know how people survive."

"Hey man," said Casey. "It's not some mystery. You just keep putting one foot in front of the other."

"You make that sound like an easy thing," said Quentin.

"It's not easy," said Casey. "But you gotta do it."

"Why," said Quentin. "Why do people gotta do it?"

Casey wasn't sure he would have been up to this question in the best of circumstances, but there in the darkness of the ruined church he felt inadequate and inarticulate. "I don't know, Quentin," he said. "I'm not Mr. Answer Guy."

"So you never struggle with it?" said Quentin.

"With what?"

Quentin just stared down at his shoes. "Everything," he said.

Casey sat down next to him on the pew. "Quentin," he said. "You got friends who love you. You don't have to be such a Lone Ranger."

"You wouldn't if you knew."

"Wouldn't what?"

"Love me."

"If I knew what?"

Quentin sat there for a long time, not saying anything. Casey watched his friend trying to put it into words, and failing.

At last Quentin just flipped open the Bible again. He laughed bitterly, softly. "*I am a brother to dragons, and a companion to owls.*"

"Hey, snap out of it," said Casey, snapping his fingers in front of Quentin's face. "That's a bunch of hooey, and you know it."

"Is it?" whispered Quentin. His voice broke. To Casey's amazement, Quentin appeared to be crying. Tears rolled down his face. "Do I?"

"Hello," said Casey. "You're not a brother to any dragon." He put his arm around his friend. "You're a brother to me."

They sat there for a while. Then they heard a voice, singing.

Quentin's face brightened. "It's Herr Krystal," he said, and leaped to his feet. "It's Nathan!"

"Fine," said Casey, sounding dejected.

"What?" said Quentin.

"Nothing. It's just that I'm here, bending over backwards to snap you out of your mood, but when Mr. K sings some stupid song, you're, like, back in the world. It's like you don't even see me."

Quentin looked at his friend. Casey's eyes were shining. "I see you," he said.

They crept forward through the dark in the direction of Krystal's voice. *I'm alone in the world.* They found him standing in Cellblock 4, gazing down the dim hallway at the abandoned cells.

"No you're not," said Quentin.

The old man's face brightened as he heard the voice of his former student. In the dark it was hard to know what any of them actually looked like.

Rachel and Maisie and Benny were standing in the Surveillance Hub when Quentin, Casey, and Krystal appeared out of the murk of Cellblock 4.

"Quentin!" shouted Rachel, and she ran forward and threw her arms around him. He put one arm around her back. "I was so worried."

"Hey," said Casey. "I'm okay too. Me and Mr. K." He looked around. "Where's Wailer?"

"They heard my voice," Krystal said.

"Slap some bacon on a biscuit," said Quentin, in the voice of John Wayne. "We're burning daylight!"

Rachel pulled back from him. "*What?*" she said.

"John Wayne," said Quentin.

"I know who it is," said Rachel.

"So why'd you ask?"

She stamped her foot. "What's wrong with you?" she said.

Quentin shrugged. "I got voices," he said.

From the end of Cellblock 1, two flashlights stabbed through the dark. "Hello?" said a voice through a megaphone. "This is the police."

"We're here!" shouted Maisie. "We're here!"

Casey bent down to look at something on the floor.

"Stay where you are," said the megaphone voice once more. "We're coming for you."

"Thank God," said Krystal. "It's the cavalry, come at last!"

"They're coming for us," said Maisie, ecstatic. "Tripper did it! We're rescued," she said.

"You have all shown tremendous character," said Krystal. He smiled at Benny, who looked from the older man's face to his sister's.

"Guys," said Casey.

The policemen entered the space where they stood, two large men in blue bearing long flashlights. One of them was wearing a name tag that read DUDLEY. And just behind them was Tripper, still looking remarkably crisp in his monogrammed Oxford shirt. "There you are," he said. "At last."

Maisie rushed toward Tripper and hugged him. "You saved us!" she shouted. "You saved us!"

"Guys," said Casey.

"What?" said Rachel. "What?"

One of the cops shone his flashlight on him so that Casey was bathed in a bright spotlight. There was a soft black lump, a cat. Its neck had been broken.

"Oh," said Benny, and fell to his knees. "Oh, it's Creeper."

Casey picked something off of the floor. It was a wedding ring: one big emerald, two small rubies. An hour ago, it had been Wailer's.

But now it didn't belong to anybody.

6

Philadelphia, Pennsylvania

SEPTEMBER 2015

Sitting at the bar of his restaurant, Casey wondered, not for the last time, whether false hope was an improvement over no hope at all.

"How you doin', boss?" said Sim, the bartender. He was wearing suspenders and had a handlebar mustache. "You wanna let me know if you need anything?"

"I'm all right," Casey said. There was an engineer's hat upon his head. Over in the corner, Cole Bloughin was playing "Norwegian Wood" on his Gibson.

They'd called him before the story was leaked to the news media, which the information officer at the Homicide Division said was "a common courtesy." Casey wasn't sure it was all that courteous. The detective, Gleeson, hadn't provided much detail about the condition of the body. Casey had been trying not to think about it, although the image he'd seen in the paper kept surfacing in his mind, like those oil bubbles rising from the sunken USS *Arizona* in Pearl Harbor. She said there were "other items associated with the body" that indicated it was Wailer's, although she wouldn't go into detail about this either. Detective Gleeson just asked that Casey remain in the Philadelphia area while the investigation continued, in case they had to "call him in to do an identification," a ritual he could barely imagine. He closed his eyes and imagined her out there in the world somewhere, hearing the news that her death had been confirmed. Wailer just laughed. *You bastards will believe bloody anything.*

"*Love craft,*" Casey whispered softly, glancing down at a copy of the *Philadelphia Daily News* that lay atop the bar. The grisly photo was splattered upon the front page.

"Boss," said Sim, urgently, taking the newspaper away from his boss. "Come on. Don't do this to yourself."

"Dude," said Casey angrily. "It's not *me* they did this to." He reached out to take back the *Daily News,* and for a moment the two men tugged at opposite ends of the same newspaper. Then Casey relented, and Sim put the paper facedown upon the bar. Casey held his forehead in his hands.

The hard thing about believing that Wailer was still alive all these years, of course, had been the obvious truth at the center of this possibility: that she'd run off into the world because she'd suddenly regretted her ill-considered marriage. Clearly something had happened that made her realize, *I've got to bloody make me escape,* and cut out while the rest of them were all wandering around the prison lost. And what more compelling motivation could there have been than taking one good look at her husband, all three hundred pounds of him? He imagined her waking up the morning after the wedding, looking at his mountainous silhouette, and thinking, *Bloody hell.* It was hard to blame her. He wouldn't have wanted to have been married to him either.

Of course there were other scenarios—that she'd been kidnapped, that she'd been struck by global amnesia, and so on, but none of these felt as likely as her simply looking at his blubber and thinking, *Right. I've married a giant marshmallow.*

"You know what I don't get?" Sim said. "How come he burns her house down at the end? You know? I mean, is he just a bastard?"

"Yeah," said Casey. "Wait, what?"

"In this song. I guess it's because he has to crawl off to sleep in her bathtub," said Sim. A waitress who called herself Shadow—a young girl with tattoos on her neck—came up and put in an order: two margaritas, a pint of Blue Moon, a pint of Dock Street Ale, and something called a Pan-Galactic Gargle Blaster. Sim knew what that was.

Casey watched the room while Sim started mixing up the drinks. The place had nearly filled.

Cannonball's, in South Philadelphia, was not the restaurant Casey had imagined when he graduated from the Culinary Institute of America in 1988, eight years after Eastern State. Back then, he imagined something much more upscale—poached bluefish, slashed with Champagne hollandaise, medallions of veal, small portions served on enormous plates in a place illuminated by candlelight. Maybe a guy in the corner playing Debussy on the piano.

Cannonball's was not that. Instead, Casey's restaurants were about comfort food. The wood-fired pizzas were his signature. Casey's best-known pie was one with a whole shelled lobster on it, with red sauce, Asiago cheese, and freshly chopped basil. That one was called Down East. Then there was Green Genie: a crust grilled on an open flame, with pesto, caramelized onions, and sweet Italian sausage. And Middle Earth: pesto, fresh mozzarella, sautéed mushrooms and red onions, with kosher salt sparkled around the rim for a pretzely finish. Pizza wasn't the only item on the menu, though. There was jambalaya and meat-loaf muffins and Belgian french fries. The Belgian fries were especially popular with the two a.m. crowd.

He'd been a guest on cooking shows plenty of times, where he was considered a kind of idiot savant. On one show he made a pie called Heart Attack Heaven: bacon, pepperoni, and ham, with cheddar cheese and Sriracha sauce. The host had mocked Casey, but at the end of the show he'd nodded begrudgingly and said, "Man can cook." There'd been talk of getting Casey his own show, but it fizzled out. His restaurants were popular in their neighborhoods, but as the leader of a food movement he was kind of a failure. The era of the three-hundred-pound chef had kind of ended with Paul Prudhomme. Heart Attack Heaven, or Burning Hot Pasta, was something you might go out for, but it wasn't exactly something you wanted to cook at home.

Casey didn't really mind, though. He felt as if he'd found a pretty good place, in spite of his losses. At least he had until today.

He turned around, picked up the *Philadelphia Daily News* again,

and stared at the photograph of the skull. Above this, the headline: OFF
WITH HER HEAD.

Sim finished making the drinks, and Shadow took them away.
"Boss," Sim said, reaching out to take the paper away from Casey.
"Come *on*."

Casey felt his eyes burning. He put one hand to his forehead and
looked down. Sometimes it was hard to remember the person he had
been before he'd lost her, and Quentin as well. Tripper had said to him,
Time heals all wounds, but instead of feeling cheered by this, Casey's
feeling was, *Well if it does, then fuck it. I don't want to be healed.*

"What do you mean, he burns her house down?" Casey said quietly, and dropped the paper onto the bar once more.

"In this song," said Sim. "That's how the whole thing ends."

"Wait. You mean, when he sings about lighting a fire and how good
it is—you think that means he burns her house down, man?" said
Casey. His eyes were still burning. He thought about Quentin, coming
to him while he was a student at the institute, the desperate look upon
his friend's face as they stood there in the graveyard. *Casey,* he'd said,
do you ever want to be—

Sim put a pint glass beneath the tap.

"Well, of course it's a song about arson," he said. "What else does
it mean?"

"I don't know," said Casey, in a broken voice. "I was thinking he
lit a fire in her fireplace. Kind of sat there thinking about her for a
while."

"No, no," said Sim. "She pisses him off when she won't sleep with
him. Like, she says she works in the morning. So when he wakes up all
by himself, he gets his revenge by burning her house down."

"He doesn't burn her fucking house down," said Casey. "Why
would you say that?"

"It's in the song, boss."

"Bullshit. He, like, sits by her fireplace and smokes a pipe—
Norwegian Wood is like, a kind of *tobacco,* man. He sits there and
thinks about this girl he's lost."

"Casey," Sim said. "There's nothing about a pipe in there."

"There's nothing about burning her house down, man!"

"*So, I lit a fire*," said Sim. "How much clearer does it have to be?"

"So it's a song about—arson?" said Casey.

Sim nodded. "It's a song about arson," he said.

From the kitchen there came a scream, followed by the sound of a pot clanging onto the tile floor. Casey looked at Sim, then put his beer down. "Uh-oh," he said, then headed across the room. There was another scream.

Casey entered the kitchen to find the place in an uproar. There was a large pile of noodles on the floor, and one of the waiters was on his rear end next to the pile, as if he'd slipped on the pasta on his way in or out. The cooks were pointing at the ceiling. Marla, the maître d', was covering her head with her hands. Deirdre, the baker, stood in front of the wood-fired oven, with her white chef's apron over her head.

DeAngelo, the line chef, stood on top of a chair swinging a large soup ladle around like a baseball bat. Something black sailed across the room. Marla screamed again.

"The fuck?" said Casey.

"We got a bat," said DeAngelo.

"A bat," said Casey. "Wait, what?"

"A bat," said DeAngelo, and at that moment the bat swept through the air again. There were more screams. "Bat in the kitchen!"

"Open that window," said Casey, pointing to the one next to the wood-fired oven. "Deirdre! Open it up all the way."

Deirdre peeled the apron away from her face, then fearfully opened the window.

There were more screams. The bat flapped over everyone's heads, then crashed into the wall. It fell to the floor, then beat its wings again and sailed up around the desserts.

"This is bad shit, boss," said DeAngelo.

The bat took another pass overhead, then swept downward and landed on top of a bowl of dough near the wood-fired oven. The creature sat there, suddenly seeming much smaller with its wings folded up, not much bigger than a mouse. Casey pulled the engineer's hat off of his head and lowered it swiftly over the animal, trapping it.

"Okay, DeAngelo," he said, handing the man the bowl. "This goes outside. Now."

"You're not going to kill it?" said DeAngelo.

"What do I want to kill it for?"

"In case it comes back."

Casey said, "It's *never* coming back." As he said this, his voice broke. Tears rolled over his eyelashes.

DeAngelo nodded. "Okay, boss," he said, unnerved by the sight of Casey's tears.

"I want this whole area cleaned up," Casey said, his voice still wavering. "Anything she touched, I want cleaned—bowls, ladles, napkins, the works."

"She?" said Marla.

"The bat!" Casey shouted, then blew some air through his cheeks. "The bat," he said again.

"Should we make an announcement?" said Marla.

"What kind of announcement?"

"You know, to reassure people?"

"To reassure people there was an animal in the kitchen? A *marsupial*?"

"Okay," said Marla. "Whatever."

"Bat's not a marsupial," said DeAngelo, walking out the back door now with the bowl of dough and Casey's engineer's hat on top of it.

"I thought they had radar," said Deirdre.

"Yeah, well maybe they don't," said Casey angrily. "Maybe they get lost same as anybody, did you ever think of that?"

DeAngelo came back in, then went over to a big sink and started washing his hands. Marla headed back out to the dining room.

"Don't yell at me!" said Deirdre, her feelings hurt. "What do I know about it!"

"You should—" said Casey, then relented. "Okay. I'm sorry. It's just—"

DeAngelo turned toward Casey as he dried his hands off with a clean towel, gave him back his engineer's hat. Then his attention fell on something just over Casey's shoulder. Deirdre was staring at it too.

"Boss," said DeAngelo.

He turned around. Two people—a man and a woman—stood in the door of the kitchen, along with a Philadelphia police officer. "Jonathan Casey?" said the man. He was wearing a name tag that said DUDLEY.

"Yeah?" said Casey.

The man took a good long look at Casey's face. "You don't remember me, do you?"

"This is my kitchen," said Casey. "You're not allowed in here. No one's allowed in here but my crew!"

The strangers did not seem impressed.

"Who the fuck are you? Are you from the Department of Health? We just got inspected a month ago. We got the highest rating!"

The man and the woman looked at each other. "Man thinks we're from the Department of Health," said Detective Dudley.

"So—you're not?" said Casey.

The detective shook his head.

"I don't *think* so," he said.

7

Philadelphia, Pennsylvania

The androgynous young man looked at her, his face placid, compassionate, transfigured. The fingers of his left hand rested upon his heart; with the index finger of his right hand he pointed toward the heavens. His eyes were widely set apart, and dark. John the Baptist's left eye seemed to look skyward. The right one looked directly into her soul. *After me will come one more powerful than I, the thongs of whose sandals I am not worthy to untie.*

Rachel Steinberg felt lightheaded, transfixed. She had seen Leonardo's *St. John the Baptist* in the Louvre a half dozen times before; she had written about the painting in the '80s, as part of her dissertation entitled *The Mystery to a Solution: Leonardo and Transfiguration*. It was one of her favorite portraits to teach in her class on Italian Renaissance at Haverford College. She'd painted Quentin in this pose, of course, back in college. She still remembered how seriously he took the job of modeling, keeping that one hand raised toward heaven for what seemed like forever. And after, how angry he'd been with the image. *That's not what I look like!* he'd shouted.

To see the Leonardo here, in Philadelphia, her hometown, seemed to change the painting yet again, seemed to make it into a thing almost painfully intimate. In Paris, she'd had to share the painting with hundreds of tourists and spectators, in a room where people had been gazing upon it for hundreds of years. Now the painting was on loan for six months in Philly, and she'd been given special permission to enter the museum an hour before opening, so that she could at last have a conversation with Saint John alone.

In the Louvre, the painting lived in a long gallery just outside the crowded chamber where the *Mona Lisa* hung. A few tourists paused beside it, or took a photograph with their cell phones. There were, sometimes, a few people gathered around it, but this was nothing compared to the hundreds squeezed around the *Mona Lisa*, a painting that, its smile notwithstanding, Rachel thought of as not Leonardo's best work. *St. John the Baptist* was the last painting he'd painted, and it was hard, at this date, to understand how scandalous it had once been. But John was traditionally depicted as a wild-eyed, locust-eating prophet, and there were more than a few medieval paintings that presented John as just this side of a raving lunatic. Instead, here was Leonardo's version: a gentle, androgynous figure, his soft lips and sexy ringlets drawing the viewer close, his face full of forgiveness and love. *Whatever this world is,* the saint implored, *its heartache shall be quelled.* He pointed toward the heavens to urge us toward the kingdom of God. But his other hand was on his heart, as if to show that the wonder of that kingdom lived within us all as well. *Love will prevail,* John said, *and make us both men and women, darkness and light.*

It was Rachel's theory—backed by computer analysis—that the animal skins that cloaked John's midsection, along with the cross above his left shoulder—had been added later, perhaps by someone scandalized by the image. As if, without the cross, the artist's intentions might be misconstrued. And what was it the animal skins were meant to obscure? Was it corporeality itself that had had to be concealed, lest the viewer's attention drift away from redemption and affix on something more carnal instead?

It angered her, even now, that the painting had been altered in this way, that someone who had missed Leonardo's point so completely had so nearly spoiled it. As if the world of flesh were not part of the world God had made. But for all that, the power of the image remained unsullied.

Oh, John the B, she thought. You sexy hound dog. There's just no quenching you.

It was the mouth that had attracted the most attention over the years. It was the same mouth he'd given the *Mona Lisa*, that tight-lipped, mystifying beam. But for Rachel, the haunting thing about John's face was the dark, soft eyes, and the long, curling hair. It was hard to repress the desire to want to reach out and run one's fingers through it. It was such a beautiful face, she thought. The forgiveness and the love that radiated out of it was confounding and humbling.

And yet, for all that, the man in the painting was not some otherworldly avenging Messiah, like the Renaissance Jesus. John had no halo. He was a human. The look on his face said, *I'm like you.* But he'd been transformed through surrender. Love came to him through that upraised finger, as if he were a lightning rod for all the compassion in the universe. Its voltage coursed through him and came out through the fingers of the other hand and consumed his heart. He looked out at Rachel with his deep, forgiving eyes, and said, *This is the world we have been given, a world in which all we know, and all we have, is love.*

Standing there alone in the chamber with him, something caught in Rachel's throat, and she cried out loud. For a moment she staggered, and she raised one hand to her temple. "Oh," she said softly. "I can't."

John the Baptist just looked at her with his soft, divine smile. *Of course you can.*

She turned from the painting and walked out of the room. A guard came toward her. "Is everything all right, Professor?"

She nodded, unable to speak, her eyes moist.

"We're opening to the public in about five minutes," he said.

"Okay," she said, and walked swiftly down the hall and into the ladies' room. She ran some water in the sink and let it fill her cupped fingers. Then she raised the water to her face.

Rachel dried off, tried to shake off some of the emotion that had engulfed her. She looked in the mirror. There she was—fifty-seven years old, her hair still long and curly but now nearly all gray. She wore no makeup. Rachel wasn't even sure she still owned any makeup, although she suspected there might have been a ten-year-old tube of mascara in the back of one of the drawers at her apartment across from campus. Her life, over the years, had attained a simplicity that gave her peace. She'd largely given up dating, owned an old Subaru wagon that spent most of its days in her driveway. She planted flowers in her window boxes, put birdseed in her feeder, and watched the black-capped chickadees and the finches as they landed and fed, and flew.

She left the bathroom, checked her watch. Her hope had been to head over to the Rodin Museum after taking in the Leonardo, but she wasn't sure she was up to it now—all that robust stone. She was a little embarrassed by her emotional reaction to Saint John—what was all that really about? There had been something intimidating about him, as if he were asking her questions he had no right to ask. Really, John the B, she thought. There had been no reason to be rude.

What can I tell you, Rachel, the saint replied. *If you're not going to hear it from me, then who? Come on. I'm one of your oldest friends. You need the people who love you, once in a while, to tell you the truth.*

Yeah? she thought. Well, I don't know about that, Johnny B. People always say that—"I'm just telling you the truth," like they have some access to the truth that eludes other mortals. Over the years she'd known lots and lots of people who styled themselves as "truth-tellers," and the one thing they all had in common was the fact that they were actually less interested in telling you the truth than in hurting you as badly as they possibly could.

I'm not trying to hurt you, the saint replied. *I just want you to become yourself.*

That's the issue here, John? That I'm somehow not myself?

Not your self in full, Rachel.

Myself in full. I'm not even sure I know what that means.

Of course you do.

This full self you're advocating. Do lots of people achieve it? You need to tell me, because it feels to me you're asking for more than most people can attain.

I'm not talking about most people. I'm talking about you.

John the Baptist? she thought. You know what you can do for me now? You can shut the fuck up.

She saw those deep, liquid, loving eyes burning at her. *I can be silent. But the question remains.*

Walking away, Rachel shrugged in exasperation at this awkward conversation. She had a pretty good sense of why she found John the Baptist haunting: she associated him with poor, doomed Quentin, of course, whom she'd loved with a passion that seemed in inverse proportion to his interest in her. She'd spent her college years hurling herself against his invisible force field, again and again—a protective boundary that was just permeable enough to let her conclude, falsely, that she was actually getting through to him now and again. There was something in Quentin that truly seemed to understand her, almost as well as she understood herself. She had never felt so safe with a man before. He was astonishingly gentle and kind to her, less interested in sex, apparently, than in intimacy.

That had been the great thing about being in love with him, of course—but it had also been the chief frustration, in the long run. They never did actually sleep together, which seemed odd in retrospect. And he could shut down just as swiftly as he opened, like some kind of flower that clamped its petals closed at sundown.

It was that last, tragic visit he'd paid to her that haunted her now. After not hearing from him for almost half a dozen years, there he was on the threshold of her place in Dorchester, down on one knee in the middle of the street, proposing marriage as Bobby Trachtenberg looked on. *We're soul mates!* he cried. For all the world he resembled nothing so much at that moment as a drowning man.

She couldn't remember the words she'd said, although she did recall asking, *What's happened to you?*, which, given the circumstances, wasn't a bad question. Later, she fell forward into Bobby's arms, after the man had done one of his backflips in the street. Or had the backflip come before? It was hard to remember.

Maisie Lenfest had been the one to call her, two weeks later, after they found the car. *Rachel,* she said. *He drove straight off a cliff.*

Rachel had just made love to Bobby. She was lying in their big bed naked, her head resting upon the man's hairy chest. *Wait, what?* she'd said. *Who?*

But before Maisie had time to explain, she already knew who it was Maisie was describing.

Quentin's death had been a hinge in her life. For the rest of her days, there would be a time after, and a time before. It was the moment she finally gave up on painting, and resolved to finish her PhD. That hadn't been an especially hard decision—her shows had gone nowhere, and the dreary landscapes she'd been doing since Wesleyan seemed to bore everyone, including herself. As it turned out, she had a real talent for the kind of scholarly writing about art that she'd always loathed as a painter. Even before she finished her dissertation she'd published a half a dozen articles in good journals. She'd been snapped up by Haverford College, tenured early, became chair of her department at the age of thirty-two. Now and again she'd look at one of her paintings, which even before she got out of grad school seemed sophomoric, pomp-ous, needlessly self-involved, and think, Ugh. She only had one in her apartment, the portrait of Quentin. Looking at it, she'd think, *When I was a child, I spake as a child, I understood as a child, I thought as a child. But when I became a woman, I put away childish things.*

Rachel Steinberg suffered from a not uncommon affliction: the thing that she actually loved—painting—was something for which, as it turned out, she had no actual talent. And the thing at which she was something of a virtuoso—academic writing and critical theory—was the thing she loathed. And so success had come to her, as it comes to so many people, not by doing the thing she loved, which she did ineptly, but by doing the thing she hated, at which she was a genius.

This, sadly, had turned out to be the case in her love life as well. There had really only been two men in her life—Quentin and Bobby—

and her passion and her talent for these two loves had mirrored the same heartbreaking mismatch she'd experienced in her professional life. She'd adored Quentin, just as she'd adored being a painter—but outside of the adoration itself, every aspect of this one great love of hers had been a disaster, ending in a collection of ugly canvases, ending in a suicide.

Bobby Trachtenberg hadn't seemed like a natural boyfriend at first, what with the backflips and the beer belly. But in a strange way, Quentin's death had touched him too, even though he'd only met the man the one time. In the weeks after, he kept turning to Rachel and asking her things like, *Do you think I could have helped him if I hadn't been such a jerk?* Rachel had assured him that whatever Quentin had been haunted by, it wasn't the gymnastics of Backflip Bob, but there were times she asked herself variations on the same question, blaming herself for not pulling Quentin back, somehow, from the cliff that waited for him.

Bobby went into therapy, stopped drinking, and eventually wound up getting a master's in social work. When Rachel got the job at Haverford, he'd found a job in the Dean of Students Office, eventually becoming the dean in charge of the sophomores. Slowly, inevitably, they started talking about marriage, a union they kept strictly theoretical until after Rachel's tenure decision. Then, the morning after the college president told her the good news, she felt a strange hollowness. She poured herself a whiskey at eleven in the morning, and stared out the window at their backyard in Bryn Mawr, where there was a rusted swing set left by the house's previous owners.

The dean of sophomores gave her a perfunctory kiss. Then he said, "We're not going to make it, are we?"

Within two years, he'd married someone else, another one of the deans, a girl with the ridiculous name of Bronwen. They'd even invited her to the wedding, there in the Bryn Mawr Presbyterian Church. But Rachel didn't go. She was in Paris, gazing upon Saint John in the Louvre.

Now she walked through the museum toward the Impressionists. *You know what you never told me, John the B. You never told me that the one whose coming you foretold would also turn out to be a man whose love I could not keep.*

There was a time when all of this had made her angry, that the love she wanted she had lost, and the love she could have kept was one she did not desire. She'd kept her eyes open in the years after she and Bobby broke up, on the off chance that there was a third love waiting for her. Who knows? It was possible that the one whose coming had been foretold had, even now, not yet arrived.

But so what, Rachel thought. If the love of her life arrived now, it would still be too goddamned late. Fifty-seven was not ancient, but it was old enough for her to have settled into a life that revolved around academic research, around the *Times* crossword, around her old dog Moogus. Uptown Spinsterville, she thought. The likelihood that her life would alter much from what it had become was pretty small. From here on out, what she had to look forward to was mostly diminishment.

Starting with Moogus, a Springer spaniel well beyond her sell-by date. The week before, Moogus had lacked the energy to even climb out of her dog bed, and just looked at Rachel with her wet, disappointed eyes. Rachel should have had the dog put down by now. But she lacked the courage to take the dog for that last ride.

Now and again she'd make eye contact with someone—a young man in a museum, a stranger at a conference—and wonder whether this was the person she was still supposed to be waiting for. She read them all like clues leading her toward her real life, a life that after all these years still felt to her as if it had not yet begun. A life still frozen at the moment Wailer disappeared.

Died. Not disappeared. She supposed she'd have to start saying it now. Until they'd found the body, there'd been the possibility, remote as it was, that Wailer had given them all the slip. That had been Casey's theory anyhow, and she'd been too kind—or cruel—to tell him any different.

Rachel stopped in her tracks. Before her, taking up an entire wall, was Cézanne's *The Large Bathers*. She sighed. Perfect, she thought. Now this day's complete.

Tell me what you see, said John the B.

They've changed, she thought. Even those big bathers are not what they once were.

It's not the bathers that have changed, Rachel Steinberg.

Oh, John. When I was young, I thought these enormous women were eternal. The embodiment of the feminine sublime.

And now?

Now I see them for what they are.

Which is?

Oh, there's nothing eternal about any of us anymore.

Rachel, John said, looking at her with his sweet, forgiving eyes. His hand on his heart. The other one pointing toward the heavens. *We are here for more than this.*

"*More?*" Rachel said out loud, angrily. She stamped her foot. "What more exactly?"

8

Cold River, Maine

In the morning, I found my husband asleep with his arms around the dog. There was soot all over Jake's face, meaning that when he'd come home from the fire he'd been too exhausted to wash up. My husband was perhaps the last man in New England to wear a union suit unironically. His clothes were in a pile on the floor, right where he'd dropped them in the middle of the night, before slipping into bed beside me. Jake, as handsome and placid asleep as awake, held Gollum in a loving embrace.

Sunlight reflecting off the lake rippled across our ceiling. Jake and I had built the house ourselves, back in 2005. It was all post and beam—there was hardly a nail in the thing except for the ones that held the pumpkin pine panels to the wall. I loved lying there in the mornings, watching the light, listening to the man I loved snore beside me. I felt so safe beside him, immune to whatever cruel fates were out there in the world. I'd have stayed there all day if nature hadn't called.

Instead I eased myself quietly out of bed—Gollum opened an eye, then closed it—picked up Jake's clothes off the floor, and went to the bath- and laundry room. I was just about to drop them into the drum of the washer when I thought twice, and raised his shirt to my face. It didn't smell like smoke.

I went through his pockets. I found about a dollar's worth of change, a half a pack of Life Savers, and a crumpled-up receipt from the Downeast Roadhouse Barbecue, in Augusta. It was dated the night before.

I threw out the receipt, put his clothes in the washer, and hit the Start button. I stood there for a moment listening to the sound of water filling the drum.

Later, I took a cup of coffee down to the lake and sat in the hammock and watched the water. It was early still, not quite seven. The coffee was hot, and the day was clear. A few fishermen drifted north on the opposite side of the pond with their trolling motors. I watched as they cast out with their lures.

A pair of loons floated past, maybe the same ones I'd heard the night before. One of them disappeared beneath the surface, diving down for fish. The other one called out softly.

I thought about my trip to New York and the story on Hart Island I'd been trying to do, a story that I now suspected I'd never write. The image of the skull that I'd fleetingly seen on the front page of the *Daily News* flickered before my eyes and I remembered Wailer, and Casey, and our hopeful young selves.

I wondered, as I sat there drinking my coffee, my husband and son and dog happily snoring away in our little post-and-beam house, if meeting people with creativity and passion when you were at an impressionable enough age actually kind of ruined you for life among normal people.

For a long time, I'd searched the world, thinking I could start up new friendships like the ones I'd had before. But I never met people like that again. I know people will think that's what everyone believes about their college friends, but it's true. Maybe we're like flowers that open up at that brief moment in our lives, and after that, we close up again, one by one. I know this is a cheesy thing to say. But I think it sometimes.

My cell phone came alive with the dog-barking sound I use as a ring tone—a sound folks find adorable if they're dog people, not so much if not. I didn't recognize the number.

"Hello?"

"Hello, who's this?" She was young.

"This is Judith Carrigan, who's this?"

"So your name is Judith. He wouldn't tell me your name."

"Who?"

"Karl."

"I don't know any Karl."

"Seriously?" she said, already fed up with me. "It's going to be like that?"

"I'm hanging up," I said.

"Don't you dare hang up on me, Judith Carrigan," she snapped. "I know what you're up to."

My heartbeat quickened in my throat when she said this, because of course I *was* up to something. The question was how this woman knew about it, how she could possibly have information on things that had happened over thirty years ago.

"What's *your* name?" I asked her.

"As if you didn't know," she said.

"Miss," I said, trying to keep my voice steady. "I think you have me mixed up with someone else."

"Ugh," the woman said in exasperation and contempt. "Just admit it."

"Admit what?" I said.

"Look, my boyfriend woke up with your phone number scrawled on his chest. In lipstick."

I took this in, then repressed the urge to laugh.

"I don't wear lipstick," I said, and hung up.

"Who was that?" said a voice behind me, and suddenly there he was: the man I loved. Jake stood beside me, his hair still tangled from sleep. He had a tennis ball in one hand and a cup of coffee in the other. Gollum sat beside him, his attention absolutely affixed upon the tennis ball in Jake's fingers.

"Some lunatic," I said.

Jake sipped his coffee. "Don't narrow it down much, does it." He threw the tennis ball out into the water, and Gollum ran after it. Although the old dog was arthritic and senile, he was beautiful in the water. He reached the end of the dock and gave a magnificent leap off the end, his front paws tucked in like a steeplechase horse. There was a mighty splash as Gollum hit the surface of the lake. Then he swam toward the place where the ball floated.

My husband sat down next to me on the hammock and put an arm around me. My heart melted a little. We'd been apart for three days. We kissed, which was nice, but I wrinkled my nose as well. Because he looked like a chimney-sweep out of *Mary Poppins*.

"You've got soot all over your face," I said.

"Yeah," he said. "Big barn fire last night. Up in Smithfield."

"What time did you get in?"

"Four a.m." He sipped some more coffee. Jake was wearing a pair of jeans over his union suit. At fifty-seven, he still had a full head of black hair. The only gray on him was in his mustache.

"When did you get the call?"

"About five. We were there half the night," he said. "Me, Dave, Cooper-Dooper, the whole crew."

I watched as Gollum, tennis ball in mouth, reached the shore and shook himself. Water sprayed in every direction. "Did you get any dinner?"

He didn't pause. "Nope," he said. "Ate some of that pie when I got in."

Gollum drew near, dropped the tennis ball at my husband's feet.

I looked at Jake. His eyes were focused on the horizon. I tried to plumb those depths, but I didn't see anything there, just the man I'd been married to for fifteen years.

"Come on," I said. "I'll make you breakfast.'

He turned to me and said, "Darlin' girl." Then he folded me into his arms again and held me and I put my face in his neck. I still didn't smell any smoke.

We walked toward the house, holding hands. A car hauling a bass boat came down our dirt road, and the driver waved at us as he passed the house.

"Go on, you get a shower," I said, "while I sauté some onions."

He nodded at me again and those twinkling black eyes sparkled at me, and he said, "I love you, Judith Carrigan," and I said, "You should."

Then he padded back upstairs. A moment later I heard the water running in the shower.

I chopped up a red onion and put it in an iron skillet with a generous slab of butter. There was the sound of an ancient paw against the porch door. *Gollum*.

He has some part to play yet, for good or ill, before the end, I thought, although what part Gollum had to play at this point in our lives was unclear, unless it involved falling over and lying on the floor with his paws in the air.

I slid open the glass door to let the old dog inside, and I was just about to close it again when I saw that something had happened to our barbecue grill during the night. The stainless-steel grill surface had been dislodged, and the shards of charcoal briquettes were gathered in a small telltale pile. As if someone had intentionally taken some of the charcoal and crumbled them in his hands. I stood there for a moment thinking all this over.

Then I smelled smoke from the stove, and rushed back to the kitchen to find the onions burning.

I reached to move the skillet off the heat, but the iron pan had gotten so hot while I was looking at the mess on the porch that I burned myself on the handle, and the whole thing fell to the floor with an enormous clang. Onions and butter were everywhere. I raised my burned hand to my lips and felt the tears coming to my eyes.

After breakfast, I drove the boat out to the center of the lake and killed the engine. The world seemed so quiet after the roar of the outboard, but there was sound still. I heard the creaking of crickets in the reeds. Waves lapped against the hull.

Late summer is my favorite time of year in Maine. The tourists are mostly gone, but the warm, bright days still continue. Most of the mosquitoes and blackflies have been eaten by now, snarfed down by bats and chickadees and crows. From my position midlake I could see the silhouette of Arnold's General Store, and the long set of docks beside it. There was one aluminum bass boat tied up there. The rest of the docks were empty.

I stood up and pulled my shirt off over my head, and then stepped out of my shorts, leaving me in my black Land's End one-piece, the kind of "sensible" bathing suit moms my age are partial to. The bikini days are over, I reckon. But that's all right. I had my fun.

Standing in the bow of the boat, I raised my hands over my head, then dove headfirst into the lake. The top six inches of the lake were warm as could be; the next two feet down were cool, and the next six feet shockingly cold, even here in the first week of September. I didn't open my eyes. A few moments later I burst back onto the surface, and filled my lungs with air. While I was under, the boat had drifted away a little, and I swam toward it and reached up and grasped the stern. On the hull was written the name of our boat, the *Red Wedding*. Falcon thought it up. People who knew those *Game of Thrones* books thought this was very funny. I hadn't. Using the outboard as a ladder, I stepped on the housing just above the propeller and hauled myself back up. Then I stepped onto the boat again and wrapped myself in a towel.

The towel was pink, and on it were the words "Exeus Travel," which was the company that arranged my trip to Easter Island, one of the first travel pieces I ever did for Condé Nast. It was that piece, in fact, that had won me my first award, and which secured my place as a working freelancer, at least for a little while. I still remembered getting up before dawn to climb the volcanoes on Rapa Nui, to see the sun rise from one of the ancient quarries where those now-vanished people had carved all those giant stone heads. As I climbed up the volcano all by myself, I'd felt my heart beating, feeling like I was trespassing on a cursed, sacred site. The mountainside was covered in predawn fog, and the stone heads loomed out of it now and again when the path led past them. There'd been a sudden movement before me, a pair of shining eyes, and I'd cried out loud. I was probably more fearless than a lot of other women my age, the result, perhaps, of the man's life I'd lived until I was twenty-nine, a half a lifetime of male socialization and privilege. I was perhaps more blind to the perils awaiting me in a lot of situations, which was good for me as a travel writer, and bad for me as a woman. As those eyes came toward me through the haunted fog I had cursed myself for my stupidity, for the way I constantly mistook my own blindness for courage. A pebble rolled down the path as the approaching footsteps kicked it loose.

Then a horse stepped out of the fog and stared at me. We stood there frozen for a full minute, each of us afraid to move. Then the horse stepped off the path and walked off among the mountainside tableau of ancient staring stone faces. I swallowed, and continued my ascent.

I dried myself off with the pink Exeus towel and lay in the bow staring up at the sky. I felt the sun on my face and on my neck, and it felt good.

I thought about the Hart Island story again, and wondered who would ever want to read such a thing. I had a pretty good idea for the lede, an anecdote about the captain of the Department of Corrections ferryboat meeting me at the dock on City Island and elegantly taking my hand to help me on board as if we were about to visit some exclusive resort.

"Welcome aboard, Miss Carrigan," he'd said, and I countered, politely, "Mrs."

I sat up and looked back at the shore. I could just barely see the outline of our house. Jake's truck was gone, meaning that he and Falcon had headed out. Jake knew that I didn't like Falcon riding in the septic-tank truck with him, and so the two of them had waited until I'd driven off in the boat before departing on today's disgusting adventure. Not that I objected to Jake's means of making a living; the septic-tank business had paid for the boat I was sitting in, among other things. He made three times as much each year from sucking the poop out of people's tanks as I did writing for Condé Nast, a fact which he was not shy about reminding me. He got another $25,000 a year working for the Kennebec County fire department, so if you added it all up, most of my travel writing hardly made a dent in the overall budget of our household. It was effluvium and fire that would pay for Falcon's college, assuming he went. But in my heart I feared that Falcon would jilt the liberal arts in favor of his father's suck truck. That was one reason I objected to Falcon heading off with Jake on these runs; it made his future seem all too predictable. There'd come a day when they'd repaint the trucks, Carrigan and Son, and then it'd be my son driving around Kennebec County, digging a hole in people's side yards and pumping out the effluvium through the big, nasty hose. On the back of the truck, then as now, would be the words: *Your Business Is Our Business.*

Falcon, of course, was not my biological son; I met Jake less than a year after his first wife died, on a night when I'd been clever enough to set my house on fire. I'd fallen asleep dead drunk, leaving a pot of macaroni and cheese on the stove, which was enough to send smoke out the window and set off the smoke detectors, while I lay passed out in a vodka stupor on the couch. Jake and the others had come through the door in their yellow coats and black boots and fire masks, holding axes and hoses, while I sat up on the couch looking at them. I'd fallen asleep with my shirt off, so the first time my future husband ever saw me I was sitting there in a beige bra with my hair tangled over my head. The guys saw it wasn't an emergency right away. One of them went over to my stove and put the mac and cheese pot in the sink and filled it with water; there was a huge cloud of sizzling steam. Another guy reached up and reset my smoke detector. They were already wrapping up the hoses as I was pulling my shirt back on over my head.

"You all right, miss?" said Jake, taking his mask off.

Tears trembled in my eyes, because clearly I was not all right. "Yeah," I said. "I'm sorry."

"Don't be sorry," said Jake, and there was such incredible kindness in those eyes. I remember thinking how odd it was that a fireman would have such beautiful and delicate eyelashes. You'd think that, given the profession, they'd get all singed off.

A couple days later, he knocked on my door. I didn't recognize him at first out of uniform. Then I saw the eyelashes.

He was holding a cardboard box of Kraft macaroni and cheese. "I figured maybe you needed a replacement?" he said.

Before we got married I had to figure out what to tell him. I wanted so much to be able to reveal the whole harrowing story, to begin with the day I rolled the Volkswagen off the cliff in Nova Scotia, and take him right up to the evening I drank all that vodka and passed out on my couch and set my house on fire. I knew it was the right thing to do, and I set out to do it nearly a dozen times. Once, I even got as far as saying, "Look, you don't know about my past," and he just waved me off. He said, "I don't want to know about your past," which was his way, I think, of saying that he didn't want to talk about his either, especially the relationship he'd had with Falcon's mother, Sarah. I knew that they'd been unhappy for years, and that having a child had been the last Hail Mary pass of the marriage.

But sparing me the details of an unhappy marriage, with all its infidelities, was different from somehow never coming right out and saying, Listen, I was born a guy, okay? I hope you don't mind. Although that of course is the wrong language for talking about it in the first place.

But Jake *would* mind. You know how I know this? Because back when I was a guy—though, like I said, that's the wrong word for it—if a woman I'd been in love with didn't tell me *she* was trans, I would have minded. It wouldn't have made any difference to me, of course, but it would have made me angry that she didn't tell the truth.

And yet, I never told him. I've never told a soul. Maybe this makes me a coward, but it's my secret to keep. So far as the world knows, I'm a woman who grew up in Pennsylvania, the only child of parents who died young. I know he thinks it's weird that I don't have any friends from childhood or college. But once I moved in, the three of us became the only family any of us knew, or needed. Less than a year after Jake first found me passed out drunk on the couch, I was holding Falcon asleep in my arms, Jake's arm around my back, as the two of us watched *Survivor* on TV. Jeff Probst took the idol from one of the players, and announced, "Once again, immunity is back up for grabs."

And so, there was a whole world of things that Jake would never know.

He would never know, for instance, about my hitchhiking from Nova Scotia back to America. Who picked me up? The guy in the monster truck called Dondi's Inferno. His name, indeed, was Dondi, and he'd been at some Canadian truck rally, and he was on his way back home to West Virginia. Dondi was a sweet man, considering he drove a monster truck for a living. He could tell I was in trouble. Didn't ask too many questions. Dropped me off at Hyde Park, New York, not far from the Hudson River. Casey was a student at the Culinary Institute of America then, "majoring in sauces," he'd said. I knocked on the door of his house. We hadn't seen each other for a few years, but Casey didn't seem surprised to see me.

"Dude," he said.

"Casey," said Quentin. "I—I'm fucked up."

"Yeah okay," he said. "Well come on in."

Quentin lay down on his couch. Casey made him a Spanish omelet with chopped red onions, goat cheese, and something called scapes, which is halfway between a green onion and garlic. He chopped fresh basil and sprinkled that on top. By the time he came out into the living room, Quentin was already asleep. Casey woke him up, and Quentin ate the omelet without saying anything. It was good. He put the empty plate on the coffee table. He didn't know what was going to happen next.

"I need money," Quentin said.

Casey looked at him, then nodded. "Okay," he said. He picked up the plate and took it back to the kitchen.

"Don't you want me to tell you how much?"

He rinsed the plate, dried it with a checkerboard dish towel. "Figured you'd get around to it."

"Twenty thousand dollars," Quentin said, a figure he made up on the spot. He didn't know how much it cost to change genders. Was that figure high or low? Even though it was the central question of his life, he had no way of knowing the answer, not then, in those days before the Internet. Where would a person go to find the answer to such questions? Whom would you ask?

"Yeah," said Casey. He thought it over. "Whatever." Then he went to his desk and wrote out a check. He handed it to Quentin. "There ya go."

Quentin took it from him. "Seriously?" he said. "That's it? Just like that?"

"You said you needed money," Casey said.

"Don't you want to know what it's for?"

"You want to tell me?"

Quentin looked at his friend—no longer the adorable fatso of his youth, but still sweet-faced and round. He could see—or imagined that he could see—the horrors of Eastern State upon him. But maybe that's just because Quentin knew what to look for.

He figured he ought to tell Casey what the plan was. To speak it out loud for the first time in his life. *I've always felt like a woman inside,* he wanted to say. *I need to go away and deal with it. It's not about being feminine. It's about being female.*

But of course he had no language for any of this, only the endless, strange desire that felt like a knife in his heart, at every hour of every day. He felt the sweat trickling down his temples, and his heart pounding in his chest. He wanted so dearly to tell Casey what he felt. But where would one begin?

Casey smiled. "You're sure you don't want to tell me what's the what?"

Quentin looked at his friend, the adorable fat fuck. He loved him like a brother. But he did not have the words.

"I want to tell you," Quentin said.

"Tell you what," he said. "You get yourself a good night's sleep. We'll take a drive tomorrow, okay? You want to talk, you talk. It's all fine."

Casey sat down next to Quentin on the couch, and he touched the side of his friend's face, a strangely intimate gesture considering what awkward men they both were. "You got gears," he said. "Spinning away inside you, man. I seen it. Long as I've known you."

Quentin nodded. Tears welled up in his eyes. "I've got gears," he said.

"I got gears too," Casey said. Then he stood up and he turned off the lights.

"Not like mine," said Quentin.

Casey started up the stairs. "I know," he said.

The next day, Casey made Quentin pancakes made from cornmeal—tiny little cakes about two inches in diameter, topped off with fresh raspberries, crème fraîche, and real maple syrup. Quentin was still lying on his couch. After he cleaned up the breakfast, Casey said, "I'm thinking we should take some acid."

Quentin had never been much of a druggie, in part because he was always afraid his secret self would somehow leak out while he was in some psychogenic fugue. But that morning he felt like, What the hell. Let it out. What's the difference now?

"Okay," he said.

"Yeah," said Casey. "You know, just to be on the safe side."

"Right. Just to be on the safe side."

Three hours later, they were walking around Woodlawn Cemetery in the Bronx. It was high noon in the city of the dead. Casey had brought his ukulele.

Casey stood before a headstone, peeing. "Who's this Elizabeth Cady Stanton?" he said. Quentin checked the pamphlet. He'd picked it up on their way in. The thick, shiny letters oozed across the page like motor oil. *You shouldn't be peeing on someone's headstone,* Quentin noted, *especially hers,* but since they'd entered Woodlawn his voice had become audible only to dogs.

"Man," said Casey, giving it a shake. "There's nothing like it, is there?"

"We're in *trouble!*" Quentin said, using the Common Speech.

The raw fingers of the dead clawed through the earth like red flowers.

"Easy now," said Casey. He was looking at the stream his pee had made. Steam was rising from the torrent. The air filled with metal dragonflies, drawn toward the warmth. He strummed his ukulele. "*Way down upon the Swanee River,*" he sang.

"*Eeeeee,*" Quentin said in the dog pitch, and started laughing, remembering the closing lines from James Joyce's "The Dead." *It was eeeeeeeeeeee for Gabriel to set eeeeeeeeeeee on his journey eeeeeeeeeeee.* They took a few steps, then paused to stand like funerary statues. From Yankee Stadium, a mile away, they heard the sound of a thousand weeping angels.

"What is that?" said Casey. "What *is* that?"

"The *eeeeee* is *eeeeeeeeee* all over Ireland," Quentin said.

Casey shook his head. "Can't you hear that? The screaming?"

Quentin stood there listening to the screaming. He was so skinny for a moment he thought he was a scarecrow. He could hear it all right.

They had paused in front of the tomb of F. W. Woolworth. This was a vast Egyptoid pyramid guarded by two sphinxes with remarkably supple breasts.

Then the screaming stopped. Quentin checked the map but it was impossible to know what it had to do with their current situation. "It says Herman Melville is buried here," he said.

Casey played his ukulele some more. "*Way far away,*" he sang.

Quentin joined in. "*That's where my heart is yearnin' ever.*" Casey stopped. The music echoed around and around.

"I never read any Melville," said Casey. "I always figured, what's the point?"

"The boy stood on the burning deck!" Quentin said, trying to be helpful.

If Melville's headstone hadn't called out to them, they might not have found it. "*Allo, squire!*" said the headstone. The accent was surprising. "I thought he was American," said Casey.

"Yeah, well, for a while he lived with cannibals," Quentin said.

They sat down before the tomb. It had several unusual aspects. For one thing, it was dominated by a large stone page, all blank. Beneath the blank page was an engraved quill pen. And all across the top were dozens of pens people had left, as a token they'd been there-o.

"Is *Moby-Dick* the one with Captain Quick?" said Casey.

"No, it's the *eeeeee*. The great white *eeeeeeee*." Casey covered his ears, as if the inaudible pitch was piercing his eardrums.

"Sorry," Quentin said.

"I saw that, with Humphrey Dumpty. Clacking his metal balls." Quentin did his Humphrey Bogart imitation, which came out like James Cagney. "*You dirty rat.*" Casey knew what he meant though.

Quentin was down on the ground now, facing the sky. Melville was six feet below. From Yankee Stadium, a thousand strangers wept again. Casey picked a pen off the top of the grave. "Here ya go, old buddy," he said kindly. "When you write the story of your life, write it with this."

Quentin put the pen in his pocket, but he didn't think it was going to make any difference. He stretched his fingers toward the blue. It eluded him. "How does anybody do anything," he asked Casey, like he was some great authority, but when Quentin looked over at his friend he was wearing his veins on the outside, which was disgusting.

"Excuse me, is that Melville?" said a voice, and there was a shy little man with a raincoat.

"*Olé, hombre!*" said the headstone.

"Now, that's weird," said Quentin. "For us, it was Brutish."

"This is him," said Casey. "You want a hit?"

"We're all done," Quentin said. He took his hand out of his pocket, but the pen Casey had given him had leaked. Quentin's fingers were shiny with the plasma.

The stranger stepped forward. He reached toward the stone, his fingers trembling. "Ah! Ah! Ah!" he said, like Frankenstein's monster. "Ah! Ah! Ah!"

"Well, *we're* just gonna mosey on *outta* here," Casey said, and they left Melville where he was, alone with the Frankenstein. Later they wound up back at Woolworth's pyramid. Quentin kept looking at those sphinxes and their beautiful breasts. He wondered if, once he was female, he'd look like one of them. It was so strange. He knew he was a woman on the inside, but he had no idea what he would look like, or who he would be, once he turned inside out. The thought that he would, when all was said and done, be pretty much himself, the person he'd been all along, was, incredibly, one that had not yet occurred to him. The future would take its own sweet time revealing itself.

"You ever go to a Woolworths?" asked Casey. It was a stupid question; of course Quentin had been to a Woolworths. Who hadn't been to a fucking Woolworths?

"Casey," Quentin said, his voice all blubbery. "Do you ever want to be——?"

He wanted to cry again, but he was too tired. Quentin wanted to shout: *Listen, I'm going to be using the name Judith from now on.* But how could you say such things out loud? He looked at the sphinxes, wondered what their names had been.

Casey played his uke. "*All the world is sad and dreary,*" he noted. "*Everywhere I roam.*"

"Call me Ishmael," Quentin said, but he was back in the dog pitch again, and it came out, "Call me *eeeeeeeeee.*" It was just as well. Ishmael wasn't what he wanted to be called anyhow.

He wondered what time it was. It was impossible to know how many days they'd been walking around these headstones. Pretty soon the two of them were going to be in worse shape than this, if they got locked in again. What would they tell the dead, if they asked the living who they were, and what it was they wanted?

And then they heard it, that dying scream. It swirled in the air between them, bouncing back and forth like an echo between two canyons. They'd heard this sound before.

The cry echoed and died out. "I'm going to go away for a while," Quentin said, after a while.

"Probably a good idea," said Casey.

"You won't tell anybody you saw me?"

"Not if you don't want."

"I'm serious," Quentin said. "If cops come asking, you have to say you never saw me."

"I don't see you now, man," he said.

"I know," Quentin said. "I'm trying to—I want to—" He decided to tell him. *I'm going to become a woman, and live an actual life instead of a fake one.* But once more his words just came out as ear-piercing silence. *Eeeeeeeeee.*

Casey held his hands to his ears. "You're hurting my brain with that," he said.

"It's not my fault," Quentin said, his voice catching. "None of it's my fault."

Casey came over to his friend. He spread his big arms and hugged Quentin. It was like being contained by the universe. There was Quentin, against all odds, sitting in the middle of a great, forgiving sun.

Then he pulled back, and he put his hands on Quentin's cheeks, and Casey brought his face forward and he kissed Quentin on the lips—softly, gently, sweetly. "You're going to be okay," he said, but strangely, the voice did not sound like Casey's. It was the voice of a commanding ghost, someone speaking from beyond the grave. "All right? You're going to be okay."

"I love you," Quentin said. It was the only thing he could possibly say, plus it had the benefit of being profoundly, painfully true.

Casey smiled. "Well, fuck," he said. "Why *wouldn't* you?"

They stood there in the graveyard for a couple of years, looking at each other, feeling the warm glow of everything left unsaid. And then I said the brave thing.

"I guess I have to find my way," I told him.

"Am I going to see you again?" said Casey.

"I don't know."

For a moment we stood there, looking at each other.

Then I turned my back on my friend and left him there among the dead. As I approached the gates of Woodlawn Cemetery, I saw the Frankenstein guy again. He'd gotten away from Melville at last.

"Ah! Ah! Ah!" he moaned. "Ah! Ah! Ah!"

There stood the stranger in his raincoat, beseeching me, his hands held outward, desperately grasping for a thing he could not name.

9

Philadelphia, Pennsylvania

"I want my phone call." Casey sat in the interrogation room with the two cops, Detectives Dudley and Gleeson. Gleeson, an African American woman with short-cropped hair, looked at Dudley uncertainly. Casey remembered Dudley now from Eastern State. He'd been the one with the megaphone, the one whom Tripper had brought in like the cavalry coming to save them all. He'd shone his light on Casey as he squatted there on the cement floor, looking at Wailer's ring, torn from her finger and dropped there, as if to say, *Well, we won't be needing this anymore.*

"Relax, Mr. Casey," said Gleeson. "You're not under arrest."

"So I can just go? Seriously?"

"Well, if you want to play it like that."

"Play it like what? What are we playing? You are messing with me! It's not—nice!"

"We just need to ask you some questions."

"Yeah?" said Casey. "Well, I want a lawyer, and I want to make my phone call."

"Okay, okay, okay," said Gleeson. "I think maybe we got off on the wrong foot."

"Mr. Casey," said Dudley, "you're not under arrest. You don't need a phone call."

"The wrong foot," said Casey, shaking his head. "Yeah, you could say that. You embarrassed me in my own kitchen! In front of my staff! They were makin' people's *dinners.*"

The room had a single fluorescent light hanging from the ceiling. The walls were beaten-up wood paneling. In the corner was a bulletin board with no bulletins on it, not even a thumbtack.

"Mr. Casey, tell us the last time you saw your wife?" asked Dudley. He was a fat man with a ring of short gray hair around his bald head. He sounded tired.

"The last time?" said Casey. "You know. When we were all in Eastern State."

"Specifically," said Dudley. "You all were wandering around?"

"We weren't wandering around," said Casey. "We were trying to get the fuck *outta* there, man."

"Were you with her when she disappeared?" said Gleeson.

"What?" said Casey. "How could I have been with her when she disappeared? If I'd been with her she wouldn't have disappeared. It never would have happened, thanks for reminding me. What's *wrong* with you?"

"Maybe you could just explain it," said Gleeson.

"I told you this story thirty-five years ago!" said Casey.

"I was in kindergarten," said Gleeson.

"Ask him," said Casey, pointing at Dudley. "He knows the whole story."

"It's been so long," said Dudley. The man was sweating. "I need you to help me remember."

"Fuck you, I want my lawyer," said Casey. "I've seen cop shows. I get a lawyer, and I get to make a phone call, and the rest of this is fucking *bullshit*."

Dudley looked at Gleeson. "Man says he's seen cop shows."

"Yeah, asshole," said Casey. "And you know what, on cop shows the Philadelphia Police Department is always the worst. Did you ever notice that? If the cops are from Philly, they're always corrupt. Like on *Better Call Saul*? Or that Harrison Ford movie about the Amish? It's always the Philly cops that are the crooks, man. I know all about you guys."

Gleeson sat down in a chair across from Casey. "Why don't we start over?" she said. "Just tell it from the beginning."

"And tell the truth this time," said Dudley. "Spare us the lies you gave us last time, okay? I lost decades of my life on this case, thanks to your bullshit." Something about the way he said this—*decades of my life*—made it sound very personal.

"You're doing that good cop/bad cop thing now," said Casey. "I'm supposed to fall for that?"

Detective Dudley slammed his open palm down on the table. The sound of it echoed throughout the room. "You want me to give you bad cop, asshole? You want that?"

Gleeson stepped forward and put her hand on top of Dudley's. "Actually, my colleague here isn't on the force anymore. He retired years ago."

Dudley heaved a heavy sigh and wiped the front of his face down with his open palm. He closed his eyes.

"If he's not a detective, what's he doing here?"

"He's trying to help," said Gleeson, although from the way she said this it almost seemed possible that she'd have been just as happy without the old man's help.

"I want my lawyer," said Casey. "I want my phone call."

"We already told you," said Dudley. "You can leave anytime."

"Do you have a lawyer, Mr. Casey?" asked Gleeson.

"Hell yes I have a lawyer," said Casey. "He's Tripper Pennypacker. He's a top guy!"

"Tripper Pennypacker," said Dudley, with a smile. He turned to Gleeson. "One of his friends from prison."

Casey's forehead crinkled. "Why would you say it like that? Like I was in prison, rather than somebody who got trapped in one? Like it was my fault we all got stuck in there."

"Well, somebody chained that front gate closed, didn't they?"

Detective Gleeson nodded thoughtfully. "And somebody unlocked it too, right? I mean, they never would have wound up in there if the gate hadn't been unlocked in the first place."

"Right," said Dudley. "And then locked it, once everybody was in there."

"You think I locked my friends in Eastern State? And then killed Wailer?"

"Locked, but first unlocked, I think is how it goes," said Gleeson. "Then locked. Then murdered. I know, it's a lot to take in. The order of the whole thing."

"Why would I kill Wailer?" said Casey. "I loved her." His voice quavered. "I still love her. We just got married the night before!" He sniffed, and tears shimmered in his eyes. "We were married, man."

"Jon," said Gleeson, putting a hand on his. "Just tell us how it was. One last time. So we can close the books on this. Don't you want closure?"

"I want it all to never have happened," said Casey. "That's what I want."

"We can't help you there," said Gleeson. "But we can try to help put an end to it, to all the suffering you've been carrying around." She patted his hand. "You're a brave man. I can't imagine what it's been like to carry this all around, all these years."

"It sucked," observed Casey.

"Can I ask you about the wedding?" said Dudley.

"The wedding?" said Casey, looking up. "Sure. The wedding. That was the night before. It was fun. I made these little hot dogs for appetizers."

"Why'd you get married at your friend's house?" said Dudley. "Miss—Lenfest. I never understood that. Wasn't your wife Irish? I thought they were all Catholic. You'd think her parents would have insisted."

"Her parents were dead."

"Dead," said Gleeson. "But she was so young. How did they die so young?"

"They were in a plane crash, man," said Casey. "While we were at college."

"A plane crash?" said Gleeson. "That's terrible. So she was left to fend for herself, alone in the world."

"She got by okay. She had me to look out for her! Plus there was family money. She inherited it all from them after they died."

"Money, really?" said Gleeson. "Was it a lot of money?"

Casey shook his head, smiled grimly. "It was a shitload. They were rich people."

There was a long pause, as the detectives gave each other a meaningful glance.

"And what happened to all that money after she died?" said Dudley. "It all went back to some other distant relative, someone back in Ireland I guess?"

Casey felt the blood coming to his face. He felt hot. "No," he said. "It went to me. I was, you know. The widower."

Dudley opened the folder that was on the desk and began to spread out some photographs that had been bound together with a paper clip. They were large, glossy photos, the size of a piece of notebook paper. There was one of the skull, a glossier and grislier version of the one that had been in the paper. There was another of the skeleton, still wearing the black jeans. Then there was one of the hands, the skin shriveled and dried like that of an Egyptian pharaoh. The nails of the corpse were painted with still-visible black polish.

"I think this one's really interesting," said Dudley, pointing at a rusted Swiss Army knife, the blade out and caked with dried, black blood. On the shaft was a monogram with the initials J. C. "Fingerprints are on that one, Jon Casey," he added.

"You want anything to drink, Mr. Casey?" said Gleeson. "You want some coffee, maybe?"

Casey looked at the photo of the knife, feeling the blood in his face, the hot tears in his eyes. "Coffee'd be good," he said quietly.

"Cream?" said Dudley. "Sugar?"

Casey nodded. The door clicked as Detective Dudley went out into the hall. Casey pushed the photos away. "You have no right to show me this shit," he said. "It's not right."

"Mr. Casey, I am so sorry," said Detective Gleeson. She gathered up the photos and put them back in the folder. "Maybe you could just tell us what happened."

"I told you," Casey said. "Why don't you believe me? Why would I hurt her? She's the only person who ever loved me. Her and Quentin. Everything's *sucked* since they disappeared. It's like *I'm* the one who vanished. It's me, man, not them."

"Died," said Gleeson. "You mean died, not vanished."

Casey opened his mouth, then shut it. Blood rushed to his cheeks.

"Well, I always had . . ." said Casey. "I always had hope." He shrugged. "Sometimes I imagined the two of them, off somewhere together. Livin' the good life?"

"But I thought Mr. Pheaney's car went off a cliff," said Gleeson. "In Nova Scotia?"

Casey was silent for a long moment. "Yeah," he said. "That happened."

"Mr. Casey," said Gleeson, looking at him sympathetically, and lowering her voice. "I am wondering—if you ever saw your friend after that?" She reached out and touched his hand again.

"After—?" said Casey. "After he died, you mean?"

Gleeson did not take her hand away. Her eyes were wet and brown.

"Yes," said Gleeson. "*After* he died."

"You mean, like, as a ghost or something?"

Detective Gleeson looked pained, as if she herself had seen more than a few ghosts in her time. She nodded softly. "You tell me," she said.

Casey was sitting in a room in Philadelphia, beneath a softly buzzing fluorescent light. But he was also in a graveyard in the Bronx, near the headstone of Herman Melville, where clawing fingers broke through the earth like young flowers. He had turned to his friend, who was dissolving before him. He kissed him on the lips, softly, gently. *You're going to be okay,* he'd said, and a voice came from him that was not his own.

I love you, Quentin had said.

The door opened and Detective Dudley reentered the room. "Got you that coffee," he said.

10

Cold River, Maine

We lay together in the big bed after sex—*wahoo!* Light reflecting off the surface of the lake shimmered on the wooden ceiling. Jake, out of breath, sat up and propped some pillows behind his head. "Well, you *are* a hellcat." He smiled. "For an old lady."

I rested my head on his chest and ran my forefinger in a circle around his navel. "Miao," I said quietly. I hadn't detected anything different about him while we made love. I'm not sure what I was expecting— some strange new move he'd learned from the woman he was having an affair with, if he was. Was he? Had I imagined he'd suddenly cry out her name at the height of his passion? But none of this had happened. All in all he seemed unchanged, still the man I had known and loved.

"Mm-hm," he said. He reached over with one hand for the remote control and flipped on the TV. Just like that: the opening credits for *Return of the Jedi*.

"Holy shit, my lucky day," said Jake. "First sex, then Star Wars." He pretended to sniff. "It's like every dream I ever had—suddenly came true!"

The bed bounced, and there was the Labrador beside us, looking at Jake and at me with his weary old face.

"Gollum," said Jake. The dog lay down beside him.

I sat up as Jake watched the words in the title card march at an oblique angle into the infinite universe. He felt me staring at him and grinned.

"Are you hungry?" I asked.

"Yeah, kind of."

"How about I make you an omelet, bring it to you in bed?"

He looked at me with love. "You sure I haven't died? 'Cause this is pretty much what I always imagined heaven would be."

"You're not dead yet, Jacob Carrigan," I said, and got out of bed. "But we can try again later." I pulled my nightie over my naked body, then stepped into a white terrycloth robe. I went back to the bed and kissed Jake on the lips. He made a sound like a satisfied Wookiee. I headed down the stairs.

It was a beautiful day in late summer. The first floor was full of slanting amber light. I opened the door to the deck. A cool breeze blew in. I stepped outside.

There were chickadees and goldfinches on the feeder. Loons called from the lake. And, nearer at hand, came the sound of clashing swords.

Two trucks were in the driveway. Both of them were marked CAR-RIGAN SEPTIC SERVICE. Beneath this, the tag: *Your Business Is Our Business*. Next to the trucks, in the big open space beside the lake, were two young men in blindingly white fencing gear, their swords pointed at each other. Their free hands were raised in the air, like dancers.

One of these men was my son, Falcon. The other, his friend Caeden. They were the co-captains of the fencing team at Torsey Pond School, and they were beautiful to watch. They stood there like statues for a moment, then suddenly Caeden pounced toward my boy. But Falcon was ready with the riposte, and then charged right back at his friend. They advanced and retreated, these two, as they fenced in the dirt road and the sun shone down. Then Caeden shouted, as Falcon scored a touch. They returned to a neutral spot upon the *piste* they had drawn in the dirt, and then faced each other again.

"*En garde!*" shouted my son.

"Boys!" I shouted. "Are you hungry? Do you want some break-fast?"

"Morning Mrs. Falcon!" said Caeden, pulling up his mask.

"Mom," said Falcon, not removing his, "we're kind of in the middle of something here?"

"I just want to know if you want breakfast. I'm making eggs?"

"We'll have eggs," said Falcon, his sword still pointed at his friend's heart.

"Thank you, Mrs. Falcon!" said Caeden with a big grin. Then he put his helmet back on.

I walked out into the drive, past the trucks, past the fencing boys, to Coakley Lane, our dirt road. The *Mid-Maine Morning Arsenal*, for which I had once been a reporter, lay in a neat bundle next to the mailbox.

Our neighbor, Josephine Reisert, drove past in her Subaru. Josie was a minister at the local Unitarian church, a place where, she joked, they "believed in one god, at most." We'd gone to services at her church a couple of times, mostly to be good neighbors to Josie rather than out of any particular religious faith. Of the two of us, I was more spiritual than Jake. Even now, I viewed the second chance I'd been given in life as such a preposterous series of blessings that it seemed impossible that it was all not the result of some plan. You couldn't blame me for my faith: over and over I'd seen love turn the world inside out.

I walked back up to the house.

I made a cup of coffee, then sat down in the living room as the boys dueled each other. The sound of their swordfight reached me as I sat in my comfortable chair. "*En garde!*" my son shouted again. Caeden had been Emily until sixth grade, came out as trans at the Torsey Pond School to the general support of the other students and the faculty. I can't say I know all the details. But he'd left school in June five years ago as Emily and came back as Caeden in the fall, and everybody rolled with it.

Falcon hadn't been that close with Caeden before his transition, but they'd drawn close once they began fencing. That was ninth grade, almost three years ago. The first time Caeden came over to the house I didn't even know he was trans. He called me "Mrs. Falcon," which

I thought was kind of adorable. He was a jovial, bouncy guy, always laughing and smiling. He was a bookworm too, which I hoped would be a good influence on Falcon. Caeden was my secret weapon in the plan to ensure my son went to college, instead of signing on to be the newest partner in his father's septic-tank business.

"That was a foul!" my son shouted.

"Dude, it wasn't!" said Caeden.

"Fuck you it wasn't," said my son.

"Arrrgghh!" said Caeden, and I could picture pretty well what was going on out there. Now my son and his friend were wrestling in the dirt road. In about twenty minutes they were both going to come inside and drop their white uniforms on the floor, where they would stay until the exact moment I picked them up and dropped them in the wash. Meanwhile, the boys would have retreated to the basement, from which would echo the sound of some Xbox universe in which robot warriors searched for the secret scroll of Xanadarth. Or something. Later, if they managed to catch Jake in a generous mood, they'd drive his truck around, maybe even suck someone's tank out with the hose. To Falcon and Caeden, running the septic-tank trunk was more enter- taining than a time machine.

I guess the world should shock and amaze me, with all its prog- ress. It ought to make me weep with wonder at the difference between Caeden's world and my own. He'd come out to his parents, they'd told him, *We will always love you,* and then they took him to the doctor. He grew a beard. Everybody changed pronouns. Now he was co-captain of the fencing team. Surely, if I had grown up in Caeden's world, things would have been better.

Truth is, though, I don't spend a lot of time thinking about things that never happened. I'm glad for Caeden. But I can't live in his world any more than he can live in mine. It's true I had a harrowing life. How I've managed to survive is still kind of a mystery to me. But here I am, with Jake upstairs in our bed, watching *Return of the Jedi*. My son is in the road, wrestling with his friend. It's a summer day in Maine. I have coffee in my coffee mug.

From upstairs came the sound of a Wookiee groaning happily. This was Jake. A moment later, a grumbling bark. Gollum.

Then I heard the sound of clashing swords again. The boys were back at work.

My eyes fell to the front page of the *Mid-Maine Morning Arsenal*. The headline was: CELEBRITY CHEF SUSPECTED IN 35-YEAR-OLD MURDER. There was a photo of Casey next to the story. He was a middle-aged man, but he was, to my amazement, still his same self. It made me smile. Briefly.

They'd found Wailer's body—not much of a body after thirty-five years—stuffed in a hole in a wall. *Mr. Casey used the money he inherited to bankroll his chain of high-end Philadelphia-area comfort-food restaurants.* They'd found his monogrammed pocketknife, with his fingerprints still on it, next to the body. Wailer's dried blood was on the blade. It occurred to me that Casey's initials were now the same as mine.

I put down the paper and stared through the screen door out at the lake. Through the trees, I could just make out our boat, tied up to the dock. Someone on a Jet Ski screamed past, and a moment later the wake lapped against the shore.

It's funny how you can know a person, think of him as your closest friend, and still never gain access to the secret chambers in his heart. I know I'm the poster child for that, but it's not just me. The things people carry around in silence—the shames, the weird private dreams, the things they did when they thought no one else could see—it's terrible to think about. There are times when I think it's impossible to know another soul. I don't know, maybe we're lucky that way. If we knew what really went on inside other people's private hearts it would make our eyeballs bleed.

And yet, for all that, I knew Casey was not Wailer's killer. Please. Oh, it was obvious enough he was not the happy-go-lucky, ukulele-playing walrus he pretended to be. His cheer masked a sense of sorrow, not least his conviction he was ugly. Even Casey had a private self, and surely the language he spoke in the dark caves of his heart was unknowable to any other soul.

But he was innocent of whatever harm had come to Wailer. I knew this to be true because, of course, I had been with him the whole time. We'd watched Tripper drop over the wall, then we'd walked back into one of the cellblocks and wound up in the chapel. Where I'd sat down on a pew and picked up a Bible and read to him from the book of Psalms.

I left the paper on the coffee table outside and walked into the kitchen. I got out the eggs, the mushrooms, and the cheese, sliced up a red onion. The butter melted in the skillet and I threw in the onion and the house filled with that crazy delicious smell. From upstairs, once more, I heard my husband make a distant, satisfied Wookiee sound.

I started chopping mushrooms. I cut them julienne-style. The knife rose and fell. I couldn't cut those mushrooms thin enough. My hand slipped and the blade sliced into my thumb.

I'm his only alibi, I thought. I'm the only one alive who knows he didn't do it.

Right on cue, the boys thundered into the house. They dropped their swords on the floor, then peeled off their fencing gear. "Hi, Mrs. F!" shouted Caeden. He had amazing dimples, which even his new beard could not quite hide. "I could eat a horse!"

"Is breakfast ready, Mom?" said Falcon. The two of them were now standing there wearing only T-shirts and boxers.

"Put those things in the wash," I said. "Please!"

"We're on it!" shouted Caeden, scooping up the clothes and running toward the laundry room. "As fast as lightning!"

Falcon remained by my side. "Mom?" he said. "Are you all right?"

I stared into the frying pan, frozen. The only way to rescue Casey was for me to come back from the dead.

"Hey," Falcon said. "Mom."

The only way to save his life was for me to lose my own. Which, all my love notwithstanding, was never going to happen. I loved Casey, loved him like a brother. But his life was no longer mine to save.

I remembered our parting in Woodlawn Cemetery, when Casey

had given me the money that made my life possible. I had reached forward and held his cheek in my hand, and kissed him.

Eeeeeee.

In late afternoon, I was riding with Jake in the boat, across the lake to
the house of our friend William "Weasel" Laboutillier. Jake's Tele-
caster, inside its beat-up case, lay in the bow. We were heading to a jam
with a band known as the Skidders—a group of guys my husband had
known since high school. There was Ian, the bass player, who had a
job at the L.L.Bean factory, and Weasel himself, the lead guitar player.
Weasel was a Maine Guide. The lead singer, Cassie, was married to
Ray, the drummer. They ran a bed and breakfast called Moose Landing.

I'd been intimidated by the lot of them when I first hooked up with
Jake, but they'd been generous and welcoming to me, on the whole. I
think they were relieved that their friend had finally fallen in love with
someone after Sarah died. All Jake had to do was make it clear he cared
about me, and just like that I'd been welcomed into the circle.

Now we were scudding across the surface of Cold Pond in the *Red
Wedding,* bound for the village and a jam at Weasel's camp. Jake was
behind the wheel. I sat up in the bow, watching his face. His mustache
was almost completely gray. He wore a Red Sox cap on his head. His
hair blew around in the wind.

I closed my eyes and felt the sun on my face.

The outboard sputtered once, then twice, then died, just like someone had shot it with a handgun. There was a puff of gray smoke, and
then everything was silent. We rose and fell in our own wake as the
boat slowed and drifted.

"Hellfire," said Jake.

"That didn't sound good," I said.

Another thing that didn't sound good was the roar of something called Kennebec Falls, which was the spot on the lake where all the water from Cold Pond flowed over the lip of a fifty-foot gorge and fell onto the pink granite boulders of Kennebec Creek. I looked over my shoulder in the direction of the falls. There was a small cloud of drifting vapor that hung in the air above the gorge, sparkling in the sunlight. Slowly we drifted in the direction of the precipice in our powerless boat.

Of course we had oars, so if it came to it, Jake had the wherewithal to prevent our deaths. That was reassuring of course, but in some ways less reassuring than you'd think.

My husband turned the key in the ignition. The engine sputtered but didn't quite catch. Jake tried again.

"Well, damn," Jake said. He took off his Red Sox cap and ran his fingers through his hair.

"What's up?" I said. I could make out Weasel's house on the shore of the lake opposite the falls. I saw the shapes of people gathered around amplifiers, a tent, a picnic table loaded with food.

"That's it, Judith," said Jake with a smile. "We'll drift forever. Like the *Flyin' Dutchman*! We'll be the ghost ship of Cold Pond."

"Really?" I said.

He tried the engine again. It sounded deader this time.

He spread his hands. "Naw," he said. "We'll go off the edge of the falls first. Wind up on the rocks." Jake saw the distressed look on my face. "Hey," he said. "It'll be okay. I think I been running it too rich. Flooded the engine. Give it a minute or two to cool down, I bet we'll be okay."

We continued to drift toward the abyss.

"Do you actually know what you're talking about?" I said.

"What do you think?" he said.

"Nope," I said.

He got up and sat down next to me in the bow. "You know me pretty good, don't you?"

I was still looking at the shore. "Do I?" I said.

I hadn't meant for the words to fall like heavy weights, but they did.

Jake sat there looking at me for a moment, then took my hand. "You okay?" he said.

The boat was drifting aimlessly now. The bow was moving around in the current toward the south, lazily moving toward the cloud of mist above the waterfall.

"Fine," I said. "I'm just hoping we're not going to like, you know, die."

He ran his fingers through my hair, then leaned in for a kiss. I admit that the possibility of our imminent deaths, however remote, made this moment a whole lot more erotic than it had any right to be. "What?" he said.

"You know what," I said, looking at him. I was struck by how beautiful he was. Like a lot of men, he was sexier in his fifties than he'd been in his mid-thirties. His eyes twinkled; little crow's feet, burned by the sun, accented Jake's broad smile.

He squeezed my hand. For a moment we sat like that, the sun shining down on us, the boat drifting.

"Okay," he said, then got up and tried the engine again. This time it turned over. A couple seconds later we were cutting through the waves toward Weasel's barn again. All our troubles were behind us.

We tied up at his dock. The members of the band applauded as we arrived, having observed our trouble from the land. "Good to see ya," said Ian. "Thought we was gonna have to send out a search party."

"Bastard just seized up on me," said Jake, carrying his guitar case down the dock.

"I don't envy ya, Judith," said Cassie. "You could have been stuck out on the lake for hours with this nutso!"

"Oh, I don't know," I said. "He's got a few redeeming qualities."

"Yeah, well," said Ian. "You forget we've known him since Messalonskee Middle School."

They all laughed. I could have been hurt by this, I guess, but I didn't mind. It was true enough. All those boys went way back.

The band was set up in an old chicken barn. Maine is lousy with them—remnants from the days when the state had a thriving poultry industry. But all that had come to an end once Frank Perdue got into the game, and the era of mass-produced plastic chicken began. Within a decade, the whole industry shut down in Maine. Most of the barns have been razed too, since there's not much you can do with a barn once chickens have had their way with it. The barn on Weasel's property wasn't very big, as these things go. But it was big enough for the Skidders to play at one end of the ground floor, and for there to be plenty of room left over. It had a second floor as well, still filled with the empty roosts.

"Hey where's Falcon?" said Cassie. She had curly auburn hair and freckles from the tip of her nose to her shoulders, a classic colleen.

"Back at the house," I said. "He said if he hears 'Mustang Sally' one more time he's going to have to go to a psychiatric hospital."

"Him and me both," said Gert, Ian's girlfriend. They worked together at the L.L.Bean factory. She worked on the gumboots line, and Ian worked in camping goods. Gert and I kind of shared a sisterhood— "band widows," we called ourselves. This meant that we spent a lot of time sitting in chairs drinking beers while the rest of them played "Mustang Sally," and "Brown-Eyed Girl," and "Jumpin' Jack Flash," again and again. Cassie joked that Gert and I deserved the Skidder Purple Heart—"for bein' wounded in the line of duty."

"Here ya go, Judith," said Weasel, handing me a Blue Moon ale. The rest of that crew liked to drink Bud Light, but they always made sure that they kept "the snob beer" on hand for me. They weren't stupid either; they knew it was in their best interests to keep me happy.

I twisted the cap off the beer and walked over to the picnic table. There was a slow-cooker filled with beans. Chicken and Italian sausages were slowly cooking on a grill, and a grizzled older man stood by the Weber holding a giant spatula. Grizzled, in this case, meaning an unkempt beard and a stained sailor's hat. This was "Pappy," the sire of Weasel. He nodded at me and grinned with a mouth that did not quite have all its teeth. During the summers, Pappy slept on the second floor of the poultry barn on an old mattress he'd dragged up there. An extension cord that ran from the house provided Pappy with enough juice to power a single lamp, which cast just enough light for him to read the works of Louis L'Amour.

"Got 'em sausages sizzlin' they-yah," said Pappy, in an old-school Down East accent, the kind almost no one has anymore unless there are tourists at hand.

"Are those sweet sausages?" I said. "Or hot ones?"

Pappy looked nervous, chewed a little bit with his forlorn mouth. "Got 'em sausages *sizzlin*'," he said emphatically.

The members of the band plugged their instruments into the amps and tuned up while Gert and I sat down on lawn chairs with our beers.

Then Ray shouted, "Let's do it!" and he clacked his drumsticks together to count off the time. After the short intro, Cassie started to belt out an Aretha Franklin classic, "Respect."

I sat there listening to the band. There was always a good vibe when the Skidders played. Part of it was that they were, in fact, pretty talented, especially Cassie, who, even in her fifties, had a voice that could shatter glass. But that pleasant groove was also the by-product of decades of friendship—relationships that were as well worn as an old baseball glove. There were times when I was jealous of their closeness. I'd been married to Jake for sixteen years now, but I'd never know him the way these friends did. That was all right by me—I was grateful for the relationship that I had. But it did make me think, now and again, that there was no one in my life who knew me the way the Skidders knew my husband, at least not anymore. I'd left them all behind when I'd rolled that Volkswagen off a cliff on Cape Breton.

Pappy came over with a paper plate full of Italian sausages in buns. "Come 'n' get 'em," he said.

"Pappy, did I see you on *The Bachelor* the other night?" said Gert.

Pappy smiled. "I seen that show," he said. "Fella's numba than a pounded hake!"

"You sure that wasn't you?" said Gert, taking a sausage.

"Warn't me," said Pappy. "I would'na go on no program."

"No?" said Gert. "How come?"

"Wall," said Pappy, "you got a thing like I got, you don wanna *pub*-lacize it."

"Thanks," I said, taking a sausage and biting right into that sucker. I don't know what Pappy's secret recipe was, especially if it involved his beard, but it was an amazing sausage—sweet and smoky, done just right.

"*Ausgezeichnet!*" I said.

Pappy looked confused. "Ya sneeze?"

"No, sorry," I said. "It's German. Means incredible, outstanding, great."

"Wall," said Pappy, "them's good sausages."

We ate our sausages for a while. Then I said, "What are you reading, Pappy? You still working your way through Louis L'Amour?"

Pappy nodded. "*Lonely Up ta' Mountain*," he said. "That's the one I'm readin'."

Gert regarded Pappy with curiosity. "Have you really read every one of those books?"

"Ayuh," said Pappy. "Them's good stories."

"Are there any of them you don't like?"

He worked his toothless jaw for a moment, then he said, "*Haunted Mesa*'s wicked pe-*cu*-lah. 'Bout them portals."

"Portals, what kind of portals?" said Gert.

"Them time portals they got," said Pappy.

Gert nodded. "*Ausgezeichnet,*" she said, echoing the word I'd said as closely as she could.

Pappy stood between Gert and me, hunkering for a while, then he wandered back to the grill and threw on a slab of ribs with a pair of enormous tongs. There was a flicker of flame, and a cloud of smoke rose toward heaven.

Gert and I sat in our lawn chairs listening to the Skidders having at it. They were on to "Sweet Jane" now. *Me, babe, I'm in a rock-and-roll band.*

"I didn't know you knew German," said Gert.

I nodded as the last of the sweet sausage went down the hatch. "Studied it a long time ago," I said.

"They didn't have German at Cony," said Gert. Cony was the high school in Augusta. "Just French."

"You ever use your French?" I asked.

"I used to. My grandma was Acadian. Came to Maine for the log drives." She drank her beer. The sun shone down upon us. "Used to be you'd hear a lot of French in Waterville, Augusta, Bangor. The French people all worked the log drives, lived down by the river on Water Street. I still know some folks their grandparents don't know any English. Logging days are all done though."

"Yeah," I said. I knew a little bit about the history of the log drives in Maine from a story I'd done for *Down East* magazine. The rivers used to be filled with timber, floating down to the mills. There was still a timber industry in Maine, barely hanging on into the twenty-first century, but they didn't use the rivers anymore. The last log drive on the Kennebec had been back in 1972. I was only fourteen then, still a boy, living in Pennsylvania, watching reruns of *Lost in Space* on Channel 29.

"It's sad that whole way of life is gone," I said wistfully. "When that generation is gone, nobody will remember those days anymore."

"Yah, well, those days kind of sucked, Judith," said Gert. "Used to see guys in Waterville missing an arm, a hand, a foot. And the rivers were a fuckin' pigsty. I'm sorry all the mills are closed but, you know. We don't got hog-rendering factories up here anymore either. I'm not cryin' any tears over all that shit getting shut down."

"Yeah, I know," I said. "It's just—like I said. A piece of history that's lost."

Gert shook her head. "Judith Carrigan, you're the most sentimental person I know," she said.

"Am I?" I said. "I don't think of myself as sentimental."

"The hell," said Gert. "I bet you take a dump you get all sad you gotta flush it down."

The band finished up with "Sweet Jane," then went on to "What's

Up?" They used to play in bars a lot in the '90s and 2000s, but then they got sick of it. There's a law of diminishing returns about playing out: barflies want to hear the music that was popular when they were young; since the average age of a bar patron in central Maine is thirty-five, that means the target playlist is music from about fifteen to twenty years earlier. So in the '90s, music from the mid-'70s was perfect. But like the saying goes, nostalgia isn't what it used to be. By the late 2000s, people wanted to hear songs from the '80s, even, god forbid, the '90s. That was bad news for the Skidders, whose musical knowledge peaked with the Band's "Last Waltz" in 1976. They didn't play out much anymore; the denouement of their long career was right here, in Weasel's chicken barn.

More cars arrived as the afternoon went on. A red-faced, curly-haired guy named Dave showed up with his wife, Erica. They owned a flower shop in Waterville and had three kids, all between the ages of four and eight. Dave had his Strat in a case. We all knew that after a few beers, Dave was going to inflict some Neil Young tunes upon the innocent—"Ohio" and "Powderfinger," and "Farmer John," a song I found almost indistinguishable from "Louie Louie." But Dave was a good guy. He and Jake worked at the fire department together. We'd had Dave and Erica over to the house lots of times. Dave's weakness for playing Neil Young was really his only discernible character flaw, and believe me, there's worse.

A whole bunch of people arrived from a softball game that had been going on down at the grounds of the Cold River Central School, and soon the camp was full of kids in uniforms that said GOLDEN POND FINANCIAL WARRIORS, and their parents. The kids ate hot dogs, or lay next to one another on the grass playing games on their iPhones, or ran around the banks of the lake spinning a Frisbee. Some of the adults danced to the band, in that sad but sweet middle-aged way—guys with beers in one hand, the other gyrating gently in the "thumbs-up" position. The women danced with them, or stood at the edges looking on. A few older women came in with bowls of potato salad and coleslaw.

Pappy stood by the grill with a satisfied expression. "Got 'em sausages *sizzlin'*!" he announced to the newcomers. Sparks from his grill rose into the air and drifted skyward.

I sat in my chair drinking beer, listening to the sounds, watching my husband playing rock-and-roll in a chicken barn. He was so unguardedly happy when he was playing music with his friends. Part of me wished that I'd known this sweet, goofy group of people since I was young, that I'd been able to see them before they quite became themselves. I tried to imagine Jake, or Ian, or Weasel back when they'd been twenty, but it was hard. I was the only one in this crowd except for Cassie who'd been to college.

Yeah, Jake had said to me once, when we discussed this very subject. But we don't hold it against you.

Now they were playing "Dr. Feelgood," a blues tune that really let Cassie sing her heart out. The band started this one off very softly, which really let her belt it out as they built to a climax.

Jake was playing slide, looking at Cassie like something was about to burst out of him like fireworks.

That was the moment I figured it out. He looked at her again, trying not to show his quiet inner swoon. I glanced over at Gert. She looked at Cassie, then at me, then back at Cassie, sucked on her beer. And I thought, holy shit. Everyone *already knows*. He's been fucking her for how long now, right underneath my nose? And everybody knows about it but me?

I looked at Ray, though, and saw nothing but contentment. He was sitting on the back there on his drummer's stool, keeping time. Were they keeping it all from Ray too? Or was it a thing he'd accepted long ago—they had some kind of arrangement?

I thought about that receipt I'd found in Jake's pants, the night he was supposedly off at the fire. The Downeast Roadhouse Barbecue. I pictured Cassie sitting in that dump, drinking a frozen margarita, barbecue sauce on her cheeks.

The band fell silent as she belted out the finish. *Good God almighty.*

The other Skidders all came in on the last note, and then bang, the tune was over. Along with my marriage, I thought.

But then Jake was looking at me, smiling and twinkling. Everyone was applauding. Gert looked over at me and said, "Boy, she sure can sing." And just like that my certainty evaporated like fog. I felt a little dizzy. A minute ago I knew they were fucking, and that my marriage was over. Now it all seemed like a delusion. It had just been a few hours ago that I'd made love with Jake, golden light from the lake quavering on the wooden ceiling of our bedroom, as I looked at the gray hairs in his mustache. Was that not real?

Now he picked out the opening to "Folsom Prison Blues." The rest of the band groaned, but they kicked right in after him, and moments later, there they were. Cassie stepped up and belted it out, doing her best Johnny Cash imitation.

I smiled to hear the familiar old song. There was a time when I could do that voice, back before I found my own.

Pappy came over to me, his destroyed face full of kindness. "Heyah, Judith," he said, handing me a paper plate. "I got 'em sausages *sizzlin*!"

By early evening Jake and I were back in our little boat, heading toward our home on the opposite shore. His guitar case was in the bow again, along with a Tupperware container of baked beans that Gert had forced upon us. "I'll tell you my secret," she'd said to me, although I hadn't asked for it. "I add that Liquid Smoke."

I was sitting at the bow of the *Red Wedding*, not quite Leonardo DiCaprio–style, my back to Jake. My legs dangled down over the hull. We weren't going very fast, but a little spray kicked up and flicked against my cheeks. The sun was going down over McGaffey Mountain on the far shore.

Then the engine seized up once more and died. The wake rushed past us, and the boat rose and fell. "Hellfire," said Jake. He tried starting the engine again, but this time there was no response from the outboard at all, save a repetitive metallic clicking, like the ignitor of a gas grill trying, and failing, to start a fire.

"I think we're screwed," said Jake. "Again."

"Really," I said, suddenly pissed at him, pissed at everything. "So what, we're just going to float out here for fucking ever?"

"Yeah," said Jake, his eyes flickering. "Might play out just like that."

"I'll call Falcon," I said, getting out my cell phone.

I called our home on speed dial, and listened as it rang.

"Yeah, he's not gonna be home," said Jake.

"What?" I said. The phone was still ringing.

"I told those boys they could take the truck out and do a job up in Madison for me," he said.

"You didn't," I said. I hung up the phone. "Seriously?"

"I got the call just as we were heading out. He said he could do it, make some cash for school." Jake smiled, like *Whaddya gonna do?* "Those boys sure love the truck."

"I don't want him driving the fucking septic-tank truck," I said. "What is wrong with you?"

"Kid has a thing to do he likes," said Jake. "I don't see why that's a bad thing."

"He's not going to suck out people's crap through a hose for the rest of his life," I said.

"Like me?" said Jake. Now he was pissed, which was fine with me. Let him be pissed.

"It's not about you," I said. "It's about him. He should have a future!"

"He's *got* a future," Jake said. "You should let him be who he wants, Judith. Be who he wants to be. Not some version of you."

"It would be so bad for him to be like me?" I shouted. "That would make him a failure?"

Jake didn't reply. Instead he tried the engine a couple more times. It was as dead as Jacob Marley. He opened up a side panel and pulled out an oar. Then he went up to the bow, where I was sitting, and stood there with the oar for a moment like he was going to hit me with it. He stared at me for a long minute. Then tears brimmed over his eyelashes, and he fell down on his knees, dropping the oar into the boat. He took my hand.

"I'm sorry, Judith," he said. "Okay? I'm sorry."

"Jake," I said. "I—" I didn't know how to respond. My husband wasn't much of a weeper. And he was even less of an apologizer. To have him do both at once was completely unexpected, like he'd suddenly started juggling, or playing the accordion.

"It's okay," I said, and I took him in my arms. I was still pissed off at him, actually, because, after all, we were still stuck out on the lake with a dead motor, and Falcon was still off in Madison continuing his apprenticeship as a septic-tank truck driver. But Jake had folded his cards. There wasn't much alternative to this besides hugging him, then wiping the tears from his cheek with my thumb.

"I, uh—" he said. He looked kind of panicked. I realized at that moment, he's going to confess the whole thing to me now. I also realized that I was going to have to forgive him, even if I didn't want to.

"I been kind of confused," he said. "What with the kid coming up on his last year of school. I been thinking about his momma. I miss her sometimes but I don't want to tell you about it because, I don't know. I just don't."

"You can talk about her." I said her name. "Sarah."

"Yeah," he said. "I miss her sometimes." The tears spilled over his eyelashes again. "She was the only girl I ever loved. Until you." He looked down. "I been lucky that way, I guess. The only two women I ever loved I married."

We were approaching thin ice now, and we both knew it. "You never feel bad you never got to—" I searched for the phrase. In German, you say *Mit jemandem in die Kiste steigen,* which means *to climb into the box with someone.* "Sow your wild oats?"

The wind was picking up a little now, and little whitecaps made the boat rise and fall. "Yeah," he said softly. "Well, sometimes I think about that."

We were at it now. I figured, what the hell. He was down on his knees weeping. This was as much of an opening as we were likely to have.

"Is that what you were doing at the Roadhouse the other night?" I said quietly. "Thinking about it?"

He didn't look shocked, just sad. Jake didn't say anything at first. Then he nodded. "Yah. A little."

It was a relief, I guess, that we weren't going to have to have the whole conversation in which he denied it, in which he pretended to be insulted by the accusation. Like I said, Jake knows when to fold his cards. But my heart was beating hard in my breast. For the first time in over a dozen years of marriage we were suddenly in unknown territory, quite literally adrift.

"How long?" I asked him.

The boat had twisted around so that the bow was facing the shore from which we'd come. We could see Weasel's house there in the distance, the tiny outlines of the white tarp beneath which the band had played.

"How long what?"

I wasn't entirely sure what he meant by how long what. We *were* talking about the affair he was having, weren't we?

"How long have you been seeing her," I said, angrily. "Just tell me."

"Judith—" he said.

"Are you fucking her? This is Cassie we're talking about, right?"

He ran his fingers along the edges of his gray mustache. Jake looked at me with what seemed like equal measures anger and shame, which pissed me off. *Listen, honey. If I were you, I'd go for more shame, maybe a little less anger. I wasn't the one who'd been lying.*

"It's not like that," he said.

I reached forward and slapped him. I didn't even think about it. I just did it. It made a clear, bright sound that echoed around us. It was the first time I'd ever slapped a man in my life, and it was kind of surprising that I knew how to do it without ever having practiced.

But here I was, fifty-seven years old, slapping my first man. It didn't feel good. My first impulse was to reach out and rub the cheek I'd injured, which was already turning pink. But all I could think was that the phrase *It's not like that* was the kind of thing people said when, in fact, *it was exactly like that.*

"Yeah? So tell me. What's it like?"

He looked at me, his feelings hurt, as if somehow he was the wounded party here. "You should not have done that," he said.

I slapped him again. "You're right," I said.

"I'm not fucking her," he said, and all the blood rushed to his face. "Jesus Christ, you think I'd do that?"

"You meet her at the Roadhouse, you lie about it, and you make up some story about a barn fire? You smudge your face with charcoal briquettes from the grill? You could see how I might be kind of doubtful about this story."

Now he just looked sad. "You figured all that out, then," he said.

"Yeah," I said.

"Can't pull the wool over your eyes," he said.

"What?"

"'Cause you're always one hundred percent truthful, right, Judith?" He looked at me accusingly.

"I do my best," I said, but my voice came out a little flimsy. I knew he heard it.

"Look," he said. "I'm not fucking Cassie Hudson. I'm not doing that." Jake looked off at the shoreline. The flags in front of Arnold's General Store twitched on the pole. "I'm not fucking her. I just wanted to talk to her about Sarah."

"You can't talk to your wife about her?"

"You didn't know her," he said.

"Wait. You're telling me you met Cassie in a bar in Augusta, then lied about it, because you wanted to have a little talk about your ex-wife?"

"She's not my ex-wife," Jake snapped. "She's my *dead* wife."

I paused to take my bearings here. Somehow, I'd wound up on the losing side of this argument, in spite of the fact that my husband had snuck off with a girl from high school, gone to a bar, made up a story about a barn fire, and then, to bolster this story, rubbed his face with ashes out of the Smokey Joe. He could do all of that, but as soon as he brought the question of his dead wife into things, I was outplayed. Nothing could trump the dead-wife card.

"You're not wrong about her," Jake said. "About Cassie. She did want to start something up. But I told her I wasn't going there. What I wanted was a talk about Sarah, and she said all right in the end."

"I am going to have to make a note to go bite her fucking head off."

"Aw, Judith, don't be too sore at her. She knew I'd turn her down. She's just a little messed up. Her and Ray are gonna have to sell the bed and breakfast I think. They can't make a go of it."

I nodded. "That's a shame," I said, and it was. I hated the idea they'd have to sell Moose Landing, and I felt sorry for them. Not sorry enough to forgive Cassie for dive-bombing my husband, but a little.

"So what does Cassie say about Sarah? You reach any conclusions I should know about?"

Jake opened his hands and looked at his fingers. "She thinks Sarah would have been proud."

"Of you?"

"Of Falcon. The way he's turned out."

"Does Cassie want Falcon to drive a suck truck too?"

I could almost hear him counting to ten before he responded. "She wants him to be himself."

"Jake," I said, and all at once I just felt my cards folding too. "You're asking me to believe you, and I believe you. Okay?"

He nodded. "Okay."

"But no more sneaking. And you leave the Weber grill alone. It's not dignified."

"Okay," he said. "Deal." He was still staring at me intensely. "Now it's your turn."

"My turn what?"

"Since we're being all honest here. You got anything you want to get off your chest?"

I felt my heart pounding. What did he know?

"Give me a hint, Jake."

"Maybe you've got something you've been keeping from me?" he said.

My throat closed up. I'd rehearsed this conversation in my head many times. But even now, after sixteen years of marriage, I still didn't know how to begin.

"I don't know what you're talking about," I said, and once again I felt like I was in a play. That's what you said when you knew exactly what someone was talking about.

"Judith," he said. "Who's this Karl?"

"Karl," I said.

"His girlfriend called on the phone yesterday, while you were floating on the boat."

"Karl? I don't know any Karl."

"Yeah, that's not what his girlfriend said."

"Okay, Jake, now you're freaking me out a little. I don't know any—" Then I remembered. The lunatic on the phone. "Oh," I said. "Her."

"Oh," Jake said, bitterly. "Her."

"But she's insane," I said.

"No wonder Karl wants to get away from her," said Jake.

"Wait," I said. "No. I don't know these people. She just called out of the blue."

"She says your phone number was written on his chest. In lipstick."

"I know she says that. But that doesn't have anything to do with me."

"No?" said Jake.

"Jake, this is insane. I literally don't know these people."

"Goddammit," Jake roared, suddenly, and his voice echoed around the lake. "Tell me the truth!"

"Jake, I don't know these people. That's all I can tell you."

He looked at the general store. The flag was limp now, the breeze suddenly gone. "So you really were in New York last weekend?" he said. "Doing some story about—that island where they bury dead people?"

"Well, yeah. Where else would I be?" Suddenly I had no idea where he was headed.

He looked at me, so hurt and wounded. "I thought maybe you were with him," he said. "This Karl."

"Jake," I said, my heart going out to him a little. "No. I wasn't. I was doing the story. About Hart Island."

"Yeah," he said. "So this girl—just has you mixed up with somebody? Or couldn't read the—the number somebody wrote on her husband's chest in lipstick?"

"That's the story," I said.

Jake put his hand over his mouth, stroked the gray hairs of his mustache.

"Okay," he said. "Well, I guess we're good then."

"Wait, what? We are?" I looked at him, astonished, but he just smiled.

"Well, yeah," he said. "But I guess you are still you?" It was a statement, but he said it like a question.

He flicked a switch below the starter, then turned the key in the ignition. Just like that the engine turned over. "Hey, look at that," he said. "I must have hit the emergency cut-off by accident."

He pulled the throttle into gear. "Jake, you didn't," I said. "You didn't just kill the engine on purpose so we could float around the lake and have this insane conversation?"

"Hmm," said Jake. "It's a mystery, I guess." He raised one arm and pulled me to him. "Glad we had our talk though. Clear the air and everything."

He pointed us toward home. We hugged. "So we're okay?" I said. This all seemed too easy, but then Jake is not a man who understands what it is to have a secret life. You cleared the air, and then you were done. Clean slate.

For all the world I could not imagine what this would be like.

"'Course we're okay," he said, completely at ease. He looked at me with love, and my heart compressed, as if someone were crushing it with his fist. Jake's sweetness and trust were, at that moment, almost impossible for me to bear. I remembered standing at the locked gates of Eastern State with Rachel. *I'm trapped!*

"Judith, what?"

I thought I could swallow it, but a sob convulsed me. Oh, if only I could have kept it all locked down inside of me for just another five minutes, how different our lives could have been. But it had escaped. I was shaking now, the tears rolling down, and at long last the gates were creaking open.

"Jake," I said. I could barely get his name out. He pulled back on the throttle and stopped the engine again.

A wave hit the side of the boat and the spray flicked against our cheeks. He held me. I felt his mustache against my cheek.

"I can't," I said.

"You can't what, Judith?"

Now everything was quiet again. Water lapped against the hull. Jake took my hand.

Tell me, he said.

11

Eagle, Pennsylvania

Dan Dudley, late of the Philadelphia Police Department's Homicide Division, sat behind the keys of his 1901 Steinway parlor grand pounding out Elton John's "Amoreena," and singing the tune in a voice that his own departed wife had once compared to the sound of a cement mixer. The Steinway didn't improve things much, given that the soundboard had cracked over the years and the thing didn't hold a tune for more than a week or two. The piano tuner, a Horatio Blackmun—surely one of the last Horatios of his generation—came by Dudley's house out in the green farmland beyond Exton and tuned the Steinway up twice a year. Afterward, Dudley sat behind the keys of the instrument—like a child who'd just been given a Rolls-Royce—and played his crappy old Elton John and Grateful Dead songs on the keys and felt for all the world like the beatnik Vladimir Horowitz, a feeling that would last no more than half a month before the warped, dried-out soundboard began to bend the notes out of tune, so that soon enough the thing sounded like a saloon upright in a cowboy movie, the kind of thing you'd see a minor actor playing in a black-and-white film right up until the very moment Lee Marvin swung through the swinging doors and shot everyone dead.

Sure was fun, though. He finished up "Amoreena," rolling out the big G chord at the end. "Thank you very much," he said, just like the teenager he'd once been, pretending when he'd played this very same piano in 1965 that he was a shyer, straighter, whiter version of Little

Richard, receiving the applause of his stunned and loving fans. During his marriage, he hadn't played as much, and when he did play he didn't sing very loud, but since Evangeline had passed on he spent a lot of time now pounding out the keys. It was one of the few advantages of being a widower; no one ever said, "Can't you turn that down? It's *blasting.*"

He left the piano bench—still bearing the needlepointed cover Evangeline had made almost forty years ago, stitch by stitch—and went back to the stack of yellowing paperwork from the Curtin murder. He was surprised that Gleeson even wanted his insight on the case, given that he'd retired five years ago, not to mention the unavoidable truth that *retired detective with one last unsolved case* was pretty much just another way of saying *unrelenting asshole*. He'd run into plenty of characters meeting that description over the years, guys who just couldn't let go, who tossed and turned at night over cases that everyone else had stopped giving a shit about years and years ago. He remembered one guy—Sally Scaramuzzino, in fact—who just wouldn't go away, who kept rooting through the old files every couple of months, coming up with new theories and suspects on a case that was, in fact, closed; a case in which a suspect had, in fact, confessed and for which he was now pleasantly doing a sentence of thirty years to life in Delaware County Prison. But old Sally—a bald, hugely overweight man, not unlike himself—kept coming by HQ on Friday afternoons, his belly just hanging over his pants like a loaf of bread that had been baked with way too much yeast. *Listen, Yoder isn't our guy!* he'd say, referring to the convicted killer. *Yoder's just the fall guy! The real guy is this Mc-Clintock!* And everyone could only roll their eyes, because, fuck, the case was closed. If McClintock wants to go to jail so badly, why doesn't he stab somebody else? The last he heard, Sally had died of a massive heart attack in his own bed. Probably still surrounded by the files from the Yoder murder case, a long legal pad at his side. His last words were probably something like, *But it's McClintock! I can prove it! Honest, I can—ugh.*

And now I'm that guy, Dudley thought, staring with despair at the thirty-five-year-old piles of paper, all those forms typed and signed by his own hand, many of them carbon copies, back in the day when you had to use actual carbon to make actual copies. For a while the protocol was to fill out the intake form using five sheets of paper, four sheets of carbon between them. He'd come home and kiss Evangeline and raise one hand to her face and leave a soft purple smudge there from the carbon. *Danny*, said she. *Wash your hands.*

Thing is, the Curtin murder—they had been supposed to call it a disappearance, but it was pretty obvious the girl was dead from day one—had kept him awake nights, for years and years now. This was not only because of the yawning hole in his own life now but also because of the circumstances. Eastern State Penitentiary! That humid day in that turgid summer! And all those poor kids, wandering around lost. Somebody, somewhere, had locked them in, an action you could imagine was accidental, at least until Wailer Curtin got killed.

The folder before him contained not just the formal report but also his own typed-up notes on each of the suspects. Odds were pretty good it was one of the kids themselves, of course. There they were: Jon Casey. Rachel Steinberg. Maisie Lenfest and the boy, Benny Lenfest. Tripper Pennypacker. Quentin Pheaney. The teacher, Nathan Krystal.

He knew these kids so well. It was funny; he had such a complete picture of them that they were almost like his own children. And yet they probably hadn't given *him* a second thought in thirty-odd years, at least not until the very moment he'd walked into Casey's restaurant—at Gleeson's very generous request—and watched as they hauled him off to "ask a few questions." All this time, they had thought he'd forgotten. But instead he'd gone to bed each night, thinking of each one, and what it was that had brought him or her to Eastern State that day.

He had eliminated Tripper Pennypacker from the beginning, of course, since he was the only one who wasn't there when the murder took place. The women—Lenfest and Steinberg—weren't very interesting either, since they had nothing to gain from Curtin's death. Nathan Krystal, on the other hand, was a *very* interesting character, and

he'd unearthed enough anecdotal evidence to suggest he had a very ornate private life. But nothing linked him to the victim. The same could
be said of the child, Benny Lenfest, although of all the people there
that night, he was the one whose account of things was the most unsettling. Dudley flipped through the paperwork to review his notes from
1980 and '81. He'd briefly adopted one of the feral cats and named it
Creeper. *Subject says he was given the cat by "a caveman" who lived in the
library.* He'd dutifully gone through the old prison library, mushrooms
growing through its rotten leather-bound volumes, plaster fallen upon
its reading tables. *Forensic investigation of reading area shows no sign of
caveman presence.*

Someone—not Dudley himself—had written in the margin of the
report—*No shit, Sherlock.*

That's *her* handwriting, he thought. Iris Claremont. His former pro-
tégée, and, let the record show, Your Honor: a very hot young detective.
A wave of guilt washed over him as he remembered the whole tawdry
business. Was it really a mortal sin, in the full measure of things? One
night in the Bellevue-Stratford, three sheets to the wind, her lace bra
draped over an easy chair. And then, at the hour of dawn, it was like
Hot Iris was replaced with Angry Iris, and Angry Iris blamed him for
her ruination—that was her word, "ruination." *You put something in
my drink! You bastard you bastard you're a monster you.* She stormed out,
leaving him lying there naked and stupid. *I'm not a monster,* he said to
no one. *I was just lonely.*

His face grew hot remembering the mortification of it all. But even
this wasn't the worst. The worst was the secret, keeping his wife in
the dark for all the years to come about the complaint Iris had filed,
the sanction against him. It was the reason he never got promoted, the
reason his whole career had shriveled up and died. One time he'd said
to his wife, *Listen, I know I'm a disappointment to you. I know you always
expected me to make Lieutenant.* And she'd replied: *I don't mind you being
a disappointment to me. I mind you being a disappointment to yourself.*

Well. All of that was behind him now.

All along the obvious suspect in the murder had been Jon Casey. He was the one who had profited by his wife's death—and the more you looked into the circumstances of their wedding, the more ridiculous it seemed. They were two very young people who were about to be separated for a year, and possibly two, as Curtin went off to Togo to work for the International Red Cross. She'd been orphaned at an early age, and inherited a shocking amount of money from her parents, who'd died in the crash of an Aer Lingus jet in 1977. You wouldn't know she was loaded to look at her—the pink hair, the ripped-up clothes. Dudley wondered whether her friends actually knew how much money their friend was worth.

One thing was clear: Jon Casey knew *all about it*. He'd signed the documents making him joint owner of her trust effective upon their marriage, meaning that she didn't even have to turn up dead for him to have access to her money. On the one hand, you'd think this would decrease his motivation to do away with her, since he'd already gained the legal power to sign the woman's checks. On the other, her absence meant that no one would object if one member of the couple happened to say, *Hey honey I think I want to open up a chain of restaurants that serves up meatballs and macaroni and cheese.*

They had a pretty good case against him, even in 1980, given that he hadn't been with the others when the murder was committed. If they'd had a body in 1980, in fact, they would have booked him. The hasty marriage, the money, all of that suggested that something was up. Did Jon Casey suspect that his wife would find someone else while she was overseas, someone with whom it was slightly less impossible for her to be in love?

That was the thing he kept coming back to. He picked up a photograph of Jon Casey, circa 1980. He was a morbidly obese man with a scraggly beard. The Casey Jones engineer's hat on his head made him seem like even more of a cartoon. The only possible universe in which Jon Casey was not the primary suspect was a universe in which a not-unattractive young woman might look this creature in the eyes and think, Why yes, I'll spend the rest of my life with *this dude*.

All that said, the only other possible suspect in the case had been the scarecrow boy, Quentin Pheaney, dead now nearly thirty years. Dudley picked up a photograph of Pheaney, looked at him. He remembered his interview with the young man, late that summer, how he'd twitched and squirmed in his chair, as if he were guilty as sin. *What are you so nervous about?* he kept asking Pheaney.

I'm not nervous, Pheaney had said, crossing his legs and clutching onto his elbows, like some kind of human corkscrew. In fact, given his demeanor, Dudley would have picked Pheaney as prime suspect were it not for the fact that the young man was so passive it was hard to imagine him picking up a gun—or a knife, or whatever it was they'd used to do away with the wife. He'd held Pheaney in interrogation for hours and hours, thinking he could break him, but whatever secret it was he held, he wasn't letting go.

He checked his notes. *Lives with his mother. Translating Walt Whitman into German.* A few years later, in Iris's handwriting: *Began work at Continental Bank as teller, Center Square concourse branch.*

When Pheaney committed suicide a few years later, Dudley had suspected that this had justified his theory: the guilt over what he'd done to Curtin had finally gotten the better of him. That was when they'd finally put all the documents from the case into storage and effectively declared the game over. It was neither a solution nor a confession, of course—but in the absence of a body, it was as close to resolution as they were likely to come. Officially the case remained open, but once the files went into storage, everyone stopped worrying about it.

Everyone, that is, except him. Dudley picked a pile of junk out of one of the boxes sitting on his table, blew the dust off of a checkbook ledger and an assortment of photographs. True, he didn't obsess over the case the way he used to. But now and again he'd wake up in the middle of the night and remember the way Jon Casey had looked as he picked his wife's wedding ring up off the ground. He remembered the way Quentin Pheaney had squirmed around in his swivel chair, cracking his knuckles. He remembered the way Benny Lenfest had trembled when he whispered to him, *The leader of those cats is a caveman.*

Dudley got up and sat down at the piano and played the opening chords of "Burn Down the Mission," another Elton John classic from the early 1970s. The structure of the tune was remarkable, the octaves in the left hand being so completely unlike the chords he played with the right. This piece had almost every chord in the scale—G major, E minor, and then a B-flat chord in the right and a C octave in the left. Dudley remembered those early albums fondly—*Tumbleweed Connection* and *Madman Across the Water* and *Honky Château*; it was a time when the music seemed to be more important than the character of the person playing it. Elton was just a piano-playing hippie back then. This was before he started performing wearing a Donald Duck suit. Of course, the showmanship was probably what had made Elton a star. But Dudley never was much for the giant glasses or the sequins. All of that distracted from the music, and the music was really beautiful.

He stopped playing and went to his back porch and looked out on his backyard. There was a birdbath there, and a robin was swimming in it. There was sunflower seed in his feeder, and a pair of finches were flitting around, pecking. He smiled grimly, thinking of Quentin Pheaney. The young man had been something like this, a nervous bird afraid that some predator was just about to swallow him whole.

The thing was, Pheaney didn't really work as a suspect. The suicide was curious, to be sure. But he didn't seem like he had murder in him. It was hard enough to believe he'd found the chutzpah to kill himself, let alone anyone else.

Plus, it was Jon Casey who benefited from Curtin's death. What was in it for Pheaney? They'd been each other's alibis, of course, back then. Casey said he and Pheaney had gone for a walk, and that they— what was it? Sat in a rec room or something? He went back to the dusty old folders and checked the report. *During the approximate time of the disappearance, Jon Casey and Quentin Pheaney reported that they sat in the prison chapel and had a conversation of roughly ten minutes in duration before rejoining the others at the Surveillance Hub.* It was very convenient, the most suspicious event in the entire scenario, as far as Dudley was concerned, that the two prime suspects were each other's alibi. He remembered asking Pheaney what this conversation of theirs had been about. *I was reading,* Pheaney had said, which in some ways seemed unbelievable, until you realized that this was kind of all Quentin Pheaney did. Of course he sat there in the ruined chapel of the penitentiary in which they were trapped and read—it was the Bible, in fact? One of the Psalms. It was sad. Quentin Pheaney seemed like he was hardly there at all, like he wasn't much more than a brain on a stick.

The thing that kept Dudley awake at night was this: that Jon Casey had killed not only his wife, but his friend Quentin as well. He hadn't interviewed Casey after Pheaney's death, but what were the odds that the man had no alibi? He remembered going to his sergeant, Rocky Collins, and proposing that they get a statement from Casey about his whereabouts, and Collins had just looked at him like he was insane. *Dudley,* he said. *Your suspect is dead by his own hand. You can let it the fuck go. Everybody wins.*

Two days ago, when Gleeson took Jon Casey in for questioning, she'd asked him about Pheaney's death, and the man got real quiet. Dudley had excused himself, said he'd get the man some coffee, but had watched and listened from the other side of the room's one-way glass as Gleeson did her thing. Casey, looking at the photos of the corpse, crossed his arms and squeezed himself, just as Pheaney had done thirty-five years before, as if Casey had consumed the man whole and even now his ghost was trying to get out. *Inside every fat man there is a thin man trying to get out.* It was like that moment at the end of *Peter and the Wolf,* when you can hear the bird singing from inside the belly of the captured wolf.

Did I talk to him? After he died you mean? And that was the moment the possibility finally occurred to him: Was Pheaney still alive? Could all that business in Canada have just been one big fake-out? The man's body had never been recovered from the wreck.

He remembered his father taking him to hear Tchaikovsky's *Peter and the Wolf* when he was a child. Eugene Ormandy conducting the Philadelphia Orchestra at the Academy of Music. Beforehand, they'd gone to some club where the cops all went, and had snapper soup. He remembered his father introducing him around to all the other cops. "This is my boy, Daniel," he said.

The other cops shook his hand and nodded. He'd been wearing a coat and a tie. "You gonna be a policeman like your old man when you grow up?"

He'd nodded. "Yes sir," he said. "Yes, I will."

Dudley whistled the main theme of *Peter and the Wolf* for a moment before his eyes fell on the old ledger.

Grandfather shook his head discontentedly. "Well, what would have happened if Peter hadn't caught the wolf? What then?"

He opened the ledger and looked at it. He did not remember this piece of evidence. It was an old-fashioned checkbook of the kind people used to use in the '60s and '70s—probably someone still does, somewhere: with the checks in pages of three on the right, and an on-going tally of the stubs on the left. It was the ledger from the Curtin trust, from the mid-'80s. He paged through it, looking at the stubs. Then his fingers stopped. An entry marked July 27, 1987, said *Twenty thousand and* $^{00}/_{100}$ *cents to Quentin Pheaney.*

He stopped whistling.

Dudley leafed through the files. He knew the obit was in there, but it took a while to find. Then, at last, he found it: a small entry from the *Philadelphia Inquirer*: Quentin Pheaney, twenty-nine, writer and bank teller.

The entry began "BELOVED SON . . ."

The date of death was listed as July 24, 1987. Three days *before* Casey wrote the man a check.

Dudley thought about this for a long while. A strange smile crept over his lips.

He looked through the files again, not certain if he would find the thing he was looking for, but there it was: the envelope full of Casey's canceled checks from the same era. He leafed through them—$23 to Ticketron; $33 at Bookbinders, $45 to Checkered Cloth Cooking Supply. And here: right before him. The check to Quentin Pheaney.

Twenty thousand clams. He looked on the reverse. There was Pheaney's signature. And a stamp from the bank where it had been depos-
ited: Key West Provident Bank. August 4, 1987.

"My, what brave fellows we are," Dudley said out loud. Quentin
Pheaney, dead in Canada in July, had cashed a check for $20,000 in
August, in Florida.

*And perhaps, if you listen very carefully, you will hear the duck quack-
ing inside the wolf, because the wolf, in his hurry to eat her, had swallowed
her alive.*

12

Poughkeepsie, New York

Tripper Pennypacker was behind the wheel of a Tesla dual-motor Model S. His wife, Molly, sat in the passenger seat, wearing a floppy hat and sunglasses. Vassar College was five miles behind them now, along with their son, Max, whom they'd left in his dormitory along with his new sheets and his fiddle and a desk lamp. Max had walked them out to the car and said, "You're not going to start crying now, are you?"

"No," Tripper said. "I'm good." It was a rhetorical question. Tripper had never been much of a crier.

"You think of anything you need, you text us, all right?" said Molly. She gave him a big hug, squeezed him there in the parking lot. Tripper shook his son's hand. Then the two of them got into the Tesla and drove off. Tripper looked in the side mirror and saw Max staring after them. Then the kid put his hands in his pockets and headed back into the dorm.

"Well," said Molly. "That's that, I guess."

"Free at last!" said Tripper.

Molly slid her sunglasses down her nose to give him a look. "Are we?" she said.

Shit, Tripper thought, realizing, it's going to be like that then. Not that he'd expected it to go any other way. He wasn't even sure he *wanted* a reboot with Molly at this late date, but he at least had wanted the satisfaction of her asking for it, and him saying no.

They'd been running on fumes for a long time. But they'd bit their tongues in hopes that they could at least get the kid to college. Which they had, thank you Jesus. Max was back in the Main Building, putting up posters on the wall of his dorm room for bands that Tripper did not know. While he and Molly headed back toward Philly in the Tesla. He hoped they'd at least be able to get back to the house before she started in on him.

"You tell me, Doc," he said. "You're the authority."

"I don't *think* so," said Molly.

"Is there any scenario," Tripper asked, "in which you're not a total bitch to me right now?" He punched the Tesla up to eighty-five, passing other cars on the Taconic like they were Matchbox toys.

"I don't know, Tobin," said Molly. She refused to call him Tripper. "Is there a scenario in which you're somebody else?"

Tripper thought being somebody else right about now would have come in pretty handy. But said, "I'm exactly who I was when we got married! I'm sorry that's such a disappointment."

"We were *twenty-six* when we got married," Molly said.

"I know how old we were!" Tripper shouted.

"I don't want to be married to a twenty-six-year-old," she said. "I want to be married to a grown-up."

"You know, a lot of women would be happy to be married to someone with a youthful spirit," said Tripper.

"Is that what they call it?" said Molly.

"Ugh," said Tripper. They were up to ninety now. He took a deep breath. "I guess you're not interested in straightening things out then," he said. "You want to just make it easy on ourselves, call it quits? You know, we can spare ourselves a lot of trouble. I can just call Jon Hart." Hart was the partner at Pennypacker, Martin, Williams & Hart who handled all the divorce cases.

Molly just looked out the window at the rushing greenery of the Hudson Valley.

"No," said Molly quietly.

"No?" said Tripper. "No what?"

"No, I don't want you to call Jon Hart."

"Why not? What's the point?"

"Because," she said. "I love you, you asshole."

Tripper felt like someone had slapped him with a fish. "You mean that?"

"That you're an asshole?" said Molly. "Yeah, I mean that."

"No, goddammit. That you love me."

"I love some version of you," said Molly. "He's in there some-where." She took off her sunglasses and put them in her purse. Molly had brown hair streaked with gray, cold blue eyes. "I wish you'd let him loose. But you have to do it, not me, Toby. Maybe your younger self might be willing to loosen up the stranglehold? Now that Max is launched, you could do that maybe?"

He thought about the way Max had just turned his back on them at Vassar and headed toward his dorm to start his life. Tripper's hands clenched the wheel harder. It seemed unfair, that Max got to live his life, whereas he—his father!—had to soldier on at Pennypacker Mar-tin. It's an injustice, Tripper thought. An affront.

Thirty-nine years ago, he and his parents had pulled up in front of a dormitory at Wesleyan University in a black Mercedes. "At last!" his mother declared. "College!" From the backseat, he had glowered.

"You think you'll be seeing much of Quentin and Casey?" asked his father.

"I don't know," he said.

"My thought," said his father, "is that it's best to make a clean break." Tripper's dad was still angry he hadn't gotten into Princeton. His mother unlocked the trunk. It contained a suitcase, a stereo, a box set of the complete Beethoven symphonies, and a copy of Coffin & Roelofs's *The Major Poets*. His favorite teacher, Mr. Roswell, had used it in their Modern British Poetry class, Roswell with his three-piece suit and nineteenth-century mustache. He had brought the book with him on the backpacking trip he'd taken with Quentin to Europe that summer, an adventure that his father had objected to from the begin-ning. "There's something off about that boy," said Tripper's dad, just before they left.

"What?" said Tripper, not that he disagreed. "What's off about him?"

His father wouldn't say.

It was a question Tripper would return to in the weeks that followed, as he and Quentin had boarded a flight bound for Brussels with only their backpacks, a pair of Eurail passes, and their high school German to guide them. It was odd that they had decided to travel together, given that Tripper hadn't been all that close to Quentin at Devon Boys' Latin. There was something skittery about Quentin, with his long hair and his feminine good looks and his hummingbird metabolism. He always reminded Tripper of a bird caught in a house, some creature blindly crashing from one wall to another. He didn't understand why the boy didn't just open up the window, whatever it was, and be done. It's what he would have done, if he'd been Quentin, which fortunately he was not.

The flight to Europe they'd purchased was some kind of charter run through an outfit called Capital Airways. The flight out of New York had been delayed for a day, though, with the result that all the passengers had been put up at the Taft Hotel, where Tripper read Aeschylus while Quentin argued with a group of Hare Krishnas. The Krishnas seemed to think that Quentin had potential, and invited him to eat with them at their table. "I pray and pray to God," Quentin had said to the bald-headed, pink-robed Krishnas. "But nothing ever happens."

"You see," said the leader of the group, a person whom the others called Perfect Master. "Your prayers have all been answered."

One of the other Krishnas had looked at the book Tripper was reading, and asked, "What are its teachings?"

Tripper opened the book to a passage he had underlined. It was the one Bobby Kennedy had quoted in Indianapolis. "*He who learns must suffer,*" he said. "*And even in our sleep, pain that cannot forget falls drop by drop upon the heart, and in our own despair, against our will, comes wisdom to us by the awful grace of God.*"

The monk seemed amused by this. "Is he American, this fellow?"

"Greek," said Tripper.

They landed in Brussels, spent a day or so wandering around speaking neither French nor Flemish. At one point Quentin had gone into a store, leaving Tripper on a street corner. A small boy had approached the intersection, and Tripper had said, "Hello. What's your name?" The child had just looked at him in fear. "It's all right!" said Tripper. "I'm an American!" The child ran away.

They were in Amsterdam, in a bar with some sailors, Quentin standing on top of a table while the sailors—had they been Australian?—applauded and cheered. Then they were somewhere near the Coliseum in Rome, eating pizza, which didn't look anything like the pizza they had eaten in Pennsylvania. They were together in a tent on a hillside in Bavaria as rain came down and Tripper read Aeschylus and Quentin lay still. They got so cold and wet that at last they hiked into a town, where they ordered Spargelsuppe and ate brown bread. In Munich, they stayed in a hostel on the outskirts of the city that was a large circus tent. Around a bonfire a group of young people from England were singing "Mr. Tambourine Man" and playing guitars. Tripper bought a bottle of beer for *fünfzehn Pfennig*.

They traveled the Romantische Strasse, from Würzburg to Füssen. There had been a fountain in one of those cities, maybe Augsburg, against which Tripper and Quentin leaned for a while, looking at a map. Where had they gone after that? It was all gone except for the fountain. Then, in Frankfurt, they came upon a whole section of the town that was still bombed-out. There was a memorial—underground—featuring a Nazi soldier in marble laid out like a slain man, and the words UNSERE GEFALLENEN. Tripper couldn't figure out if it meant "our fallen" or "our fall." They paused in a park and watched some old men paying chess with giant chess pieces. Quentin was whistling "Give My Regards to Broadway." One of the chess players was surely old enough to have served in the war. He had a long scar down the side of his face. He turned to Quentin and growled, *"Kein Pfeifen,"* which meant "There's no whistling." Quentin stopped. The old soldiers looked at the young men with hate.

Then they were in Locarno, Switzerland, where Tripper had a great-great-aunt. He hadn't seen her since childhood, but he remembered Tante Senta as a cool, thin, stylish woman. She'd married a Swiss Italian who dropped dead of a brain hemorrhage one afternoon, leaving her with his fortune and a house at the foot of the Alps by Lake Maggiore. But Tante Senta was almost unrecognizable to him; in the intervening years Alzheimer's had swept through her mind, leaving her unable to speak English, and appearing, at times, not to really understand who Tripper or Quentin were, or why they were in her house. But she could still cook, and she made them pasta with sauce and opened up bottles of Chianti. After dinner, they put Beethoven's Ninth Symphony on her record player, and the three of them—the two young men and the old woman—sat there listening to the music. As the chorus began to sing in the fourth movement—"O Freude!"— tears had rolled out of his aunt's eyes and down her face.

They lay in bed that night, drunk on the Chianti, mesmerized by the Beethoven, lying in two twin beds.

"*Alle Menschen werden Brüder*," Quentin said.

"Yeah," said Tripper. "It's nice to think about, isn't it? All of us being brothers."

Quentin said nothing for a long while. Then said, "I'm living in one of the coed dorms," he said.

"Thank God," said Tripper. "Maybe you'll finally get some pussy."

"Ech," said Quentin. "That's kind of a horrible thing to say."

"I want you to fucking get laid, Quentin," said Tripper. "That's so horrible?"

"I don't care about getting laid," said Quentin. "I just want to be in love."

"Aw," said Tripper.

"I'm serious," said Quentin. "I'm not fucking someone just to fuck someone. I want to be in love first."

"Yeah," said Tripper. "Maybe I should have tried that approach with Maisie. Spared myself the trouble."

"What trouble?" said Quentin.

"You know what trouble," said Tripper.

A ringing sound shook Tripper out of his memories. Molly was talking. "Are you going to answer that?" He was back in the Tesla.

"I got it," he said. Tripper held the phone at arm's length so he could read the numbers of the incoming call. It was no one he recognized.

"Hello?" he said. "What?"

"Tripper," said a voice.

"Speaking."

"It's me. Casey."

For a moment Tripper didn't say anything. Now they were in New Jersey. He looked out the window at the Meadowlands, bridges curling over the swamps. This is where they always used to dump the bodies in *The Sopranos*.

"What can I do for you, Casey?" he said. He knew he sounded cold, but there was a reason he didn't talk to any of those people anymore.

"You gotta help me man," said Casey.

"Actually," said Tripper. "I don't *gotta* do anything."

"I'm in trouble," Casey said. "They found . . . you know. The, like, *body*. They been asking me all these questions. I need—*representation*."

"What body?" said Tripper.

"Tripper," said Casey. "Come on. You know what body."

"Ah," said Tripper. He then made a number of calculations in a very short amount of time. "Okay, look," he said. "I'm having someone from the firm call you. His name is Winston O'Rourke. He'll take care of you." Tripper pictured his colleague Winston O'Rourke, a man who smelled like peppermint schnapps at ten thirty in the morning.

"But I want *you*, Tripper!" shouted Casey. "You gotta be my guy! You were there!"

"I don't *gotta* do anything," said Tripper. "As I said. I'm sending you Winston O'Rourke. That's my favor to you. Now your favor to me? Leave me alone."

He hit the End Call button on his phone. They drove on for a while. He felt Molly staring at him.

"What?" he said.

"Jon Casey?" she said. "Your friend the walrus?"

"He's not my friend," said Tripper.

"Of course he's your friend," said Molly. "That's the whole problem."

"Wait, what problem are we talking about?" said Tripper.

"This is why I'm stuck married to a twenty-two-year-old!" she said. "Because you can't let those people go! You're obsessed with them!"

"What are you *talking* about?" Tripper snapped. "I never even *think* about those people." As he said this, it occurred to him that, okay, he'd just spent the last fifty miles thinking about them. He remembered, once again, his trip to Germany in the summer of '76 with Quentin. There they were, talking about Maisie in Tante Senta's guest room, the "Ode to Joy" still fresh in his heart. He'd never heard it before.

They'd lain there in the dark. Tripper wondered whether Quentin had fallen asleep. "I thought you loved her," Quentin said at last.

"Well, now I have to," said Tripper.

"You don't have to love her," said Quentin. "You don't have to do anything."

"She had the abortion, now I'm stuck with her forever," said Tripper. "That's how it works."

Quentin thought this over. "I thought she had the abortion so you wouldn't have to stay together, unless you loved her. Which I thought you did."

"Man," said Tripper. "You really don't understand women, do you?"

Quentin laughed unexpectedly at this. He cackled as if this was hilarious.

"What'd I say?" said Tripper. "Did I say something funny?"

But Quentin just rolled over. "Maybe," he said.

13

Bryn Mawr, Pennsylvania

"Look, Aimee," said the girl's mother. "We're here at Maisie's house. It's time to play pipe organ. Isn't that nice?"

The girl showed no reaction. A string bean of drool hung from the corner of her mouth. Aimee was about seven. She had thin hair braided in tight pigtails, tied with pink yarn.

"Hello, Aimee," said Maisie. "I'm glad you're here. Do you want to play the Toccata and Fugue in D Minor for me today?"

Aimee held tight to her mother's hand, and neither retreated nor advanced toward the king of instruments. The ridiculous, ornate organ, with its four separate manuals and sixty-four stops had been custom built by the Aeolian-Skinner Organ Company back in the nineteenth century, to fit in the space at the center of the circular stairs in the Bagatelle, the exaggerated mansion built by Maisie's great-grandfather, Virgil Lenfest.

Now Maisie lived in the Bagatelle with a cat named Snowy, and gave music lessons to special-needs kids on the Main Line. She also directed something called the D'Oyly Care Company, which put on Gilbert & Sullivan operettas with casts of troubled actors under the age of thirteen.

Her brother, Ben, lived in his room on the third floor, reading books. Maisie cooked his meals.

"Let's get you up on the seat," said Mrs. Lupin. Aimee's mom was a morbidly obese woman with a languid Southern drawl. The girl did not protest as her mother stuck her hands in Aimee's armpits and lifted her onto the seat. Her legs did not quite reach the pedals.

"There you go," said Maisie. "I'm so glad you've come to play for me." Aimee's right hand was bent like a claw. The girl opened her mouth wide, her neck muscles straining, as if she were going to shout. But no sound came.

"I understand you're going to play the Toccata and Fugue in D Minor?" said Maisie. She looked at the girl's mother. "She's been listening to it?"

"Oh yeah," said Mrs. Lupin. "Pretty much nonstop for the last week."

Maisie took this in. "The whole thing? The toccata as well as the four-voice fugue?"

"The whole shebang," said Mrs. Lupin. "Got it on repeat." The woman sighed. "All Vincent Price and whatnot."

"It's unfortunate the piece has come to have that association," said Maisie. "It wasn't written to scare people."

"Too late now though huh," said Mrs. Lupin. She got a Kleenex out of her Coach bag. "Let's mop you up, darlin'." She wiped the drool from Aimee's mouth. "There. Now you're clean as a whistle."

Aimee sat there on the stool, her right hand still clenched. In the living room was the set of *HMS Pinafore*. The previous evening, a boy with Fragile X syndrome had stood in the middle of that set and sung, "*I am the captain of the* Pinafore!" And a whole chorus of other children, each with their own challenges, had shouted, "*And a right good captain too!*"

Ben had made one of his rare trips down from the third floor and stood there watching the singing children with a hollow expression, until one by one they fell silent.

"Do you want something?" asked Maisie.

Ben had stood there, wanting something. He didn't say what.

"Can you play the Toccata and Fugue for me, honey?" said Maisie to Aimee. "Your mom says you've been listening to it all week?"

"Nnngh," said Aimee.

"I'm going to just lower your hands onto the keys, okay?" said Maisie. "Is it all right if I touch your hand? Okay? Okay?"

She took Aimee by the hand and lowered her arm until the fingers of the girl's right hand rested on the A octave, thumb and pinky. "There," said Maisie. "That's where you start. Do you want to try?"

Aimee's hands were on the lower manual now, but she didn't seem any more relaxed. Looking at her, Maisie could only wonder how it was that someone so small could bear so much tension. The girl was like an overwound clock.

"You begin when you want to," said Maisie. "No rush at all. You don't even have to play. I just like being with you." She nodded. "I like your ribbons. Pink is pretty on you."

The girl's eyes did not move. She stared off above the music stand, toward the middle of the staircase that wrapped around the instrument. Aimee sat like that for a long moment, her fingers frozen upon the A octave.

"She really was listenin' to it," Mrs. Lupin said. "Round and round."

"I believe you," said Maisie, and why shouldn't she? The girl, mysteriously wired as she was, had performed all sorts of miracles on Maisie's watch. The first time she ever came for a lesson, she'd played the Goldberg—the aria and all thirty variations—from memory. The mother said she'd never played it on an actual keyboard before, but out it came, the whole thing.

It was nearly impossible to teach students with Aimee's difference, Maisie had learned over the years. You could show them different fingering, or suggest a change in dynamics—*a little softer during the canon, dear*—but often her instructions had no effect. Her students—some the survivors of post-traumatic stress, some on the autism spectrum—mostly wanted the opportunity to play the things they heard, most of which went only one way, and if you tried to get between them and the way they heard the music, you'd wind up with a student screaming at you, or collapsed into a fetal ball upon the floor, or—as was often the case with Aimee—she'd just stop, let an appropriate moment of silence go by, and then begin playing all over again from the beginning, exactly as she'd played it before.

The Toccata and Fugue in D Minor was pretty ambitious, though, even for a savant as gifted as Aimee. It was a piece that had broken many organists over the years, including ones without any additional neurological hurdles to clear. But who knows? Maisie thought. Maybe the world that Aimee lived in was a world of numbers, a land of ones and zeroes. Some of the distractions of the piece—many of them emotional—were not things that Aimee perceived, at least not in the way that Maisie understood them. But then, Maisie had to admit that, even after twenty years as a piano and organ teacher of special-needs children, she didn't feel qualified to describe what her students' inner worlds were like. All you could do was love them, after your fashion, and help them bring the music that lived inside them out into the open.

Aimee sat there, her body tense, her gaze focused somewhere far off. *What are you seeing?* Maisie wondered. Aimee wore heavy, thick lenses that magnified her eyeballs. But it was impossible to know what the world looked like through those eyes.

"What are you looking at?" Maisie asked the girl. She seemed fixed upon the staircase.

"Does anyone else live in this house, Miss Lenfest?" asked Mrs. Lupin.

Maisie thought about Ben, up on the third floor. Earlier today, when she'd brought him his lunch, he was gluing together the planes of a sphere with thirty-six sides.

"No," said Maisie.

"She's not usually like this," said the mother.

"Do you see something?" said Maisie. "Is there something on the stairs?"

"There's *nothin'* on the stairs," Mrs. Lupin said, rather firmly.

"Nngh," said Aimee, and she raised her hands from the manual and brought them to her mouth, as if she were frightened. Maisie had never seen the girl like this before—she had always seemed so affectless during her lessons. Maisie glanced at Aimee's mother. Now Mrs. Lupin was looking at the stairs, at the same spot that was transfixing her daughter.

Once, Wailer had come down those stairs, wearing her mother's wedding dress, her hair as pink as a rhododendron blossom. At the couple's request, Maisie had played "Whiter Shade of Pale" on the organ, a piece that was a kind of cousin to Bach's "Ich steh' mit einem Fuss im Grabe." A year or so later, before they'd all agreed to stop seeing one another, it was Quentin who'd pointed out that the bride had processed to a song reminiscent of a piece that translated as "I stand with one foot in the grave."

It was a piece that Maisie didn't play anymore.

But there she stood, as if alive. The twenty-two-year-old Wailer, blooming like a pink flower, looked down on her friends with an enormous smile. Light radiated from her. In her hands was a bouquet of daisies, picked that afternoon from the Lenfests' backyard, after Maisie had pointed out that she didn't have any flowers to carry. At first Wailer just gave her another blast of her exaggerated brogue: "Can I not just fuckin' swerve on it? It's so beside the point." But she seemed to like the idea of flowers yanked up out of the ground by her own hand. They'd stood there in the backyard of the Bagatelle, a place that had once had its own gardener, with its boarded-up Victorian fountain. Maisie remembered the fountain working when she was very, very small—there'd been one hot Fourth of July when she'd played in it like a swimming pool. But her father, "Lucky" Lenfest, had put an end to that with one particularly memorable trip to Vegas. Now it was just one more ruin, like the rest of the place.

There were daisies, though, and Wailer had picked a few with Rachel and Maisie, her bridesmaids. Rachel had sat on the edge of the boarded-up fountain plucking out petals, saying, *He loves me, he loves me not.*

"If you're talking about Quenty, you can fuckin' skip ahead, can't you?" said Wailer.

"Don't be mean, Wailer," said Maisie.

"It's not meanness," said Wailer. "I'm just looking out for me girl."

"When do you go to Togo, Wailer?" said Rachel.

"End o' September," said Wailer, gathering daisies. "I'm gettin' orientated in London first at the Red Cross HQ, then it's off to the Dark Continent in October."

"And you'll be—"

"What else, love?" said Wailer. "Teachin' English!"

They all laughed. "This would be the Queen's English?" Rachel said. She'd reached her last petal.

"I've got no fuckin' queen," said Wailer. "Just me king, Jonny Casey the First."

"It's going to be hard for him to be apart from you for a full year," said Maisie.

"'Tis," said Wailer. "I'm addictive." She looked at the flower with the single petal in Rachel's hand. "So? How'd you wind up then?"

"He loves me," said Rachel.

"The fuck he does," said Wailer. "He loves himself."

"Miss Lenfest?" said Aimee's mother. "Are you okay?"

Maisie snapped back. "I'm fine," she said. "Isn't that something." She looked at Aimee. "I was just thinking about a friend of mine, from a long time ago. Do you have a special friend?"

Aimee relaxed a little. Her hands fell into her lap. "Miss Lenfest," said Mrs. Lupin, sounding a little impatient. "*Y'all* are her special friend."

Maisie opened her mouth, then shut it. "Oh," she said. "Of course. And you're my friend too, Aimee. I love when you come to visit." She looked at the girl's mother. "Do you want to give it another try? The Toccata and Fugue?" But the girl just curled toward her mother, as if trying to hide.

"I think we're done for the day," said Mrs. Lupin. "I don't really understand. She was all riled up to play for ya."

"Well, you can play for me next week," said Maisie. "It's all right. You keep listening to the piece on your stereo. You'll play it when you're ready."

Mrs. Lupin stood up. Aimee held tightly on to her hand. "Very strange," she said. "Oh well."

"Do you want me to play a piece for you?" said Maisie. Sometimes this helped to loosen her students up a little.

"What do you think, Aimee, do you want to hear Miss Lenfest play the organ?"

Aimee turned toward Maisie a little bit.

"Okay," said Maisie. "Here, let me get situated." She slid onto the bench, pulled out a few stops.

Then she began to play it. "Whiter Shade of Pale." It had been a long time, but her fingers knew where to go.

"Nngh," said Aimee, her voice rising in panic. She was pointing at the landing again. But there was no one there.

"We're going to go," said Mrs. Lupin. Maisie thought about stopping, but she didn't.

"Okay," she said. "See you next week!"

Mrs. Lupin looked at Maisie, annoyed. But Maisie just kept on playing. She heard the front door open, then close.

Maisie started to sing. *We skipped the light fandango.*

She sang the whole thing, the whole bloody, incomprehensible song with its vague imagery—something about two people meeting at a party, a girl's face turning ghostly, the singer wondering whether all this life was just a dream.

As she played, she imagined Nathan Krystal, that old fuck, riding a tricycle around and around the organ, late that night after Wailer and Casey's wedding. It was quite a sight, the towering, elmlike man hunched down into the Big Wheel. She'd had to decide whether or not to have a fight with Casey and Wailer over his invite. She had seen him with little Benny at the *Pajama Game* cast party, had come upon them with the old bastard's treelike arm around the fragile boy. She'd thrown him out, then kept her silence. Later, she turned to Tripper and asked him what to do. Tripper's jaw got hard. She'd never seen him look like that before. It had scared her. *He's not getting away with that,* Tripper said. *We have to push back.*

What, she'd asked him. *What should we do?*

What do you want to have done? said Tripper.

I don't know, Maisie said.

At the reception, Casey had played "Long Black Veil" on the uku-lele. *The judge said son, what's your alibi?* They'd all stayed up until the dawn, drinking blue martinis made from that gin Casey had found somewhere containing the crushed leaves of iris flowers.

Maisie finished "Whiter Shade of Pale," and for just a moment, the house echoed with the sounds of the great instrument. Then there was a white flash, something streaking through the air before her, and Maisie drew in her breath quickly, her arms turning to goose bumps.

Snowy, the cat, hopped up on top of the organ. He looked at her curiously, then jumped down into her lap.

"*Miao,*" said the cat.

"Oh, you," said Maisie. "You scared me."

"I didn't mean to," said a voice behind her.

She turned around on the bench, and standing there like a ghost himself was Tripper, wearing khaki pants and a blue Oxford shirt, slightly wrinkled.

"Tripper," she said. Maisie looked at her teenage boyfriend, now a roly-poly middle-aged man.

"*Miao,*" said the cat, and hopped down from her lap and onto the floor.

"Did you see the news?" Tripper said. He looked at her quizzically, as if she were a student who was in the midst of failing an oral examina-tion. "No," he said, with an air of contempt and disappointment. "No, of course you didn't."

"News, what news?" said Maisie.

"What news," Tripper said, exasperated. He looked at the pipe organ, and at the circular stairs, whirling upward toward the third floor. It was aggravating. Everything here was just as he had left it.

"Listen," he said. "I think they're on to us."

14

Cold River, Maine

I felt Jake's body tense, even as I sat there encircled by his arms. Water lapped against the hull of the boat. Everything was very quiet. The only other sound was the distant roar of Kennebec Falls. "Tell me," he said.

I pulled back from him and looked into his eyes. I felt as if I were holding a bow and arrow, my fingers tensed and trembling against the bowstring, getting ready to let fly the arrow. "Um," I said.

"Judy," said Jake, squeezing my arms. "It's all right."

"Yeah," I said. "Hold that thought."

"No, honey," he said again, and squeezed my biceps harder. "There's nothing you could say that could make me not love you. Okay?"

I nodded. "Okay."

We drifted in the boat for a little bit—ten seconds? A minute? I really couldn't tell you. I'd rehearsed this conversation in my head about a million times since the day we'd met. But I still couldn't figure out how to begin.

"We've known each other for a long time," I said at last.

"Yup," said Jake.

"And I love you with all my heart. I can't even tell you how—" And just like that, my throat closed up, and tears rolled over my eyelashes and I started to cry. "Oh," I just said, and covered my face with my hands, and put my elbows on my knees. "I can't, I can't, I can't."

"Judy," said the man I loved. "Of course you can." He put his hands on my wrists. "Of course you can." He smiled, but I could see from his face he was worried. Something inside him was already taking bets on just exactly how bad this was going to be.

"Yeah, so, you're all I care about," I said. "You and Falcon. That's the life that we've built."

He nodded. Now he was just waiting for me to get it over with.

"But the thing is . . ." I said. I felt like my heart was going to pound its way out of my mouth.

"The thing is what, Judy?" Jake said, gently, lovingly, kindly. *You poor son of a bitch*, I thought. *I am just about to murder you.*

"The thing is," I said. "There's something you don't know about me."

"I know plenty," he said, and I wondered what he meant. Was he telling me that he already knew? That he'd figured it all out years ago, and it was all just fine? Was it possible, after all this time, that I had impaled myself upon a secret that was, as it turned out, not a secret at all?

"So you know?" I said. We had drifted a little closer to the falls now. Pretty soon we were going to have to get out the oars. The sound of water going over the edge grew louder.

"What do I know?" he said.

"That's what I'm asking."

"What are you asking?"

"What you know."

"About what?"

"About . . . my past," I said and my voice caught again, and once more the tears rolled down.

"Judy, honey," said Jake. "How stupid do you think I am?"

"I didn't say you were stupid," I said. "I just don't know what you . . ."

"You must have had it rough," he said kindly. "I know you did. But you're a good person. You're the kindest person I know. The way you came into my life, and made things good again, after we'd been in the dark. Me and Falcon, I just figured we'd never . . . And then, there you were." Now Jake's voice was trembling. "I never thought we'd ever look forward to getting up in the morning again, him and me. After we lost her. I just figured we'd just trudge along, you know, just doing the best we could in the dark. But instead—" His voice choked, and he stopped. It took him a long time to get himself back in one piece. "Instead one day," he said. "One day there was you."

"There was me," I said, but the way I said it, it didn't sound like I was much of anything.

"Goddammit, Judy," he said. "I love you. Don't you know that by now? Nothing's going to change that. I don't care how much trouble you got yourself in when you were young."

"Trouble," I said, and from the way he said this, I suspected, once again, that Jake didn't know the truth, that he didn't have a clue about the mystery he had long since forgiven me for.

I looked up. We were drawing near to the edge, and somebody was going to have to do something.

Jake, reading my mind, nodded, and got up and went to the hatch on the side of the boat where the oars were stowed. "Don't worry," he said. "I'll get us out of this." The oars were not the kind that connect to an oarlock and allow a person to row with purpose and dignity; they—or, it, in fact, since there was only one of them—had to be operated from the front of the boat, where Jake now positioned himself, upon the very point of the bow, and began to paddle us away from the place where the water curled over the lip. The current was swift. Jake had to put some serious effort into turning us around. I watched his muscles flexing through his shirt as he moved us away from the gorge and slowly propelled us back in the direction of our house. I could see our dock jutting out into the water about a quarter mile ahead of us. As he rowed, water flung off the oar spattered against my cheeks.

And yet, as I watched him, a strange sense of peace settled upon me. It occurred to me that after a while, the present trumps the past—that I had been a woman almost exactly as long as I had been a man, that I had been a mother for all but two of my son's seventeen years, that whatever I had been, I had been something else for far longer. Plus, I had been solid, unlike my younger self, who had been more like a ghost, or some kind of sentient mist. I thought about Casey in the graveyard, telling me, *You're going to be all right* in a voice that I did not recognize but which had not seemed to belong to him. I had wondered whom that voice belonged to, now and again, over the years, but only now was it becoming clear to me. That was the voice of my future self, the woman that at last I became, the woman that now lay in the stern of a boat as the man I loved paddled us away from danger and toward the shore.

We were about a hundred feet away from the dock when Jake put down the oar. He took off his Red Sox cap with one hand and wiped the sweat off of his forehead.

"You all right?" I said.

"I'm fine," he said. "'Course I'm fine." He turned around to face me. "What about you?"

"I'm all right. But I'm a little . . . I feel like you're forgiving me for something you don't actually know about."

"Judy," he said. "I know." He held his cap between his knees. The breeze blew his hair around. "I told you. The past doesn't matter."

"Oh, Jake," I said, and as I said it I shuddered. "I've been thinking about this conversation forever. Since the day you busted into my house with a fire hose. I was always afraid to tell you because . . ."

"Because you were afraid I wouldn't love you anymore," he said.

I nodded. The nose of the boat drifting slightly to the right as we gently, almost imperceptibly, began to spin around.

"That's what makes me angry, Judy," he said. "It's not that you, you know. Did time. It's that you thought it would make a difference."

I could see our house through the pine trees on the bank. I pictured our bedroom, the late-afternoon sunlight slanting onto the pumpkin pine floorboards. Gollum was almost certainly lying on his side in our big bed, his head on our pillows.

"Did time," I said.

Jake smiled, and the crow's feet around his eyes crinkled once more. "Yeah, if that's what you want to call it."

The front of our boat once again pointed toward the falls. I saw the mist drifting through the air behind the man I loved.

"Jake, I wasn't . . . a convict," I said, but even as I said it, I thought, *Yeah well, actually . . .*

"No?" he said.

"Jake, I'm trans."

He looked at me uncertainly, like I'd said, *I come from ancient Greece.*

"You're the what?" he said.

"I was born a boy. I transitioned in my twenties. It was a long time ago."

Now he smiled, from ear to ear. He put his hat back on. "Good one," he said.

"Jake," I said. "I'm not kidding."

"Wait," he said. "What?"

I blew some air through my cheeks. "I always knew I was meant to be, you know. Myself. Even when I was a child, I knew. But I never told anyone, because I was afraid they wouldn't love me anymore. I was afraid I'd lose everything. Because I never had anyone back then who loved me the way you do."

Jake was looking off toward the shore. He wasn't looking at me. "Like I do," he said.

"I left home when I was twenty-nine. I went up to Canada. I rolled my car off a cliff in Nova Scotia. Everybody thought I'd died. I did die, if you want to look at it like that. I hitchhiked down to Florida. Lived there for a while before I went to Thailand."

"Thailand," said Jake.

"That's where they actually did, you know. The business. I came back here, got a job at the Kennebec Arsenal. That's where I was living the night I left the macaroni and cheese on the stove, and you—"

"All right!" shouted Jake. "Enough already." He looked at me with a wild expression, like an animal with one foot in a trap. "Listen. Listen."

I listened.

"I said that I," he said, but then said nothing. He shook his head. "I said that I would always love you." He took his baseball cap off his head again and looked at it for a while, then he put it back on his head. He looked at me. "I said it and I meant it." He picked up the oar again, and turned his back to me. Jake dipped his oar in the water, and slowly started rowing us toward home once more.

I went up to him and put my arms around him and leaned my face against his back. "I'm so sorry," I said. "I wanted to tell you. I've always wanted to tell you."

"Judy, I'm trying to row the boat."

"I know," I said, hugging him tighter. "I'm just so grateful. I love you so much."

"I said I love you too," he said. He turned around and looked at me with an expression I'd never seen. "Now, *back off.*"

I sat back. From someplace I could not see, loons called to one another.

I know where you are.

"So it's going to be like that?" I said.

"It's not like anything," Jake said, and he turned to look at me over his shoulder, his face red. "I said I love you. It doesn't make any difference to me. It's fine. Just let me get us away from the goddamn waterfall so we don't tip over and die."

"Well, I appreciate you saving my life," I said.

"I'm not saving anything," he said, more to himself than to me. With the oar he spun us around again and rowed us toward our home.

"I can answer any questions you might have," I said. The loons called again. "I mean, I guess you'd have lots of—"

"Judy, I think it's kind of better if you don't say anything right now."

"Jake, I'm sorry—"

"Don't be sorry," said Jake. "Just be quiet."

And so we made our way back to our dock, and Jake dropped the oar in the boat and jumped onto the shore holding the bowline in one hand. He tied us up and then he stood there and reached out with one hand to help me back onto the dock. "Come on, Judy," he said. "I got you."

As I stepped out of the boat, and onto the dock, Jake pulled me toward him, and then he wrapped both his arms around my chest and we stood there in the twilight by the water.

"Are you still hungry?" I said. "I can make us some dinner."

"Yeah," said Jake. "I'm thinking I want to take a walk, okay?"

"Oh," I said. "Well, okay, we can do that." I nodded. "Let's take a walk."

"No, yeah, see," he said. "I want to be alone for a while, okay?"

"You're sure you don't want . . . Because I can—"

"Yeah, I think I need to think," said Jake.

"Are you all right?"

"I said I need to think, goddammit," said Jake, his voice rising.

Tears spilled out of my eyes again. "Jake," I said. "I'm sorry."

"Yeah," he said, turning his back on me and walking down the trail that ran along the water's edge. "Me too."

15

Bryn Mawr, Pennsylvania

"What do you mean, they're on to us?" Maisie said to Tripper.

They were on either side of the fireplace in the olive-green wing chairs. The one Tripper was sitting in still had an oil-shaped spot on it that marked the place where Maisie's father had rested his head in the evenings, or had, anyway, right up until the night he and his wife slid off the curve on Saw Mill Road in Newtown Square on his way back from a party at Thatcher and Nancy Longstreth's. At one end of the enormous room was the old piano, upon which he and Maisie once played a duet of "Heart and Soul" during the Ford administration.

From out in the hallway, through the big arch with its elegant keystone, footsteps creaked up the stairs. Her cat, Snowy, who had been standing on top of the piano, arched his back and hissed. The animal coughed, as if he were sick.

"I see this place is still the Haunted Mansion from Disneyland," said Tripper.

"Tripper," said Maisie. "What do you mean, they're on to us?"

"You know what this house reminds me of," said Tripper. "Those pictures of the *Titanic* on the bottom of the ocean. Barnacles growing off the chandelier. Sharks swimming through the ballroom."

"Tripper," said Maisie.

"You don't read the news?"

"I try to avoid the news," she said with an air of superiority, as if not knowing what was going on in the world somehow made her a better person.

"They found her," said Tripper. "The body. Stuffed in a hole in Eastern State. In one of the cells."

Maisie looked a little uncertain. "I thought . . . I thought your guy—Mr. Gergen—"

"Gurganis," said Tripper. "And he wasn't my *guy*, okay? He was an acquaintance. From youth."

"He was supposed to . . . I mean, I thought he said he—"

"Yes, well," said Tripper. "Here's the good news." He looked down the hallway. Snowy peered at them from a safe distance. "They're going to pin it on Casey. The merry widower. His penknife was in her."

"Wait, how is this good news?" said Maisie. "He's innocent."

He looked at her, annoyed. "Better him than *us*, Maisie."

Maisie looked uncertain. "Is it?"

Across from where they were sitting was a love seat covered with white linen. There were dark stains on the material, which Tripper knew to have once been red wine. It was impossible for him not to associate this particular piece of furniture with the night of the Bicentennial.

They had arrived back from the party at Peter Davis's house in Stone Harbor that night and lay there with their arms around each other, Maisie in the middle, Quentin and Tripper each making out with one side of the same woman. This triangulation had begun on the beach at Stone Harbor as they lay on the sand, watching the fireworks over the ocean, drinking Southern Comfort. In retrospect, it seemed curious that Quentin had decided it was just fine for him to make out with his half of Tripper's girlfriend, but then it was the Bicentennial after all, and the ordinary rules of good taste had been suspended. They'd sat there on the sands of New Jersey, the beach strangely deserted, as the fireworks exploded, Quentin's arms and his own wrapped around the same girl, and all he could think was what a beautiful night it was, what a beautiful country.

Then they drove home, all the way across South Jersey and across the Delaware, and wound up here. Maisie didn't seem weirded out that

Quentin was sucking on her left ear. Maybe she thought of it as an act of charity; he hadn't had an actual girlfriend in four years of high school, and around women he displayed a hunger that would have been affecting if it wasn't so pathetic. They wound up on the linen love seat for twenty minutes or so, and briefly, Tripper's fingers had interlocked with Quentin's. Who knows what the denouement would have been had not little Benny shown up, standing there beneath the archway, looking at them accusingly in his Liberty Bell pajamas.

Maisie, as always, had been the first one to notice him. "Benny," she said, turning red. "I didn't know you were there." It was hard to know what embarrassed her more, the fact that there were two boys making out with her at once, or that there was an open bottle of Southern Comfort on the floor.

Benny had stood there before the trio, wanting something. But what it was he wanted he did not say.

"You ever think what would have happened if we'd had that baby," Tripper said now, not looking at Maisie. "Instead." ·

"Oh, Tripper," said Maisie, looking at him with pity. "Why would you ask that?"

"You never think about it?"

She crossed her legs. "I thought that I'd have other children," she said. "When I was ready. But I wound up with Ben instead."

"How is he? Benny?"

"Ben. He lives upstairs. He reads books, folds origami. I cook for him. He eats beige food."

"Beige food?" said Tripper.

"Pasta, rice. Mac and cheese. White bread. It's a thing."

"Does he ever play the—" He shrugged. "I know you have an enterprise for the special-needs children."

"I'm not giving *him* music therapy," said Maisie, as if the idea was offensive to her.

"What, because it wouldn't take, or—?"

"I've done *plenty* for Ben already," said Maisie. "I've done more than my share!"

"I'm sorry for him," said Tripper. "I'm sorry about a lot of things."

"Well, you *should* be sorry!" shouted Maisie. "You're the one who hired the world's worst hit man. A guy you found, where, at a clown college?"

"You said you wanted revenge," said Tripper evenly. "You asked me to have someone take care of Nathan Krystal."

"I didn't say murder anyone!" said Maisie.

"You said give him a scare," said Tripper.

"He attacked the *wrong person*, Tripper," said Maisie.

"He said it was dark."

"He killed our friend. A woman we *loved*."

Tripper wasn't having any of this. "She wasn't *my* friend."

Maisie shook her head. "That poor girl."

Tripper took a breath. "My understanding is that she fell," he said. "She broke her neck when he shoved her. He didn't know it was the wrong person until after the fact."

"Well, I'm not going to jail because of what *your guy* did. Your *idiot moron*. I'll tell them everything before I do that."

"You're guilty, Maisie," said Tripper. "We are *accessories*."

"I'm not having my life ruined," said Maisie. "For something that happened thirty-five years ago."

Tripper looked around the run-down living room, the makeshift set for *HMS Pinafore* at one end. There was a ship's steering wheel and two small poles that served as masts. "Our lives are already ruined," he said.

Maisie frowned. "I didn't *do* anything!" she said firmly.

Tripper thought this over. "I heard Nathan Krystal died. Heart attack."

Maisie felt the life draining out of her. She stared at the floor. "That happened years ago."

Tripper gave her a hard look. "You're wrong about this place," he said.

"Wrong?"

"When you said it wasn't haunted." He pointed to the love seat.

"Look, we made out right there," he said. "You and me and Quentin. That night we got back from Stone Harbor."

"Oh, *Quentin*," said Maisie. It was a name she hadn't heard for a long time. "Quentin Pheaney."

Tripper walked over to the piano and sat down on the bench. "Remember that summer before college? Quentin and I went to Europe together? There was this one time we got caught in the rain and we hiked into this little village in Bavaria and had asparagus soup and brown bread. I think that was the best soup I ever had in my life."

Maisie went over to the piano and sat down on the bench. She played the first few bars of "Whiter Shade of Pale." On the piano it sounded understated and sad, like a lost invention by Bach. Then she stopped.

"Why are you talking about soup?"

"Because I thought he was a friend!" said Tripper. "We had that soup. Then we got to college and he acted like I was nothing. He was Joe Cool! While I was his straight man. A *sidekick*!"

Snowy stepped onto the strings of the piano. When he got to the center of the instrument, the cat lay down on the strings, purring. Maisie put her foot down on the sustain pedal, and the sound of the cat purring echoed and resonated in the harp.

"If we were really brave," she said, "we would turn ourselves in maybe."

Tripper shook his head. "Yeah, right," he said.

"I'm serious," said Maisie. "Maybe that's the answer. We tell the truth."

"Okay, that's enough," said Tripper. "I swear to God, if you keep talking that way—"

His voice fell. They sat there in stalemate, Maisie at the piano, Tripper in his wing chair by the fireplace. The cat purred into the harp.

"What would you do?" she said. "Tripper?"

He didn't respond, but after all this time the answer to this question was not exactly a mystery.

Tripper knew exactly what he would do.

16

Nether Providence, Pennsylvania

Even now, Rachel thought, at the end of all things, my dog still hates me.

Moogus's list of grievances was long. Rachel was always ordering the dog to do something she had no interest in. She'd say, "Come," but she didn't. Moogus considered Rachel's commands an irritant. She didn't see what they really had to do with her.

Rachel sat in her apartment in Bryn Mawr, surrounded by books. The painting of Quentin as John the Baptist hung on one wall. Her dead college boyfriend pointed toward the heavens, his eyes looking in two different directions. The Springer spaniel, lying on the couch next to her, cast a single look at Quentin the Baptist and rolled her eyes. *Oh him,* Moogus observed. *There's another one.*

"You poor old thing," she said, stroking the dog, but looking Quentin in the eye. It was the left one she was looking at, the one that stared at the viewer. The right one was fixed upon heaven.

Moogus the dog just sighed. *I still hate you,* the dog said.

"I know," said Rachel.

She'd gotten the dog a few years after she broke up with Backflip Bob, right around the time he'd married that Bronwen. When she told one of her colleagues—the medievalist at Bryn Mawr—about the dog, he'd nodded sagely and said, "Ah. A rebound dog."

Moogus hadn't provided much in the way of solace. The dog just glowered at her. *You think I like this?* the dog said. *You're wrong.*

"Well, here we are," Rachel said to the dog. "End of the line." She sighed. "I did my best, Moogus. Really I did."

Your best, the dog scoffed. *Ha!*

"Okay," said Rachel. "Let's take our ride then." She lifted the dog into her arms, walked outside to her car, and laid Moogus down in the backseat. She heard the voice of the adult Scout from *To Kill a Mockingbird:* "So began our longest journey together."

She drove down Bryn Mawr Avenue, out into Newtown Square, past acres and acres of housing developments that had once been green fields in which Angus cows had grazed. She turned right on Darby Paoli Road, then took a left on Goshen Road, traversing the old stone bridge across Darby Creek and following Goshen through Newtown Square and beyond. The country grew more rural as she drove south. There was a small stone cottage with a sign out front: BLACKSMITH. Fields of corn surrounded old barns bearing the hex signs of the Pennsylvania Dutch.

It was a long way to travel just to bid your dog farewell, but if you were going to do the thing you might as well do it right. And something in her hoped that, even now, Moogus might see that she was, as always, taking the extra time to do this properly, not that it made any difference to the dog whatsoever. *You really think this is the way to win me over?* the dog said.

Rachel looked in her rearview mirror. "I'm trying," she said. "That's all I can do is try."

You could have done a whole lot more than that, said the dog.

Her fingers fell to the radio dial and hovered there for a moment before withdrawing. Since they'd found Wailer's body the news had become intolerable, and not only because of the way it dredged up all the old horror. It also finally ruled out the remote possibility that Wailer was not dead, that instead of becoming the victim to some dark terror, she had indeed taken off, escaped, somehow made her way out into the world and begun her life anew. Of course, to pull off this caper, Wailer would have had to stage her own death, to believe that her own clean start had been so urgent that it had been worth dooming all of them to lives of loss. It would mean that she'd never loved Casey in the first place, that she saw him just the way he had, in the long years since her loss, come to see himself: as a large, bloated loser. There was no mystery why the man had developed a chain of restaurants whose fare seemed *designed to give you a heart attack*. It was food to eat if, above all, you were secretly rooting for death.

Yeah, muttered the dog. *Unlike you.*

She pulled into the Nether Providence Veterinary Clinic and sat there for a moment in the silence. Then she lifted Moogus out of the car. There was a man behind the counter with a name tag that said CLARK. He had an abundant, remarkable beard.

"I'm here about my dog," said Rachel. "It's time to let her go."

I can't wait, said the dog. *Seriously, I am so out of here.*

"You're . . . one of those kids," said Clark, with a voice of astonishment. He was wearing blue surgical scrubs.

"What?" she said.

"I recognize you," the man said. "From the television." Then his face fell, and he looked embarrassed. "I'm sorry. I shouldn't have—"

"It's all right," said Rachel, but the truth of the matter was that being outed by a clerk at the animal hospital was a little creepy. She felt her heart pounding, as if suddenly everyone knew something about her she had tried to keep secret. But why should it be my shame? she thought. I was a victim, trapped behind the walls of that terrible place while the rain came down and those moans rose and fell in the night.

If it wasn't for you, they'd all still be alive, noted the dog.

She glanced down at Moogus, the old thing still scowling at her. Rachel was tempted to yell at the dog, but there was no point. She was going to take her leave of Moogus with kindness and love, no matter what the dog said.

"It's fine," said Rachel. "It was a long time ago."

"I remember that story," said Clark. He appeared to be blushing through his beard. "I remember it when it happened. You're—uh?" He looked uncertain.

"I'm—" said Rachel. "Maisie Lenfest."

The dog sighed. *Liar.*

Rachel shot a look at the dog. *Listen, I just want my privacy. It's not fair I have to have this conversation while I'm standing here at the animal hospital.*

You want to talk fair? said the dog. *I'm the one who's getting snuffed.*

"Yeah, Maisie Lenfest," said Clark. "The piano teacher? You teach those special-needs kids."

Rachel nodded uneasily. She forgot, sometimes, in the quotidian routine of teaching classes and grading papers, that they'd all been infamous in their early twenties, although the thing that she—and the others—had been known for was something she wished had never happened in the first place.

The night before last, Moogus had had a seizure, and Rachel held her in her arms. It was like the dog was having a dream of running, a dream from which she could not wake up. When she finally came out of it, she seemed, briefly, not to know who Rachel was, or why it was this stranger was embracing her.

"Yeah, so listen," said Rachel. "I think I'd like to take Moogus for one last walk. Is that okay?"

"You take all the time you want, Maisie," said Clark. "I'll get everything ready."

Rachel hooked Moogus up to a leash and went outside again. The dog swayed from side to side. It had started to rain now. Behind the clinic was a field of green corn. The rain ticked softly against the long thin leaves on the cornstalks.

"Heel," said Rachel. The dog just rolled her eyes.

There was a scarecrow standing at the edge of the field, and it opened its eyes and looked at her and said, *Rachel,* and she cried out unexpectedly. Moogus couldn't even. *This is how it's all going to end, me standing here trying to have one last good sniff of the world, while you hallucinate a talking scarecrow?*

The dog took another drunken step, then she listed to the left and fell over, just shy of a flower bed in the clinic's backyard.

"Oh, sweetie," Rachel said. "It's all right."

She kneeled down and set her aright again. There was a stone Buddha in the flower bed, its arms raised over its head. She hugged the dog, felt her soft fur, felt the rain on the back of her neck.

She took one more look at the scarecrow, nailed there in its raggedy clothes. Then she walked back inside.

"You want to be there when it happens?" said Clark.

"I do."

Clark nodded. "That's good. Some people, they just leave their pets here. It's not right."

"Well," Rachel said. "We've been through a lot together."

You've been through nothing, said Moogus. *All this time I waited by the door. You never came through.*

They walked into a small chamber. Clark said, "Can you help her up on the table?" Rachel said, "Moogus, come," but she didn't.

Clark shaved a little place on the dog's front paw, and then he injected the drug, and Moogus gave her that look. *I waited and waited for you,* said the dog. *You never came.* Then she closed her eyes.

Clark told Rachel she could stay with her for as long as she wanted, and so Rachel stayed there and wept, the old dog in her arms. There was still a little rain on the dog's ears.

Then she took her collar off and stroked her head one last time, and said, "You're a good dog, Moogus."

The dog did not reply.

Rachel went outside and stood in the rain with the collar in her hands.

Then she drove home. The house was silent.

She stood by her living-room window for a little while, looking out. Then she made a cup of tea, and sat down in her chair, and rewrote the syllabus for her fall class, AR 351: Depictions of Christ.

That night she dreamed of the scarecrow hanging from his board, his crucified arms filled with straw. She stared down at him from a farmhouse window on a night with a silver moon. The raggedy scarecrow stared at her with such hatred. *I waited and waited but you never came home,* he said. *If I wasn't nailed here I would come into the house and*

I would slit your throat open with this scythe. There was silvery liquid like mercury dripping from his straw hands where the nails went through. Now he was struggling, trying to get his arms free. His sleeve ripped as he got his right arm free and then he tried to use that arm to get the nail out of the other one, and he looked at Rachel standing in the window and he said, *You're the one who should be dead, not me.* Now he had the other arm free and he tore his legs loose and he fell to the ground. Then he looked up at the window and started running toward the house with the scythe. She saw the blade shine in the half-light then she opened her eyes and sat bolt upright in bed.

Everything was quiet. Moogus's bed was empty, a tennis ball rolled into one corner.

She got up and went out to her living room. Her printed-out syllabus for Depictions of Christ lay in a pile near her easy chair. Quentin looked at her from his portrait. *Do you remember that time at the quarry?* he asked, as if she could possibly forget. It had been almost forty years ago, at Wesleyan, the first week or two of their senior year. There they were one hot September afternoon, tripping and swimming naked in a quarry. She and Maisie were naked, Casey was naked, Wailer was naked, even Tripper was naked, everybody except Quentin. They'd sat on purple rocks and watched a copperhead swim through the water. It had freaked Rachel out. *I just hate snakes,* she said. Wailer said it wouldn't bother them if they didn't bother it, but Rachel doubted this was true.

Casey stumbled out of the woods. He had lost his clothes. He was covered with mud and there were cuts and scrapes on his legs and the blood was running down his calves. In his arms he held a bunny. "Look," said Casey joyfully. "I got a rabbit friend!"

Tripper looked over at Casey disapprovingly. "Let that creature go," he said.

"Okay, man," said Casey. "You don't have to get sore." He kneeled down to free the bunny, but as he laid it down the rabbit closed its eyes and died.

"Whoa, whoa, whoa," said Casey.

"You squeezed it," said Tripper, accusingly.

"No way," said Casey. "I didn't." He looked around in panic. He was still naked. "Maybe it had a heart attack."

Rachel had been furious with him. "You always wreck *everything*," she said.

"Don't be pointin' fingers," said Wailer.

Casey hung his head, naked, gargantuan. "Naw," he said. "She's right. I suck."

Rachel turned to Quentin. "Make it better?" she asked.

Quentin was feeling pretty self-conscious about not being naked.

"I can't," he said. Then he went over to the rope swing and Rachel watched as he soared through the air. In that moment he was so beautiful: a young man in flight. He was fully clothed but he was headed toward the water.

Quentin landed in the water with an astonishing splash, and waves rippled out in every direction. He disappeared underwater after impact. For a moment the surface was just ripples.

The copperhead slid out through the water toward the place where Quentin had submerged. It opened its mouth. All the others watched this happen like it was a nature show.

Quentin surfaced. His lungs sucked in oxygen and he yelled, "I'm alive! I'm alive!" Then the snake sank its fangs into him.

"Fuck," moaned Quentin, and his head went under. He resurfaced and said "Fuck" again, and then Tripper stood up.

"Dear Lord," said Tripper, and ran toward the water. It made sense that Tripper would save him. He was always saving everybody.

Wailer watched all of this with disappointment. "Jaysus," she noted. "He's poisoned."

The rope was still swinging back and forth from the long tree limb, like the pendulum of a clock.

Maisie looked at Rachel, and her face was wild. "This is *not* happening," she said.

Rachel said a mean thing then, although it did not seem mean to her until years later. "It is *so* happening Maisie," Rachel said. "It's happening right now." She pointed at the quarry, where naked Tripper was dragging Quentin toward the shore. Behind her, Casey was crying about the bunny he'd squeezed. "Don't you see this?" she said to Maisie. "This *unbelievable bullshit* is what makes up our actual lives."

It was all a long time ago.

Sometimes, Rachel thought, all I want is to find every person I've ever known and say, *I'm so sorry.*

But maybe everybody feels like that, convinced it all could have been more fun, if only you'd been more forgiving, if only you'd been more full of love.

As they sat there on the rocks at the edge of the quarry, Maisie had started crying. Rachel already regretted what she had said to her about the nature of their lives.

"No, wait," she said and put her arms around her friend. Tripper had hauled Quentin to safety now. He would not die, at least not yet. It had occurred to Rachel at that moment that maybe she didn't actually know any of her friends all that well.

She hugged Maisie as if she were her own sad self. "Seriously," she said. "I'm lying."

17

Cold River, Maine

There was a hole in our front yard as I walked up to the house from the dock. A pile of dirt was next to the hole, and a shovel was stuck in the pile. One of the septic-tank trucks was parked just off of the turnaround for the driveway, and a hose ran from the truck, across the front yard, and into the hole.

If I understood things properly, Falcon and Caeden, having been to Madison and back with the truck, had decided—their enjoyment somehow still being incomplete—to suck out our own tank. I guess it was better than shooting heroin.

"Boys?" I shouted. There was no answer.

I turned my back on the house. There, through the trees, was the path that led down to the lake. I could see our dock and the *Red Wedding* tied up against it. In the distance, as always, was the hush of water pouring over the falls and vaporizing on the rocks. Jake had said that he wanted to be alone for a while, and now, I presumed, he was sitting on the bench overlooking the falls, thinking about his pledge to always love me. Jake is no philosopher, but I knew he was probably considering, even at this moment, the question of exactly who it was he'd made that promise to.

The vows we'd made, all those years ago, were to love, honor, and obey. At the time, we'd had a lot of feisty conversation about these, especially that word *obey*, with all its creepy antifeminist undertones. And yet, as it turned out, loving, honoring, and even occasionally obeying had not been the tricky part.

The tricky part was *thee*.

How much could the person you love change, and still remain the same person to whom you'd made your promise? We don't expect our lovers to remain the same over the course of a long relationship. In fact, if you're married at sixty-five to the same person you married when you were twenty, your marriage has probably failed. But there are changes, over time, that spell doom for a marriage, although exactly what these are, and to what degree, varies from couple to couple. For some people, vast changes over time make no difference to the fundamental sense of devotion one soul has for another. But for others, relatively small changes can push things to the breaking point: gaining or losing weight, gaining or losing faith, gaining or losing wealth. How does any relationship survive in the end, when change is the only constant?

"Hi, Mrs. Falcon!" said a voice, and I turned to see Caeden standing next to the hole in the ground. The shovel was now over one of his shoulders.

"Hi, Caeden," I said.

"This is my favorite shovel!" Caeden shouted. It had never occurred to me, that a person could have a favorite shovel, but then Caeden, with his exuberant, joyful buoyancy, seemed to have a favorite everything.

"Have you boys had dinner?"

"Yeah, we nuked up some Hot Pockets!" said Caeden.

"Where's Falcon?"

"I'm down here, Ma!" said the voice of my son. I looked around but I did not see him.

"Falcon?" I said. "Where are you?"

His head popped out of the septic tank. "I'm here," he said, grinning from ear to ear. "Down in the hole."

Caeden took a spadeful of dirt and shoveled it onto Falcon's head. "Dude," said Falcon. "Quit it!" Caeden threw some more dirt at him, and laughed, and then Falcon climbed out of the hole, and tackled Caeden, and the two of them fell into the dirt pile and started wrestling.

"Boys," I shouted at them, but either they didn't hear me, or (more likely) my pleas were of exactly zero interest to them. They had sucked out a septic tank all by themselves. One of them had climbed into the tank. The other had shoveled earth onto his head. Now they were wrestling in dirt. It was twilight on a day in late summer. They had everything they could want.

"I want you to wash before you come inside," I shouted at them as I walked toward the porch. "Falcon! Caeden! I mean it! Go jump in the lake!"

They stopped wrestling for a second, looked at me, then each other, then leaped to their feet, and began running toward the water's edge. "Okay, Ma!" shouted Falcon. "Okay, Mrs. Falcon!" shouted Caeden. The young men disappeared through the pine trees. As I reached the porch, I heard two splashes, first one, then the other.

❦

When I got inside, Gollum was sitting mournfully next to his dish. *Gollum,* he said.

"Oh, you poor thing," I said, and picked up the dish and carried it out to the mudroom, where I keep the bag of kibble. I gave him two scoops and then came back into the kitchen and put it on the floor. Gollum looked at me thankfully, then lowered his sad gray face into the dish.

Now he was crunching.

The kitchen was a complete ruin, especially considering that the boys had only microwaved some Hot Pockets. But they'd done more than this, apparently, during the hours while Jake and I were (1) enjoying rock-and-roll music in a chicken barn, and (2) having the conversation that might have ended our marriage. There was an empty plastic bag of tortilla chips and a skillet in the sink in which scrambled eggs had been fried. The bowl they'd scrambled the eggs in was piled in the sink as well, and the butter and the egg carton and a spatula and two dirty plates were scattered across the countertop. I looked at this mess, and thought about cleaning it up, then thought better of it. I'd have them clean it up themselves, after they got the lid back on the septic tank and covered up the hole with the dirt and retracted the hose and got the truck off the lawn. As one does.

This is my favorite shovel.

Gollum had finished his dinner, and now he was looking at me with hope. "Okay, come on," I said, and we went out to the porch. "Let's take a walk."

The dog's ears perked up and he scampered around the deck until he found a tennis ball. Then he came back to me, and the two of us, mistress and hound, walked off the porch and into the sunset.

Our house is on a dirt road that gets almost no traffic, so I didn't bother with a leash. Plus, Gollum is so old that if a car does come, it's pretty easy for me to just grab him by the collar. My main concern is just to keep him from falling over. In that way he's not so unlike other individuals I might mention.

I stepped over the hose from the truck that still was spooled out in the front yard. Out in the lake, Caeden and Falcon were splashing. I could hear their voices, shouting, falling. And always, like a low roar in the distance, the sound of water going over the falls. I couldn't see my husband, but I knew he was still sitting there, still trying to figure out the unanswerable, unavoidable question of *thee*. My heart went out to him.

Because if I wasn't who he thought I was, then maybe he wasn't who he thought he was either.

"Come on," I said, and whistled. The dog looked at me in mortal despair. "*Gollum,*" I said.

As we walked along the road together, the old dog and me, I thought about the bar called Outlaws in Key West. That's where I'd landed after taking my leave of Casey in 1987.

Gollum squatted down to take a dump, but his old legs were so frail that he was trembling. It's hard when you get old. Everything's a production.

A year after my surreal farewell to Casey in Woodlawn Cemetery, I was pouring out margaritas, wearing a halter top, and wearing my hair up in a bun. I don't know why I wound up there, although maybe something in me thought that, since my last voyage as a man had taken me to the far north, perhaps my female future might begin in the sun-drenched south. My parents had taken me to Key West for a vacation once, a long time ago, before my father died, and for all the obvious reasons, I had never forgotten Outlaws, where we had lunch one day. They had female impersonators there.

Looking back, it now seems to me like I'd discovered something like the French Resistance. In those days the only way to find your way forward was by trial and error, trying every door until you found the low gate in the garden wall—the one that led, against all odds, to the secret world.

Of course, "female impersonator" was the last phrase I'd have used to describe myself. For one, the thing I'd been impersonating all these years was maleness; my womanhood was a fixed certainty I had carried within my heart at all times. For another, I had exactly zero interest in drag or performance, although I made plenty of friends who were fine with that language. But speaking just for me, I didn't want to create some sort of illusionary self. I was in search of my own.

What I wanted, even at the beginning, was to become myself, to have the reality of my heart reflected in the body in which I dwelled. And so I waited tables at Outlaws, or poured out drinks behind the bar. I lived with another one of the MtFs, a girl named Myla. She was a lot further along than me. She did a lot of sex work, like most of the women I knew in what I came to think of as *the resistance*. Almost surely I would have wound up in the same place, if Casey hadn't given me all that cash. It was only the generosity of my friend that stood be-tween me and a much more dangerous place.

It was Myla who connected me to Dr. Schecter, an endocrinologist with wild, crazy hair, like Einstein. Schecter prescribed progesterone and Premarin, connected me to an electrologist named Sandra who worked on all the girls in that Key West clique. By Easter of '88, I was well on my way. "I knew you had it in you, Judith," Myla said to me after I began to morph. My second adolescence, as if one were not bad enough.

I heard someone say once that if you start hormones in your twenties, you generally revert to the shape of most of the women in your family, minus one cup size. My mother, and both my grandmothers, had been large-busted, big-hipped women, so I don't know, maybe I had the genes for it. But there I was, at age thirty, going through puberty. The area around my nipples got sore. I needed a bra within six months. I needed a *good* one before the year was out. I let my hair grow long, and after a while went to an actual salon. That made a difference too. Sandra zapped my beard, pore by agonizing, horrible pore. I experienced a thing called *fat migration,* which meant that the fat on my body moved away from my belly and my neck and took up residence on my hips. One day, about two years after I'd landed in Key West, I caught a glimpse of this pretty young woman in a window on the street. When I realized that I was looking at my own reflection, I stopped there, stunned. I thought of an old line of Groucho Marx's. *Outside of the improvement, you'll never notice the difference.*

A friend of Myla's got me the driver's license of a girl named Cassandra Horton, who'd died in a car accident. She looked a little like me. All Myla said was, *I got somebody who works in the ER.* She had somebody in the ER; she had somebody everywhere. I used Cassandra Horton's ID to get my other papers. For a couple weeks everyone at Outlaws called me Cassandra, and I went with that, thinking that maybe I'd get used to it. But Cassandra always felt like an alias, whereas Judith—well, that just felt like me, even though it was a name I had never spoken out loud. I got my driver's license changed without showing anyone a birth certificate, which technically they weren't supposed to do, not in 1989—but they did it. Somehow, I slipped past the gates. I got myself to Thailand. There were surgeons in the United States, of course, but

even with the plane fare, it was cheaper to go overseas. That was where
most of the girls I knew from Florida had done it—those who did it at
all, although plenty of those women did not.

For me, the whole thing was like a dream. I stepped off the plane
and they put a lei around my neck.

Two weeks later I was on my way home, although in some ways,
now that my body matched my soul, I had already arrived at the place
I'd been dreaming of, one way or another, for most of my life.

It's worth saying that no one does this anymore, or almost no one—
the flight into anonymity, the assumption of a new identity, and most
of all, of course, the histrionic fake suicide, which even by the fairly
high standards of melodrama for trans people, I think represents a particularly narcissistic high-water mark. I think of Caeden, coming out
in sixth grade, transitioning before seventh. Being trans, of course, is
hardly a road to safety these days, and depending on race and class it
can still be almost as hard a journey as it once was for me. But at least
it's something that people have heard of, and many people have begun
to understand. Back in my twenties, there were times when I feared
I was the only one of me in the world, that the entire condition was
something I'd invented out of sheer loneliness.

I had no idea back then that the world was full of people just like
me, that the process of coming out and going through what is now
called "transition" would become an increasingly well-worn path, a
trail marked by blazes that in years ahead others—including young
Caeden—would find waiting for them. But back then, all I knew of
other people like me was what I had seen on television—a few curi-
osities on talk shows like *Donahue* or *The Jerry Springer Show*. Trans
women back then were always portrayed as wildly exotic freaks of nature, and the idea that we were simply one more variety of human, a
variation occurring with far more frequency than anyone imagined,
was not yet part of contemporary discourse. I knew that there were

other people like me in the world, but before I arrived in Florida I had no idea how to find my way to the trailhead. That such a transition could eventually come to be something less culturally scandalous and farfetched seemed inconceivable to me then. I don't know. Maybe to some people it still seems inconceivable.

Sometimes it exhausts me though, when people say they can't imagine what such a thing must be like, as if the dream of becoming someone else is a fantasy unique to transgender men and women. But surely the idea that one might slip away unseen and take up another life is nearly universal. Is there anything more fundamentally human than the desire to live in another world, as someone other than our own earthbound selves?

I had, of course, felt myself to be female from my earliest memories, although I lacked for many years a language for describing the difference that I felt. When I was very young the difference between men and women was itself unclear to me. But in time I came to understand the feeling that I had, to give a name to it, and almost at the same time came to realize exactly how strange and unusual that sensation was, to others at least. As I lay my head on my pillow at night I would pray, alternately, for two contradictory things—one, that I would wake in the morning miraculously transformed to female, or two, that I would rise from my bed with the desire to be female just as miraculously quelled.

I hoped, as I grew older, that a great love would take me out of myself and make me content to stay a boy. I think it's very human, the hope that an all-encompassing love will change us into someone else, someone better. That this hope usually turns out to be false makes it no less human; the world is full of hopes far more unlikely than being transformed by love.

Ironically, it had been my female spirit, I think, that women found so alluring in me, and which made me so attractive to a certain kind of vulnerable, thoughtful girl, especially the kind that I met at college. Rachel Steinberg was not the last girl to find me infuriatingly passive, in spite of her best efforts at hurling herself at my impenetrable walls.

I could love her, which of course I did, but it was also impossible to be with her—or anyone—as long as I knew I was lying to her. Plus, I had a softness in my heart for boys—not that I could imagine being with them, or anyone, for that matter, while I was still in that male body. It seemed to me as if my life was just a series of unbearable, unanswerable questions.

When I think about my drive up to Boston in '87—what I now think of as Quentin's Last Voyage—it makes me cringe. I thank God Rachel had the good sense to turn me down, not that there was much chance of her accepting my proposal, given all the abundant evidence that I'd kind of lost my mind. Still, something in me hoped that I'd be able to tell her the truth about the nature of my soul, and that it wouldn't make any difference to her. But of course it *would* have. Straight women love a feminine sensibility in a man, but that love only goes up to, and un-fortunately does not quite pass, the fact of his being an actual woman.

For a long time I waited, assuming that the new name and the social security card I'd gotten from Myla would inevitably lead to charges of fraud and jail, but no knock ever came. I moved to Maine, where I filed my taxes, where I got a job as a reporter for the *Mid-Maine Morning Arsenal*. Later, I freelanced for Condé Nast, and for all intents and purposes the person I had been was dead and gone.

Trans people used to call this "going stealth," and for a long time it was the standard way of going about transition. You were supposed to do the switcheroo, then move someplace where no one knew you, and start life over, without a soul knowing who you had been. Among mental-health-care providers—the few who thought that the troubles of people like me were worth their time—it was the recommended course of action, as if the idea of being sundered from everyone you had ever known, as if lying about your own past, was a path to whole-ness. The age of the Internet, as well as the slight movement in the cul-ture toward compassion for the whole spectrum of LGBT people, has made "going stealth" a rarity. Given the digital footprints that we all leave behind now, it's very hard for anyone to effectively erase her past.

Sometimes I think I must be the last trans woman on Earth who went stealth, but then who knows? I could be surrounded by fellow travelers to whom I am invisible, just as they are to me.

I felt joy at having leaped the divide, in those early years. But no one can live without a past, and that sense of having been stripped of history weighed on me heavily sometimes. I was a woman without a girlhood, a person who had to improvise wildly whenever questions about my past arose. I got pretty good with the story, so I could tell a consistent narrative. But I mourned the past. I missed my mother. I missed Casey, and Rachel. I missed, even in all of its squalid, eccentric sadness, my youth.

I had always imagined that if only I could live as my actual self, that life itself would be its own reward, and provide solace for anything I had had to give up. And that was mostly true. But then, late-winter days in Hallowell, Maine, walking up Front Street, with the frozen river off to my right, the wind howling over the ice, I'd get into a state. Sometimes I'd get back to my house overlooking the Kennebec, and I'd drink vodka and listen to John Coltrane records and watch the ice floes.

One night, I did a short Internet search for Casey, found his restaurant, Cannonball's, down in South Philly. I called the number, and he answered. *Casey,* I said, before my throat closed up. In the background I heard the sound of people talking, glasses tinkling.

Hello? he said. *Do you want to make a reservation?*

I didn't say a word, just sat there listening.

Hello? said Casey again. *Is anybody there?*

We were heading back to the house now, Gollum and me. I was hoping when we got back, Jake would be sitting on the porch, waiting for me. I was hoping that he'd have figured things out, and that as I approached him he would spread his arms. I knew that he loved me, and that his devotion ran pretty deep. Still, I suspected it might take a long time for him to come to terms, and why not? It took me almost thirty years.

It's funny that Caeden had said that thing about the shovel, because I've spent a great deal of time thinking about this very issue. Of course, the reason Caeden loves the shovel is because Jake told the boys one day how *he* loves the shovel, for the very reason that it will "last forever." "I've had this shovel twenty years now," he said. "I've replaced the handle twice and the blade three times."

Yeah, great shovel. It'll last forever.

The boys loved this story, and I've since heard them tell it to other boys when they come over and throw Jake's tools all over the yard. Part of what the boys love is the absurd sense of it. But the reason it gets my attention is that it's almost a word-for-word embodiment of a philosophical dilemma known as the Ship of Theseus. A shorter version of the koan is called Abe Lincoln's Ax. In the short version, a museum keeps Lincoln's beloved ax behind glass. "The ax was passed from Lincoln's father down to his son," the docent says. "Since Lincoln owned it, the axe head has been replaced twice, and the handle four times." Virtually every museum I've ever been to has some version of this—the reproduction furniture meant to suggest what such-and-such a room might have looked like at some other point in history. In Independence Hall, in Philadelphia, the room where the Declaration was signed is filled with eighteenth-century desks, from *exactly the same period* as when the founders wrote the Constitution—although not, in fact, the very same desks. In Rome, the Keats house has lovingly re-created the room where the poet died, in a bedroom overlooking the Spanish Stairs, although of course it's not the same bed in which Keats died: since the young man died of tuberculosis, everything in the house was taken out and burned, even before Keats was in the ground.

But it's a different matter to say that Abe Lincoln's ax is the *same ax,* when its original essence has been removed and replaced so many times. By what logic can anyone say it's the same ax? By what logic is Caeden still using the same shovel that Jake bought twenty years ago?

The longer—and not a whole lot more boring—story provides an answer. Theseus, the great warrior maze-doer and Minotaur-slayer, had a ship, and upon this he sailed the seas. But as time went by, he fixed it up as things broke down. One year, he replaced the mast; another he changed the sails; still later pieces of the deck as they warped and splintered. But—in the story at least—someone is saving all of these pieces as they're removed, and assembling them one by one. So that after twenty years a second ship has been built, with all the original masts and sails and planks. Now there are two ships, one made out of all the original pieces, and the other, the one with all the new parts, which Theseus has been sailing. And the question is, which is the true ship of Theseus?

I was wondering how Jake would answer, if I told him this story and asked him this question. Gollum and I arrived back at the house, and I poked my head in. From downstairs I could hear the sounds of the Xbox. My son and his friend were blowing things up in some other dimension.

I let Gollum off the leash, then filled his water bowl. The dog took a few halfhearted laps, then stumbled to the bottom of the stairs, and looked up. I knew he wanted to make the climb and get into our bed, but it seemed like such a long, hard journey. My heart went out to the dog because, of course, I knew exactly how he felt.

"Come on," I said, and I helped Gollum up the stairs. Mostly it was just a matter of getting him started. I lifted him by the collar and pushed on his hindquarters, and then Gollum was making a Herculean effort to ascend. When we reached the top, I followed him as he stumbled through the hallway and into our bedroom, where he stood by the bed and groaned. "Okay," I said. "Good boy." I lifted the dog up and got him settled. His head was on my husband's pillow.

My husband, I thought. Outside it was nearly dark. I could hear the water falling.

I descended the stairs and walked back outside and into the woods. The path to our dock forks about halfway to the water, and I took the turn to the right. Among these trees it is not easy to see, but I hoped that on the way back I'd have Jake with me. He had a small flashlight on his key ring, and on the return journey, he might use this to light our way.

But I don't think there will be a return journey, Mr. Frodo.

He was right where I thought he'd be, sitting on a bench by the falls, leaning forward, watching the water. His hands were folded on his knees.

"Well?" I said. "Have you made up your mind yet?"

He turned halfway around to look at me over his shoulder.

"What'd they used to call you?" he said.

"That's what you want to know? Of all the questions you've got, that's where you want to start?"

"I don't think it's a bad question," he said, and turned to look at the waterfall again. There was a fence before us, separating the bluff upon which we sat from the drop-off. To our right was the long ridge along the gorge; to our left were the falls and the placid lake beyond. The moon shone down upon the still water. Mist drifted through the air.

"My name was Quentin," I said.

"*Quentin?*" he said, as if this was the final insult. "Seriously?"

I sat down next to him on the bench.

"Jake—" I said.

"No, don't start," he said. "I don't want to hear it."

"What don't you want to hear?" I said.

"Any of it. I can't stand it. I feel like grape jelly is gonna come out of my ears."

"You think I shouldn't have told you?" I said. "Would you have been better off not knowing?"

"I don't know!" Jake shouted. "I don't know."

"We agreed when we got married we'd keep some things about our earlier lives secret. We said it would be better that way."

"Yeah, I was thinking along the lines of, like, maybe you'd been in the circus or something. Not—"

"It was like being in the circus," I said. "Every fucking day."

He shrugged. "I don't know," he said. "Maybe it's not such a big thing, you know, the world's changed. Look at Falcon's pal, Caeden. He's all right."

"They left the truck out," I said. "The cover's off our tank. The hose is in the front yard."

Jake sighed. "Yeah," he said. "I reckon."

We sat there and listened to the water pour down upon the rocks. We sat there for a long time, not talking.

"I'm the same person," I said to him at last, and put my hand on his.

He looked at me, wounded. As if he didn't want to hurt me.

"In what way exactly is that true?" he said. And took away his hand.

"Listen," I said. "I want to tell you something. Have you ever heard the story of Abe Lincoln's ax?"

"The what?"

"Okay," I said. "So there's a museum. And behind glass they have this ax that belonged to Abe Lincoln. And the docent goes, 'This is Abe Lincoln's ax. The handle's been replaced two times, and the blade—'"

"Judy, I don't want to hear about Abe Lincoln's fucking ax right now."

"I'm trying to explain something."

"You've explained *enough*," he said. "It's not the gender thing, I mean, well, no it is the gender thing, but the gender thing isn't the point. The point is the lying. Every time I've looked at you for the last fifteen years you've been lying to me."

"I haven't lied to you once," I said. "Stop it. The lie was the time before."

"The lie was in your silence," said Jake.

"You said you didn't want to know about my past!" I shouted. "We said we weren't going to talk about it, that we were going to accept each other as we are!"

"Yeah, well there's past," said Jake. "And there's past."

"The person you're all upset about," I told him, "doesn't exist. He disappeared off a cliff in 1987."

"Yeah, so you said. You actually what—staged your own death or something?"

"Yes, as a matter of fact."

"So wait, there are people in the world who knew you—back in the day—who thought you'd died, people who had to grieve you? Friends, family? Parents? You have parents, Judy?"

"My mother," I said.

"Your mother," he said firmly. "Burying her—son. Who wasn't even dead. You put her through that?" He shook his head. "Boy, you just keep getting more and more entertaining, don't you honey."

"I didn't know how else to do it," I said. "I had to find my way. I didn't know how to go about it."

"Yeah, so I guess faking your own death would be kind of the fall-back position," he said. "That makes a lot of sense."

"Yeah, okay, next time I come out as trans I'll do a whole lot better job," I said. "Thanks to this conversation."

"But you didn't come out," he said, and he looked at me. "That's the thing. You just lied."

"I'm telling you *now*," I said. "That was the point."

"Wow," said Jake. "Nick of time."

"Jake," I said, and I took his hand again. "Am I not me?"

He looked at me and tears shimmered in his eyes.

And at this moment his plectron radio went off, the sound of a sharp alarm piercing the night. He picked it off his belt. "Carrigan," he said.

"Five-alarm blaze," said the dispatcher. "Cold River, downtown."

"On my way," Jake said, and leaped to his feet.

"Gotta go check out a fire," he said.

"Jake," I said. "Am I not me?"

He looked at me, his eyes still wet. Then he put his Red Sox cap back on his head and ran away. In a moment he was lost in the dark trees.

His truck rushed up the hill. I stared into the woods for a little while, then walked toward the falls. There below me, the water pounded against the pink rocks.

18

Key West, Florida

Detective Dan Dudley (Ret.) stumbled out of the insufferable sunlight into the light-blue nave of Mary Star of the Sea. Even here it
was brighter than a Catholic church had any right to be, but Dudley
wasn't going to complain at this hour. He collapsed in a pew at the
back of the empty church, loosened his tie, and clutched his chest. It
was some place, Key West. Before him, the blue wall behind the altar;
on either side of the aisle leading up to it, a half dozen slender white
columns with golden capitals shaped like crowns, holding up a vaulted
white ceiling. Dudley took off his coat and laid it down on the pew next
to him, mopping the sweat off of his brow. The sunshine, the light,
the way everything twinkled and shone. He didn't see how people endured it.

Behind the altar was a stained-glass window showing the virgin
mother in white, a dark-blue veil or scarf falling from her shoulders.
Beneath this, and on every side, were palms, giving the church an air
of tropical mystery, as if the whole thing was just one or two degrees of
separation from the Enchanted Tiki Room at Disneyland.

In front of the altar was a grand piano. It was so quiet in here.
He imagined going up to the front of the church and sitting down on
the bench and playing a tune on the piano. "Come Down in Time,"
maybe. Or "Love Song." All those old *Tumbleweed Connection* tunes.
But of course he'd do no such thing. The blessed virgin was not known
for her partiality to '70s glam rock. More's the pity.

Dudley sighed. The air-conditioning was doing its trick now, and the former detective could feel his skin slowly cooling as the sweat trickled down his temples. He looked at his watch—2:30 in the afternoon. It felt like high noon. Mary Star of the Sea was deserted, although the church still bore the scent of recently extinguished incense. He remembered this smell from his childhood church, Corpus Christi in New York, on 121st Street. A decade before him, George Carlin had been a student at Corpus Christi School, and some of the nuns and priests would still turn red if you asked them about George. Sister Mary John would only say, "The Lord loves George Carlin, even if the feeling is not mutual." He liked that.

He missed going to mass. He'd sworn he would never go back, the bastards, but it was hard to deny that something felt empty since he'd foresworn the faith. *I said I was sorry,* he'd told the priest. *I've done my penance. Why isn't that enough?*

Perhaps because you do not truly regret your actions, said the priest, which, if you thought about it, was a less forceful version of *Perhaps because you Roofied that girl and fucked her in the Bellevue-Stratford? You really thought a few Hail Marys would balance the ledger?*

He had not been able to see the priest behind the screen, of course, but the unmistakable voice belonged to Father Kreider, a man who would less than five years later find himself defrocked on account of his relationships with several parish gentlemen. There were times when Dudley wondered whether he'd actually learned more about sinning from the priests than anyone else.

George Carlin had once said something about the church giving him—what was it?—the religious instruction that he needed exactly in order to reject his faith.

"Hello?" said a voice, and Dudley looked up to see a young priest in his long robes.

"Hello," he replied, feeling self-conscious.

"Welcome to Mary Star of the Sea," said the priest.

"Hello, Father," he said. "I just came in—it's so hot, I couldn't—"

"You aren't from Florida," the priest said. It wasn't a question.

"Philadelphia," he said. "New York, originally."

"I went to New York once," said the priest thoughtfully. The man—was he Cuban?—shrugged. "Once was enough."

"I was just—" said Dudley. "There's a bank near here—Key West Provident?"

"Down the street," said the priest, and smiled like something was funny.

"What?" said Dudley. "I say something funny?"

"You were looking for a bank," he said. "But you came into a church."

"Yeah, well," said Dudley. "It's easy to get the two mixed up some-times."

The priest's features fell. "Oh," he said. "I see." He nodded. "God bless you," he said, and walked down toward the altar, and then ducked into a side door.

"Hey, I didn't mean to—" said Dudley. But the priest was already gone. He could hear the man's footsteps scurrying down a hallway. Anyway, he did *mean to*. He didn't want to waste the man's time. Whatever I've done it's on me, he thought.

He looked at his watch. He ought to get down the street and talk to this lady at Provident, Mrs. Livingstone. She'd been very forthcoming on the phone. *Oh yes, I remember Quentin Pheaney! The journey that poor thing went on. But in the end she wound up kind of pretty.*

He'd sat in his chair in his kitchen feeling his heartbeat triple. In the end wait what? he'd said. The next day he was on the plane, bound for Florida.

Now, sitting here in Mary Star of the Sea, Dudley's heart was still beating fast. This is how I'm going to go, he thought. One of these days he'd just drop like a stone, and that would be that. He'd told his son to sprinkle the ashes in the Delaware River, but what were the odds Franklin would carry out his wishes? The boy hadn't done such a good job of obeying them while he was alive. Carrying them out after he was dead seemed like a stretch.

All right, Dudley thought, we're done here. He folded his jacket over one arm, slid out of the pew, faced the altar. He was about to head out when, for no apparent reason, he kneeled down, facing the altar, and crossed himself. Old habits die hard, he thought.

He got back up, but he didn't turn around. The sunlight was coming through the stained-glass window. It was time to head to the bank, hear more from this Mrs. Livingstone about Quentin Pheaney, and his so-called *journey*. But Mary beckoned to him. *Blessed art thou among women,* said the voice inside.

You know, Dudley thought. Sometimes I get tired of hearing about women all the goddamned time. Iris Claremont, and his own Evangeline, and Detective Gleeson. And Jesus Christ, Quentin Pheaney now too?

Be with us now and in the hour of our death.

Right. An hour which, if the women of the world had anything to say about it, would be coming up any moment now.

The virgin looked at him. *Come on,* she said. *Auld lang syne.*

"Oh for Pete's sake," he said, out loud, then approached the altar. Now he could see her more clearly. The virgin was robed in white, covering a blue dress. The Christ child was in her arms. Behind her was a blood-red horizon, ablaze. And on every side were the masts of ships. Some of them looked like they were sinking. A stone lighthouse over her left shoulder shone out over a turbulent green sea.

You want everything, everything, *everything*! he thought. It's not fair!

Above the woman's loving face was a piercing white star. Dudley raised one arm to shield his eyes, as if its radiance had left him blind.

19

Cold River, Maine

Jacob Carrigan crept forward in a crouch, breathing compressed air through his mask. The smoke was thick in the top of the barn, so thick that Jake could not see more than five feet ahead. He followed the line, moving gorilla-style on his hands. They were using a two-and-a-half-inch hose on this one, the task-force nozzles. He checked his regulator. He had ten minutes.

Stay on course, he told himself, shining his light to the right. Through the smoke he saw chicken roosts, barn wood, some old egg crates. There were no flames up here yet; the fire itself was still on the first floor of the chicken barn. *But it's coming.* Even if the rest of the crew did its job perfectly down below, the odds were still pretty good that the whole barn would go up before the end.

He raised his mask for a moment and called out. "Pappy?" he shouted.

He listened carefully, but he didn't hear a response. All around him Jake heard the roaring of the blaze, shouts of the other firefighters on the ground level, static from the hand radios crackling in the air. Jake pulled his mask back down over his face and inhaled. A bell went off somewhere in the smoke before him.

A moment later, Dave came crawling back toward him. He pointed at his regulator, its bell still chiming. Jake nodded. Dave was almost out. He had to work his way back to the outside by following the line of the hose. Jake moved close to Dave's ear, and shouted, "Any sign of the old man?"

Dave shook his head, then headed out. Jake took another look at his own regulator, then moved forward through the smoke. He smiled grimly. The last time he'd seen Dave had been at the jam, singing "Powderfinger" into the mike, something about a white boat on the river.

The party seemed like another lifetime ago. Was it only just that afternoon that they'd all been standing around the first floor of the chicken barn, playing music, eating baked beans and sausages, drinking beer? He remembered watching Cassie as she sang "Dr. Feelgood." The little catch in her voice.

Okay, so he'd never slept with her. But the idea had crossed his mind, especially in the last couple of years when Judith spent so much time traveling to these exotic places, doing research for her stories. He didn't mind that he never got to go, not even when she went to Turks and Caicos and stayed at Parrot Key. Apparently it was halfway between Keith Richards's house and Christie Brinkley's. He imagined Keith pulling up to Christie's house in his Jaguar. *Hey, do you mind if I borrow a cup of heroin?* Judith came back from that trip all tan. She'd received what she called "treatments" in the spa, went scuba diving on a coral reef, drank drinks with little umbrellas in them. While he drove the septic-tank truck around central Maine. It would have been nice if she'd have asked him to join her, maybe even once.

His foot punched through the floor. Jake fell to one knee, then he righted himself once more and pulled his foot out of the hole. Smoke billowed up. *It's coming.* The hole was just a weak spot in the old barn floor; it was not the result of the blaze. He shone his light off to the left. Still no sign of Pappy. Jake felt his heart pounding. If the old man really was sleeping off the party up here among the old coops, there wasn't a lot of time left. The smoke would get him long before the flames. *Look out, Mama, there's a white boat comin' up the river.*

He'd been sitting on the bench by the waterfall for a couple hours when Judith finally came out to find him. It had been good for him to have a while on his own to try to sort this shit out. He liked the sound of the falls, the solitude. But it was also true that he'd been waiting for her to come to him, and she hadn't, at least not until it was way too late.

It was impossible to sort through his feelings—rage, humiliation, confusion, love. There was part of him that wanted to just rush up to the house and tell his wife that he loved her, no matter what. But the fact was that he really didn't understand. He didn't understand about transgender people, even though he knew that Falcon's friend Caeden was a decent, joyful guy. He got that Caeden had done what he felt he needed to do. But there was still a lot of confusion in his heart why Caeden—or for that matter, Judith—would feel it was necessary. Changing genders seemed like a very complicated way of solving a problem that was more simply solved by accepting the body that you had.

Above all he couldn't understand why she'd lied to him, why she had hidden this essential truth from a man who had given his life to her. It was, after all these years, like being married to a complete stranger. So while part of his reaction was, *It doesn't make any difference to me, I love you,* another very considerable part of him also felt, *What the fuck, go to hell.*

The worst of it was that the woman he thought he'd known better than anyone in the world had, in a single moment, become someone he found incomprehensible.

Judith had come down to the falls at last and said to him, *I'm the same person.* But wasn't this only possible if, in the end, there was no real difference between women and men? It all made his brain hurt. He wanted to shout at her, *The same as what?* But he felt too exhausted and wounded to argue.

The question was what to do now.

That was the thing he'd been wrestling with when the plectron went off. He'd left Judy standing there alone, which on some level felt just about right. There wasn't a whole lot more to say than, *Gotta go check out a fire.* Some part of him even felt relief, that he'd been given a reprieve from what felt like a conversation that, no matter how it ended, would lead to disaster. Fighting fires, as terrible as it was, was a thing he knew how to do. At least, he thought, this is something I've been trained for.

The dispatcher had told him the address, but for some reason it hadn't struck him until he pulled up in front of Weasel's that the fire was at the house of his own friend, that it was, in fact, at the very barn where they'd been playing crappy rock-and-roll songs not five hours before—"Brown-Eyed Girl" and "Mustang Sally" and "Somebody to Love."

He thought about the sparks flying off of Pappy's barbecue. There hadn't been much wind during the party, but it had picked up after the sun went down.

Tommy and Lou Falco had driven the pumper over from the firehouse, and they were already setting up when Jake had arrived. He jumped out of his truck, then got his gear out of the back: bunker pants, rubber boots, Nomex fire coat, neoprene hood. The firefighters in Cold River used old-school Ben Franklin helmets with the big brim across the back. Tommy's and Lou's hats were yellow. As captain, Jake's hat was red. Another pumper arrived from Messalonskee, manned by three men Jake knew pretty well—a short, strong guy named Artie; a huge dude named Rupert; and a nerdy fellow with glasses they called Cooper Dooper. Rupert was the captain of the Messalonskee crew, and the two of them did the initial 360 as the others attached their hoses. Smoke was billowing from the back of the barn. Rupert grabbed the nozzle and followed Jake in. Tommy stayed back and ran the intake hoses to Cold Lake, the water source. Lou flicked the PTO switch, which moved the power of the engine to the pump, then he ran to the side of the truck and began flanking out hose.

Weasel was half out of his mind. He was still wearing his flannel nightshirt. "I think it was a stray spark from the barbecue," he said. He grabbed Jake's arm tightly. "My pop's up in the loft," he said. "You gotta get him out of there. You gotta!"

"We'll find him," said Jake.

The sheriff, who'd arrived by then, pulled Weasel away from the house, and made him stand at a safe distance with the other onlookers. He'd looked at his watch. *It's coming.*

Working his way through the thick smoke in the dark, breathing through his mask, made Jake think about what scuba diving would be like. It would be nice someday if he and Judith went together. On the ocean floor before him, now discernible through the haze, was a stack of Louis L'Amour books, an old Naugahyde easy chair, and a floor lamp. There was *The Quick and the Dead* and *The First Fast Draw* and *Showdown at Yellow Butte* and *Dark Canyon.* Some of the books had been read so many times the pages were falling out, the spines broken. He pulled his mask off again for a second to shout, "Pappy!" But there was no response. *Oh you sweet, stupid old bastard,* Jake thought. *Where have you put yourself?*

"What does she have that I don't have?" Cassie had asked him at the Downeast Roadhouse Barbecue. "I mean, Judith's nice and all, but there's something stingy about her, if you ask me. You know what I mean? It's like she holds herself away from you."

The waiters were line dancing, singing a song called "Tumblin' Tumbleweeds." Now and again they would *yee-haw.* The young people clapped their hands, slapped their faux chaps, raised their ten-gallon hats in the air. It made Jake grimace. One of the reasons a person lived in Maine, he thought, was to ensure that you never, ever had to witness anything even remotely like this.

"How do you mean 'stingy'?" he'd said, although he sort of knew what Cassie meant.

"I mean she doesn't exactly give herself to people," said Cassie. "The way you do. The way I do."

Cassie had reached out and taken his hand and squeezed it.

"Cass," he'd said. "I told you we're not going there."

"Oh, what's the difference?" she said. "We've known each other for thirty years. You've thought about it. I've thought about it. It's like we've been doing it for years already."

Jake had sipped his margarita with one hand. He hadn't snapped the other one away from Cassie. It had felt good to have his hand in hers.

"Just because I want to," he said, "doesn't mean I'm going to."

"Aha," said Cassie. The dancing waiters went, *Yee-haw* once more. "So you admit it. You do want to do it."

"Of course I want to do it," said Jake. "Who wouldn't want to fuck you, Cassie? You got plenty of charms."

"Charms," said Cassie, and laughed. She took her hand back and then waved at a passing waitress, one of the few who wasn't dancing around in fake chaps. "I'll have another 'rita," she said. "Hornitos." Cassie grinned. She still had those dimples. "You feelin' a little hornito, Jake? I am feeling *totally* hornito."

"Don't you gotta drive?"

"I'll stay in the motel, fuck it," said Cassie. "Watch porn off the plasma screen. What's the difference?"

"I don't like seeing you this way," said Jake.

"Well, let's *fuck* already," said Cassie. "My spirits will lift right up. I'm serious, you'll see a real improvement."

"Yeah? Where's Ray in all this?"

"Ray? Ray's back at Moose Landing, attending to our guests." She sighed. "What few of them we got. You know we're going to have to close the bed and breakfast. We been losing money for years. Now, we just gotta get *done*."

"I'm sorry."

"No, you're not."

"I'm sorry you're going to have to close Moose Landing. But I'm not sorry about deciding not to mess around with my friend's wife behind his back." Jake heard the sound of his voice and hated it. It was no fun, being the voice of reason.

"Then why did you come?" said Cassie. "You're kind of sending me a mixed message, don't you think?"

"Yeah, maybe," said Jake. "Maybe I wanted to make sure."

"You should just fuckin' go, Jakey," said Cassie.

"Yeah, maybe I should," he'd said. The waitress came by with two margaritas, set them down.

"Are those both for you?" he had asked.

The bell on his regulator went off, and Jake, brought back to the present, looked at his gauge. He was down to five minutes of air. He looked around the floor at the scattered Louis L'Amour books, at the beat-up Barcalounger in which Pappy did his research. Fuck, Jake thought. Where could the old man be? The bell continued to chime.

That was when Jake realized he had lost the line. The task-force hose was the only real way he had of keeping himself oriented in the thick smoke, and now it was gone. He felt his heart pounding in his throat. The bell on his regulator continued to chime.

Okay, easy, he thought. *Follow the procedure.* He got down on his hands and knees and squinted through the thick air, played his light off the floor, looking for landmarks. He could see the planks of the barn wood on the floor. They were laid parallel to the length of the chicken barn. So he just had to move in the same direction as the planks and he'd cross the line of the hose—if not that, then he'd come up against the wall that faced the street; the ladder to the lower level was on that side.

Slowly, carefully, Jacob Carrigan moved through the smoke on his hands and knees.

He remembered the first time he had seen Judith, the night he'd come on a call at her house. She'd been passed out on her couch, an empty martini glass on her table. She'd been lying there in her bra, a pot of macaroni and cheese burning away on her stove. He'd seen all sorts of things during his years of answering calls, and an unconscious woman with her shirt off was not the most dramatic.

But there'd been something particularly haunting about her. Maybe it was her sadness; but it was something else too. Even before he woke her up, he'd known that this was someone with a history. She'd opened her eyes, looked at him in his mask and fire coat. Jake had thought she would scream to see a stranger standing in her kitchen in full rough-neck gear, but instead she'd just smiled thoughtfully, as if the presence of the stranger from Mars in her living room had confirmed some private theory of her own about the nature of the universe.

When Sarah lay dying, she'd turned to Jake one afternoon in the Waterville hospice and clasped his hand like she was going to squeeze the life out of him. "Don't sit around crying in the future," she'd said, in a whisper.

"I don't think so," he'd said.

"If you just sit around crying, I'll come back and fucking kill you," she whispered. "Falcon needs a mother. And you need—someone to kick your ass."

He'd nodded, although he wasn't agreeing. Decades could pass, he then believed, and he'd never open his heart again.

Then, a year later, Judith had fallen asleep while making macaroni and cheese.

A gray wall emerged out of the smoke ahead of him. He played his light off of it. This was the far end of the chicken barn, but it didn't look familiar. Everything seemed strange, wavery, indistinct. The borders between things were disappearing. It was as if he'd somehow strayed into a completely different world, a place where things were neither one thing nor the other, but instead dwelled in some gray, smoldering middle zone. He didn't like it.

There was a sudden *whoomp*. Jake recognized it instantly. It was the sound of the fire coming alive, in a single explosion. *It's here*. Light from the blaze below now streamed angrily from the cracks between the floorboards of the barn. The air glowed. Jake could see the smoke moving now, billowing furiously. He felt the heat through his suit.

Okay, Jake thought. *Game on.* He played his light against the wall, then searched the floor for the ladder that led below. But there was no sign of it, and no sign of the hose line that ought to be at this end as well. He staggered from one side of the barn to the other, but there was no sign of the ladder. That was when he realized his mistake: he'd followed the floorboards to the wrong side of the barn.

This was the back of the barn, not the front. He had to turn around and get all the way back to the other side. Soon.

Jake moved swiftly now, scrambling in a crouch, following the planks in the other direction. After a minute he came upon the Naugahyde chair again. He wondered again, where, in all this smoke and flame, was goddamned Pappy? It was the old bastard's fault he was up here in the first place.

Now the wall behind him erupted in flame. He turned back to look at it, feeling the heat through his neoprene mask. Then he turned and ran, as fast as he could in the crouch, along the barn floor. The bell on his regulator was still ringing.

He saw something on the floor in front of him, and with a shock of relief, he realized it was the line he'd been searching for, at last. Now all he had to do was follow the hose back to the ladder and outside. He was saved.

Jake was in the midst of that thought—*I'm saved*—when his foot punched through the floor again. This time the boards around the hole splintered and broke, and he fell through space into the fire below.

He landed with a *thud* on a flaming bale of hay. He felt the heat scorch through him. Jake stood up, feeling lightheaded, and took another step. But his foot punched through the floor again. He fell another ten feet, and crashed into the old cement basement of the chicken barn.

Lying on his back, he stared straight up at two stories of burning barn. The flames on the first floor were gathering in intensity. Smoke billowed toward the loft.

His regulator stopped chiming. Okay, that's bad, he thought. Out of air, or nearly. He got to his feet, feeling dizzy. It was possible, however, that falling into the basement had saved him for the moment— the cellar wasn't on fire, at least not yet. But he was down in a hole, hemmed in on all sides by concrete, except for one wall, which was a heavy wooden gate, locked with a chain.

It's a pigpen, he thought. After all these years, I'm going to die in a pigpen.

Sarah used to tell a story about her grandfather, who'd been such a wicked drunk that they used to find him in the morning passed out in the ditch. This was up in Aroostook County. Her grandmother always feared that pigs were going to eat her husband. Sarah had had to begin many mornings by grabbing the old bastard by the arms and dragging him over to a pump well and splashing water on him until he revived. Years and years later, Sarah still called those days the worst ones of her life. Sarah's grandfather had vanished by the time she was an adolescent, ran off for good. Her gram didn't talk much about him after that, except to say, *He must have found someplace where there was no one to save him from the pigs.*

He realized he'd started to drift off. Above him now he thought he saw other firefighters, lowering a ladder. He recognized Tommy and Lou Falco, along with Rupert. He wanted to ask why Tommy wasn't with the pumper. That was his post. Chain of command. The foot of the ladder met the earth next to the place where Jake lay.

He got to his feet and reached out for the ladder. A torrent of water knocked him off his feet, and now he was swimming once more in the blue waters of the Caribbean. His face mask, as it turned out, worked just fine for scuba. There were hundreds of orange clownfish, a turtle. A manta ray swept toward him on majestic gray wings.

There was another spray of water, and Jake was washed up on a beach that was on fire. He saw the legs of the aluminum ladder next to him, and he understood that this was the way up. So he grabbed the sides of the ladder and took a step. Then another. As he ascended, though, something weird happened to gravity. He was hanging off of the ladder like a ring-tailed monkey. Each ascending step made him feel more upside-down. From overhead he heard another bell go off, the alarm on one of the others' regulators—Lou or Tommy, maybe Cooper Dooper. They were shouting at him now: *You're on the wrong side,* and Jake had just enough wherewithal to think, I guess that's true, I guess that's been true for a long time. He tried to take another step, but his feet slipped off. He was holding on to the underside of the ladder with just his arms now, like a chin-up bar in high school. The floor was alive with tongues of flame, and when he fell he landed in the heart of the fire. There was another wave of water that washed over him, and again he saw the enormous turtles and the ray.

Some rays could sting you, but this one looked all right. A wave picked him up and he rose, a luminous soul, to the surface. He broke through to the light and there he found Judith, wearing her polka-dotted bikini, sitting in a beach chair. Next to her was a platter with two pink cocktails on it. There were little umbrellas sticking out of them. A white boat was coming up the river.

Are those both for you? he asked.

20

Bryn Mawr, Pennsylvania

They left the funeral home around noon. Rachel had made most of the arrangements, and Casey wrote the check. The undertaker, a strangely jolly man named Owen Kennedy, seemed discouraged only by Casey's insistence on cremation, even though it was already a done deal. "That's what she *wanted,* man," said Casey. The urn with the ashes in it was sitting on his desk. Owen Kennedy, in a rough but lovely Kerry accent, simply said, "And what is it you want now, Mr. Casey?" he said. "Perhaps a monument in our garden of remembrance? Some find that lessens the pain."

"What do I want?" Casey said. He looked around the strangely ornate office, decorated with small collectible pug-dog figurines. "I want her alive again, asshole."

It was strange being together again, Rachel thought, but in some ways they'd fallen right into the patterns of thirty-five years ago. She'd gone down to Casey's house that morning in South Philly to pick him up, found him thick as thieves with the lawyer that Tripper had recommended, a Winston O'Rourke. Rachel wasn't sure, but the man appeared to be drunk, at ten in the morning.

"What's the strategy?" Rachel had asked O'Rourke as they all walked outside to their cars.

"We don't need a strategy!" O'Rourke said. He was wearing a worn-out tweed coat, patches on the elbows. "He's not under arrest! And even if they do bring him in, it'll never go to trial!"

"That's not what Detective Gleeson said," Casey said. "She seemed pretty sure I was going to jail, if I would only be patient."

"Trust me," said O'Rourke, swaying. "It'll be fine."

As they drove off together in Rachel's car, she thought, but did not say, *Fine in what way exactly.*

Now they were in her car, heading out to Maisie's. The urn with the ashes lay on the seat between them. The plan was to make arrangements for the reception after the memorial service.

"Do you remember that time we were at the quarry?" said Rachel.

Casey looked uncertain. "What quarry?"

"We were swimming. I think we were on drugs. Quentin got bitten by a snake, and Tripper dove in to save him."

"Oh yeah, yeah," said Casey. Then his features fell. "Oh, that bunny." His voice cracked. "I killed a bunny."

Rachel looked over at him. "I shouldn't have said anything. I'm sorry."

"Oh, that poor bunny," said Casey, shuddering.

"Casey," said Rachel. "Are you crying? About a rabbit you killed by accident, thirty-five years ago? You're actually crying?"

"I didn't kill it!" said Casey, almost shouting. "It had, like—a heart attack! It was scared!"

"You're actually crying," said Rachel. She looked in the rearview mirror. A woman with gray hair looked back.

"Well," said Casey. "It's sad."

They pulled into the driveway of the Bagatelle. The mansion looked like a good, strong wind could take the whole thing down; its Victorian towers listed, and it appeared not to have been painted since the Kennedy administration. But Maisie had offered, and it made some poetic sense, to have the reception for the funeral at the same place where Casey and Wailer had been married, and so here they were: full circle.

Many years had passed. But now, in the early evening of their lives, they found themselves gathered around the kitchen table, three middle-aged people, eating everything bagels with chive spread.

"These are really good," said Casey thoughtfully. "It's hard to make a bagel. Harder than you'd think. You go to California, you can't get a real bagel anyplace, even in Los Angeles. It's sad."

"I wouldn't have a clue how to make a bagel," said Maisie. She still had that beauty mark on her cheek. "Except by defrosting of course."

"You have to boil 'em," said Casey. "You boil 'em, then you finish them off under the broiler."

They considered the bagels. There was lox and chive spread and chopped red onions in small plastic containers. Maisie had bought enough bagels to feed a rugby team. The bagels were in a large wicker basket lined with a blue linen napkin. A sharp serrated knife lay crosswise on a cutting board.

"You know I can play organ at the thing," said Maisie. "If you want."

"That is really nice," said Casey. "Except, like, there's no music at a Quaker service. We just sit there all quiet-like, and if anybody feels like talking, they get up and say it."

"But—?" said Maisie. "Whatever would a person *say*?"

"Whatever they want, man," said Casey.

Maisie shrugged. "I'm sorry," she said. "But do you guys ever feel like—" She sipped her coffee. "I mean, it was all so long ago. Sometimes I don't really remember what she looked like. We were all so different."

"I'm not," said Casey. "I'm exactly the same."

Maisie looked at him skeptically. "Are you?" she said.

There was silence for a little bit. From the old stairwell came a series of soft creaks, like the sound of footsteps.

"Is that—is that Benny?" asked Casey.

"That isn't anything," said Maisie. "Ben is in his room."

"Oh," said Casey. "I thought I heard footsteps."

"Well," said Maisie firmly. "You were mistaken."

They sat there chewing for a little while. On one wall was a clock shaped like a cat. Its tail, the pendulum, wagged back and forth as the seconds ticked by.

"You said you saw Tripper last night?" asked Rachel.

"Yes," said Maisie. "He was here."

"How was that?" asked Rachel.

Maisie opened her mouth to respond, but nothing came out. Her eyes shone.

"He's a terrible person," she said. "You know. The same."

"Yeah, but his wife is pretty hot," said Casey. "The doctor? They came to the restaurant one time and I made them dinner. She had the lobster jambalaya."

"He's just relentless," said Maisie, more to herself than either of them.

"Relentless how?" said Rachel.

Maisie looked at the two friends of her youth. They flickered before her eyes. One moment they were their former selves, the unformed teenagers, fueled by the dream of what they would become. The next they were these husks.

"Relentless how?" Rachel repeated.

Maisie appeared to be struggling with the exact nature of Tripper's relentlessness. She opened her mouth, but nothing came out. She turned her head this way, then that way, as if trying to get a running start on the thing she wanted to say. Then she sighed.

"He asked me . . . about the fall of our senior year. When I was at Conestoga and he was at Devon Latin. If I ever considered what it'd have been like. If I'd had the child, instead."

Casey took this in, sucked on it like a lollipop for a little while. Then said, "What child?"

"Casey," said Rachel.

"Well, I do think about it," said Maisie. "What she'd have been like. The things I could have taught her. She'd be in her thirties now. I could have been a grandmother."

"Maisie," said Rachel, taking her hand.

"Wait," said Casey. "What child?"

The women gave him a look that was not quite a glare.

Casey stood up. "I'm gonna just . . . you know," he said, and walked out into the main hall, gazed up at the stairs circling the pipe organ. The old brass pipes were built into the wall. He reached out and touched one, a long pipe for one of the organ's low notes. It was almost six feet tall.

The pipes rotated up the stairs, all the way up to the second-floor landing, where there was a deep windowsill. Casey climbed the stairs, one hand on the creaking banister, until he reached the landing. He remembered this window. It was so deep you could sit on the sill, like you were sitting in the car of a Ferris wheel. On the day of the wedding, he'd sat on this sill reading a book by Tom Robbins, *Even Cowgirls Get the Blues,* a book that at the time seemed like the handbook for a new world. Now he could barely remember it: something about some clockworks? At one point he'd put the book down and gazed through the glass into the backyard, where Wailer and Maisie and Rachel were gathered around an old fountain, gathering flowers. Rachel was plucking the petals from a daisy, one by one. Wailer was holding forth. *That's the girl I'm marrying,* Casey thought.

He'd never had a girlfriend in high school, and the fact that he'd gone out with Wailer at all still struck him as something of a miracle. On move-in day, freshman year, he'd been in his Butterfield dorm room, listening to *American Beauty* on his stereo. He was hanging up an Indian-print tapestry on the wall. Phil Lesh was singing.

The next thing he knew, a girl with short pink hair was standing in his room. "What in fuck's name is this ungodly shite?" she asked.

"It's the Grateful Dead, man," said Casey. " 'Box of Rain'!"

"Is it not the music of the mentally ill?" she asked.

"Mentally—wait, what? It's the Dead! It's about loving people!" She rolled her eyes. "What?" he said. "You're against loving your brothers and sisters?"

"I love plenty of people when the situation calls for it," she said. "Other times, I lean towards kicking 'em in the arse."

He stood there on top of his bed, tacking his tapestry to the wall. "Which situation am I in right this second?" he asked her.

Wailer looked at him mischievously. "I'm thinking," she said.

It was Wailer who had gotten him to change his view of the world.

He'd always felt like an outsider, not least because of his ungainly size. "I don't know what you like about me," he'd said to her, right after they started dating. "I've always thought I was kind of, you know. Ugly and fat."

"Oh, for fuck's sake, Jonny," she'd said to him once. "Don't you know there's a lot more ways of being beautiful than by being beautiful?"

"What? That doesn't make any sense, Wailer."

"Fuck you and your sense," she said. "In all the world I can hardly think of a soul more beautiful than yours, you fuck."

Then she'd kissed him, and with the kiss all the hairs on the back of his neck stood up. That, he'd thought, even while they were still kissing, was what it felt like when the whole world changed in an instant.

Four years later, he was in this windowsill, watching her in the backyard picking flowers. He remembered sitting here in this old house—which had not yet started falling to pieces. He'd been filled with a joy he could barely contain.

As he'd sat there, all lightheaded, Quentin had come up the stairs and stood by his side for a while. Casey turned and saw that his friend was looking at the same thing he'd been looking at—the three young women out on the green lawn, picking flowers. He expected to find Quentin wearing an expression not unlike his own, a look of love and jubilation that the world contained women like these. But instead, he saw upon Quentin's features a look of utter despair. When Quentin realized that Casey was staring at him, he put that expression away, and his face regained its usual look of irony and detachment. For a moment Casey wanted to ask Quentin, *What in the world about gazing upon three beautiful women could possibly fill you with such remorse,* but he also sensed instantly that Quentin was embarrassed at being caught red-handed in his sorrow. So he said nothing.

He thought about the expression he'd seen on the face of his friend, now and again, in the long years that followed. Sometimes he wished he'd said something. *Hey, man. Why the long face?*

A door off the landing stood open, and Casey peeked into a room he'd never entered before. It looked like an old office, although it didn't appear as if anything had been touched in there for years. One wall was all bookshelves, with titles from the 1950s and '60s. *Inside America* by John Gunther. *Aku-Aku* by Thor Heyerdahl. A collection of books from Time-Life about science and nature: *The Universe. The Insects. The Sea.*

There were trophies on a shelf. There were photographs of Maisie's parents with their son in a baseball uniform. There was a plaque that said RADNOR TOWNSHIP SPELLING BEE. CHAMPION. The room was wall-to-wall with Benny memorabilia. But there was not a single photo of Maisie.

There was the sound of something electrical coming to life, out in the stairwell, followed by what he recognized as air filling the bellows of the old pipe organ. From the floor below him, he heard the sound of Maisie Lenfest playing Bach. "Ich steh' mit einem Fuss in Grabe."

He pictured Quentin at the tomb of F. W. Woolworth. A pyramid with sphinxes with beautiful marble breasts. Way far away.

He came out on the landing, took one last look out into the back-yard. There were no flowers there now.

From the third floor he heard a sound.

Casey walked to the bottom of the stairs and looked up there. For a moment gravity was reversed. He felt like he was staring down into a pool.

"Benny?" he said. "That you, man?"

Casey climbed the creaking stairs. Halfway up the staircase, he had to stop and hold on to the banister. His heart was pounding wildly, and sweat was trickling down his temples. For a moment he thought he was going to pass out. Is this how it began, the heart attack that in some ways he had been planning for years? Casey clutched the banister for a long moment. He looked up at the ceiling above him. A trapdoor on the third floor led to the attic, and a single cord dangled down from it. He had never been up there.

The fit passed, and he carried on up the stairs to the third floor. There were four rooms up there, plus a bathroom at the far end of the hall. Cobwebs hung from the ceiling. One door was slightly open, and a dim light shone from it.

"Hello?" said Casey, and stepped forward.

A man sat in a chair reading a book. His hair was thin and greasy, and there was a bald patch on his crown. He had scabs on his hands where he'd picked his hangnails. The man was wearing a hooded sweatshirt that said MUHLENBERG. The room was full of books. Something that looked like an illuminated manuscript was open upon a messy desk. There was also a menagerie of origami animals—cranes, horses, a unicorn. Next to these were the forms of multisided polygons, all glued together from rice paper.

"Benny," said Casey. "It's me, man. Jon Casey?"

The man looked up. He studied Casey's face but didn't say anything. On Ben's lap was a closed volume. On the cover were the words *Winnie Ille Pu.*

"Is that—Winnie the Pooh in like, Latin?" said Casey.

Ben's face fell to his lap, as if ashamed.

"I read that when I was a kid," said Casey. "Though, in English and everything."

Ben just looked embarrassed.

On the table before him was a plastic thumb and a faded blue handkerchief.

"So, like, Rachel and me are visiting Maisie? There was, like, some trouble. At the prison. They found—uh—"

Ben stared at him, hard. He shook his finger at him, then let it fall in his lap, as if he were exhausted.

Casey took this in. "Do you remember Wailer? My—my wife? We got married here, in your house. Did Maisie tell you they found her? In that prison?"

Ben smiled privately, as if laughing at a joke known only to himself.

Casey looked annoyed. "You think that's funny? That she's dead?"

Ben held up a golden ring. Casey looked at his finger. His wedding band wasn't there.

"Hey!" said Casey, suddenly furious. "That's my ring! Wailer gave me that!"

Ben smiled, as if he were not responsible for the way things were.

"Jesus. You're still a criminal, little dude," said Casey. He took a breath. Ben handed the ring back to him.

"I played a trick on you," Ben said softly. With his left hand he picked at the cuticles on his right thumb. "I had a cat, its name was Creeper."

"You did," said Casey. "And me, I had a *girl*. Her name was Wailer."

Ben Lenfest's eyes shone. Suddenly he leaped to his feet and spread his arms and wrapped them around Casey. Casey, caught off guard, raised his hands like he was the victim of a stickup. Ben made a sad, heaving sound.

"The things we loved are gone," he said.

21

Sidney, Maine

The spanking new Mid-Maine Medical Center in Sidney is filled with space-age devices that can print a 3-D image of a crenellated brain from space. But the waiting room of the ER comes from some whole other era. There they are: the same miserable copies of *Family Circle* and *Highlights* magazine from my childhood, each one worn and crinkled by the fingers of the distraught. When you read a copy of *Family Circle*, you have to wonder why they even bother printing a different issue each month. Would anyone notice if they just ran the same recipe for making slow-cooker chili as the month before? This copy of *Highlights* has simply got to be the same one I read in 1965, when my mother took me to the optometrist for the first time. Dr. Rankin, who looked a little like Professor Marvel, put drops in my eyes. It was hard to see. But I could still make out the stories in *Highlights*. Maybe because even then, I already knew how they'd go.

I stand up and pace the room. Falcon is holding his head in his hands. There's just the two of us here at six a.m. on a Friday morning. There's a fish tank with no fish, and a poster on the wall that says DO-MESTIC ABUSE HURTS EVERYONE. There's a television with no volume tuned to CNN, and a very blond anchorwoman talking in what looks like a busy newsroom. I wonder if the story about Casey is still in the rotation.

At eleven o'clock last night I stood with my husband by a waterfall. Loons called out in the dark. He was struggling, and maybe I should have just let him struggle. It took me almost thirty years to figure it all out; there was no reason he should be expected to do all that work in his head in a single day. But then he said, "Gotta go check out a fire," and dashed off. I stood by the water for a while, then walked back up to the house. Falcon was waiting for me in the kitchen.

"What's going on?" he asked. His friend was on the couch.

"Caeden, I need for you to go home," I said.

"What?" said Falcon. "What are you—"

"We need to talk," I said. Caeden didn't need to be asked twice. "Don't worry, Mrs. Falcon!" said the buoyant young man. "It's gonna be fine!"

"I'll text you later," said Falcon to his friend. A moment later it was just the two of us.

"What is it?" said Falcon, looking genuinely worried. I looked at my son, whom everyone said looked like me. But in that moment, I saw nothing of myself in him. I only saw Sarah, whom I had never known.

So I told him of my past.

Falcon was thoughtful. For a while he didn't say anything. Then he asked me, "How's Pop doing?"

"He's pissed," I said. "Not about my being trans, I don't think, although he doesn't really get it. He's just angry I didn't tell him the truth."

"Do you blame him?"

I shrugged. "I don't know."

"You don't know?"

"Maybe I was hoping he'd say, *Wow, you must have had a hard life. I'm sorry for everything you suffered. You know I'll always love you.* Something like that?"

"But you lied to him," said Falcon. "And to me. About who you were. About who you are."

"You know who I am!" I yelled. "I made your lunches for school. I taught you how to drive a car! I'm your mother! Who else would I be?"

"It's not about who you are," said Falcon. "It's about who you were."

"What difference does it make? You weren't even alive then! Why do you care!"

"It's about being honest," said Falcon. "My best friend is trans! It's just not a big deal anymore. No one cares. But if you lie to people— that's what hurts."

"I've never lied to you," I said, although I wanted to go back and challenge him on the whole *no one cares* business. Plenty of people cared. The world was still full of people who would kill me for being my own self. "When I was—who I used to be—then I was lying. That whole life was a lie. This—the life we have—this is the truth."

"I get all that," said Falcon. "But Dad's old-school. You should have told him the truth from the beginning."

"He'd have slammed the door in my face!" I said. "He'd *never* have understood. This whole life we have would never have happened!"

Falcon shrugged. "Maybe it shouldn't have," he said. "If it was all built on a lie."

I slammed my open palm down on the kitchen counter. "Your life," I shouted, "is not built on a lie!"

We just stood there for a long moment. Then he came over and hugged me. "It's okay, Ma," he said, and as he did, my whole body convulsed with tears. "We'll figure it out."

The phone rang at four thirty in the morning, the Waterville fire chief on the line. *Judith,* he said. *Jake's been hurt.*

I didn't say anything. The words echoed around in my head.

Pretty bad, he added.

Five minutes later, Falcon and I were headed here.

"Can we watch something else?" Falcon asks, as I stand there in front of the wall monitor.

"Sure," I say, switching the channel. There is Fox News and ESPN and a movie channel showing *Mutiny on the Bounty.* Marlon Brando stares out at the sea. Then there's a cartoon.

"Leave that," says Falcon.

A fish with glasses is talking to a hermit crab. Another fish, exaggeratedly female, curls around the fish with glasses.

"*The Incredible Mr. Limpet*," I say.

"What?" says Falcon.

"It's a classic piece of schlock. Don Knotts."

"Who?"

"You know, he was Barney Fife, the cop, on *The Andy Griffith Show*."

Falcon just shakes his head. "You know, sometimes it's like you're from a whole different era in history," he says.

"Don Knotts," I say. "He was this nerdy guy. This is *The Incredible Mr. Limpet*. It's Don Knotts's *Citizen Kane*."

"Citizen who?"

The doors to the waiting room open, and in comes Cassie. Her eyes are red. "Judith," she says, spreading her arms open wide, and then hugging me in my chair. As she hugs me, I think, *She doesn't know that Jake told me about them*. She turns to Falcon and hugs him too.

"I am so sorry," says Cassie.

"Thanks for coming," says Falcon, and he says this in a voice so like his father's it takes my breath away. The thought flashes through my head—if Jake dies, Falcon becomes the man of the family. I can see him now, giving up on college, staying in Cold River the rest of his life. I can see him on a cold February day, digging through the snow to get to someone's septic tank.

"What do we know?" Cassie asks. I want to yell at her: *We know you poured margaritas down my husband's throat and tried to haul him into a motel room in Augusta, the state capital that is more accurately called Disgusta.*

"He fell through the floor of the barn," says Falcon. "He inhaled a lot of smoke. The doctors are working on him. He's burned." Again, he says this with authority and calm, a steady, grim patriarch-in-training.

"Oh God," says Cassie, dissolving in tears. "Oh no." She starts to shake and to sob. Falcon gets up and sits down next to her and puts his arms around her. Cassie collapses on my son. He holds her.

"It's okay," says Falcon. "We're all here." I want to ask my son, *Who's this "we"?* But instead I count to five under my breath and look up at the TV monitor. Cassie weeps on Falcon's shoulder. I stand up and turn on the volume so I don't have to listen to her. A chorus is singing to Mr. Limpet. *Be careful how you wish.*

"Judith," says Cassie, wiping away her tears. "Are you okay?"

"I'm hanging in there," I say, which is, of course, the thing you say when you're not.

I get up and walk over to the fish tank. It has green gravel on the bottom, a fake photo of tropical plant life taped to the back. There are two plastic trees, and a deep-sea diver. Air is bubbling out of his diving helmet.

"I wish I were a fish," I say, in the voice of Don Knotts. Most people wouldn't recognize a Don Knotts imitation these days, but I know who it is.

There's a concerned silence, then Falcon says, "Come on over here and sit with us, Ma."

"I wish I were a fish," I say again. I don't know who I'm talking to. The little plastic deep-sea diver, I guess.

"Why do you wish you were a fish, Judith?" says Cassie, in her oh-so-sensitive voice.

I turn around. "It's not *me* who wants to be a fish," I snap. "It's Don Knotts who wants to be a fish. Mr. *Limpet*." I point at the movie on the TV screen. "*He* wants to be a fish." Cassie looks a little frightened, like *The Incredible Mr. Limpet* is the most horrifying movie she's ever seen. "He goes, '*Oh, how I wish I were like you,*' and then later he falls into the ocean and they turn him into a fish and he swims around and he's happy." Both Falcon and Cassie are looking agitated. "Tell me that's so wrong," I shout at them. "What, he should have stayed a human being? Seriously?"

"No one's saying that," said Falcon. "Come on. Sit down. You're freaking us out."

"Oh, well, I'd hate to freak anybody out," I say. "I mean, I just want to make sure everybody gets through the day without being uncomfortable."

"Mom," Falcon says, and again he sounds like Jake. "Stop it. Sit down. Jesus Christ."

I sit down next to him, but I'm still fuming. A nurse opens the door and walks into the waiting room, looks at us.

"What?" I say, getting to my feet.

"What what?" says the nurse.

"What *what* what?" I say.

"Do you have any news for us," says Falcon hurriedly, perhaps to stop the nurse from going, What *what* what *what?*

"Who are you waiting for?"

"My husband," I say, going over to her. "Jake Carrigan."

She doesn't quite follow. "I'm not sure I—"

"The *firefighter,*" I say.

"Oh," she says. Then her face falls. "*Oh.*"

"What's '*Oh,*'" I say.

"They're working on him," says the nurse.

"Who? Who's working on him? We've been here for hours!"

"The whole team," says the nurse. She straightens herself up. "I'm sure the doctors will be out to give you an update when we know more."

Then she turns and walks swiftly away, as if afraid to engage with us further.

"I can't believe this," I say.

"What happened?" says Cassie. "I heard there was an accident?"

"Dad was fighting the fire at Weasel's. The chicken barn. He was looking for Weasel's father."

"Pappy," I say. "He was trying to rescue fucking *Pappy.*"

"Is Pappy okay?"

I laugh bitterly. "Pappy's fine!" I shout. "Pappy was down by the lake jerking off in a hammock! Don't be worrying about Pappy!"

Falcon leans forward. "Mom," he says. "Pull it together."

I just look back at him, furious. "Why would I *do* that?"

"Because you're making everything worse," he says. "By being out of control."

"*I'm* out of control!" I shout at him. "*I'm* out of control?"

"Yeah, kinda."

I sit down in a heap next to him and heave a sigh and the tears spill out all over the place. "Oh, brother," I say, reaching into my purse for a tissue. "Oh, brother."

Cassie looks at Falcon. "You haven't heard anything so far?"

"No," says Falcon. "He got here in an ambulance around five a.m. We got here around five thirty. They've been working on him for"—he checks his watch—"almost two hours."

"Oh no," says Cassie. "Oh Jakey." And I think, *Jakey?*

"Who called you?" I say. "*I* didn't call you."

"Weasel called me," she says. "He called everybody."

"It's good you came," says Falcon, all paternal. I am wondering why Falcon isn't keening and sobbing, but then I kind of remember the drill. Back when I was a boy, pretending to be strong for other people—especially for women—was one way of dealing with grief. It wasn't that I didn't feel the same terror and sadness as the women in my life—my mom, Rachel, Maisie; it was that, sometimes, imitating strength actually made me feel something pretty damned close to it. But then, I was always good at doing voices. I remember after Wailer disappeared, performing a kind of Strong Quentin persona for Rachel. *The important thing is that we all have each other,* I said to her, in a voice much more authoritative than my own. I held her in my arms and let her cry.

It makes me wonder just how many supposedly brave people in the world are just men and women trying to imitate someone more courageous than themselves.

I dry my eyes, and I feel someone's arms around me, out of nowhere and I look up, and it's Cassie. She's crept up and sprung a hug on me. I think about smacking her for a second, saying something like, *It's all well and good you being all kind and thoughtful, but if you were all that maybe you shouldn't have been trying to fuck him.* But I relent, and allow myself to be held, even by her. If people can find courage by imitating bravery, it's possible that others can pretend to be moved by them.

Who knows, maybe imitating someone who has found solace will actually help me find it.

I exhale noisily, and with this breath comes more tears. "Ohhh, okay," I say. "Okay, Cassie." I pat the arm that is encircling me. "It's okay. We'll get by."

And the funny thing is, I really do feel better. For the moment, it is as if I have been healed.

After a while, Cassie releases me, and then she turns to Falcon. "And how are you doing, young man?"

"Tell you the truth, I'm kind of fucked up," he said. "But I'm hanging in there."

"We're all hanging in there," I add. We all sit in silence for a while. I pick up a *Highlights* magazine. There's still the Bear Family, just as in days of yore, and Find the Hidden Pictures. And Goofus and Gallant, of course. It's funny, when I was a child I always identified with Gallant, because all I wanted was to be good. But now that I'm in my fifties, my heart goes out to Goofus. It must have been awful, having Gallant as a brother. He had that whole good-boy thing all sewn up. What could you do, if your brother was Gallant, except give yourself over entirely to evil?

I look across the room at the fish tank. "I guess those fish died," I said. "That's the only explanation for it."

"What?" says Cassie.

"Mom, don't start up with the fish again, okay? Just don't."

"I'm just saying, that's the only explanation. They had some fish, then the fish died. Maybe they figured it's easier just to have the tank. It's less work."

"Deep breaths, Ma," says Falcon.

"We're all pretty stressed out," says Cassie.

"Jake and I were having a fight when the alarm went off," I say.

"A fight?" says Cassie. "What were you fighting about?"

"Guess."

The doors swing open, and a man in scrubs steps out. "Mrs. Carrigan?" he says. He's looking at Cassie. We all stand up.

"*I'm* Mrs. Carrigan," I say. He comes over to where we are.

"I'm Dr. Payne," he says, and I think, *He's doctor pain!* "Your husband is out of surgery. He's resting now. He breathed a lot of smoke, and he was unconscious for ten minutes. But he's conscious now. We don't think there was any brain damage. He has some burns on his legs, but he's mostly fine. The protective equipment he was wearing saved his life. He'll have to rest for a day or two, but he should be up and around soon enough. He's a very lucky man."

"Oh my God," I say, the tears running everywhere once again. Falcon and I hug each other. Cassie stands a short distance away. "I was so worried. I was *so* worried."

"You see, Ma?" says Falcon. "It's going to be all right."

"I'm so glad," I say, my voice cracking. Cassie comes forward and puts her arms around both of us, and for the moment, it's just fine. Let her hug us. Why shouldn't she? Jake's going to be all right. Our lives together will continue.

"You can see him now," says Dr. Payne. "Would you like to come with me?"

"We'd love to come with you," I say. We follow Dr. Payne through the swinging doors. As we leave the waiting room, I see one last shot of *The Incredible Mr. Limpet* on the big TV. Limpet's wife, now widowed, is weeping in her kitchen. We walk down a long hall. We can see patients in various stages of distress. Some are sitting up and eating; some are reading books. Others lie there like dead people. Some of them might actually *be* dead people. My brothers! My sisters!

I am glad Jake is not one of the dead ones. All I can think of is the day he knocked on my door—a lifetime ago—and there he was, standing on the threshold with a box of mac and cheese. I make a vow to make him mac and cheese for the first meal he eats once he comes home.

We enter his room, and there he is, sitting up. His right leg is bandaged, and his face seems red. But on the whole, he is my husband, the man I have loved for sixteen years now. My heart rises right up into my throat. For a moment I am thinking it will come right out of my mouth and I will stand there with my own pink heart beating in my hand.

Then his face contorts. He points at me. He's shouting. At first I can't understand him. His voice seems distorted and strange, like it's coming from underwater.

But the words come clear. They pop like little bubbles. "No! No! Not *her*!" he shouts. "I don't want her in here! Not *her*!"

Yeah, I think. *See, this is why I didn't tell you.*

22

Nether Providence, Pennsylvania

Clark scrubbed himself clean as a whistle. First he used the regular soap, then the special disinfectant. He used the brush to get under his fingernails, but he still felt a little wavery. He checked the chart. The clippers and the razor were already on the stainless-steel table from the last one. Sometimes, he thought, the world seemed to be a place without mercy or love, a place that was punctuated only by its terrible, heartless injustice. So what could you do, in the face of this endless cruelty, except try to proceed with gentleness and forgiveness? It wasn't much, but it was the thing he had.

Clark went out to the pound. The air filled with the sudden opera. He checked the clipboard at the cage. Buster was sitting there, head cocked. *They always know,* Clark thought.

He opened the door and Buster wagged his tail. Clark patted him on the head. "I'm sorry, pupper," he said. Buster didn't seem convinced. "You're a good boy." He clipped the leash onto the dog's collar and led him into the chamber. Buster looked around, then cast a glance at Clark. *Is that all there is? If that's all there is my friends, then let's keep wagging.*

"It's okay," said Clark. He urged the dog onto the stainless-steel platform. Then he pressed the button that slowly raised it. Buster lay down and put his head on his paws. Clark shaved a small area on the dog's front leg, then swabbed the area with rubbing alcohol.

"You're a good boy," said Clark, patting the dog on the head. He picked up the syringe and pierced Buster's leg with it, found the vein.

Clark got out the stethoscope to check. "Okay," said Clark. "Off you go, into the wild blue yonder."

His sister Cyndy used to sing that song. Now, in thinking about the place where Buster had gone, he concluded: *Well, it's not wild. But it's blue.*

He got out one of the bags, pulled the body into it, then sealed it up. He wrote the stats on a yellow-colored tag, then affixed this to the outside. Then he picked up the bag and carried it out to the sterile chamber. There were seventeen other bags already there. Clark checked his watch. Hink was supposed to come by with the van any time now. They didn't do the cremations here at the shelter. That was done at Hink's garage, out in Fairfield. He didn't like to think about that too much. Hink used to have a cow. Not anymore though.

For families that were having their pets put down, Hink got paid extra to gather the ashes in a small box. Hink made a small impression of the dog's paw in plaster, etched the dog's name into the plaster right next to it. But there wouldn't be any such ritual for Buster. *There will be no books written about my mother. But she was a saint.*

He got another syringe ready, checked that the clippers were clean, that everything was as it should be for the next one. Next up was a pug. Clark opened the door, and again the air filled with the sounds of barking. Francis was at the end of the second column of cages, where they kept the smaller animals. There were some rabbits down there and a ferret as well. He'd get to them later, but he preferred to do all the dogs first, then the cats, then come back for the miscellany. There was a structure in that. Francis looked happy to see him. He opened up the cage and bent down, and attached the leash to his collar. "Okay, pupper," he said.

Francis made the grunting, heaving sound that is the trademark of the breed. Clark tried not to let his own opinions enter into it. When he was a young man, he feared that the world was out to get him. Now, in late middle age, he'd learned the horrible truth: the world barely knows you're here.

"Gurganis," said a voice, and Clark looked up to see a middle-aged man standing by the table.

"Toby!" said Clark. His entire face brightened. He rushed forward and threw his arms around his friend. Francis ran around the legs of the two men in a happy circle. It was a big-ass party, right there in the small-animal euthanasia chamber.

"It's so good to see you!" said Clark. "Gosh, I've missed you!"

Tripper seemed a little distant, businesslike. "I guess you've seen the newspapers?" he asked.

Clark's shoulders fell. "Oh," he said. "That."

"Oh," Tripper said. "That."

They'd gone to the same nursery school. Every day Clark's mother made him a peanut butter and honey sandwich. On the weekends Clark and Tripper shot off model rockets. A Big Bertha. A Black Widow. A scale model Gemini-Titan.

Tripper looked at Clark with barely contained rage. "You said that you sank her in the Schuylkill," he said. "You swore to me."

Clark's eyes fell to the floor, and his face colored. Francis looked up at him hopefully, wagging his tail. Tripper waited for Clark to explain, but the man just stood there. Slowly, his eyes began to shine.

"Well?" said Tripper.

"You know, I get tired of being yelled at," said Clark.

"They found the body!" Tripper shouted. "You fucking *idiot*."

"This is what I'm talking about, the shouting," said Clark. Francis barked at Tripper angrily. Then he barked again. Clark squatted down and picked up the dog and patted his wrinkled face. He hugged the little dog, then put him down on the metal table, and shaved a little area on Francis's front leg.

"Clark," said Tripper, "we're in trouble."

Clark patted the head of the pug. "It's not right the way you boss people around." He pierced the little dog's leg with the syringe, plunged in the sodium thiopental. "You're a good little boy," he said. "It's okay. You're gonna be okay."

Francis did not shut his eyes. He looked at Clark the whole time as life drained out of him and the glimmer of dog soul visible in those wet eyes disappeared.

Tripper ran his palm down across the length of his face, from his hairline to his mouth. "Listen," he went on, in a softer voice. "Clark. I think you're very brave."

Clark patted the late Francis for a little bit. "I'm not brave," he said. "You just do what you have to do."

"Considering what you've had to carry," said Tripper. "I think you're one of the bravest people I know. I'm proud we're friends."

Clark cast a shy, embarrassed glance at Tripper. He ran his fingers through his giant beard. It was like a haystack in a barn for Clydesdales.

Clark got out a bag and slowly pushed the late pug into it. "You should call me on the phone sometime if I'm such a friend," he said.

"I know, I know," said Tripper. "The last couple of years have been crazy for us. It's been nuts."

Clark stared at the bag with the dog in it. "That little kid of yours is a college student now?"

Tripper nodded. "Time just rushes past," he said. "It leaves you with nothing."

Clark looked wistful. He opened the door to the sterile room and put the bag with Francis in it on top of the others. Then he came back to the chamber.

Clark nodded. "I miss us being friends," he said. "You and me."

"Clark," Tripper said again. "Do you remember Maisie Lenfest? My old girlfriend? That's kind of what I need to talk to you about."

"Maisie, sure. She was in here the other day. I saw her."

"Wait, what?" said Tripper, uncertain. "Maisie was *here*?"

Clark put his hands on his hips like Superman. "I knew who *she* was," he said proudly. "But she didn't know who *I* was."

Tripper had a fleeting image of Snowy wheezing atop the piano. It didn't surprise him that the creature was unwell.

"See, the thing is," he said. "Maisie's having issues, I think. Now that everything's all stirred up again."

Clark wiped his hands on his pants. "Issues," he said. "What do you mean, issues?"

"See, Maisie gets these dark nights of the soul," said Tripper. "On account of the idiot brother, I think."

Clark looked accusingly at Tripper. "You shouldn't call him that," he said. "He's doing the best with what he can. The way he was born. I hate the way you judge people, Toby. You look *down* on them."

Tripper took a deep breath and exhaled slowly. He appeared to be thinking very sincerely about what Clark was telling him.

"Maisie has been saying some unsettling things since that girl's body turned up, like maybe she's going to tell someone something. The police, for instance?"

Gurganis's eyes grew wide. "But she can't do that!" he said. "After all this time? Why would she?"

"I think she feels it'd be more *just* if we were all in prison. That we've all evaded judgment somehow, and that we really ought to come clean."

" 'Just'?" said Gurganis, clapping a hand to his forehead. "You know what they do to people in jail, people who've put animals to sleep?"

"Yes, well," said Tripper. "It's not a place I'd like to see you wind up."

Gurganis looked at the door that led to the sterile chamber. He thought about all the bodies in their bags.

"I wish I hadn't killed that kid's cat," he said.

"Yeah," said Tripper. "That always struck me as a little baroque."

Gurganis looked ashamed. "It was after I drug the girl into that hole. I was so angry."

Tripper looked very mournful. He put his hand on his friend's shoulder. "What you've been through."

"That tunnel was filled with some bad things," said Clark. "The things I saw. I think about them sometimes."

"You need to just put all that behind you," said Tripper.

"I was trying to help," said Clark. "But you know what happens when you try to help? You make everything worse."

Gurganis hung his head dejectedly. A dark world closed around him.

"Clark," said Tripper, "you have to have hope. Believe in the goodness of things."

Gurganis swung his hands forward and back. "That's easy for you to say, you have a life," he said. He left the room.

Tripper stood there in the empty chamber for a moment. There was a metal paper-towel dispenser on one wall. It reflected his image back at him all warped and exaggerated. Tripper thought, I don't look like that.

Clark Gurganis returned a moment later with a Siamese cat in his arms. It was purring softly.

"So—do you think you could pay her a visit?" said Tripper.

Clark looked angry. He pointed at Tripper and jabbed him in the chest with his finger.

"You are asking me to do a terrible thing."

Tripper nodded. "I know."

"Is that who you are? The guy who goes around asking people to do terrible things?"

"No," said Tripper, raising his hand as if he were a cop trying to stop traffic. "No. I'm not. This thing between us, this history. This isn't who we are."

"No? Who are we?"

"Clark. We're just two good men in very unfortunate circumstances. This is just *residue*. The vestigial remains of some other time. We can't let that time define us. We are more than that, both of us. You and me."

Clark shook his head angrily. "You're some talker," he said.

"We get to decide who we are, Clark," said Tripper. "Not these other people." He put an envelope in Gurganis's hand. It contained a lot of money.

Gurganis shaved a small portion of the cat's leg. Then he picked him up and cradled the creature in his arms. The cat's purring grew loud. He could feel the vibrations through his body.

"Do we?" he asked.

Clark and his sister, Cyndy, had a cat, back when they were kids. Her name was Sneakers. Near the end, Sneakers disappeared into the woods. That was back when they lived in the country, next door to Tripper and his family. Nether Providence, in Chester County. A couple days before Cyndy died, the cat came back out of the woods. *Look,* he told his sister. *Look at the mouse she's got.*

23

Philadelphia, Pennsylvania

Rachel pulled up at Casey's house in South Philadelphia, tooted her horn a couple of times, and out he came, all three hundred pounds of him. A police officer who'd been leaning against her squad car, smoking a cigarette, threw her butt into the gutter and climbed behind the wheel in order to follow them. Casey sat down next to Rachel and handed her a small brown paper bag. There were stains on the bottom, and the bag was slightly warm.

"I made these for ya," he said, struggling to pull the seat belt across his large belly. "Chocolate-chip cookies."

"Thanks Casey," said Rachel, casting an eye into her rearview mirror as they pulled out into traffic. "I guess we're being chaperoned?"

"Detective Gleeson," said Casey, turning around to look at the cop car behind them. He waved. "She's persistent."

Rachel reached into the brown bag and pulled out a cookie. She bit into it. "Whoa," she said.

"I'm telling you," said Casey.

"No, it's just, jeez, Casey. Even your stupid cookies are amazing."

"Hey, they're not stupid," said Casey. "My cookies are totally sincere!"

"I know, I know," she said. The soft chocolate oozed onto her lips. "It's just like, I wish I had one thing I could do as well as you can cook everything."

"Hey, you got your art!" said Casey.

"I haven't painted in years," said Rachel. "You know that."

"Yeah, but you're a good teacher, right? That's not nothing!"

Rachel sighed. "I hate teaching."

"I don't know man," said Casey. "Making other people smarter is kind of like having a superpower, isn't it?"

She finished the cookie. There was a little melted chocolate on her cheek.

"I guess," said Rachel.

They drove through the city, past the art museum and onto the Schuylkill Expressway. The towers of Eastern State flashed into view for an instant. Casey looked at the place's dark silhouette.

"You think we'd have stayed together, her and me?" said Casey.

Out on the Schuylkill, a half dozen crew shells were being rowed upriver by young men. Casey looked at their strong arms, flexing together. The boathouses on the far bank were decorated with flags.

"What?" said Rachel. "You and Wailer? Of course you'd have stayed together!"

"You don't know," said Casey.

"Well, of course I don't know," said Rachel. "But you two loved each other. Everybody knew that."

He nodded. "There's another cookie in that bag," he said.

"I'm good," she said.

They drove west. On a far hill to the right were the tall antennae towers of Roxbury. Each one was topped by a glowing red light.

"Sometimes I think she'd have never come back," said Casey. "From Africa. That's why I wanted to get married. I wanted to make her keep her promise."

"Why wouldn't she have come back from Africa?"

"I don't know," said Casey. "I just look back on it, man, and it's like everything just seemed all doomed. Like, how do you think people in Togo were going to react to a girl with pink hair? Don't you think they'd have been freaked out?"

"If anybody could have won people over, it was Wailer," said Rachel. "She was a force of nature, wasn't she?"

"She was," said Casey. He grabbed the paper bag. "You sure you don't want this?"

Rachel nodded. Casey bit into the still-warm chocolate-chip cookie. "Hey, these *are* good, man," he said. "I must really love you."

"I love you too, Jonny," said Rachel.

"Ha," said Casey. "That's what Wailer called me." He stuffed the rest of the cookie into his mouth and chewed it up. He looked wistful. "Wish I'd brought some milk I guess."

"You want me to stop?"

"Nah," said Casey. "Detective Gleeson said not to make any weird stops. And, you know. I wanna keep Detective Gleeson happy." He looked over his shoulder at the car tailing them again, then he looked at Rachel. "Hey man, you got a little—" He indicated the spot of chocolate on her cheek. She didn't immediately seem to know what he was getting at. Casey licked his forefinger, rubbed it against the small smudge of chocolate. Then he licked his finger again.

"See, the thing is," said Casey, "I think Wailer was kind of fucked up. You know her mom and dad died? Yeah. That's why she was all punked-out, man. She was so pissed off and sad."

"She wasn't pissed off at you, Casey."

He looked out the window for a long time. "You know that crazy accent of hers wasn't exactly real either, right? She always said it was half Ireland, half Tyneside, but I don't know, sometimes I think it was three-quarters bullshit. She just wanted to be a character."

The cop car behind them fell back a little. Rachel looked at Detective Gleeson again in her rearview.

She drove down Gulph Road. They passed the Hanging Rock, a huge piece of shale suspended over the roadway. Washington was said to have passed beneath it en route to Valley Forge in 1778. It looked like it could fall.

Maisie sat at the grand piano in the rotting old parlor of her house, her fingers resting on the keys. All around her were the caterers and the florists, swirling around like the arms of a spiral galaxy. Maisie played

a C-sharp-minor chord. Beethoven's favorite. She played the first couple of bars of the Moonlight Sonata, then stopped. A young woman—
maybe eighteen—was setting up a bar at the far end of the living room.
Next to the bar was the wheel from the HMS *Pinafore*. The bartender
had long blond hair, a dewy complexion, freckles, a black apron. For
a moment she looked over at Maisie and they locked eyes. Then, embarrassed, the girl continued with her work—arranging the bottles,
stacking up the plastic glasses.

For a moment Maisie and the young woman swapped bodies. It was
awkward, being young all at once like that. Just like that, all of Maisie's
years still lay ahead. It lasted only a second. Then they were themselves again. She started in on a Bach two-part invention.

"Oh, don't play that," said Tripper. Once again he had materialized
out of thin air, a regular Captain Kirk. "Play the Beatles again."

"I don't know that song," she said.

"You were just playing it. That John Lennon tune, 'Because.' "

"Yeah, I know. The irony." She turned to look at him. He was
wearing a black suit. "Don't you ever knock? Or, I don't know, call, to
let people know you're coming?"

"You told me to get you at two. It's quarter of."

She leaned over and smelled him. "You're not drunk. Are you?"

"Not yet," said Tripper. He sat down next to her on the bench.
"Looks like the caterers are on the job."

"Main Line Hospitality Company. They're the same ones we used
for Wailer and Casey's wedding, thirty-five years ago."

"They had to have the reception here?" said Tripper. "You really
think that's appropriate?"

"I couldn't bring myself to tell Casey no when he asked," said
Maisie.

"It's not that hard," said Tripper. "You just open up your mouth
and tell him."

"I guess I should have had them call you."

Tripper nodded to the far side of the parlor, where the young
woman with whom she'd switched bodies for a full three seconds was

now once more assembling the bar. "You know, I hate to be the one to tell you this, but there's a wheel for an ocean liner at one end of your living room."

"HMS *Pinafore*," said Maisie. "I teach these kids Gilbert and Sullivan, the special-needs kids. Don't you know this? This is what I do for a living. I help kids with music."

Tripper just shook his head. "You're something," he said.

"So are you," said Maisie, and just like that, the two old lovers were strangely intimate with each other. It was hard for Maisie to know if she felt real desire for Tripper, or if it was just the memory of that desire. The two of them drew close, eyes locked. Maisie's lips parted.

Snowy jumped up on the piano, breaking the moment. His tail waved around like a charmed cobra. Maisie smiled sadly. "So—where is Dr. Pennypacker today?" she asked. "The good wife?"

Tripper rubbed his chin. He was freshly shaven. "She's meeting me there."

"Mrs. Lenfest?" said a young man, holding a bouquet of summer flowers—black-eyed Susans, Queen Anne's lace, petunias. "Where do you want these?"

Maisie looked at the man like he was an image on a screen. He was fresh-faced and handsome. "It's Miss," she said, and pointed to the bar near the *Pinafore*.

"Is Benny ready?" asked Tripper.

"He's upstairs," said Maisie.

"You want me to go get him?" Tripper's gaze went out to the parlor and the old staircase. "I can go get him if you want."

"Tripper," said Maisie, quietly. "We really should tell the truth."

Tripper touched the side of her cheek. A look of piercing sorrow crept over his face. "You think?" he said.

Tripper looked around the room. A harp stood at an angle to the grand piano; Lenfests from the nineteenth century stared out from their dark oil paintings; two leather wing chairs were placed on either side of the fireplace, the linen couch across from them. Tripper pictured his nineteen-year-old self smoking a cigarette in one of those chairs. Young Maisie, six weeks pregnant, looked at him from the piano bench, her fingers poised above the keys.

Here he was now, in the place where she had been.

In his upstairs room, Ben Lenfest was hard at work. In one hand was a clipboard with a yellow legal pad, covered with ink: all the different strategies. He was wearing a hooded sweatshirt that read MUHLENBERG. There were footsteps on the stairs and Tripper Pennypacker came into the room. He took in the scene, took in Ben. On one wall there was a print of a cat drawn by Louis Wain, the Victorian schizophrenic. The cat's elaborate mane was abundant with tongues of flame.

On the desk in front of Ben was an icosidodecahedron he'd been building. It had twenty triangular faces and twelve pentagonal ones. The triangles were purple. The pentagons were black. He was only two triangles away from finishing, although he had to wait for the glue to dry on the last pentagon first.

"What are you doing?" said Tripper. "You're making notes?"

"I've been figuring something out," said Ben.

"Can I see?"

"No," said Ben. He didn't want Tripper Pennypacker to see any of the plans he'd sketched out for rescuing Jon Casey. He knew how Tripper's mind worked. The man wouldn't be happy until he'd burst every last balloon.

"Fine. Whatever. You ready to go?"

The walls of Ben's room were eighteen different intersecting planes. By the transom was a peeling place where water from the attic leaked through. This distorted the plane's resonance. Sometimes light shone through the window at a fifty-two-degree angle. That light was so beautiful. It broke his heart to think about it.

"Benny?" asked Tripper.

As a child he'd lain in his bed in this very room and listened to the footsteps in the attic going round and round. It sounded like someone pacing. It was creepy, not least because ghosts did not exist. But he listened to the pacing anyway without believing in it. It was company of a sort. The loneliness is really the hardest part about it all, Ben thought. It was hard living in a world with only one person in it.

The thing in the attic took a step. To Tripper Pennypacker it just sounded like the house settling. To Ben it said, *You're nothing*. It was a mean thing to say, but he knew what the thing was getting at. Maisie had all these kids over every week to perform Gilbert & Sullivan songs in the living room, kids who were a lot more messed up than he. But no one ever asked Ben to sing, even though he knew the music.

"*I'm called little Buttercup,*" he noted. His voice was sweet. "*Dear little Buttercup. Though I could never tell why.*"

It was true, he was nothing. What proof would there be after he was gone that he had ever even been here?

Now he sat in his chair with the fifty-something-year-old version of Tripper Pennypacker. *If I can save Jon Casey, that will be proof enough.* But how? It was impossible to do anything without friends.

He remembered when Tripper and Maisie were boyfriend and girlfriend, back in the 1970s. Jimmy Carter was wearing a cardigan. His brother Billy had his own brand of beer. His mother was called Miss Lillian. *There's a lid for every pot!* his mother used to say. But he doubted this was true. There were some pots that had no lids, because the shape they defined could not be duplicated. His mother had insisted this was part of the beauty of the world. You are you! she'd gushed. You are you uoy era uoY. She had long since circled the drain.

"You're called what?" said Tripper.

"Nothing," said Ben.

The Thing in the attic took another step. Tripper paid it no heed whatsoever, but then he didn't have to, did he?

He's a real nowhere man, Ben thought to himself. *Residens in patria sine domo.* Making all his *omnia consilia sine domo faciens nemini.*

He smiled, thinking about the word. *Neminem*. Then he thought it backwards: menimeN. John Lennon had lived in the Dakota. Which was where they filmed *Rosemary's Baby*. Which was directed by Roman

Polanski. Who had been married to Sharon Tate. Who was killed by Charles Manson. Who was inspired by "Helter Skelter." Which was performed by the Beatles. Who were led by John Lennon. Who lived in the Dakota. Which was where, et cetera, et cetera.

"You coming, Buttercup?" said Tripper.

"I don't believe in you," Ben said. Tripper looked confused, but Ben wasn't talking to him.

That's okay, the Thing in the attic replied. *I don't believe in you either.*

24

Atlantic Coast

By noon I was on the Tappan Zee, crossing the Hudson. There were derricks and cranes floating out on the river, evidence that a new bridge was being built. I didn't really know what was wrong with the old one. Peter, Paul, and Mary were on the satellite radio, singing "In the Early Morning Rain."

Light rain pattered on the windshield. The wipers kept time.

I thought about the hate in the eyes of the man I loved as he gazed upon me. *Not her!* Falcon stood between us. One of the machines Jake was wired to started beeping, like my mere presence was enough to give him a heart attack.

"Listen, Ma," said my son. "I think you oughta go."

"Judith," said Cassie.

For a moment I stood there, paralyzed. Another machine started beeping. "Mom," said Falcon more insistently. I turned and fled, leaving my family in the capable hands of Cassie Hudson.

I passed Brunswick, Freeport, Portland, Kennebunkport, heading south. I crossed the Piscataqua River and into New Hampshire. In Massachusetts, I saw the sign for Bonker's, somewhat the worse for wear after almost thirty years. But it was still there, urging the moms and dads of Boston to take their kids down below for pizza and pinball, although it was hard to imagine anyone playing pinball anymore.

Casey, I thought, and remembered sitting there with him in the ruined chapel of the prison. I had become the companion of dragons, a friend to owls. Casey had shook his head. *Dude, you're not a friend to any owl. You're a friend to me.*

I hoped he would be more forgiving than my husband had been. I imagined myself arriving in the meetinghouse, pulling off the veil, and Casey's kind face turning to anger. *Not her.* And the thing is, I couldn't blame him. It wasn't being trans that had made me the companion of dragons. It was my certainty that the people I loved were incapable of understanding—a certainty based not on random fear but on actual experience. Exhibit A? The reaction of Jake, the only person in the world who loved me even more than Jon Casey had. Even my son: *Listen, Ma. I think you oughta go.*

I wanted to yell at everyone. *You're all so sure what the right thing to do would have been. What if there was no right thing? What if you'd been born with a condition that, by its very nature, stuck you with an unsolvable philosophical puzzle, from your earliest recollection of childhood to the present? Is it so impossible that you might imagine what it must have been like to have felt the things I've felt, and not known what to do?*

Of course, there's a road map now. But when I was growing up there wasn't any map, there was nothing. I was fifty years old before I ever saw anyone like myself on television, or on a TV show, or in a book. In the absence of story, the very clear message was, *People like you do not exist.* The only transgender women I ever saw in the big mirror of the culture were murder victims in detective shows; or sad sacks on talk shows being ridiculed or held up as circus freaks; or drag queens with comical stage names. There weren't any moms, or teachers, or cops—people who just wanted to move on. To disappear into the anonymous, loving gray of a normal life.

I'm a relic, though. That's what I realize now. The world has become a safer place for trans people, for some of us anyhow. Maybe it's become safer as a direct result of people coming out, being visible, living openly in the world. But I was never that brave. *I set out to save the Shire . . . and it has been saved. But not for me.*

"Gollum," I said. "Gollum."

I still remember going into Olin Library at Wesleyan when I was a student there, looking for books about the thing I was struggling with. What I found, of course, was nothing—or, in some ways, worse than nothing. The only books I found were full of theories that were just hilariously, ridiculously wrong. There was one that said people were trans because our "fathers were too passive." Or we "wanted to be closer to our mothers." Or that we were fetishists. I remember reading those books and thinking, Gee, that doesn't sound right. Are they sure? It reminded me of a cartoon I saw once of a woman reading a book called *All About You*. The author of the book: *Not You*.

I have a different theory, which is even more harebrained. It goes like this: Maybe we should all just love one another, even if we don't completely understand the things that people bear in their dark, strange hearts, even if the stars that other men and women are following seem invisible to us. If we make ourselves open to the humanity of others *first*, maybe understanding will follow. An incomprehensible theory of the universe isn't necessary if your only ambition is to embrace another soul. What you need, maybe all you need, in fact, is the willingness to love.

I crossed the Delaware River. To my right was the iron bridge with its sign: TRENTON MAKES. THE WORLD TAKES.

Yeah, well. Sucks to be you, Trenton, I thought.

25

Devon, Pennsylvania

The Old Devon Quaker Meetinghouse sat in a green field populated by dead Friends. The oldest stones were made of granite and adorned with hand-hewn images of skulls, goblins with wings, gruesome femurs, wide-faced moons. More recent ones were made of marble, and bore the carvings of willow trees. And were more likely to be unreadable, as the marble melted in the acid rains of Pennsylvania. In one corner of the cemetery were graves for the members of the 141st Pennsylvania, wiped out on the second day of Gettysburg. The Peach Orchard.

The interior of the meetinghouse was plain. There was no organ, no piano, no stained glass, no altar. Instead the room was set up with three sets of pews all facing one another. At the center of the room on an easel was a blown-up photo of Wailer, as she had been in 1980. Pink hair, big smile. Below the easel on a small table was the urn.

A car with Maine plates arrived late to the parking lot, and a tall middle-aged woman got out. She seemed dispirited. For a moment she stood by her car, looking at the meetinghouse, at all the old headstones. Then she slung her purse over one shoulder and moved with determination down the gravel path.

About twenty feet from the front door, however, she stopped. She raised one hand to her lips and took a step back. Then she walked off the path and stood before a grave. It was a modern stone bearing two names. JOHN MOYNIHAN PHEANEY. 1928–1974. GRAINNE ANNE PHEANEY. 1930–1990.

The woman fell to her knees, then reached out with one hand and touched the letters on the stone.

Rachel Steinberg, her hair gray, walked up the path and paused to look at the stranger down on her knees.

A man with a large beard walked up the path behind Rachel, and smiled to gaze upon her.

My head was reeling by the time I got into the meetinghouse. I'd left the key fob for the Prius in the car, but I wasn't thinking about that once I saw the headstone. Who had come to that service, the day they buried my mother? Did Grainne look out the window on her last morning and say, *Quentin, I'm going to be with you?*

All I could think, as I stood by my mother's headstone, was that I had done this.

There were sounds of a scuffle behind me, raised voices, which I ignored. There wasn't room for a whole lot else in the world right then. When at last I turned around, I saw a man with a beard and a woman about my age walking away from the graveyard back to the parking lot. Second thoughts, I figured. The coin of the realm.

When I finally sat down on one of the long benches inside the Quaker meetinghouse, it was impossible not to look around at everyone and think, This could have been my life, this could have been my pew, if I'd stayed a boy, stayed in Pennsylvania, just kept trudging year after year living the life I was born to. I saw an older man who could only be Tripper Pennypacker come in with Maisie Lenfest, and I almost cried out. Time had beaten them down to nothing. My heart was still aching from staring at Grainne's stone, but it also occurred to me that if I hadn't left here, I would look like Tripper by now: a ghost.

I looked around for the others, but I didn't see them. Fleetingly, I wondered if Wailer might come. It would be good to see her once more. *Ah mate, yer a savage.*

People in gray clothes sat on the long, hard benches, their eyes closed, hands folded.

I had forgotten the austerity of a Quaker funeral. There was no music, no singing, no nothing. We all just sat there in contemplation. I imagined Wailer's response. *Are you not a bunch of bloody wankers. Will you not begin the party, then?*

There was a photograph of her on an easel at the front of the meetinghouse. It was shocking to see her: she was not much more than a child, really. Beneath this, an urn that contained the ashes.

Someone groaned, and then I saw him: Jon Casey, my dear old friend. He was shaking gently, and I realized the reason he was shaking was because he was crying. I wanted to go to him, to tell him, *Dude: it's me, back from the dead. Also: I love you.* But the oppressive air in the room kept me frozen, unable to help the man whom I had come all this way to see.

Maisie turned around on her pew and glanced toward the door, as if looking for someone. Her eyes briefly fell upon me, then moved onward. Even to this friend of my youth, I had become invisible: a middle-aged woman in gray.

"*Ugh,*" said Casey.

His moan sent a silent jolt around the room. He cleared his throat, then said it again.

"Ugh, like . . ."

Casey, I thought. I wanted to go to him, and put my arms around him, and tell him I was sorry: sorry I was the way I was, sorry for the losses he had suffered, sorry for the whole goddamned world.

But then he staggered to his feet. Casey walked to the center of the meetinghouse, and addressed us all, as if we were the ones in need of solace, and he were the one called upon to provide it.

"So I appreciate everyone being here and everything," said Jon Casey. "I know some of you didn't know Wailer and that kind of sucks because she was awesome. She was like this very bright light that kind of blinded anybody who was in the same room as her.

"But she was also, just, like, a very good person. When she died she was about to go to Togo and work for the Red Cross, teaching kids English, which would have been funny because, you know, she definitely had a way of talking. I don't know what they'd have thought about her in Togo. I mean, I always worried a little bit that maybe she'd have freaked everybody out.

"But maybe they'd have thought she was a person with a very big heart and that everyone would have seen how strange and interesting she thought everything was. She had all this love inside her. If she hadn't died, I don't know, maybe we'd have had some big crazy family, and she'd have been a mom to a whole bunch of kids, her and me and I'd have made everybody, like, Belgian waffles."

Big beads of perspiration rolled down the sides of Casey's face. He paused for a moment, as if trying to figure out what to say next.

"I really did love her and stuff," he said. "You know at first I could hardly believe it, I mean, that someone actually loved me? Up until then I didn't think I was a person who really deserved to be loved, I mean—you know, on account of being. But she used to go, like, *Aah, yer a bloody walrus, mate, but you're all right.* And because she said it, it was true, I *was* all right. I stopped being that, like, *Oh, nobody loves me* guy and instead became an *I love everybody* guy! And when she died, it was like I went back to being a—no, actually it was like I turned into a *Nobody can ever again* guy."

Casey went over to the small table on which the urn was resting. Now he was talking to the urn.

"Wailer, everything after you died has *sucked*. I'm so, I'm just so— aaarghh—I'm so *mad*!" He was almost yelling now. "And not only because you're gone, but because—"

He looked around the room. His glance fell from face to face.

"I don't know how people survive, man," he said. "I used to have all this love in me, but all the world does is just crush it like it's . . ."

He looked into the pews again, and then his eyes fell upon me.

Casey.

He raised one hand to his chest, and his face contorted.

"*Kwuh*—" he said, and then, unexpectedly, sank to his knees.

His left arm shot out wildly. With his right one he clutched his heart.

"Ugh," he moaned. His arm knocked the pedestal upon which Wailer's ashes rested. The urn teetered back and forth.

I watched the pedestal, and the urn containing all that was left of Wailer wobbling back and forth, back and forth. Then—slowly, agonizingly—it tipped off the edge and plummeted to the floor. When the urn hit the stone tiles, it shattered with an ear-piercing *smash*, and Wailer's ashes scattered in every direction.

"Casey," I said.

He said, "Ugh," again, and rolled over.

"Park anywhere," said Gurganis. "They got lots of spaces."

A banner hanging from the front of the prison fluttered gently in the breeze. TERROR BEHIND THE WALLS, it read. OPENING NIGHT. Eastern State was a museum now. From late summer through Thanksgiving the place raised money by putting on a show. THE WORLD'S LARGEST HAUNTED HOUSE INSIDE THE WALLS OF A REAL PRISON. It was very popular within a certain cohort: teenagers and ghostbusters and LARPers.

Rachel pulled in behind a VW bus covered with hippie bumper stickers and rainbow decals.

"Why are we here?" said Rachel. Gurganis sat next to her with the Walther PPK in his lap. He looked regretfully at the high stone wall before them.

"I bet you think I'm an evil person," he said.

"I don't know anything about you! I don't even know who you are!"

"I'm a *vet*," said Gurganis.

"Were you in Afghanistan?" said Rachel.

Gurganis looked at her like she was insane. "What would I go *there* for?"

Rachel was still behind the wheel of his car. He'd insisted. She'd found herself frozen before the grave of Quentin's parents, watching a woman she did not know weeping by the stone.

That was when the man with the beard pointed the gun at her and said, *Make a sound and kaboom.*

Now, at Eastern State, young men and women in costumes walked down the sidewalk toward the entrance. There was a Frankenstein monster and a mummy, a Richard Nixon and some Minions.

"You said you were a vet," Rachel said, looking at the stranger. She had seen him before.

"Not *that* kind of vet," he said.

"You're—that guy from the *animal* hospital," she said as the penny dropped at last. "You're the one who put down Moogus."

"Poor pupper," said Gurganis.

Gurganis released the safety on the Walther PPK. It made a mechanical sound, like the teeth of gears meshing together.

"So you're kidnapping me because—I had my dog put down?"

"Ha," said Gurganis. "You're so funny."

"Who's making you do this?" asked Rachel.

"You know who," said Gurganis, angrily. "Your ex-boyfriend. The criminal mastermind."

Rachel thought this over for a while. "Backflip Bob?" she said.

Gurganis blinked. "Is that supposed to be a joke?"

"I really don't know who you're talking about. That's the only ex-boyfriend I have."

"You know where I was when Tripper called me up? Bucknell. Summer of 1980. He goes, *We have to teach someone a lesson.*" He shrugged. "Never went back after that. Never *could* go back."

"Tripper Pennypacker called you?" she said slowly. "And asked you to do what?"

"And teach that guy a lesson!" Gurganis shouted.

"What guy?"

"Yeah, like you don't know the whole story. The only thing you don't know about is *me*. I'm the one who's suffered! I had to carry it, all these years."

"What did you have to carry?"

"It was hard to see in the dark," he said. "I thought that girl was that teacher. Because of that, I have to pay my whole life long? Is that how the rules go?"

Rachel, who was not following what the man was saying at all, eyed the gun in his lap, and wondered what would happen if she made a sudden lunge for it. "I think all of us struggled after Wailer was killed. If that's what you're saying."

"Yeah, you all struggled," said Gurganis bitterly.

"It was pretty horrible, yeah. You think it wasn't horrible?"

"Aw," said Gurganis. "'Course, you didn't spend your evenings watching television with the barrel of a gun in your mouth, though did you, Maisie? 'Cause that's what it was like. That's what it's *been* like."

Rachel blinked. "Maisie? You think I'm Maisie Lenfest?"

"Fuck you," said Gurganis. "As if I don't know who you are!"

"But—I'm Rachel Steinberg! You—you've kidnapped the wrong person! If that's what this is. Is this a kidnapping?"

Gurganis just shook his head. "Nice try," he said.

"I'm telling you the truth!" she said. "That day I had my dog put down, I was—I was embarrassed you knew who I was. I just wanted my privacy. So I gave you the wrong name."

He pointed the gun at her. "You're a piece of work."

"Look, you get a second chance," said Rachel. "You can admit your mistakes and start over. You don't want to hurt the wrong person again, do you? I get it now. You weren't trying to kill Wailer, you were trying to kill Nathan Krystal. Weren't you?"

"I wasn't trying to *kill* anybody! I'm not a murderer!" he shouted, waving the gun around. Then he paused in hopes of gaining some perspective. "I'm just Tripper's friend. I was trying to help him. He's a good guy!"

"He is *not* a good guy," said Rachel. "He's a liar."

"Like you should talk."

"But I'm not who you think I am," said Rachel. "Why won't you believe me?"

Gurganis shook his head in contempt. "I know who you people are better than you do," he said.

"That doesn't mean anything."

"No?" said Gurganis. "You know what that girl sounded like, after her neck was broken? She was going, *Please tell Jonny that I love him please,* and you know what, she didn't have any accent at all. I'm the only one who heard what she really sounded like, the sound of her actual voice, but I'm the one who had to make the decision." His eyes flashed angrily. "*Please tell Jonny, please tell Jonny,* and I kept telling her, *Shut up, for God's sakes, it was just an accident I'm sorry,* but then she starts making this sound, wet like a boot in mud. I was going, *Shut up, shut up, I'm sorry.* But she just keeps on going, *Please tell Jonny,* in this voice like she came from Atlantic City. I heard someone's footsteps on the stairs up to the tower so I put my hand on her mouth, just to go, *Be quiet and I'll get help for you.* I was going to help her! That was what I wanted. Then that sound stopped and I saw it all, the whole terrible thing from one end to the other. So what would you have done if you'd been in my shoes? Called your friends? Called your idiot brother? I can tell you exactly what you'd have done, you'd have tried to put it all away in a hole and crawl out through the tunnel, which is what I did. Like it never happened, except it happened." His shoulders shook. "I don't even know why we're even *having* this conversation. There's no point to anything. Everything just goes where it wants."

"You still have a choice," said Rachel softly.

"Ha, funny," he said, and pointed the gun at her. "Get out slowly."

She did as he asked. Men and women walked down the sidewalk in their costumes. "Why *are* we here then?" Rachel said. "If there's no point?"

"Duh," Gurganis sighed, as if the answer was obvious. "You want to hide something," he said. "You leave it out in the open. That was the mistake I made last time."

"What do you want to hide?" Rachel asked.

"Gee," said Gurganis. "I wonder."

EMTs rolled Casey onto a stretcher. They'd come swiftly. Tripper and Maisie followed the gurney out to the ambulance. "I'll go with him," said Tripper's wife, Molly. She wasn't really asking anyone's permission. "I'm a doctor."

"Okay, Doc," said one of the guys, and then climbed in. The door was shut and the beacons flashed and off they went, over the green hills of the graveyard.

Inside the meetinghouse, one of the Quaker elders was sweeping Wailer's ashes up with a dustpan and a broom. A few stunned mourners were still sitting in their pews.

Outside the meetinghouse, Maisie stood still. "Where's my brother?" she said. Tripper was looking at the graves of Friends.

"What?" said Tripper. He seemed surprised to see her. "What's this now?"

"Ben," said Maisie. She was looking all around the graveyard, but there was no sign of him. "He never came in. He was behind us in the graveyard, then he said he wanted to take a moment to look at the old headstones."

"Oh, for fuck's sake, now he's *lost?*" said Tripper. He took the pocket square out of his jacket and mopped his forehead with it. "Jesus fucking Christ," he said. A tall woman standing next to him was looking at Tripper curiously.

"I'm sorry," said Tripper. "Do I know you?"

Drivers honked their horns angrily at Ben Lenfest as he swerved from one lane to the next. The car he had stolen had license plates from Maine. He hoped the owner would not mind. Of course, if they'd minded so much maybe they shouldn't have left the key fob in the cup holder.

Cars honked again. It hurt his feelings. What did they expect? Maisie had driven him when he was little, but then she said, *You're not my problem anymore.* He used to enjoy their drives together in the morning. Listening to Joe Garagiola on WFLN. And a guy named Ralph Collier, who did a little monologue each day called *One Man's Opinion.* He felt a little bad about taking the car, but he'd had to make a spur-of-the-moment decision. He'd been lucky—the plan was never going to work without a little serendipitous assistance. But then, *Gratias agimus Deo!*—here it was! Inspiration from on high! The hairy man had yanked Rachel Steinberg into the car and made her drive off through the graveyard, and Ben was the only one who'd seen. And so just like that room had opened up for a hero, and that hero was himself.

He turned on the radio. WMMR in Philly. Once it had been run by mixed-up hippies but now it had been taken over by corporate assholes, same as everywhere. They were playing a song by the Beatles.

Hey, Jude. Ne facias aliquid malum. Cantum tristem elige, et fac meliorem. The minute you let her under your skin. Res meliores facere incipis.

They'd piled into the Tesla, Tripper behind the wheel, Maisie beside him in the passenger seat, the tall woman from Maine in the back. She'd introduced herself as Judith. Now she was monitoring their progress on her cell phone.

"I'm so mortified," Maisie said.

"All I want is my car back," said the woman. "So I can leave. I shouldn't have come here."

Tripper looked in the rearview mirror. "I swear I know you from somewhere."

"Were you a friend of Wailer's, Judith?" asked Maisie.

The stranger thought about it. "I knew her when I was young," she said.

Maisie turned around and gave Judith a hard once-over. "Did we know you?"

Judith shook her head. "Not really."

"Where's he now?" said Tripper. They were on the expressway. The woman looked at her phone. When she'd realized her car was missing, she also remembered that her iPad was in the trunk. She used the tracking app to see where her iPad was, and there it was, a moving blue dot on the highway. "He's near the art museum," the woman said.

There was a long pause. "What the fuck is he up to?" asked Tripper.

"I should call the house," said Maisie. "Tell the caterers the reception is off."

Tripper shook his head. "You're really thinking about the caterers? At this moment? You don't see what he's done."

"Ben, you mean?" said Maisie. "What's he doing?"

Tripper muttered under his breath. "You didn't see—ah—*Rachel* before we left did you?"

"I didn't," said Maisie.

"Rachel?" said Judith from the backseat. "This is Rachel Steinberg you're talking about?"

"Yes," said Maisie. "Did you know her?

"I used to."

Tripper looked at Judith in the rearview mirror once more. A strange expression slowly spread across his face.

"Of course," said Tripper to himself.

"Of course what?" said Maisie.

The Schuylkill River came into view on their right. Out on the water young people in boats strained against their long oars.

"You want to tell her?" said Tripper, glancing in the mirror at Judith once more. "Or you want me to do it?"

26

Philadelphia, Pennsylvania

We pulled up at the prison and got out of the Tesla and then stood there on the sidewalk looking up at the old towers as adults walked by in costumes. A banner fluttered from the high stone walls. TERROR BEHIND THE WALLS. OPENING NIGHT. The sun was sinking low.

"Why would he drive here?" said Maisie. "Oh my God, this horrible place."

Tripper grumbled to himself. "You see your car?" he asked.

"Yeah, there it is," I said, nodding toward the Prius with the Maine plates. We walked over and found the vehicle unlocked and empty. The key fob was in the cup holder, right where I'd left it.

"God, look at you," Maisie said, taking me in.

"Yeah, well," I said. "Look at *you,* Maisie."

Tripper shook his head. "Un-fucking-believable."

"It all makes sense now," said Maisie. Her eyes were shining. "And—you're happy?"

"Well," I said, "maybe not at this exact second."

Tripper rolled his eyes. "Un-fucking-be-*liev*-able," he said again.

"You didn't have to vanish, though," said Maisie. "That was mean, Quentin. A lot of people cried a lot of tears over you."

I stood there thinking about how to respond. Maisie wasn't wrong. "It's Judith," I said.

Maisie turned to Tripper. Now he was looking up at the prison. "What do you think, Tripper?"

"Of what?"

"Of *her*."

"Let's just go in and get Benny, okay? Have our big reunion later maybe?" said Tripper. "I want this to be—" He took a step toward the entrance, then he stopped. The car next to mine had a decal in the back window: NETHER PROVIDENCE ANIMAL SHELTER. And a bumper sticker: KEEP THE TAILS WAGGING! SPAY YOUR PET!

"I still don't see why he'd come here, of all horrible places," said Maisie.

"It's like a salmon going upstream to spawn," Tripper said. "Back to where it was—" He looked at the car with the bumper sticker again. "Aw, no, no, *nooo*!" He clutched his forehead with one hand. "You've *got* to be kidding me," said Tripper. "Oh for fuck's sake."

"What?" said Maisie. "Tripper, what's wrong? Whose car is that?"

For a moment Tripper stood there, gears whirling around in his brain. "It's all happening," he said, stunned. "It's happening again."

"Wait," I said. "What's happening?"

Tripper didn't explain. He rushed toward the entrance, and Maisie and I followed behind. A moment later we were going down the stairs into the sunken foyer. Where once there had been rubble and the eyes of feral cats there was now a gift shop selling costumes and T-shirts and fashionable tote bags. Tripper ran straight through the gift shop and up the stairs on the other side, out into the prison yard. A moment later Maisie and I were alone in the stone foyer.

"Listen," said Maisie. We were at the bottom of the stairs. I thought we were going to rush after Tripper, but instead she turned to me.

"What?"

"I'm thinking," she said. "Maybe it isn't such a good idea for you to be here."

"You think I want to be here, Maisie?"

"That's not what I mean. It's Tripper. I think he's—" She looked up the stairs. "I don't know."

I followed her gaze. I could just see the far wall from here, out on the other side of the prison yard. A searchlight played against it.

"It was you, wasn't it?" I said. "You and Tripper."

Maisie opened her mouth, then shut it. Her eyes shimmered. "I said you should go."

"But why?" I asked. "Can you tell me that? Wailer never did anything to you."

"It wasn't supposed to be Wailer," Maisie said. "It was supposed to be that *asshole*, Nathan Krystal."

I thought about my old teacher. He had seen something in me, a long time ago, when I had seen nothing of value in myself. It was Herr Krystal who had woken me up, made me take myself seriously, even when I lacked a name for the thing I felt.

"He wasn't an asshole. I owe my life to him. He lifted me up."

"I thought I saw him do something to Benny, okay?" Maisie explained. "At a party. I wanted to send him a message to leave my brother alone. Tripper was supposed to hire some guy to rough him up. Instead he found this *idiot*, who . . . It was an accident. None of it was supposed to happen."

I took this in. "So we should tell the police," I said. "We should call them right now. Tell them the truth."

I wanted to reach out to Maisie, to embrace her for the first time as a sister. It was strange to be talking to her now at the age of fifty-seven, without any walls between us. But then I wondered if this was true. There are plenty of walls between people, and gender, in the end, may turn out to be the least of them.

"Listen to you," said Maisie.

"Yeah, goddammit," I said. "Listen to me."

Maisie nodded grimly. "If telling the truth was so easy, I bet it would be more popular."

"I didn't say it was easy. I said you should do it."

"Oh, Quentin," said Maisie. "You really shouldn't have come back."

She leaned forward and kissed me on the cheek. Then she turned her back and climbed the stairs into the prison yard, following in Tripper's footsteps.

"It's Judith," I said.

There was a long moment of silence. Then a voice said, "Or Cassandra."

I turned around slowly, slowly. An overweight man, sweating profusely, stood in the door.

"What?"

"I said Cassandra," he said. He was out of breath. "Cassandra *Horton*. You've used that one too."

"I'm sorry?" I said. "Are you here for the thing, the . . . Terror Behind the Walls?" I pointed into the prison yard. "It's through there."

"Terror behind the fuckin' *walls*," he said contemptuously. He handed me a card. *Daniel Dudley, Philadelphia Homicide (Ret.)*.

I stared at him, and the card, and then back at him again. "You're not in costume," I said.

The prison yard of Eastern State was full of monsters: Frankensteins, Reagans, Creatures from the Black Lagoon. A group of guys walked by wearing prison stripes. They were all chained together. A guard with a handlebar mustache had his plastic gun trained upon them all.

"Help!" Rachel shouted. "Somebody!"

"Nobody's helping you now," said the guard.

"This is real!" Rachel shouted.

"*This is real!*" the prisoners shouted back.

"You like cats, Maisie?" asked Gurganis. They were walking around the inner perimeter.

"Do I what?"

"Like. Cats." He sounded irritated with her. "That retard brother of yours always wanted a cat, why didn't you just let him have one? Could have spared everyone all this bullshit."

"He's not my brother," said Rachel. "Why don't you believe me?"

"You'd say anything right now to get away. Wouldn't you?"

"Let me go! Fuck you, let me *go*!"

Rachel wrenched her arm away from Gurganis's grip and began to run, but he grabbed her again. He yanked Rachel down along the prison yard as she screamed without pause. A trio of college students looked over at them—there was a Harry and a Hermione, and a Ron. Good times.

"He's trying to kill me, somebody, *help*!"

Hermione pointed her wand at Gurganis and said, *"Avada Kedavra!"* The spell didn't work.

"Stop it, Maisie," said Gurganis. "Enough."

Rachel kept screaming. Gurganis pressed the gun to her temple. "I said *stop it*." Rachel stopped screaming, but she was breathing hard now, and tears were running out of her eyes. "You can get out of this, if you act like a good girl."

Rachel choked on a sob. "Can I?" she said.

Gurganis didn't respond. He stared at her for a long beat, then pushed her forward again.

"I didn't *do* anything," said Rachel.

"Exactly," said Gurganis. He stuffed the gun into his belt. Ahead of them was a small marble statue of a cat, its tail raised, poised by the high wall.

These words were engraved upon a plaque next to it:

IN HONOR OF Dan McCloud, Caretaker of Eastern State Prison during the years the property lay abandoned. He fed the pride of feral cats that lived on these grounds for twenty-one years. This statue is placed here in memory of the man who cared for this historic property, as well as to the animals that he loved.

Gurganis reached into his pocket and got out an Almond Joy bar. "Here, you want half of this?"

"I don't want a fucking *candy* bar," said Rachel.

"No?" said Gurganis, chewing. "What *do* you want, Maisie?"

"I want you to know who I am," she said.

"Yeah," said Gurganis. "Join the fuckin' club."

A man wearing a hooded sweatshirt marked MUHLENBERG rushed past them, collided into Gurganis briefly, then kept running. "Help," Rachel cried out again. "Help me!" The hooded man did not stop.

They continued along the perimeter once more. "You said I could get out of this if I was good?" Rachel said.

"It's not me who's doing this," said Gurganis. They approached a door marked DEATH ROW.

They walked past a half dozen cells, then entered a larger chamber. Gurganis and Rachel moved forward slowly in the dark room, stumbling over pieces of fallen plaster until at last the chair was there before them.

"Okay, pupper," he said.

Tripper walked around the perimeter of the prison yard, the high stone wall to his right, the constellation of cellblocks to his left. His face was hot. He entered Cellblock 1 and for a moment stood in the entrance, staring down the long hall, remembering the last time. That was when everything went once and forever all to shit. It was amazing that one decision, made in haste thirty-five years ago, had been enough to divert the course of his entire life, had been enough to make him into *this* instead of the man he was supposed to be.

But *nothing* had broken the right way, he thought, walking down the cellblock. He should never have gone to Wesleyan, for starters, which even then turned out to be full of pompous freaks and patchouli squirters. The original blueprint had called for Princeton. But it had been a hard year, said Mr. Woodward, his college counselor, and the trouble with Maisie in the fall of his senior year left its toll upon his grades. So instead he followed Quentin and Casey to Wesleyan. And four years later his friends were this ridiculous group of punks and hippies, instead of other young Turks like him. He'd thought of his friends with a kind of detached amusement, as if he were studying them the same way an anthropologist might make notes on a primitive culture.

So he'd learned the strange tongue of Casey, with his marijuana pancakes; and Wailer, with her pink hair and affected brogue; and Rachel, with her boring paintings; and Quentin, the pretentious *fuck* whom Herr Krystal had always loved more than he'd loved Tripper himself. That long summer in Germany had given Tripper the illusion that Quentin had cared for him, that they were friends. But once they got to Wesleyan, he'd made his contempt clear once more. So many times, he'd wanted to say, remember that night with my Tante Senta, in Locarno? The three of us listening to the Ninth Symphony as that poor old woman wept? Remember what you said to me that night, *Alle Menschen werden Brüder?* I believed you when you said that. I thought you were my friend.

But you were never anybody's brother.

Someone cried out from a locked cell to his right. "Hey! Let me outta here!" said a withered old man in tattered rags, an actor. "I didn't do it! Can't you help me, please? I'm innocent!"

"Fuck you," said Tripper.

"You gotta help me!"

"It doesn't matter whether you did it or not," he said. "No one cares." He kept on walking down the hall until he reached the Surveillance Hub. Tripper stood at the center and looked down the long arms of the cellblocks. There were distant shouts, a few moving shadows. He didn't see Rachel, or Gurganis. Tripper looked at his watch.

"Fuck," he said out loud. "Fuck, fuck, fuck." Maybe Maisie was right. They should have turned themselves in years ago, just explained that things got out of hand. But it infuriated him, the whole idea that he'd have to finally accept being someone other than his true self. He'd have to become this joke—a man who'd paid to have someone beaten up years ago, then tried to pass the blame for everything that had gone wrong onto someone else.

"But I'm not that guy!" he cried out loud, and his voice echoed in the Hub. *I'm just someone who was trying to protect a child. So I paid a bully three hundred dollars to punch Nathan Krystal in the nose. It was a good cause, defending poor Benny from Krystal, who should have known better, who should have left that boy alone, who ought to have been paying more attention to which of his students actually had promise, and which ones were just—*

There had to be a way of turning it around, even now, he thought. Of being the person he actually was, instead of this fraud, a man who'd been shunted aside from his actual character on account of a single mistake, a mistake not even his own. He thought of Quentin Pheaney, standing in front of their AP German class with Herr Krystal, Quentin using his skills of mimicry to imitate someone so much more sensitive and scholarly than his actual self. And Herr Krystal had fallen for it! *Can't you see,* he'd wanted to shout. *He's not really that guy! He's imitating a perfect student! And you're falling for it! How can you be so blind? He's not that guy!*

He thought of Quentin and felt the rage seethe up in him again. Of course Quentin had turned out to be a fucking woman. Of *course*! The man that all the women were in love with because he was so sensitive *had never been a man in the first place*! It made him want to scream and laugh and cry out with rage all at once. It wasn't fair that Quentin had had everything that he, Tripper, had ever wanted: looks and charm and the love of others, when they were young—but he had not wanted any of that charm for himself. All along he'd just wanted to be someone else, someone hidden.

"And now he just gets his way!" Tripper shouted. He ran his fingers through his hair. Quentin Pheaney, who had never been here in the first place, got to make his getaway, and live his actual life—while he, Tripper, who had never wanted anything other than to embrace his own greatness, had wound up a clown. And now here I am, he thought, at age fifty-seven, wandering around a fake prison trying to find Clark Gurganis. A man who appeared, after all these years, *to have fucking kidnapped the wrong person.*

It's like I've got a clown magnet, Tripper thought. Some kind of magnets are attracted to iron. *Not mine though!* It makes you wonder: what's the point in even trying to be yourself? The universe doesn't give a shit who you want to be. *You're very clever, young man, very clever.*

But it's clowns, all the way down. He spun and looked down Cellblock 2. He spun one hundred and eighty degrees and stared down Cellblock 9. He spun ninety degrees to the right, and stared down Cellblock 6. Everywhere he looked was another steaming helping of endless stupid.

For a while he just stood there at the center, spinning and thinking. Then he stopped.

"Hey!" shouted the man in the cell down the hall, an actor pretending to be a prisoner. "Is anybody there?"

It was funny how a person got angrier the older they got, Ben thought as he walked through the ruined cafeteria holding the gun. They hadn't done much by way of restoring this part of the prison. It was almost as awful as it had been back in 1980, as best as he could recall, which wasn't very well. He didn't like to think about it.

When he was very small, maybe five years old, he'd gotten frozen outside one time—he'd lost his glasses sledding, and he wandered around in a blur and by the time he got home he couldn't even talk he was so cold. All he could do was cry: *Ahenh, ahenh, ahenh.* Maisie had found him on the front doorstep. He'd been full of shame at how cold he was. Ben wasn't even able to open the door. So he rang the doorbell, and Maisie found him, and said, *Oh you poor lost lamb,* just like that. Then she picked him up and put him down at the kitchen table and she made him some Campbell's Chicken Noodle Soup. It was so hot he couldn't even taste it. She put an ice cube in the bowl to cool it off and he watched the cube shrink and disappear.

There were still bowls and cups here in the old cafeteria. Some of them looked like they'd been put down on the long tables one day in 1971 and left there. He'd read that on Easter Island in Polynesia the hand tools the Rapa Nui people had used to make the giant stone heads were still lying all around the ancient quarry, as if one day the carvers just thought, Fuck this, we're not making giant heads anymore. There'd been an article about it in *Condé Nast Traveler* magazine.

He peeked into the kitchen. "Here, kitty kitty," he said.

Nothing.

She'd sung him "The Whiffenpoof Song" as the ice cubes melted in his chicken noodle soup. It was a long time ago now. *We're poor little lambs who've lost our way. Bah, bah, bah.*

He walked back out into the long hallway with the Walther PPK. Once he had thought it was bizarre, the whole idea of one person taking a gun in their hand, and shooting someone else with it. Now it made more sense, the crap he'd had to listen to over the years and pretend to tolerate. Life on Earth was just one insult to the brain after the next one. It was a shame that you couldn't make everything vanish. Even his magic trick "The Disappearing Egg" didn't really make an egg disappear.

He walked down the cellblock in the direction of the Surveillance Hub. Fallen plaster crackled against the bottom of his shoes. He could hear his footsteps, just like on the stairs of the Bagatelle that time. Maisie, are you there? He'd made plenty of noise going up the steps. But she and Tripper Pennypacker were deep into it, and his sister was moaning and yelling and he just stood there in the doorway. He imitated the sound. It didn't sound the same when he made it; it came out like the sound a leopard might make if it got one of its paws caught in a trap. It was okay that she'd chosen Tripper over him, her own brother. That was the way things worked.

But it would have been nice if just once she'd asked him to sing.

He walked down the long, empty expanse of Cellblock 6. This was another one of the ones they hadn't fixed up yet.

It hadn't been all that hard to find the caveman. There he was, with Rachel Steinberg, looking at the monument to the man who'd cared for the cats. The caveman had fished a candy bar out of his pocket. It had been simple to sneak up on them. The trick, as always, was to divert the subject's attention.

Now he held the Walther PPK in his hand. It was surprisingly heavy. "I played a trick on you," he said.

A voice called out: "Hello? Is someone there?" It was impossible to know if it was from an actual human.

Shannon Savage, a sophomore from the University of Pennsylvania, heard the sound of someone groaning. Oh for Pete's sake, she thought. How had it gotten so late?

People in costumes staggered down Cellblock 1. It was opening night for Terror Behind the Walls. Shannon had hoped to catch up on everything she'd had to leave undone when the body turned up. But she'd forgotten about the Terror thing. THE WORLD'S LARGEST HAUNTED HOUSE BEHIND THE WALLS OF A REAL PRISON, the posters read. And now she was stuck here, her work still undone, people in stupid costumes on every side. She hoped that Professor Sweney would understand. It was just the latest in a series of obstacles to getting anything done at all.

Not the least of which was the body she'd found last Friday, stuffed into the opening for the old escape tunnel. Among the people who'd originally dug that tunnel was the famous bank robber, Willie Sutton, the man who said he robbed banks because "that's where the money was." Sutton and the others had emerged into the streets of Philly, covered with mud. They were only out for an hour or two before the cops rounded them all back up again. Now there was a small exhibit on the 1945 escape. She'd helped write some of the text herself.

She hadn't known it was a body at first. There were things that looked like sticks and some cloth and an old Swiss Army knife. There were initials on the shaft: *J. C.* A round thing had rolled across the floor and stopped at Shannon's feet. She'd looked at the skull. A little hair still clung to it.

Shannon let the skull fall to the floor. "*I am inosant,*" she said.

"But you heard Maisie," I said to the detective. "She admitted it. It was her, and Tripper. Didn't you hear her?"

"I heard her," said Dudley, not that he seemed all that happy about it.

"So you know I didn't have anything to do with the murder," I said. I was sitting in the front seat of his car. "Neither did Casey. It was Tripper, and the guy he hired. It was all an accident."

"Yeah, you know what wasn't an accident?" said Dudley, mopping his neck with his handkerchief. "You rolling that car off the cliff in Canada. People crying their eyes out over somebody who wasn't actually dead."

On the sidewalk in front of us were the members of the Beatles, the early ones. Behind them, a Lady Gaga. One thing led to another.

"It was so long ago," I said.

"Doesn't make it right, Quentin," he said. The poor bastard, I thought. At last he had the solution to Eastern State. But he couldn't let go of Nova Scotia.

"You know," I said gently. "You can use my real name. There'd be no sin in that."

"And you had that legally changed when?" said Dudley crossly.

I felt heat in my cheeks. "Can I ask you one question," I said. "What do you care? Why do you give an *actual fuck*?"

Dudley looked at me, a beaten man. I almost felt bad for him. Whatever it was he'd been expecting, this wasn't it. He'd arrived on the scene after chasing me, apparently, for years, only to find out at this exact moment that someone else was guilty of the crime he'd had his heart set on arresting me for. After all this time, Dudley was so accustomed to pursuing me that my actual innocence just got on his nerves.

He began to speak to me in a different voice, one tinged with defeat. "You like the Animals?" he asked. "You know, the band? They had a song 'We Gotta Get Out of This Place.' You ever hear that song?"

"Everybody knows that song," I said.

"Well, you're somebody who did," said Dudley.

"Did what?"

Dudley nodded, as if the world were beginning to make sense to him, although not in the way he had hoped. "Got *out*," he said.

"Detective Dudley," I said. "Are you—like me? Are you trans too?"

"What?" said Dudley. "Me? Ha!"

"It's funny?"

"I like women, all right?" said Dudley.

"Good on you, Detective Dudley," I said.

"I've *always* liked women," he went on. "It's just—they've never liked me. That's why I, you know."

"What did you do?" I said to the man. A mummy, trailing gauze, disappeared into the entrance to Terror Behind the Walls, and now the area outside the old prison was deserted again. All at once we were the only people in the world, retired old Detective Dudley and me. "Dear God. What did you *do?*"

"It doesn't matter," he said. "People do all kinds of stupid shit."

"Whatever you did," I said. "You should forgive yourself. Whatever this is. It can't be worth all this grief."

"You don't get to forgive yourself!" the detective shouted, suddenly as angry as I'd ever seen anyone. "That's not your job!"

"What are you talking about, of course you can."

"You can forgive others," said Dudley. "Only the Lord can forgive *us.*"

"Really?" I said. "The *Lord*. Is that what they taught you?"

"It's the truth," said Dudley. "What, you think the world should go like, everybody just does whatever the fuck they want, and then, it's all fine, because they forgive themselves? That's not how it works. You can forgive everybody else for what they do, but you don't get to let yourself off the hook. Everything you've done is yours to carry."

"Detective Dudley," I said. Everything was very quiet. "You're forgiven." I made the sign of the cross, touched my thumb to his forehead. "There. I absolve you."

Dudley swore at me, and pulled out his gun, and pointed it at me. His hands were shaking. "Don't make *fun* of what I believe."

"I wasn't," I said. "I was trying to help."

"Fuck you. Just because you rose from the dead doesn't make you Jesus," he said.

"Well, I'm not him," I said. I reached toward him and gently lowered the muzzle of his service revolver. "I'm not him."

"You're fucking right you're not him. You're the *opposite* of him."

"Now, now," I said. "I absolved you. There's no reason to call people names."

He heaved a long sigh. "So what am I gonna do? Just let you go?"

"It'd be one solution," I said.

We sat there in stalemate.

But then he said, "I'm not like you. I could just use a little vacation once in a while. From myself, I mean."

"Yeah?" I said. I opened the door. "Who else would you be? Instead of you?"

"Oh, I'd still be me, Judith," said Dudley, in a tone of voice that suggested I was stupid not to know this already. "I just wouldn't feel so *crappy* about it."

❧

The light was on in the library. A girl was dusting the books. This room had been fixed up since 1980. The girl looked over at Ben fearfully. She was standing right where the caveman had stood all those years ago.

"I'm not . . . you, who are you?" she said.

"What?" said Ben.

"I'm sorry," she said. "I'm not very good at talking."

"I, uh, I'm not, that either so good." He looked around nervously. "Henh, heh, henh." He picked at the cuticles on his fingers.

"I'm Shannon."

"Ben."

"You're not wearing, uh a costume, Ben," said Shannon.

"No costume except my costume," said Ben. He held up the gun. "And this."

"Wow," said Shannon. "That looks so realistic."

"It is realistic," said Ben. "I took it off some caveman guy."

She smiled gently. "Can I help you with something?" She stood there with books in her arms.

"I, uh," said Ben. He looked around the library. He remembered that guy standing in the corner, him and his beard. *You tell anyone you saw me, I'll cut you.* "I'm so tired."

"Do you want to sit down?" said Shannon, nodding toward a leather chair in the corner. There was a little table next to it, and on the table a lamp. The room was like something out of Sherlock Holmes. She'd fixed it up. There were books by Calvino and Hobbes. In one corner was a heavy iron safe.

"Yeah, okay," said Ben, sitting down. He felt the air go out of him. "Ahenh," he said, convulsing with a sudden sob. "Ahenh, ahenh, ahenh."

"Wait," said Shannon. "Are you crying?"

Ben nodded. Shannon got some tissues out of her purse and handed him one. "See, I had a cat one time," said Ben. "But somebody. This guy."

"I'm sorry," said Shannon. She was looking at him carefully.

"People just take things from you," said Ben, looking at the gun he'd stolen.

Shannon nodded. She looked down at the book in her hand. *The Princess Bride.* "Have you read this?" she said.

Ben wanted to respond, but now he was crying again. He wiped his eyes with the tissue. Then he said something so softly Shannon could not hear it.

"What?" she asked.

"*The Cliffs of Insanity,*" he said softly.

"You really are all broken," said Shannon. "I thought I was broken, but you're *really* broken. You must be the all-time champion."

Ben nodded. "I didn't have to be," he said.

"It doesn't make you the only broken person," said Shannon. "That's what I learned. Everybody's black and blue, somewhere. I never met anybody who wasn't."

"Not like me."

"No," said Shannon. "Everybody gets broken all their own way." She smiled bitterly. "That's what makes you, you: the pieces you're smashed into aren't like anybody else's. They're all yours." She blew some air through her cheeks. "I told you I can't talk," she said.

I'd taken my leave of Detective Dudley. Ten minutes later, there I was, wandering around the prison yard, surrounded by young men and women whose sole source of joy was irony. I tried not to hate them. There was a time when I too had thought everything was hilarious, and who can say who's cornered the market on the truth of such things, the young or the old? It might well be that the young, in their monster costumes and their Sexy Nurse fishnets, were closer to the life force at this hour than my own ragged self. So what could I do but pass them by, and keep on looking? It was the thing I knew.

Still, no sign of Rachel, which was just as well, perhaps. I'd had my chance back in the day, hadn't I, night after night at Wesleyan U in the dark in a Foss Hill dormitory, as she whispered to me, *Quentin, I'm yours,* and I'd failed to follow through. Following through, such as it was, was hardly even on my radar, to be honest. All I'd wanted—then as now—was to be in love.

So I don't know, maybe I wasn't entitled to a mulligan, especially what with the vagina and everything. My experience up until this point had suggested that life allowed for plenty of do-overs, of course, but it was not impossible that I'd never really understood the fundamental indignities of time travel, that I'd failed from the beginning to get my mind around the difference between the first go-round as tragedy and the second go-round as farce.

But then I heard her voice. *Help me! Somebody!* All at once, she was close at hand. A door before me led into a small cellblock built between the others. There were a few abandoned cells on the right and a big fuse box on the wall from which cables spewed like a collection of aortas.

I drew near. "Who's there?" she said, and just like that she was in the shadows before me: the girl I had been searching for, in my own blind way, all these years. *I am so sorry*, I wanted to say to her. *I didn't have the words.*

"I'm not Maisie!" she shouted. "You have to believe me!"

"I know who you are," I said.

There was a long pause. Then she said, "Quentin?" as if to even call me by my deadname was an embarrassment, as if she were admitting that she had given herself over entirely to hallucination.

Now it was my turn to pause. What could I say to her now? "I'm here," I said at last, but even as I said it, an inner voice inquired, *Ya think?*

"You're not—dead?" she asked. She couldn't quite see me in the dark.

"Dead?" I said. It was a good goddamned question. "No," I said. "Not anymore."

"How can you possibly be here?"

"I'm not sure I can explain that," I said.

"You're not going to hurt me, are you? Please don't hurt me."

Of all the things she could have said, this was perhaps the saddest, the idea that, returning from the dead, I could have brought her anything other than love. "No, Rachel," I said. "I'm trying to save you."

I got closer. I reached forward like a blind person and felt her face with my hands. The cheek and nose and eyes. She was strapped into the chair.

"Quentin!" she said. "It *is* you!" She knew me from my fingers.

I felt around for the buckles on the straps.

"I'm so sorry," I said. "I didn't know how to do it."

"Do what?" she said.

I thought about Jake yelling at me. *Not her!* I wanted to open my heart to her, but experience had taught me better.

A sudden sob convulsed Rachel. I wanted to take her in my arms and say, Yeah, that's what it's like exactly. But I had to keep my distance. It wouldn't help anyone if I took her in my arms.

"I'm confused," she said. "I can't see you."

"I don't want you to see me," I said.

"What happened, are you—deformed?"

"Yeah," I said. "No. I'm sorry. I just—"

I thought about it, but at this point all I could feel was exhaustion with her, with the whole teeming world of people who are not transgender, with their endless questions and interrogations. Enough already. I'm sorry, but I have to ask: What is wrong with you people? Does every human soul really require an explanation before she can be deemed worthy of human kindness? Does compassion for one's fellow humans really demand a test first?

"I'm sorry I said no," Rachel said. I was struggling with her straps. "Back then."

"I'd have wrecked your life," I noted. She had her right arm free now.

"I'm sure that's not true," said Rachel.

"I'm sure it is. You don't know how lucky you were, winding up with that Backflip Bob."

"Backflip Bob," she said, like I'd said Clarabelle the Clown. "He wasn't the one. It was you. Who was my soul mate."

"There's no such thing."

"Oh. I don't—"

I undid her final strap. "Look," I said. "You're free."

She reached for me in the dark. Her fingers brushed my cheek.

"Don't come closer," I said, pushing her back. "Don't touch me."

"Why not?" she said. "Quentin—"

"Remember me like I was, okay?" I said. Somehow, freeing her from her bonds just pissed me off. Maybe I was jealous, that for her it was simply a matter of unbuckling some straps. Nice work if you can get it, I thought. For the rest of us, things weren't so simple.

"What are you?" she asked. It was a good question.

"Just go," I said. "Don't make me explain. Spare me."

"But I love you—" she said. "I've always loved you."

"If you love me, just go. We had our time. Okay?"

"But—"

"Go!" I was so angry I didn't know what to do. She heard it in my voice. Rachel wandered out of the chamber and down death row and then out into the prison yard. I watched her leave.

As she emerged into the light, she looked behind her, but I wasn't there. A young couple walked by, a man and a woman, their arms around each other. A searchlight from the high tower played against the wall. For a moment it paused upon the couple. They stopped to kiss each other, illuminated.

27

Philadelphia, Pennsylvania

As he walked around the prison yard, looking for Gurganis, Tripper was put in mind of one of those old-fashioned percolators, the kind with the glass bubble in the top. He'd had one back in law school. You'd plug it in and pretty soon brown liquid was squirting against the dome like Old Faithful. Sometimes he'd put on Stravinsky's *Rite of Spring* while the thing was percolating, and he'd pace around and around listening to the violent music and sucking back mug after mug of black coffee. There was a part of the Stravinsky that sounded like the whole orchestra was one big percussion instrument. Like in *Fantasia* when the volcanoes erupt with lava. That, Tripper thought, that is exactly what it feels like now.

He paused to lean against the side of the prison, put out a hand to steady himself. *Easy, Trip,* he thought. Now was not the time for panic. The situation was unfolding, and everything depended on precision and logic. It was just like filing a case with the court of appeals. You figured out the argument and you made it. Part of figuring out the argument, of course, was anticipating the argument of your opponent. Sometimes you could just dismiss them in cross. But it was better to anticipate the defense, so that by the time they even did their opening you'd already made them sound ridiculous.

A guy with tattoos and his skanky girlfriend walked past. For a moment he thought they were in costume. He nodded at them. "Hey," he said.

"Fuck you," the dude replied, and his girlfriend laughed.

"Wanker," said the girl.

Tripper was going to reply in kind, but held his fire. He had to stay on the case. Where was Gurganis? Where had he taken Rachel? He'd take her somewhere private, he guessed. But that didn't narrow it down. The prison, in its half-restored, half-ruined state, was still abundant with private nooks and crannies. There were whole cellblocks that hadn't even been touched yet. They could be anywhere.

The tattooed dude and his girlfriend opened the door into Cellblock 2. A chorus of desperate cries greeted them. "Help me!" yelled a prisoner, or someone imitating one. "I didn't do it!"

"Hey," he said in the direction of the now-vanished couple. "Fuck you too." He said it quietly. Once, when he was about seven years old, he'd been driving in the Volkswagen Beetle with his father and his mother. Tripper was in the kangaroo pouch, in back. They'd gone to a Burger King for dinner, which was a big deal back then: fast food was new in 1965, the whole idea shiny and entertaining. His father had gone to the counter and tried to order "a black-and-white milkshake," and the woman at the register had no idea what he was talking about. It's vanilla or chocolate, she tried to explain, but his father just got infuriated. He was talking to her as if he were still a boy in 1935, talking to the soda jerk behind the fountain. "It's vanilla ice cream with chocolate syrup," he said, enraged. The woman behind the counter started to cry. It's just vanilla or chocolate, she sobbed. Those are the flavors. Tripper's dad was like that, always disappointed that the world he lived in kept on changing.

On the way home that night they'd been stopped at a red light, and a guy on a big Harley had pulled up next to them. They waited, tensely, at the light for a long time, the Harley's engine going *potato-potato-potato*. There was an Atlantic station on the corner that a few years later would become an Arco. On the opposite corner was an Esso station that would soon become an Exxon. The old signs down, the new ones up. The guy on the Harley turned to Tripper's dad and said, "Fuck you." The light changed, and he roared off on his hog.

Dad put the car in gear. They drove home in silence. Clearly if a greaser said *Fuck you* at random on the way back from a Burger King, there was nothing else to do except endure it stoically.

But Tripper had been amazed, that the world contained people who could just tell your own father to *fuck off,* and then be on their way.

"Wanker," observed a voice once more. He looked up, but he saw no one. Tripper looked down the long, and now-empty prison yard. From inside the decaying penitentiary came the cries of the incarcerated.

For a moment he stood there, looking down the yard. The tree he'd climbed, all those years ago, was visible at the far corner. He remembered crawling out on that limb as the rain came down.

I should climb it now, he thought. I should climb that tree and get the hell out of here. Why should Quentin Pheaney be the only one to get free? I could drive to Nova Scotia my own self, push my car off a cliff. If Quentin could do it, anyone could do it. All you had to do was have the dream of a life bigger than—

"Ye fuckin' *yob,*" said the voice again. Tripper spun around. There was no one.

"Wailer?"

"Cunt. Arsehole. Dog shite."

"Where are you!" he shouted.

"Well, why not use your eyes for once in your life ye insufferable fucking fuck."

He turned toward Cellblock 3, and there she was, leaning against the wall. She had a Richard Nixon mask on.

"How are you alive?" he said.

"How are *you* alive, you fuck?"

Tripper raised the gun and pointed at her. "Take off that mask," he said.

"You take yours off first."

Tripper rushed toward her. Wailer ducked into Cellblock 9. This was one of the blocks that had not been restored. It was dark. Parts of the ceiling had fallen in. There were piles of plaster on the floor. Tripper heard her footsteps receding, then they stopped. He stood still for a moment, listening, but he heard nothing except the sound of his own breathing.

Then, following his long, reluctant habit, he stepped once more into the dark.

"Thank you, Detective," said Maisie into her cell phone, then put it back in her pocket. She heaved a long sigh. The deed was done.

She sat down on a crumbling wall near the overgrown baseball diamond. She felt strangely relieved, a burden lifted from her, in spite of what she knew might be the grim consequences. She would tell them the whole story now, and let the chips fall where they may. It was possible they'd let her turn state's witness, but who knew? None of that mattered. *Someone will have to take care of Snowy,* she thought. *Someone will have to show Aimee Lupin the proper fingering for the Toccata and Fugue. And someone will have to show Alison Tieter how to perform the role of Little Buttercup.* The world will go on without me. But it will all just be just fine.

It was seeing Quentin—now Judith—that had tipped the scales. She could hardly imagine what the woman's life had been like. But the idea of being so driven by desperation that you felt you had no hope except to erase yourself and start over—well, she thought, maybe in the end that was the rule rather than the exception. There probably wasn't a soul on Earth who hadn't imagined what it would be like, at some point, to get a complete do-over, to head out like Huck Finn, one step ahead of the hellhounds. And yet, Judith seemed like someone solid, unlike Quentin, who at times seemed so close to not being there at all it was a surprise the wind didn't blow through him. There was a sadness to her, but then, you don't get to be a fifty-seven-year-old woman without bearing some sorrow. Really, if there wasn't any melancholy in your heart by this point, you simply weren't paying attention.

She remembered a little song she used to sing for the special-needs kids. It went to the tune of "Dixie." Quentin used to sing it, back in the day. *Oh once I sang a song about a man who got turned inside out, he had to jump, into the river, because it made him so very sleepy.*

"Maisie, this is Shannon, she's my acquaintance now," said Ben, and Maisie turned to see her brother approaching with a pale girl about twenty years old.

"Hello," said Shannon.

"Oh for God's sake," she said. "Ben." She rushed toward him and put her arms around him. "You had me so worried. What were you thinking, taking—ah—that lady's car?"

"He's here, the caveman," said Ben. "He killed Creeper. I stole his gun."

"What did we say," Maisie asked. "About telling stories."

"He's telling the truth," said Shannon. "He took the bullets out. We put them in the safe, in the library."

Maisie looked at Shannon, uncertain. "Who are you again?"

"Shannon. I'm a sophomore," she said.

"I didn't go to college," said Ben. "But I have many of the insights."

"He does have insights," said Shannon. "Ben told me some of what happened here. We learned about—what you all went through—as part of our research. Doing the history of the prison." Shannon seemed strangely self-conscious. "It's a famous case. It's right up there with Willie Sutton and the Escape of '45!"

"Ben, you took that lady's car," Maisie said, as if Shannon had not spoken. "That was a bad thing you did. *Very* bad."

Ben looked down, pulling into himself. He cast a fearful eye at Shannon, and spread the fingers of his hand, as if to explain the situation to her. Ben chewed on his lower lip. He trembled a little bit, his eyes darting around. Shame was creeping up on him.

"I stole someone's car once," said Shannon, giggling. "When I was sixteen. The school principal. He left his keys in the ignition, and I took it to a car wash with the windows open." She laughed wickedly. "I got in *so much trouble!*"

Shannon felt a little dizzy. Why would she mention that business with the car wash now? It wasn't helpful. Still, she had taken a rather strong dislike to Maisie Lenfest. She felt absolutely no compulsion for staying on the woman's good side, assuming she had one.

"It is not easy, doing the right thing," said Maisie, almost to herself. "You can spend your whole life weighing the options. Sometimes people do the right thing kind of as a last resort."

"Ben says—you're a music teacher?" said Shannon.

"Yes," she said, and Maisie's face softened a little. "I teach pipe organ and light opera to special-needs kids."

"That's so cool," said Shannon. "And has Ben ever been a student of yours?"

Maisie looked astonished, as if Shannon had just proposed they all take a voyage to Alpha Centauri. "*Ben?*" she said, incredulously.

"Well, yes," said Shannon, embarrassed that she'd clearly said the wrong thing again, although what exactly was wrong about her question she did not know. "I'd think he might have um . . ."

"Not *Ben*," said Maisie dismissively.

"Oh," said Shannon. "I just thought . . ."

"It's okay," said Ben. "My needs aren't that special."

"You shouldn't say that!" Shannon said. "You should never say that!"

"Why shouldn't he say that?" said Maisie.

Shannon looked down the long prison yard. A guy trailing gauze bandages, like the mummy, was lurching toward them. He said *Rrarrrr*.

"Everybody's needs are special," Shannon said.

This phrase hung between them for a moment, like a helium balloon.

"Aw," said Maisie, bursting it with a pin. "That's adorable."

"It's true!" Shannon flushed. She was going to hold her ground.

"You're an expert on human need?" said Maisie.

Shannon's face turned pink. She didn't like being pushed around by this Maisie Lenfest. It was no wonder Ben was like he was. How terrible to spend your whole life thirstily waiting for the love of someone like this, a person who had no sense of affection or decency.

"I tried going out on the Walt Whitman Bridge and jumping," said

Shannon. "I mean. And jumping." She felt her throat close up. Maisie Lenfest didn't seem moved by Shannon's story—the opposite, in fact. She looked like she was going to smack her. Oh, I've said too much, Shannon thought. I have to get out of here, and quick. These two are in a lifelong headlock, and I can't get between them.

"*Iiiii,*" said Ben, suddenly. It was a long, drawn-out note. Maisie looked at him uncomfortably. Then at Shannon. Then at Ben again.

"Very nice, Ben," she said. "Now. Shall we get out of here? The police are coming. They'll find your caveman."

"*Iiiii,*" Ben groaned again. "*I'mmm—*"

"Ben, what is this noise?"

"*I'm called little Buttercup,*" Ben began again. He turned toward Shannon. "*Dear little Buttercup.*"

"What are you doing?" said Maisie. "Stop it."

"*Though I could never tell why!*" he sang, more confidently now.

Maisie stood there, stunned. Ben folded his fingers together and put them next to his cheek and looked at Shannon adorably.

Shannon Savage stood there entranced. "He's called Buttercup," she observed, delightedly.

"Ben, I asked you what you think you're doing?"

But Ben just smiled from ear to ear. He reached into his pocket, and then he waved his hands around. Out of thin air the broken man produced a blue silk handkerchief.

"*Still I'm called Buttercup,*" he continued. "*Dear little Buttercup. Sweet little Buttercup, I!*"

"Maisie," said Shannon. She couldn't believe she had to explain it. Wasn't it obvious? "He's *singing.*"

28

Philadelphia, Pennsylvania

There I was, sitting behind the wheel of my car. I had no idea where I was headed next. Where could I go? The prison in which I'd once been trapped stood before me, its doors wide open.

I imagined the long drive north, a ferry ride across the Bay of Fundy, the drive along the coast ending with the car rolling off a cliff again. This time I could do the thing right and stay in it. I pictured myself ringing the doorbell at the Whitakers' bed and breakfast. They'd be old now. *Ah, Judith,* Mrs. Whitaker would say. *We've been expecting you.*

This time I'd try their fucking jam, all right. *Is there anyone you want to call? You can use our phone.* But I was all done with that.

As long as I'd lain in the heart of my family, with Falcon and Jake, making dinners and walking Gollum, listening to the loons on the pond, I'd remained invincible. But there was my mother's name on that stone. I'd reached out and touched the letters with my fingers.

I remembered Grainne looking at my passport photo, before I went to Germany with Tripper. *Is there something you want to tell me? You know I will always love you, no matter what.* Why had I not taken her at her word? Why had I thought that she'd have closed her heart?

Then I thought of Jake, pointing at me and crying out with that terrible voice. *Not her!* I had wanted so dearly to believe in a world in which love would prevail. But day after day I was brutally reminded of the many ways in which that world was not this one.

On the other hand, I thought, I appeared to have just saved Rachel from something. I'd found her in the dark, undid the straps, and set her free, the woman that I once loved, the person who, a long time ago, had first shown me what it might mean to live a woman's life with art and grace. It wasn't exactly an antidote for the trouble I'd brought about with my husband. But it was, in some small way, setting a wrong to right.

The doors of the prison swung open and a man came stumbling out of Eastern State. He was a short, squat man with a big head of hair and a beard like shredded wheat. He looked up and down the street, raised one hand to his forehead, then ran it down over his face. He staggered over to the wall and put one palm on the stone, a tableau of mortal sadness. I had done something like this myself when I touched my mother's headstone.

I put my fingers on the button to start the ignition. But I couldn't quite press it.

The hairy man was shaking now.

I know I should have left him alone. His trouble was not mine. But old habits die hard. I got out of the car. "Excuse me," I said. "Are you all right?"

The hairy man raised his head to look at me. "Oh, I don't guess so," he said.

We had a little standoff for a few moments. Then I said, "Is there anything I can do for you?"

The stranger thought it over for a while. "A time machine would be good."

I wondered what his story was, what he'd gone through to reduce him to an idiot weeping by the side of the walls of a former prison. The sign above his head read: TERROR BEHIND THE WALLS. I went back to the car and got a roll of Breath Savers out of my purse and then returned to find the man still standing there staring. I handed it to him.

"I don't have a time machine, but here's a breath mint."

"Okay," he said. He crunched into the Breath Saver. It was gone quickly. He blew some air through his cheeks. "I hate this place," he said.

I nodded. "I hate it too." I paused. "You mean, the prison? Or, like, Earth?

"Ha," he said. "The prison, I meant. Every time I come here I wind up facing the truth," he said. "Which is what I hate."

"What's this truth?" I said.

He didn't want to say. Tears quavered at the edge of his eyelashes.

"Hey," I said, and pointed toward the passenger door. "Why don't you sit down for a minute." He walked to the far side of my car and sat down in the bucket seat. "Here you go," I said, handing him the mints again. He pulled another one off and crunched it up. "I want you to keep that whole roll."

"You're a nice lady," he said. For a moment he sat there snuffing. A few people wearing costumes came out of the prison, laughing. A sexy nurse. A Romney. There was a girl in fishnets who looked frightened. She was trying to hide it from her friends.

"How come you hate this place?" I said.

"Why *wouldn't* you," he said.

"What happened to you?" I asked. "Did something happen to you in there?"

He sighed, like a broken man. "I messed something up. Like I always do. Every single time!"

A police siren wailed in the distance. "You have to forgive yourself," I said to him.

"Does that work?" he said.

I shrugged. "I don't know," I said. "I'm still working on it."

A cop car turned onto the street that led up to the prison. The blue and red lights blinked against the high prison wall.

We sat there for a moment. The stranger looked restless.

"Can you take me somewhere?" he asked.

"Where do you want to go?" I asked him.

He pointed toward the horizon. "Wild blue yonder."

"Okay," I said. I figured if I did this one good thing that at least there'd be one gesture that might count in my favor. It wasn't enough to counter all the trouble I was responsible for, but it was one more thing, like that operatic gesture I'd performed for Rachel in that nasty-ass electric chair. An act of charity.

"How about Atlantic City?" I said. It was closer than Nova Scotia.

"Yeah okay," he said. He pulled an envelope out of his pocket, stuffed with cash. "I got all this money."

I kind of blinked at the wad of cash. "Wow, you're loaded," I said. I remembered hitting the jackpot, all those years ago, when I took the ferry to Canada. That girl in the satin top had asked me, *What's your secret,* and what could I tell her? *Just lucky I guess.*

I started the car and we pulled out. I looked at Eastern State Penitentiary in my rearview mirror. We wouldn't be coming back.

"Atlantic City," he said. "It ain't wild. But it's blue."

❧

The heart monitor was beeping, one for the systolic, one for the diastolic. Casey heard it in his dreams even before he woke up. He heard it as he traversed the dark territory leading away from the dream-space. When he realized he was awake, he opened his eyes. A woman was sitting in a chair next to him. She was reading a clipboard.

"Hey," he said. "I'm alive and junk!"

The woman looked at him and smiled. He was wired up to a number of machines. She looked at the green LED readout next to his hospital bed. "Yes," she said thoughtfully. "You are alive and junk."

There was a movement at the door. An African American woman came in and looked at him. "Detective Gleeson!" said Casey. "Are you okay?"

"Mr. Casey," she said. "You're awake." She looked at the woman. "He'll live?"

"He's doing just fine," said the woman.

"Do I know you?" said Casey.

"I'm Molly Pennypacker," she said. She put down her knitting. "I'm an ER doc. Tripper's wife."

"Oh yeah, yeah," said Casey. "I made you the lobster jambalaya that time!"

"I'm glad you're feeling better," said Detective Gleeson. She nodded, and then went back out in the hallway, taking a position outside the door.

"I'm gonna make you some biscuits!" Casey shouted at the detective.

"Yeah, maybe hold off on the biscuits," said Molly.

"Yeah. Last thing I need's another heart attack. One was plenty!"

"It wasn't a heart attack, Jon Casey. It was a panic attack."

Casey looked ashamed. "Oh yeah," he said. "The funeral. I passed out in the middle of my speech. Oh man. I feel terrible about that. I let everybody down."

"Jon," said Molly. "I need to talk to you."

"Yeah?"

"You're killing yourself," she said. "Is that something you're doing on purpose?"

"What?" he said. "What are you talking about?"

"You're about a hundred fifty pounds overweight. You live on pizzas and lamb chops. You don't exercise."

"I'm busy," said Casey.

"You're going to die," said Molly.

"Yeah," said Casey a little self-consciously. "I guess."

"Well," said Molly, "you shouldn't."

"Why not?" said Casey dejectedly.

Dr. Pennypacker went over to the bed and looked at the patient. She smacked him hard against his big jowly cheeks.

"Wake up," she said.

The heart monitor they had him wired up to started beeping more rapidly. "Okay," he said. "Okay." The monitor's beeping increased. "Hey wait, no way!" he said excitedly. "I just remembered why I passed out. You know who I saw? You know who was there at the service?"

"You need to calm down." Molly looked at the cardio stats on the machine. "Take a deep breath."

"The fuck I will. It was Quentin," he said. "He was sitting in the back of the meeting house. I saw him. I mean, her. I mean—he's, like, I don't know the word for it, but you know, those people, trans-lesbuh-*change-o*-blasters, or whatever? Molly! He . . . She, I mean. She was sitting there, looking at me. And I was like, No way!"

"I'm serious," said Molly. "You need to relax."

"Don't you get it? She's my *friend*. I got her *back*. I was like, *Of course!* Good for you, man! I was so glad for her, and so pissed off, and woo-hoo! It was definitely wonkaly. I am telling you." He took a breath and lay back. "And she can vouch for me too. So I don't have to wind up going to jail. Which, you gotta admit, would be totally bogus." He yelled out into the hallway. "Hey! Detective Gleeson! Get in here! I got a witness!"

But Gleeson was on her radio. She poked her head in the door and raised one finger. "Yeah, okay," she said to the person on the radio. "Okay."

Dr. Pennypacker checked her clipboard again. "I have to say I've been hearing about this Quentin for years," she said. "I hope she's happy now, if the person you think you saw really was her." Molly looked at Casey over the top of her reading glasses. "Did she look happy?"

"Yeah? I think so? I mean, she was at a funeral, so that probably brought her down some." He looked alarmed. "Hey, what happened to Wailer's ashes? Did somebody get the ashes?"

Molly Pennypacker nodded at a paper bag in the corner. "The Quakers swept her up for you."

Casey smiled. "Fuckin' Quakers!" he said. "Awesome!"

Gleeson poked her head back into the room. "I need to head over to Eastern State," she said. "There's an incident in progress."

"What?" said Casey. "No, wait, listen! I got a witness. My friend Quentin Pheaney's alive! I got somebody to prove I'm innocent, okay?"

Gleeson nodded. "That'd be good news for you, if it's true. But I have to go." She looked at Molly Pennypacker. "Can you keep an eye on him?"

She nodded. "I can do that."

Gleeson headed out. "An incident," Casey said. "I wonder what's up."

Molly sighed. "I'd be surprised if my husband wasn't at the center of it, whatever it is."

Casey thought about it. His heart monitor started beeping just a little more swiftly again. "What's the deal on him, anyway?"

She nodded. "Listen, Casey," she said. "You might as well know. He's a bad man."

"Well, hell," Casey said. "*I* could have told you that."

She nodded. Her eyes shimmered a little bit.

"But you know what?" said Casey. "*I'm* not a bad man."

"No," said Molly. "You're not. Just a very large, unhealthy one."

"Yeah," said Casey. "I know." He thought about Quentin, about how she had looked, sitting there at the back of the meetinghouse. He remembered the last time they had been together, back in the cemetery. He'd said, *You're going to be okay,* and Quentin had said, *I love you.* And Casey said, *Well, why wouldn't you?*

"Wish I had my ukulele," Casey said, looking over at Molly Penny-packer. She had sad eyes. A lot of people had them.

29

Walt Whitman Bridge

We crossed the Delaware by way of the Walt Whitman Bridge, *die Whitmanbrücke*. The tires of my car hummed below us. I saw the lights of a tanker on the river. A big ship, headed out to sea.

"Boats against the current," said Clark contemptuously.

I remembered my Whitman translation project from the summer of 1980, how I'd worked on that fucker day after day in my bedroom on the third floor of my mother's house with my door locked. As I worked I wore a bra and a blue knit top and a black skirt. So I wouldn't get distracted. When I wasn't wearing that gear I'd kept it stashed in a secret panel below my window. A nice thing about growing up in an old house: all the hidey-holes. In addition to the skirt and the top I had a few other things stashed in there. A pair of clip-on earrings. A copy of Betty Friedan's *The Feminine Mystique*. I can still remember the opening paragraph, in which she lamented the sense of dissatisfaction in the hearts of American women. I was well aware, as I sat there translating *Leaves of Grass* into German, that Betty probably wasn't thinking of me as someone who was suffering from the problem she was describing.

But you should have, Betty, I thought. *You should have.*

"What's that?" I said.

"Boats against the stupid *current*," said Clark Gurganis. "From the ending of *The Great Gatsby*. Isn't that how it goes?" He ran his hand through his beard. "Something about how we're all rowing boats against the current but we're idiots if we think *that's* going to do anything."

I thought about it. At one time I could have recited the passage. But now I couldn't quite come up with it.

We reached the other side of the Walt Whitman Bridge. I remembered how once there'd been a liquor store situated on the Jersey banks of the river, back when the drinking age had been twenty-one in Pennsylvania but eighteen in New Jersey. I'd made the Jersey run with Casey a bunch of times in high school. We'd felt so sophisticated. We drove back across the bridge bearing our treasure: bottles of Southern Comfort, sloe gin, Kahlua.

"That has got to be the worst book ever written," Clark said.

I remembered the first time I ever went into a bar—I was with Tripper and Casey and this other friend of ours, Otto. Atlantic City, New Jersey, summer of 1975. We went into a place called the Sand Bar, underage, thinking we were very tough. Ordered four white Russians. Which was Kahlua with milk. A hooker in the corner cast an eye our way and smiled. Four preppy boys from the suburbs, drinking milk at the bar.

"Wait, what?" I said.

Clark pressed the electric window of my Prius all the way down and stuck his head out like he was a St. Bernard. The wind blew his hair and beard around. He opened his mouth and the air filled his cheeks. Then he pulled his head back in and shook his head and said, "Blugh, blugh, blugh."

"Why do you hate *The Great Gatsby*?" I said.

He ran his hand down his puffy face. "It's bullshit," he said.

"*The Great Gatsby*?" I said. "Why is it bullshit?"

"All that crap about how you can't make yourself into somebody else, of course you can. Isn't that what we're doing right now, you and me, Judith Carrigan? Takin' a mulligan! You know, I thought I was a loser because of a thing that happened. But now I realize it was a gift. A chance for me to finally be myself."

"Yeah?" I said. "Who's that?"

"A *veterinarian*," he said.

"That's your true self, a veterinarian?"

"Yeah," he said. "I was *gonna* be one, then I got mixed up in all this bullshit."

The road divided before me. I had to choose between the Atlantic City Expressway and the Black Horse Pike. I went with the latter. Because it was more deserted.

"I don't know," I said to Clark. "I guess I look at it a different way."

"Yeah," said Clark. "You're some expert?"

"I've seen some things," I said.

"What do you know, about what I gotta be," he snapped, then heaved a sigh. "I'm sorry," he said. "I didn't mean to be. I'm like, whoa. You can't imagine what I been through. At that place."

"You want to talk about it?"

"No," he said. "I don't think so." He was considering some issues. I took another look at him. Even though he was my age, or nearly, something about the man seemed like an overgrown baby, beard notwithstanding. He was puffy and pink. It had seemed like an act of mercy, giving him a ride. Now I wondered.

He laughed. "You know, even the name of that book shows you how stupid it is, Great Gatsby. He isn't so great."

"What, you think they should have named it, like, *The Above Average Gatsby? The Pretty Good Gatsby?*"

He laughed again. Clark raised and lowered the window on his side of the car like he had never seen electric windows before. Then he reached around to scratch his left shoulder blade with his right hand. He was certainly twitchy, I thought. I remembered how he'd squirmed when he saw the approaching beacons of the police.

"*The Stupid Gatsby,*" he said. "*The Lousy Gatsby.*"

"I wasn't trying to insult you before," I said. "When I asked you about it. I'm just curious why you think it's such a bad book."

"Seriously?" said Clark. "It's like he says, whoever you are when you're twenty years old, that's who you're stuck being forever. Gatsby leaves Fargo or whatever, turns himself into a billionaire so he can impress this girl, right? And that means he has to die? I mean, fuck. I would love a million dollars. What's the point of living if you have to stay in North Dakota forever? Our whole lives are just one big second chance!"

"I don't know if that's true," I said to the stranger. "Sure, you can start over. But everybody needs a past. Otherwise you just turn into a ghost."

"That's not true!" said Clark angrily. "Don't be fuckin' talking that way!"

"I'm not talking any way," I said. "I'm just saying, you have to be careful. Or you wind up having two lives instead of one."

"I *want* to have two lives," shouted Clark. "That's the whole point!"

"Nobody gets to live twice," I said.

"So what, you think everybody just has to stay the same, forever? Whatever awful thing you did, that's who you are for good?"

"Not exactly," I said. I thought about my mother. I saw her name on that stone.

"Then what?"

"Where I live in Maine," I said, then paused. "Where I *used* to live in Maine, there's a marina. By the marina there's a sign: YOU ARE RESPONSIBLE FOR YOUR WAKE."

"Yeah, so?"

"So. It's like that."

I reached down to the radio and turned the switch. I found WXPN, Temple University's jazz station. It was playing old tunes from the 1930s—Coleman Hawkins, by the sound of it. "You carry the past with you. Even if there's a before, and an after, in your life. It's still the same life. The trick is to build a bridge between that and what comes later. So you have a sense of wholeness? I mean, everybody needs a past."

"Depends on the past," said Clark.

I stared into the beams of my headlights. "We are who we have been," I said.

"Man, I hope not," said Clark.

The Coleman Hawkins tune on the radio ended, and something else began. It sounded like a player piano. Old-time rinky-tink. Clark cracked his window again. The wind rushed in.

I stared into the beams of my headlights. "But the past still makes us who we are," I said.

"Just stop it," said Clark. "You're trying to trick me."

"Of course I'm not—"

"Just be quiet. I don't want to hear about it!"

"You don't have to shout."

"I do have to shout!" he shouted. "You're trying to tell me I can't start over! But you don't get to make that decision! I do! Okay, Judith Carrigan? I do. So you can shut the fuck up."

"There's no reason to get angry."

"You're the one who made me angry!" said Clark. "You and your Lousy Gatsby." He reached down and snapped off the radio. "And this music from a hundred years ago! You're trying to suck me back into the past, Judith Carrigan. Well, I'm not fucking going."

I didn't say anything, but I could feel my heart pounding. We drove for a long time, not talking. I stared into the dark, and I realized how far we were from anyone. All around us now were thick forests.

"I'm not trying to suck you into the past," I said quietly. "I'm just saying you have to make peace with it."

His leg started thumping, up and down. I couldn't tell if he was aware of it or not.

"Pull over," he said.

"What?"

"I gotta go," said Clark. "Pull over."

I could feel my heart beating in my breast. "Why don't we wait until we get to—"

"I gotta go now, goddammit," said Clark. "Pull over."

I slowed the car and pulled us over to the side of the road. There was an old barn there, its roof caved in. I put the car in park.

Clark got out of the car, then paused to look at me. "You go too," he said.

"I don't have to go," I said, although this was not actually true. It was well past time.

"Come on now, Judith Carrigan," he said. "We should go together. To show we trust each other."

There was a silence between us. I turned off the engine and got out of the car and walked toward the barn. "Okay," I said. "I'm going to go on this side, and you go on that one."

"Sure," said Clark. "Whatever." I walked around the back of the barn through tall grass. The night was full of sounds—crickets and cicadas, creatures croaking from the woods. Over my head, the sky was abundant with the stars of late summer. I looked at my watch. It was midnight.

I squatted in the tall grass. Then I headed back to the car.

Clark wasn't there when I got back. I got behind the wheel and looked toward the barn. But there wasn't any sign of him.

The Prius didn't make any noise as I inched it forward. I was on battery power, and the car was almost silent.

The car edged toward the curb. I looked back at the barn, but there wasn't any sign of him. I punched the pedal to the floor, and the car took off down the Black Horse Pike.

Okay, I thought. So that was a mistake. I'd been so freaked out from the funeral, and from my surreal rescue of Rachel, that I'd allowed myself to become stupid with self-pity. So many terrible things had happened to me, many of them the result of my own choices. I'd acted all along like being trans was some terrible curse, and that dealing with it demanded all this insane subterfuge. But half of the trouble that had befallen me was a result of that subterfuge itself. In so many ways, I had simply traded one secret for another. Maybe, I thought, there would be hope for me yet if I simply lived my truth out in the open. It was possible that the biggest transformation in my life was not going from male to female; it was going from a person burdened by secrets to a person who had none.

My heart felt like a human hand was squeezing on it. I rolled down the windows and let the air blow my hair around. I smelled pine trees, and tar. I raised one hand to my chest and held it there. In that moment I remembered that portrait that Rachel had painted of me in college. I would never be a saint, of course. But I had known what it was like to feel the presence of something larger than myself.

Something moved in the rearview mirror.

I looked up and saw his face, grinning at me. Gurganis was in the backseat.

I wanted to tell him about the thing that I felt in my heart. It was so large. But I couldn't talk. His fingers wrapped around my throat, and with those fingers he squeezed my life to nothing. He cried out with a low moaning sound, as if he were the one whose life was ending.

A loon called to its mate from a dark pond. *I know where you are.*

⤞⤝

Tripper stood before the old X-ray machine. He had been there before.

"Wanker," said the voice. He looked around the destroyed infirmary room. It hadn't been touched. The sheets of plywood still stood against one wall. The rotted beds for the sick were all in a row.

"Show yourself," he said. His shoe stubbed against something, and he reached down. A perfectly round white rock was there on the ground. He picked it up. It was heavy.

Now everything was quiet. He remembered Casey being moved to tears by the old operating theater, the long table, the dark stains of blood on the floor. He'd been annoyed by Casey's weepiness back then. *What are you crying for?* he'd said critically. He would have liked to have been able to tell Casey that he'd been wrong, back then. There'd been plenty to cry about.

Now everything was silent again. He stood still, listening, but there wasn't a sound except the far off wailing of a police siren.

"Hello?" he called. Tripper felt sweat dripping down his temples. She did not respond.

"Look, I'm sorry that you're dead," he said.

She didn't respond.

"It was an accident. You know that now. I was trying to protect Benny from harm. Was that so unforgivable? Because of that you're going to haunt me now?"

There wasn't even an echo of his voice in the old medical wing. The broken plaster and the rotted beds sucked up all sound.

"Maisie says we should tell the truth, just come clean. Is that what you're trying to tell me? That we should just come clean?"

He stood there with the white rock in his hand, looking into the near darkness. Something creaked in the corner.

"Who's there?" he said. "Is that you?"

The footsteps came again.

"Show yourself," he said. He stood there listening. The sirens drew nearer. Water was dripping somewhere.

"See, I don't know if telling the truth makes any difference anymore. We've lived our lives. I didn't get to live the life I wanted either. You're that, and I'm this."

There was another creak in the corner. Tripper said it again. "You're that, and I'm this." He turned toward the corner. A cold wind blew across his face.

"You want to punish the guilty party?" he said. "Show me the guilty party and I'll punish them."

Then something white flashed past his legs. Tripper shouted. Now a figure was before him, raising its arms out in the shadows. It was coming for him. He raised his arm and threw the rock toward the specter. The words on the shimmering wall read INCOMING PATIENTS HAVE THE RIGHT OF WAY. The mirror shattered as the stone hit it. The shards flew in every direction.

"Ugh," said Tripper as one tore into his leg. He collapsed on one knee. There was another slash in his belly, and Tripper rolled to the floor. He put his hands on his wound, the blood gushing into his fingers. Then he raised his hands to his face and looked at it, his own blood.

A white cat crept back into the room and stood by him. She reached out tentatively with one paw, then batted him in the face. "Ow," said

Tripper. The cat batted him again, as if slapping him first on one cheek, then the other.

"Bloody hell," said a voice, and the girl tiptoed into the operating room. In one hand she held the Nixon mask. Her boyfriend, the guy with the tattoos, was right behind her.

"What's all this?" he said.

"Wanker busted the mirror," said the girl. "I was just fuckin' with 'im, and now he's bloody murdered himself."

"Ugh," said Tripper, turning to the couple. He had seen them before. "Help me."

"Should we 'elp 'im?" said the girl.

"Fuck this," said the boy. "Let's bolt. Come on."

"Help me," said Tripper again.

The girl took one last look at him, then threw the Nixon mask onto the floor. Her boyfriend grabbed her hand, and then the two of them ran down the hall.

Tripper listened to the sound of their steps receding. He reached down once more and felt the blood pulsing into his fingertips. He was surrounded by the shards of the broken mirror. "Help me," he whispered. "Someone."

There was a quiet purring. The cat looked at Tripper with her green, unforgiving eyes. She touched the empty mask on the floor with one paw, to see whether there was anything inside.

30

Cold River, Maine

JULY 2016

Before my first death I was a child, a scarecrow. In summers I mowed the lawn and after I mowed the lawn I drove the machine back to my parents' garage and parked it between the blue-and-white '66 Pontiac on the one side and the green '58 Buick on the other. Then I pulled the throttle to the off position, and the engine slowly died. I sat there on the tractor for a moment, still feeling the inertia of the blades spinning beneath me. The garage was full of the smell of gasoline, of freshly mown grass, of fertilizer in burlap bags. Then I walked into the house and opened the refrigerator and stood there for a while feeling the cold air drifting around my neck and my bare, grass-stained legs. I reached in and pulled out a tall green bottle of Wink, poured it into a glass my father got at the Esso station, the same one that promised to *put a tiger in your tank.*

A boy named Kevin Walsh and his older brother Tick were playing baseball in the block beyond our house. The ball made a sharp socking sound as it landed in Ticky's mitt. In just a few years, Tick would head off to Vietnam. We would go over to the Walshes' house and listen to reel-to-reel tapes Tick sent back from the war. Sometimes there was the sound of gunfire.

From my mother's bedroom came the soft tinkling of a music box. There was a small ballerina figurine in her jewelry box that pirouetted and danced to the music when the box was opened. When no one was home, sometimes I went into my parents' bedroom and wound up the music box, and watched that ballerina dance.

My father was building a wall in the side yard. There was a *chunk* as he hit the slate with his hammer. Then he pulled it over to the wall and found the right place for it. There was a soft flinty *snick* as he struck his butane lighter and lit up an L&M filter. On his transistor radio was the sound of the Phillies game, the boys playing over in old Connie Mack Stadium, the sound of the distant crowd roaring as Jim Bunning hit a fastball. Quietly I imitated the sound of the announcer's voice: *A blooper to right.*

It was a boyhood, and it was mine, and it was typical, with the exception of the business inside my heart. My mother stood on the threshold of the front door, and rang a copper cowbell. The sound of that bell—clanky and slightly obnoxious—had the ability to reach my ears, wherever I was, and get me to run toward home.

I wasn't there when Grainne died, or when her house was sold, and so I'll never know where her things wound up after they were auctioned off, but I do wonder what happened to that cowbell. Did someone pick it up at a yard sale, take it home? It's nice to think that if a stranger stood on her back porch and rang it that my younger self might magically appear. Maybe my father, gone for decades now, might show up as well, covered with dust from his stone walls.

My boyhood, like others, ended over a period of years. Even the melodramatic and salacious event of my first death didn't represent the moment it all finally ceased, assuming that there even was such a moment. Sure, you could conjure such a passage up out of nothing, if you wanted—say, the day I dropped out of Boy Scouts because I was tired of the angry, ex-marine Scoutmaster lining us up for inspection every Wednesday night and yelling at us, telling us we were all soft, that we were weaklings. Or, maybe you could say it all ended when Grainne packed up the Oldsmobile Omega and drove me and my Grateful Dead albums the five hours north to Wesleyan, in the fall of 1976, there to link up with Rachel and Wailer and the others. Maybe you could nominate the day of my first kiss, or the day Jake Carrigan appeared at my door with a box of macaroni and cheese, or the day Falcon first called me Mom. There are many such days.

But most of the time I think that the boy that I was still lives inside me, in spite of the woman's life that came after. I hear his voice when I tell a joke, or raise my voice to sing some song, like "Early Morning Rain." I feel his loneliness, sometimes, when I hear children calling to one another as twilight falls at the end of a day in summer. And sometimes, when I hear the ringing of a cowbell, I'm tempted to get up from the place where I lie and run like a ghost toward home.

On a summer afternoon in Maine, Casey and Rachel and Molly Pennypacker sat in the *Red Wedding*. They'd taken the boat out to the center of Cold Pond, and there they sat, the two old friends and the one new one, with a box bearing letters on the outside that read CREMATED HUMAN REMAINS. This was a year after the Troubles. Tripper was in jail, on the basis of Maisie's confession, although it wasn't clear if the case would ever go to trial. The main culprit, Clark Gurganis, was beyond the reach of punishment now, and Tripper, his lawyers had argued, had already suffered enough. Casey, for his part, wasn't convinced, but it was also true that revenge was really not his strong suit. He'd gone in to visit Tripper in the Detention Center in Philly, bringing with him a dozen double-chocolate brownies. One time, Ben and his friend, Shannon, had come with him too.

Molly Pennypacker, Tripper's ex-wife, sat with her small hand on Casey's broad back. "Are you ready?" she asked. Casey looked over at Rachel. "Are we?"

Rachel touched the side of her face. "Casey, you have a little . . ." He reached up. There was some maple syrup on his cheek. Before they got in the boat he'd made everyone breakfast—waffles with Maine maple syrup served with spare ribs rubbed with cayenne pepper and cumin. He hadn't lost any weight since he'd started dating Molly. She was a little heavier, though.

"Yeah, okay," said Casey, and picked up the ashes. The black box was fastened with a clasp. Casey opened the box and looked. Water lapped against the hull of the boat, and loons called from a great distance, one to another.

"Well, like Wailer would have said, *Fuck you and your sense*," he said, using an accent that proved, if proof were still necessary, that I had not been the only one among us who could speak in tongues. "*In all the world I can hardly think of a soul more beautiful than yours, you fuck*."

Then he poured Wailer's ashes over the side of the boat and into the waters of Cold Pond. There was a soft trickle, and finally a high *ploop* as Casey took the wedding ring from his finger, after thirty-six years, and dropped it gently in after the rest.

"Well," he said. "There she goes."

In the side yard, back on land, Falcon was balancing on a unicycle, wearing headphones, listening to a band called the Cat Empire. Many years from now, after he graduated from the University of Rochester and became a mechanical engineer and moved to Texas with his wife, he would think back on these summer days, when there was nothing to do but ride a unicycle, or lie on his back staring up at the blue Maine sky.

I am hoping that the boy Falcon has been will always live inside of the man that Falcon becomes. I am hoping that the trauma of my own unveiling isn't what he remembers when he thinks of me: the story of the way the Prius skidded off the road when Gurganis put his fingers around my neck, the sound of the crash as I hit a gray tree, the fire that engulfed that car moments later, a fire that Jake was not there to extinguish.

≈≈≈

There are so many things I'd like to explain. That when I was young I did not have the language to describe the workings of my own heart. That if I had it all to do over again, I would have told my truth from the beginning. That the struggle to find a connection between the people we have been and the people we become is not some crazy drama unique to people like me. It's all of us.

Rachel fires up the engine, and the *Red Wedding* points once again toward land. They don't speak as they approach the dock. The wind whips everyone's hair around. Casey's eyes are on Molly, and her eyes are on him. Rachel, who has quit her job at the college and returned to painting, is watching the shore.

She sees the tall trees that stand upon the banks of Cold Pond. She sees the mist that drifts above Kennebec Falls. She sees our dock jutting out into the clear water. And there at the end of the dock, she sees me. After all this time, I am still waiting for her.

Jake comes out and the two of us join hands and look out at the water. Gollum sits by our side. As the *Red Wedding* draws near, Molly throws the bowline and Jake catches it. Falcon, who has jumped off of his unicycle to lend a hand, secures the lines to the cleats.

"Hey, man," says Casey. "All ashore that's going ashore."

And I reach forward and take Rachel by the hand, to ease her passage back to land.

"*We choose to go to the moon!*" I say, in the voice of John F. Kennedy. "*And do the otha thing! Not because it is easy, but because it is hahd!*"

Casey shakes his head.

"Dude," he says.

After a while, we turn and walk slowly up the path back to the house together, the seven of us: Casey and Molly, Rachel and Falcon, Jake and me, Gollum. Casey is going to make lunch: lobster salad, and roasted beets with goat cheese, and salted caramel ice cream.

Jake puts his arm around me. He walks more slowly than he used to, but then this is true of both of us.

We're still finding our way forward together, Jake and me, but in most ways, we are who we have always been, two people who love each other: diminished, a little bit, by fate and by time.

When I was in the hospital, after the wreck, they'd called him. The same impact that killed Clark Gurganis had propelled me through the windshield and into the air. I'd landed with a shattered hip and a broken arm, but my heart still goddamned strong.

They'd found Jake in the hospital in Maine, where he was still recuperating from the barn fire. My husband considered the situation. Then he rose from his bed and drove through the night: through New Hampshire and Massachusetts, through Connecticut and New York—all the way down the East Coast, until he arrived at the hospital in Atlantic City, New Jersey. Which was where he found me at last, staring blankly out the window considering the days of summer: the smell of gasoline, the sound of a distant cowbell.

He'd appeared in my doorway just after dawn, wearing his Boston Red Sox cap, holding a bouquet of daisies.

"Jake," I said. "How are you here?"

"I was wrong," he said.

"But I am—" I said. "I am not—"

"Judith," he said. "Are you not you?"

He'd climbed out of his hospital bed the night before and pulled on his pants, a fireman sliding down the pole, as was his habit, when the alarm went off.

"And just where do you think *you're* going?" Cassie Hudson asked. Falcon had smiled as his father headed out into the night.

"Gotta go check out a fire," Jake said.

Acknowledgments

This book was made possible by the support of the Amtrak Writers-in-Residence program. I'm also grateful to Mary Karr, Richard Russo, and Timothy Kreider for helping me out of jams. I owe Tim a particular debt; over glasses of *Delirium Tremens* at Burp Castle he came up with the title, reminded me of the mnemonics for the proper pronunciation of Nietzche, and provided a seemingly endless reservoir of jokes to steal.

More information on Eastern State Penitentiary is available at easternstate.org. Information and resources for LGBTQ people may be found at the home of GLAAD, the media advocacy nonprofit: glaad.org.

Thanks to Captain Lana Moore of the Columbus fire department; to Kerill O'Neill, David Greene, Deb Spar, Mary Gordon, Chris Baswell, Lisa Gordis, and Timea Szell at Barnard and Colby; and Kris Dahl, Lindsay Sagnette, Rose Fox, and Rachel Rokicki at ICM and Penguin Random House.

I have a website, jenniferboylan.net, and an email address: jb@jennifer boylan.net. I try to answer all correspondence except when things get backed up.

Most of all, I send love to my family: Deirdre, Zach, and Sean. Years ago, when I first came out as trans, my mother responded to the news of my unveiling by quoting First Corinthians and saying, "Love will prevail." In the lives we four have created, we have made this hope come true. I love you.

ABOUT THE AUTHOR

JENNIFER FINNEY BOYLAN, author of fourteen books, is the inaugural Anna Quindlen Writer-in-Residence at Barnard College of Columbia University in the City of New York and is special advisor to the president of Colby College in Maine. Since 2013 she has been a contributing opinion writer for the Op-Ed page of the *New York Times*. Jenny also serves on the board of trustees of the Kinsey Institute for Research in Sex, Gender, and Reproduction, and is the national co-chair of the board of directors of GLAAD. Jenny lives in New York City and in Belgrade Lakes, Maine, with her wife, Deedie, and their two sons, Zach and Sean.